Millie's Lyme

by

Ann Barton Langley

Grosvenor House
Publishing Limited

This book is published by
Grosvenor House Publishing Ltd
28-30 High Street, Guildford, Surrey, GU1 3EL.
www.grosvenorhousepublishing.co.uk

A CIP record for this book
is available from the British Library

ISBN 978-1-908447-88-3

This book is dedicated to the memory of my mother Molly Hobbs, who so enjoyed the first half of Millie's Lyme, but sadly did not live to see its completion.

INTRODUCTION

Millie's Lyme, a romantic historical first novel, is set in and around Lyme Regis in Dorset, and based on a piece of poetry I wrote some time ago, the content of which conjured up pictures of time gone by.

Characters danced in my head and begged to have their story told... and *Millie's Lyme* was born. The area is now one close to my heart although I was born and still live in Somerset. My characters are entirely fictitious, and extensive research of life in the eighteenth century is subject to some literary licence.

My sincere thanks to family and friends for their patience, encouragement, and support; and for help with my limited computer skills.

Also my thanks go to museums, and libraries for their valued assistance.

The sequel *Millie's Fortune* is due out in 2012.

Ann Barton Langley

OLD LYME

Well salted herrings, and barrels of grog
Endlessly lining the walls of the Cobb;
Pig iron, French lace, barrels of tar,
Silk for the ladies
Spice from afar,
Trawlers and Schooners plying their trade
Galleons at anchor, stately or staid.
Beggars and seadogs
Scurrying there,
Full creels, fishwives, screaming their ware.
Slanting grey walls, with stories to tell
Captain and cabin boy
Noisy ship's bell
Mooring rings covered with seaweed and rust,
Hustle, and bustle, from dawn until dusk.
Sea-faring tales of yesterday,
Salty old sea town in Lyme Regis Bay

Ann Barton Langley

1765... Millie loved walking on 'The Cobb.' The harbour arm stretched out protectively, half encircling the Dorset port of Lyme Regis.

Built originally as a giant breakwater against the storms of the south west, the high wall on the seaward side gave protection from the roughest sea, the lower walk in constant use for mooring, loading, and unloading.

Tossing her curls she walked on, stopping occasionally to examine the pools of water and bits of seaweed for small living things. The sun was shining warm and bright on the deep, ever changing sea. Watching the silver sparkling movement on the surface, dreamily Millie likened it to 'dancing diamonds.' She was nothing, if not a true romantic and imaginative young lady.

Long red gold curls and striking blue-green eyes, she was attractive rather than pretty. Her slight build, belied the strength of character and determination learned at an early age from her Ma.

Now at fourteen she considered herself a young lady in the making. Millie had dreams and plans. It was as well she had no idea what lay in store for her. Moving slowly on, The Cobb stretched out in front of her. To her left lay the harbour where her Ma cleaned and sorted fish alongside other fishwives, full creels proof of the menfolk's successful fishing trips.

Millie fervently hoped her future wouldn't echo that of her Ma's. She couldn't bear the thought that working in the cold smelly harbour was all she had to look forward to. Not sure why, a deep rooted feeling nudged her into believing there was more to life than this.

She wandered on in the sunshine, the waves lapping the seaward side of the old stone wall, the occasional spray, feeling cold on her warm fair skin.

Turning to look back beyond her dawdling young brother, she glanced to the left where the grey shale and limestone cliffs and under- cliffs, stretched away into the distance. They were renowned for frequent falls of rock, and Lyme Bay for the 'curios' found there.

She stared at the line of shingle and sand and shuddered, remembering the scary stories her grandmother used to tell of the aftermath of the Monmouth rebellion. *The twelve men hanged on the beach on the very spot the Duke of Monmouth landed;* that was long before even her granny was born, she was glad all was peaceful now.

Further along was her home, tucked into the small row of grey stone cottages, where she lived with her Pa Jack, Ma Fanny, and young brother Jamie.

The town consisted of harbour, customs house, tavern and a few cottages on the west side. To the east was the main street leading off Town Square, with shops, cottages, boarding houses and hostelries, while beyond St Michael's Church lay larger houses where sea captains and people of note had their homes. On the outskirts of the town was the all important Town Mill. East and West were like two bookends, linked by a long shingle beach.

Millie turned back to continue her lazy walk towards the end of the harbour arm. Suddenly she was pushed roughly forward, exclaiming loudly, "Jamie. I told you it's dangerous here, stop larking about."

"I'll reach the end 'afore yer!" Her young brother grinned, and skipping ahead, was off like the wind, racing against the warm breeze now whipping the crest of foamy waves across the bay. Millie sighed – *best go after him or we'll both be in trouble.*

Jamie was always curious to the point of danger, and saw little fear in anything. All of seven years old, he was as dark as she was fair, the image of his Pa and like him in so many ways; while she felt so...different. Millie caught up with him and roughly grabbing his already torn jacket steered him around to face the long walk back.

White clouds moved more quickly now and the pair quickened their step; Jamie intent on leaping from slab to slab and keeping ahead of his sister. He had spied the old seadog Lazurus, and knew he was always good for a bit of liquorice dug deep from fluffy pockets; but it tasted good! Calling out that was where he was heading; Millie nodded, allowing him to run ahead to the old man.

Knowing Jamie would chatter long enough to have his fill of liquorice; she slowed down, her own thoughts taking over.

Thinking back over her childhood she smiled, remembering how *she* used to slip away from her Ma to wander on the long stone wall, taking advantage of the hustle and bustle and becoming 'lost' in the general activity. Climbing nimbly up and down 'Granny's Teeth,' the protruding stone steps set into the wall of the Cobb, was perilous in the extreme, but still hadn't deterred her.

She smiled at the memory. The local fisher folk had all known the young Millie, and had kept an eye on 'Fanny's girl.' Sure footed and without fear, she had moved like quicksilver along the high wall and the low walk. *It seemed so long ago. What would life hold in store for her?*

Lyme Bay was renowned for its changes in weather, and multiplying clouds were now bubbling on the horizon and drifting across the sky. The seagulls circling and screeching, flashes of yellow beaks and feet, amid a rush of flapping feathers, the breeze increasing to become a gentle wind. Millie arrived at Jamie's side smiling at his blackened lips.

"I see you got yer sweets! I 'ope you thanked Lazurus."

"Yea I did, I'll 'elp you wi' yer nets next time." Jamie grinned, turning to the old man.

Lazurus chuckled and flipped his ear. Millie nodded, "Are you alright? I'll tell Ma we seen you."

"Aye, I am that maid; I'm 'appy yarning to young 'un 'ere." They hurried on and Millie turned to wave.

The old mariner gazed thoughtfully after the youngsters and resumed mending his nets, his fingers as nimble as his thoughts. Half the year he was kept busy with odd and assorted jobs, the other half, part storyteller part casual help, in return for a meagre meal. Approaching his sixtieth year, his old bones grumbled from the rheumatics set in, from many a drenching and many a bitter wind.

Couldn't I tell a tale? He murmured. But Fanny, the daughter of his best friend didn't deserve that. He'd always tried to look out for her. She'd been kind to him; saved him from many a cold starving night, with many a dish of warming broth and a shaky down on the stone floor, before a glowing fire.

His mind wandered back over the years, remembering the handsome sea captain who had won her heart. Fanny's head had been filled with promises. Lazurus continued with his line of thought.

The outcome of that caused some trouble an' no mistake; She'd waited a long time for her sea captain she 'ad. Alone with the child, bringing her up special like and all that time waiting! Well I could have told her. Gentry don't want the likes of us. Not long term anyhow; aye, a quick fling when the galleons lay at anchor. Turned 'er 'ead with ribbons and silks! An' Fanny stayed true to 'im too! 'til she got tired of waiting and Jack finally won 'er 'round. That was the making of 'er it was.

Lazurus sighed; he had a lot of time for young Jack. He had taught him most of what he knew, and the rest the lad had picked up easily, mixing with fishermen and sailors in the taverns. *Now look at him! Aye, he deserved a lovely lass like Fanny, along with a readymade daughter like; an' then young Jamie come along to complete the family.* Lazurus brought his thoughts back to the job in hand.

As the pair reached the cottage, its grey walls almost propping up the steep rise immediately behind, Millie stopped and Jamie slipped inside to examine his curios. At least they were home again without him finding any more trouble to get into. Millie slipped through the door after him, calling cheerily, "we're back, Ma."

Fanny had been waiting for them. Still an attractive woman, in any other clothes she could have been called elegant, but poverty sets its own restraints. Her often rough tone covered a kind, gentle, and above all fair personality. Her close family were the centre of her world.

"Aye, so I see. Take these crabs up to the tavern, there's a good maid. Rosie knows how much I want for 'em; the price is agreed an' she knows I'll send 'em on to Coaching Inn if she quibbles."

"I'll go now Ma afore the rain sets in."

Millie picked up the wooden tray of assorted crabs from the stone floor, and hung it around her neck.

"Tuck this flannel rag under yer collar, stop it rubbing." Her Ma made it comfortable, and carried on, "Rosie knows 'ow much I want."

Millie thought quickly, *if I can by-pass Rosie and take 'em straight to The Coaching Inn, I might get to see the young gentlemen that drink there! Ma should be pleased if I get more for 'er crabs.*

Millie set off, singing softly to herself as she started up the hill. She'd walked to the inn many times to see Emily her friend who worked in the kitchen, *and* to get a look at the 'young gentlemen' in their fine clothes. Emily told her stories of their extravagant fun, and wild partying, as she listened wide eyed.

The sky was darkening around the bay and she hurried her step, before the on-coming storm caught her out. As she came alongside 'The Harbour Lights Tavern' Rosie appeared in the doorway.

Rosie was loud and common, but strong and loyal. Her life running a thriving Tavern made her so. She stood for no nonsense nor hint of trouble. After her husband's death, she continued the same way with the help and respect of her regulars. No doubtful stranger took advantage of the female alehouse keeper, or if he tried, there were many drinking there, who would quickly quell any disturbance, or see off trouble makers. Rosie's slim build and ready smile belied her tough character. To count her as a friend was indeed useful and Millie knew better than to upset her; she'd have her Ma to answer to.

"Is there anything there for me, Millie?" Rosie enquired.

With the tray in full view Millie could hardly expect Rosie to believe otherwise. With a quick change of heart she called back, "of course Rosie if you're paying Ma's price," whilst thinking, *there's always another time for the Coaching Inn; aye an' the young gentlemen!*

As she stood in the darkened doorway of the tavern, a coach rumbled slowly by. Millie glanced up and caught the eye of the occupant. *I wonder who 'e is; 'es' got a nice face!* Followed quickly by, *'e's looking straight at me.* She felt colour rush to her cheeks...

His thoughts were in a similar vein, as he in turn wondered about the pretty young girl. Unknowingly he echoed Millie's thoughts; *another time perhaps.*

Jack made several sea voyages, Fanny worked hard on the Cobb and Jamie was close to finishing at the church school. Millie, now a glowing, tawny- gold young woman, had perfected the art of by-passing Rosie. With the help of her threadbare cloak and choice of the smallest of the crab trays, she covered her good dress and the crabs in one fell swoop.

Her Ma had become used to the extra money and didn't question the time it took her to sell on the crabs. Millie chose wet or windy days to go the extra distance, when others chose to dispose of the catch closer to home. Wrapping her cloak around her, concealing her secret and keeping her dress dry just in case she should 'see anyone'...

Millie wasn't quite sure she even *knew* what she wanted, but somewhere deep inside she felt the fishing life and the Cobb's hustle and bustle, wasn't quite the future she had in mind. Her Ma's raw hands and the constant smell of fish made her inwardly shudder. Millie had other expectations of life. 'High falutin' and airs and graces' her Ma laughingly chided her.

Millie shivered, feeling more than a little guilty. *Hadn't the busy harbour always been good to her and her family?*

Loud laughter and a squeaking sign heralded her arrival at The Coaching Inn tired and thirsty. Gentlemen in smart colourful clothes ruffled at neck and wrist could be seen through the main doorway, there was evidence of money there. Millie didn't want to be seen delivering crabs!

She picked her way carefully around the side of the building and through the cobbled stable yard, thus avoiding the main entrance.

The Coaching Inn had something of a reputation for the variety of victuals offered. As in most hostelries in Lyme and beyond, it was well known that buying smuggled stock was widespread; but getting proof was almost impossible. Such was the very nature of it that no-one ever heard anything, no-one ever saw anything, and those with most standing in the community were often those most deeply involved.

Coming across the yard towards her was Danny the stable lad. He worked long and hard at the stables, under the direction of old Abraham who was responsible for the smooth running of the yard. He had taken over many of the heavy tasks, and was adept at taking care of horses and coaches, whilst gentlemen slaked their thirst on the best French brandy, whisky and fine ale.

Danny had lost his Pa to the sea, and his Ma worked as cook at the Inn until her death. Until then he and Millie had met at the Sunday school each week and played together as children.

He was tall, slim, and tanned; a ready smile lighting up amazing blue eyes. His fair wavy hair was caught mostly at the nape of his neck, some escaping in curly tendrils around his face.

"I 'aven't seen you for a while Danny, you all right?"

"I am that, Millie, 'ow about you?" Hardly waiting to hear the response she rounded the corner and came to the kitchen, the smell of food making her realise just how hungry she was.

Pushing back her cloak she tapped on the door and as it opened was pleased to see Emily.

"'ello Emily I brought these, quite a few this time!"

"Bring 'em through Millie, we 'bin 'opeing you'd come, put 'em on yon table and I'll go tell the Mister." Millie watched as Emily disappeared through to the bar calling, "crabs is 'ere mister, crabs is 'ere".

Placing the empty tray on the table Millie slipped off her cloak, and let it fall onto a rough wooden chair as she waited for Emily's return. Smoothing down her dress, she thanked heaven she had remained dry, for now the rain fell in silver rods, splashing back off the cobbles outside and covering the small window with dancing raindrops.

She gazed around. Fresh baked pies and jars of cider, could be seen on the marble slab, through the open pantry door. After a few moments Emily clattered back down the stone passage.

"Mister says to give you summat to eat; payment'll be ready afore you go."

"I was 'opeing 'e would say that," smiled Millie, as Emily went off again to fetch bread, a bacon slice, and a large tankard of ale; the latter for them to share. At that point Danny stumbled through the open back door.

"I come over for our cider, Emily." He nodded at both girls, and took the jar Emily handed him, wishing he could think of something clever to say, and knowing it may be another week before Millie came again. He disappeared as the girls chuckled good naturedly at his embarrassment. Emily reached out and gave Millie a quick squeeze.

"My word Danny's sweet on you! 'e's always asking when you'll be back, or if I've seen you an' such. You only 'ave to smile special like, an' you'd be walking out with 'im in no time. As for me, I smiles morning noon and night an' a fat lot of good it does me!"

"I suppose I could be drawn to 'im, a bit like, but we bin friends for so long, an' 'e don't wear nice clothes or...

She knew that was unfair and felt a bit mean. He had long been harbouring dreams of her, and a future together.

Danny was eighteen, and had been ten years in his present work. He had as many years instruction and many a boxed ear, from Abraham, who had done a good job on the orphaned youngster. Millie sighed.

Emily cast her friend a puzzled look and proceeded to cut a thick slice of bacon and an even thicker wedge of bread.

The same age as Millie, she was very different in all respects. No high hopes of a better life for her. She deemed she had all she needed, with a roof over her head, cheap clothes on her back and a small wage to take home once a month on her few hours off. While she cleaned rooms, waited at table, and skivvied in the kitchen, her hard earned coins were turned into liquor and swilled down the throat of her lazy drunken father, along with anything he could beg, borrow, or steal!

Millie had what Emily termed a life of leisure, she had only to shop, cook, and look after the cottage and her young brother, enabling her Ma to work longer hours down at the harbour.

As Millie finished eating, Emily set the ale in front of her and they took turns drinking from the heavy tankard until it was empty.

"Go on then Millie, go an' get yer money. I know you're itchin' to see 'em out there."

They both knew Millie loved to hold her head high, and with a toss of her curls, walk out through the front door. She had watched enviously many a time as Millie turned certain heads and *one in particular!*

Millie walked through to the bar smiling, and collected the coins from the stout, ruddy faced Mister Murkin. Quickly slipping them into her pocket she thanked him, agreeing to call again soon. She was glad she took the trouble to change into her pink dress; she felt more confident wearing it. Fanny Drew would not have been so pleased had she known its main use would be to impress the young gentry

Millie smoothed down the coarse pink material, and tucking a stray curl behind her ear, slowly walked the length of the saloon; looking neither to left nor right, the front entrance ahead of her.

Enjoying her exit she reached the open door, knowing certain eyes were upon her and glancing sideways her eyes met and held briefly, the dark twinkling eyes of the most handsome gentleman she had ever seen. The fact that she had never met any other gentlemen, handsome or otherwise escaped Millie completely.

Or had she? She felt warmth seeping into her cheeks and neck, and was glad to step quickly into the cool air. Had he noticed?

It certainly didn't go unnoticed by Mister Murkin, who himself had an eye for a young woman. But Millie was still just a pretty young girl. Emily, who stood behind him, heard his muttered words.

"It's to be 'oped that smile on Master Gerard's face, don't bode ill for the girl; 'e got a bit of a reputation 'ere abouts, same as 'is father up at Manor. Now young Danny, 'e'd like to take care o' Millie and that's a fact."

Millie stepped out of the front entrance feeling pleased with herself, her heart beating faster. Then she remembered; she must do a quick detour around the back to collect her cloak and crab tray, before beginning the long walk home.

The sky was getting lighter and weak ray's of late afternoon sunshine heralded a dry end to the day. Millie breathed in the fresh damp air. Here, halfway down the hill, just above the town it seemed different; the air was sweet and fresh. *As soon as I get within sight of the 'arbour and the fish shambles, it'll smell all salty and fishy again!*

By the time she reached the bottom of the hill, the feel of cobbles through the thin soles of her boots, made her wince. She was brought up with a start as Rosie shouted after her, "it must be nice to be a lady." Rosie guessed she was up to something.

Millie smiled, waved and continued on her way lost in thought, until she reached the busy, noisy bustle of the harbour.

She reached home and changed out of her pink dress. Donning the old one, she completely forgot she was to meet her Ma at the harbour; instead she curled up in the window seat to daydream. Totally unaware that today's foray to the inn had the desired effect on the young gentleman with the dark eyes; she would have been horrified had she been privy to his chain of thought!

Fanny arrived home flustered!

"I thought you was going to come down an' meet me. I got the fish bundle, an' the crabs to juggle, an' I'm 'ot an' tired." Millie was contrite.

"I'm sorry I forgot. But give it here, I'll stir the fire and set 'em on to fry. Sorry Ma."

Later Millie slipped away and wandered down to The Cobb, walking alone in the warm summer evening, weaving fantasies about the dark young man. She was at an age to tingle deliciously at her forbidden thoughts. Tonight was no exception.

Fanny looked out at the darkening skies and not for the first time decided she must speak to Millie about her growing habit of wandering alone late into the evening. *She used to be so sensible, but lately, well;* heaving a sigh she had the feeling she would have to keep a closer eye on her daughter. Nobody knew better, how a young girl's head could be turned. It was at times like this she missed being able to talk to Jack, but he would be home soon and maybe she was imagining things.

She decided to see Jamie to bed and wander down to the Cobb to find her. *Millie used to be so good at looking after things, including her young brother but now;* again Fanny sighed. *It all starts with dreams... Aye it starts with 'em!*

Fanny brought herself back to the present with a start, suddenly spying Millie halfway along the Cobb staring out to sea in the gathering darkness. Picking her way carefully, Fanny hurried over the uneven stone slabs, all the time aware of the sea swelling high against the sea wall. "It's a high tide," she murmured to herself, the sound of the waves drowned her voice. As she drew abreast of Millie she reached out and holding on to her arm, pulled her gently away from the edge.

"Millie luv, what you doing down 'ere? It's late an' we should all be getting our sleep ready for the morrow. Lord knows the days are long enough, without you tacking more on the end. Jamie's on 'is own an' all. Come on now maid we'll 'ave an 'ot drink when we get in, an' get ourselves off to bed."

Millie turned and clung to Fanny with a sigh.

"Oh Ma, I was just thinking; life's funny, in' it?" Fanny squeezed her arm and inwardly agreed. She had still ended up as a fishwife despite all her own longings and grand ideas.

Later on Millie would find out just how 'funny' life could be. But tonight she hugged a secret to her. *Aye he did smile!*

CHAPTER TWO

Gerard Elliot downed his glass of fine malt whisky and slowly stood up, pushing back his thick dark hair tied neatly at the nape of his neck. Smoothing down his expensively embroidered long coat, he moved towards the door.

After engaging in some light hearted banter, and amid shouts of approval from several of the other young men who had been eyeing Millie, he left the inn in time to watch as she disappeared down the hill. She attracted him; in fact he'd go so far as to say she *fascinated* him.

Unlike his father, Gerard had a gentler streak and had many a time been lambasted for being soft. He stood now in the doorway of the inn, and watched as the slight figure of the young girl disappeared from view. Her appearance at the inn on several occasions convinced him she was the same young girl he had seen over a year ago, as he had been driven past Rosie's Tavern.

Gerard was drawn to her bright curls and her lightly tanned skin, unacceptable in the circles he moved in; the ladies prided themselves on their pale and fragile appearance.

He felt sure that if he once approached her there would be little chance of rejection, but was it fair? He stared at the spot where Millie had disappeared; she seemed somehow vulnerable and innocent.

He was deep in thought. *The wench will be taken down soon enough by one of her own kind. At least I'll add some refinement to the process.* Gerard began to fantasize. *She'll look good wearing satin, or lace. I could introduce her to fine wines and good food. In fact there's a lot I could teach that young lady! Not around here; maybe further down the coast; Seaton or Axminster, it's certainly something to think about.*

Gerard, the son of the local squire was used to getting his own way. His early years were marked by a definite coolness between his parents, consequently affecting relationships within the family. He and his sister Clara had been looked after by a succession of nannies; the children's behavior ensuring they never stayed long.

The squire had been more absent than present. Always a 'ladies man' and happy to be known as such, it soon became clear his wife's disposition didn't fit at all with his work and play ethic. She, being painfully aware of the part her inheritance had played, in his attraction to her, and their subsequent marriage.

As the years passed Squire Elliot's wife slipped into a decline, her escape from the duties as wife of a successful business man. The squire's London trips to the shipping company of which he was part owner, were a regular feature of his working life, and where he found solace in the charms of the London ladies.

She watched as her son started exhibiting the same tendencies as his father, and wondered for the umpteenth time if there was anything she could have done to change things.

Clara his sister was a tall, slender young woman. Pale skin, dark hair coiled lavishly at the nape of her neck. She cultured a demur look, but in essence her personality was anything but.

The young gentlemen, sons of family friends, looked wishfully upon her, and never gave up hope of winning her affection. They little knew of the longing for adventure that lurked beneath her surface calm.

On one of Millie's excursions up to The Coaching Inn, Danny had witnessed her 'staged' departure, and resolved to speak out the very next time he saw her. After talking with Emily he was becoming worried about Millie's interest in the drinking and gambling 'young sirs.' If he had anything to do with it she would be steered clear, before any harm was done. But Emily didn't agree.

"We all 'ave to find our own way, Danny."

"Aye, deep down I know when Millie makes up her mind about anything; it'll take more 'un a friendly word to change her course. Maybe I should talk to her Ma?"

"Don't you go letting on Danny; she won't thank you for it."

"You're right I s'pose; it could be enough to end a *special* sort of friendship afore it starts. Only one sensible thing to do, I'll speak to Millie. Ask 'er to walk out with me on our next free Sunday; aye I'll do that. Thanks Emily." She stared wistfully after him.

Feeling better for making a decision Danny went back to work with an easier mind.

Millie woke at daybreak to the familiar sounds of the sea and the gulls. She half remembered something nice had happened, and then memories came flooding back, of the dark haired young man. *I'm sure to see him again, and when I do I'll smile back at him.* She was still deep in thought as Fanny called up the steep and narrow stair, "Millie, hurry yerself up! There's some warm water left to wash; aye and give Jamie a shove afore you comes down."

"I'm coming now Ma." Millie quickly shook a grumbling Jamie, before hurrying down the stairs into the kitchen with her clothes over her arm.

"You're getting too old to dress by the fire now maid."

"I know it Ma, but it's so cosy 'ere, an' so cold upstairs." Fanny glanced round at her blossoming daughter, struggling into her dress, realising her girl was fast growing up. Millie picked up the wooden spoon, no longer listening, and already several steps ahead of herself.

She stood beside the range, stirring a pan of thickening oats and water. Working out the best way to carry out her plan, she casually said, "I'll 'urry though me jobs 'ere and go to town for you Ma, I'll 'ave enough time to get back and collect the crabs." To herself she thought, *then I'll change me dress when the 'ouse is empty, an' take crabs up to The Coaching Inn; maybe I'll see...*

Fanny was pleased with the idea and said so.

"That'll 'elp Millie, going to town early." she took the old tin down from the mantle shelf and rummaged for some coins to give her. "Fetch bread from yesterdays baking. One loaf, coarse, brown; we won't be needing flour for a couple of days. Then get some dripping and fat bacon from the butchers. Aye an' don't take all day about it, there's work a plenty waiting on the Cobb."

"I'll go over to the bakery first, then come back to see Ned the butcher's lad." She knew he had taken a shine to her, and would give generous weight. Everyone knew old butcher Samuels was a real skinflint with his weighing. Millie's plans were fresh in her mind as she tied her hair and made ready. Stepping out into the windy morning she was glad of her shawl wrapped warmly around her shoulders, beneath the thin cloak.

Setting off at a brisk walk across the shingle, she headed for East Gate and the town. The sea was grey this morning, matching the dreary low cloud. White crested waves were ebbing and flowing, louder as they broke on the shore, then softer, moving the shingle to their own slow rhythm.

Millie looked back and saw her Ma and Jamie in the distance. She knew their day would be the same as yesterday, the same as the morrow. Her Ma always working hard at gutting and selling fish for someone else's greater profit and Jamie wasting his time and her Ma's coins, by *not* learning at the Church school. *Three mornings a week wasted! At least I can read an' write even if I don't get much practice!*

Usually, he got a ride with the next market load going over to town, mostly it made him late, but Mister Lane held off a caning knowing it wasn't the boy's choice. At going on eight, he really needed to toughen up. Little did he know how this was going to change with the company Jamie would later choose!

Deep in thought Millie was surprised to find she had reached Bell Cliff, and made her way across the square. The town was already alive and busy and had been for several hours. There were small cart deliveries to shopkeepers, and the chandlers. Vegetables and fruit brought in by the farming folk, kegs of liquor being unloaded at various inns and gin shops, and impatient horses and barking dogs, joining in the general hubbub of the busy working day.

Millie crossed the square and walked down the narrow ally, and along the lane leading to Town Mill. Here old Joshua the miller was taking delivery of more grain. Millie remembered when she was very small and used to come with her Ma to buy flour.

They were lucky enough to have a bread oven in the old kitchen range, but sometimes they couldn't bake, if there wasn't enough wood to keep the fire burning and heat the oven. Then they took the dough to Maisie, who baked it in the large bakery oven, on the site of the old malt house, just across the leat. But this took three journeys, one to buy the flour, one to return with the dough for baking in her oven, and another to collect the fresh baked loaf.

Now Old Joshua and his Missis had branched out and opened up a bakery selling their fresh baked bread, which for Fanny and her family was an occasional luxury, one they could ill afford, but which saved considerable time.

"'Ello there Millie," called Joshua as she approached, "come on in and keep an old feller company for a few minutes, you always liked to watch the grindin'. My you're growing into a lovely maid and no mistake."

"Hello Joshua, I mustn't be too long." Millie followed Joshua into the cool dark interior of the old stone mill. It was so old and dusty it always made her sneeze. They passed the full flour sacks on one side of the ground floor, separated from the newly delivered grain on the other, and preceded up the rickety wooden steps to the next level. This was the stone floor, so called because it housed the grinding stone.

Adjusting the stone was a fine art perfected by old Joshua, ensuring that he could produce flour of varying qualities and textures. From the cheapest and most coarse, dark flour, right down to the purest and finest white.

Here a rope and pulley hoisted the sacks of grain up through the trap door in the centre, and on up to the floor above. It was then tipped by the miller into the hopper, fed down to the grinding stone below, to reappear again on the ground floor as flour. The miller's boy was kept busy all day, running between floors and filling sacks.

"There you are Millie, grain in, flour out; long as farmers keep me supplied with grain, I could be a rich man."

"You must be rich Joshua, if you own all this!"

With a deep belly laugh that made Millie smile, old Joshua went about his business chuckling away to himself.

Millie always thought he looked a bit like a ghost. The milled flour left a powdery layer over everything, settling on his hair, beard and whiskers; she smiled again. Looking around she felt this could be quite a ghostly place, with all the cobwebs covered in white, the old beams and the windows all with a fine layer of white flour, she shook herself.

"Much as I like talking to you Joshua, I came over to buy bread today, so I'm off over 'tother side of leat to see Maisie in yer bakery; but I'll be by again day after the morrow." Millie turned, and ran back down the stairs to the sound of the miller's loud chuckle.

"Aye that Millie's a rare 'un and no mistake," he murmured to himself.

Millie crossed the cobbled yard, and the wide flagstone bridging the narrow leat, and found that Maisie, Josh's good lady, had already finished one baking.

"You've not got much to carry Millie! No flour today?" enquired Maisie, her cheeks rosy with the heat.

"No, I just bin talking to Joshua; I only want a yesterday's coarse dark loaf please, if you got any left. I'll be getting the flour, day after the morrow, when Jamie comes to help carry." She selected the largest looking loaf and paid for their 'once in a while' treat. Shouting her thanks and goodbye's, Millie started the walk back to the square, pleased with her purchase.

Young Ned the butcher's lad saw her before she saw him, and blushed, even though she was still outside the shop. He had taken a shine to her, although Millie was a whole year older. Entering the shop she shifted the loaf to the other arm and found her coins in her pocket.

"Some fat bacon and as much beef dripping as I can have for this please Ned." She showed the coins, and gave him her most winning smile, knowing it doubled the amount young Ned would weigh up for her; especially as butcher Samuels was around the back and out of ear shot.

"I give you a bit extra there Millie." he winked and tapped his nose with his finger.

Millie smiled again, "Thanks Ned," and left the shop with her purchases.

As she rounded the corner by the small shop that sold everything, from sailcloth to tobacco, who should step out in front of her but; No! Oh no! It can't be! Not with me dressed like this, all windblown an' all. More an' likely flour in me hair too I shouldn't wonder!

Poor Millie was thrown into total confusion by the same dark twinkling eyes of the gentleman from The Coaching Inn. Instead of pushing past her he inclined his head, and with a slight bow quietly said, "We meet again!"

Millie stared open mouthed and wide eyed, in an instant he had stepped around her and slowly walked on.

Millie could have cried. It wasn't meant to be like this, I was goin' to smile. I shouldn't have been caught *carrying goods; I should 'ave 'ad me pink dress on!* The colour rushed to her cheeks. *He'll never look at me again,* she railed inwardly, but as she dared to risk a quick look over her shoulder he *did* look again, *and* he smiled.

Millie ran down the steps of Bell Cliff and across the square, turning the corner onto 'The Walk' to retrace her steps home. She had to get away from all the noise and people. She felt as though everyone could see inside her head, as though they could all see her burning face, as though they knew. *But there was nothing to know was there?*

Her thoughts went to Jamie in the schoolroom, to her Ma salting herrings, talking and working; to old Joshua at the mill. Everything was still the same.

She had to slow down, walk back with the bread and such. No need for her pink dress now. Rosie would get the crabs today; that was for sure! Then she would get herself onto The Cobb to work alongside her Ma. Everything would work out.

Feeling her composure returning Millie chided herself out loud, "Fancy getting in such a state, an' me going on sixteen! I'm going to 'ave to take meself in 'and."

Chapter Three

Jack Drew was a hard worker, no doubt about that. But was he always on the right side of the law? In the close knit community, many turned a blind eye and kept their mouths shut; though most knew exactly what was going on.

Such were the circumstances that found Jack agreeing against his better judgement, to row the small boat ashore, when the cargo vessel stood off further along the coast at Charmouth. There the cliffs and rock falls made for more caves and inlets, inaccessible from land to all but the most experienced of men.

At pre-arranged signals, goods were hauled up the rough cliff face with the help of ropes and climbers. Then most was loaded onto carts and pannier horses, for distribution up and down the coast. Tub men, strapped small barrels or 'tubs' to their chest or back, then headed inland. The rest was taken quickly away by those receiving the illicit goods. Where money changed hands no questions were asked!

Such was the task in hand to-night. Conditions being good, a quarter moon and a cloudy sky, the crew of the 'Amity Jane' set about their individual tasks, with only a scarce word or sign passing between them.

Lying at anchor awaiting the tide, seafaring men, for the most part honest and hardworking, had been forced to eke a living from smuggling goods bought cheaply in the French ports or Channel Islands. Landed illicitly at pre-designated locations, they were to be collected or retrieved at a later date, thus avoiding the crippling taxes. Smuggling had become an industry beginning to thrive.

Customs officers kept a half hearted look out, but the laws being what they were, nothing above high water mark could be seized. It was left to 'riders' to patrol the cliffs, but there were nowhere near enough of them, and Jack, along with the crew of the 'Amity Jane,' looked on this as almost an invitation to bring goods ashore.

Generally all that was needed was a stray word in a tavern, to send the revenue men on a wild goose chase, while the real contraband was smuggled in at a completely different location.

With the first small boat loaded, and the lookouts in the rigging giving the all clear, Jack took his place at the oars. Slowly at first and then finding his pace, the boat moved forward running with the tide, the shoreline getting closer with each passing minute.

Jack never failed to work up a good sweat, which was only partly due to exertion. The trouble was he was in possession of knowledge he wished he didn't have, that was the worst part of the business. He stared up at the dark cliff face.

A keg of fine brandy would soon be on its way to the old Vicar of the Parish church. He was a hypocrite when all was said and done; preaching hellfire and fury in the pulpit, and then supping smuggled French brandy by the fire in the vicarage along with his cronies.

Then there was 'The Vaults.' He'd given up drinking there. The place was awash with smuggled goods, and not *just* smuggled. Some stuff there was stolen on dry land; he knew that for a fact.

The company got rougher by the day, Jack knew too much to settle for a tipple there; the Gulliver brothers were on their way to an early grave by all accounts. They would pick on the wrong one soon, or get themselves hanged for the carrying of weapons. Violence had no place in Jack's scheme of things.

As they neared the shingle beach several hands jumped into the cold water, the ebb and flow of the tide making the shingle crunch and sink under their boots. Jack drew in the oars and stood up; watching as they swung oiled sacks onto their shoulders, all the while scanning the cliffs, rocks, and shingle, for a sign of light or movement.

Whispered commands and oaths were lost on the breeze. Suddenly at the top of the cliff a sound, a low guttural voice growled, "Ropes is 'ere lad's, this-a-way." The small boat's cargo of illicit tobacco, in manageable bundles, was tied and hauled up the cliff face. Half a dozen men worked swiftly and surely.

Hardly a word was spoken, each knew his role and each was intent on it. Several pairs of hands pulled up goods, and loaded the sagging panniers on sturdy pack horses. The young lad gently holding the bridles kept them still and quiet, talking softly to them until the tobacco run was finished. The second boat beached as the first was emptied; the changeover quick and faultless.

Men and packhorses were replaced by others taking over, the first crew now resting or helping where needed. Hauling boxes of liquor up the cliff face was an even more difficult task. At last the final box was raised and stowed.

Quietly the horses were led away and just as quietly Jack took his cue to set the oars in place. As the boats made the return trip, each man heaved an inward sigh of relief; a long night, and not over yet. As dawn was breaking the 'Amity Jane' with her crew safely aboard, boats raised, and anchor hauled, made her way onward to Lyme harbour. Captain Fawsey, well pleased with the nights work dipped into the keg of rum, and bade the crew do likewise; thirsty work indeed!

With legitimate cargo still to be unloaded, each and every seaman would take home his pay and choice of 'extras.' Not until all tasks were complete would he make his way home to wife and family; there to thank his stars and sleep his fill.

Jack told himself that as he only rowed the boat and kept a look out, he wasn't as involved as most, though the revenue men might see things differently.

He had given it all up when he wed; until his baby son arrived. With Fanny not strong enough to work through that bad winter, he had been forced to rethink. He remembered all too well the meagre living; never enough food on the table, never enough warmth in the small cottage, despite the drudgery of young Millie collecting driftwood. Fanny had been at her wits end, and his heart was heavy each time he left them for duties aboard ship.

His seaman's pay kept them from the poor house, but he owed it to them all, too again take the chance of easy money when it came his way. And so he had succumbed. Fanny was surprised but pleased with the extra coins and goods, and never again asked questions.

Slowly the smuggled goods had begun to take the form of a length of silk or good cotton. Sometimes velvet trims or lace. Fanny had a lovely French lace collar tucked away until such time as she possessed a good dress to stitch it to!

Since Jack had taken to doing the voyages over to France or the Channel Islands, he brought back small amounts of perfume and bottles of brandy to sell on. Dried fruit and black tea for Fanny, along with some very welcome candles. She knew not to brag about it.

Although most family's benefited from their menfolk's exploits, it was an unwritten law not to mention the origin of any 'extras.'

Lazarus was watching as the 'Amity Jane' sailed into harbour, remembering the days when *his* ships sailed in; unloading their cargos of pig iron, barrels of wine, and fine brandy. He also remembered the days when he too, could heave a barrel onto his shoulder and walk down a slippery gangway with ease.

Although the harbour had been busy since dawn, he was aware that trade had fallen off over the years. When he was a lad there was no shortage of work.

As a mariner he had travelled the world, seen more foreign places than many knew existed, loaded and unloaded assorted cargos in assorted ports, and seen a few sights not connected with the sea! He chuckled inwardly.

Lazarus watched as Fanny's girl approached at a run, looking flustered. Millie arrived at his side by the harbour, out of breath, "its Pa's ship. It is, it's the 'Amity Jane! She's coming in now, on the tide."

"Aye she is that, maid," they watched as it drew closer. Resting his gnarled old hand on her shoulder he muttered, "reckon I 'ad seawater running in me veins once! Not any more though. Seems as you get older, the sea gets crueller; couldn't do it now. Making and mending lobster pots and mackerel nets, is about all I'm good for, aye an' that a damn sight easier in summertime!"

"Poor Lazurus," Millie murmured in an absent minded way, before setting off again, not even giving him chance to answer.

As the ship negotiated the harbour, there was great excitement as she weighed anchor and the deckhands went about their work. Soon The Cobb was transformed into a hive of activity.

Barrels of liquor lined the walls, along with kegs of assorted sizes. Stacked chests filled with tea, and smaller packets of spices, so prized by the gentry. Transferring and reloading wagons and carts, and pannier ponies. The clanging and clanking of metal, as iron hit stone. Stacks of imported goods growing ever higher propped up against the high, grey stone wall.

Millie continued on, climbing the steps and edging her way along, scanning The Cobb for her Ma and the ship for her Pa. It was nigh impossible to pick out anyone at this distance, dodging through, and around small groups of people, just as intent on their business as she was on hers.

Rounding the elbow of the Cobb, she picked out the tall strong figure of her Pa approaching the ship's gangway. Effortlessly transferring a large barrel from shoulder to deck, and then deftly rolling it down the gangway to a deckhand, who had taken his place at the bottom. Millie shouted at the top of her voice.

"Pa, over here, here I am." She waved both arms above her head. As he looked over and caught sight of her, his face lit up. Here was his girl, his lovely Millie; he thought how she'd grown, even a few weeks made a difference at her age!

"Where's yer Ma?" he yelled. Fanny appeared, waving and shouting. Millie picked her way down the protruding steps, to arrive at her side.

The noise was multiplied by the shouted commands of workers, and greetings from wives and children, all anxious to catch sight of their men folk. The general bustle drowned out the sound of the sea and the gulls.

It was always the same when the cargo boats moored in the tiny harbour. Whilst the cargo was unloaded, word was sent to various other carters and wagoner's; seemingly keeping up an endless procession of transported goods.

Eventually Jack collected his dues and heaving his sea chest onto his shoulder reached their side. Setting it quickly down again, he gave Fanny a big hug, swinging her off her feet; she would have to follow on later, when her share of work was done. She and other fishwives would be the last to go home to their families.

With Millie clinging to his arm, the chest again on his shoulder, they made their way back to the cottage. Life was hard, even for those born to it. Jack looked forward to his sea leave; a few days on dry land spent with his family would set him up for the next set of duties.

When they arrived at the cottage he kicked off his sea boots and stretched out on the wooden settle, having been up all night! In a few minutes his even breathing, declared he was in a deep sleep, as a slightly disappointed Fanny found him on her return.

Experience had taught her not to waken him, and to stay her longing to ask questions until such time as he awoke refreshed. All that remained was for young Jamie to come home, and they would be altogether as a family again. Fanny treasured these times.

As Jack slept, Millie opened the old battered sea chest with the key that Jack had given her. It was her special treat, to find the hidden surprises her Pa always brought back; one she never grew tired of, nor got too old for. She pulled out a length of silk, and fingered deep purple ribbons. Almost before Fanny had come through the door, Millie thrust the ribbons under her nose.

"Look Ma, these an' the silk would trim a plain bonnet a treat."

"Lovely maid, but I'll see it all proper, later on; I got other things to think of just now." Fanny noted the extra coins on the table too, along with ribbons, lace, and a length of lilac silk that lay on the old low cupboard.

"*And* there's a good length of green cotton material on the chair there! You could make a real good dress Ma, I'll help; You never know what's going to come out of Pa's sea chest next, do you?"

Millie's excited chatter came to a halt, suddenly aware her Ma's mind wasn't on the 'extras.' Fanny looked around saying quietly;

"Where's Jamie? 'e should 'av bin 'ome more than an hour since." Millie looked up,

"You're right Ma, even if 'e dawdled 'e should a bin 'ome by now!"

Glancing at the old mantle clock, Fanny realised the time was getting on; his lessons always finished by noon.

"I'll go an' look for him," volunteered Millie, and set off to the town for the second time that day.

Jamie's time at the Church school was coming to an end. Soon he would have to turn his hand to many more tasks than he was used to. Fanny had postponed the day when he'd be responsible for putting his share in the purse.

She hated the idea of him going caulking, he was small enough, but lying under the boats helping to make them water tight was a dangerous job. Accidents resulting in permanent injury or even death happened that way.

As Millie crossed the shingle beach again, and came in sight of Bell cliff, her attention was taken by a figure coming down to meet her.

"It's Danny, what's he doing down this far" she mumbled to herself. As he came up to her, he gave a half smile and said.

"You're not looking for your Jamie, are you?"

"Yes, 'e never come back from 'is lessons. Why?"

"Well, 'im an' some other lads - not from the Church school, have been trying to get into 'The Vaults.' It seems like one of 'em followed a group of men that were loaded down with bundles an' such. Now they've all gone in to find cellars, an' your Jamie's with 'em" Danny lowered his voice, "its known stolen stuffs been stored there, till such time as it can be sold on!"

Millie knew the old pub at Cobb Gate. 'The Vault's' had a bad name for violence, drunkards, and illicit goods changing hands. The Revenue men had raided it more than once. She had heard tales of the cellars too, where ongoing passages led down to the sea, *their Jamie at 'The Vaults'?* Her heart skipped a beat.

"I must find him Danny. Pa's home from sea and Ma's worried already. If they find out where he's bin there'll be real trouble, our Jamie never learns." Millie thanked Danny and hurried on, not realising immediately, that Danny was staying close on her heels.

As they reached the side entrance, Jamie was thrown out unceremoniously onto the street, followed closely by three or four other lads. His face red and smeared with grime, he was suffering from fright and a pair of boxed ears. A burly seaman, responsible for their hasty exit, appeared behind them. Judging by his face he was an angry man.

"Keep 'em clear!" he glared at them, his eyes alighting on Millie. "You're Jack Drew's girl 'int yer? No good'll come of lad's snooping; e'll get more 'en a thick ear next time. Aye if I catches 'im 'ere again, Jack'll 'ere of it! An' that goes for all of yer!" He waved a fist in the air and disappeared again, leaving Jamie to face Millie, and the others to scarper.

Danny stepped forward grabbing Jamie by the shoulder, while slipping a protective arm around Millie. Partly to stop her doing battle on Jamie's behalf, and partly because it felt right! Quietly he drew her back.

"Nothing to be done an' nothing to be said; except, you're gonna 'ave to decide whether to tell yer Ma or not! But remember, if Jack is faced with how much snooping lad's bin doing, it might put 'im in an awkward position!" Millie stared at Danny,

"What do you mean Danny? Pa knows about 'The Vaults' being a bad place – but more than that? What you getting at?"

Danny shrugged his shoulders and said quickly, "Nothing; there's nothing for you to fret about. Let's just get Jamie home and yer ma can stop worrying."

Millie didn't *want* to talk about it anymore, afraid of what she might hear; so with strict instructions for Jamie to say nothing, all three hurried back across the shingle walk, heading for home.

Leaving Millie and Jamie at their door, Danny continued up the hill to The Coaching Inn. Now he would have to give Abraham a good reason for being so long in town. Millie stared after him.

Danny was a good sort, the sort you could trust! She had been thankful for his presence back there. Inside the cottage Jack and Fanny were waiting, Jamie rushed to hug his father.

"Sorry Pa, I didn't know you were back till Millie said." he turned to Fanny, "sorry Ma, for being so late," staring at the ground, he haltingly mumbled something about being kept late in the classroom, then going climbing at Gun cliff. Fanny was all for giving him a good shaking, but Jack intervened, glad to see his son. Millie just wondered how he got away with his tales.

"No harm done, an' anyways we don't want to waste time grumbling. I'm home; back for three or four days, not a minute to lose. After we finish supper, we'll 'ave a walk by cliffs, stretch me legs on firm ground. Jamie can show me where he's collecting 'is curio's now! Aye it's going to be a nice evening; 'specially with yer Ma's cooking to fill me belly!

Come on look lively young Jamie, you can make yerself useful oiling me boots, till foods on table. Both yer Ma an' Millie looks as though they could do with a rest from what I can see of 'em.

Millie, casting her mind back over the events of the day, couldn't have agreed more; but deciding that her Ma could do with help after her own busy day, set about preparations for the meal.

On reaching The Coaching Inn, Abraham called out to Danny, "Where you bin? What you bin doing Dan lad? There's 'orses in, wants watering, there's a change over waiting, and I can't work as fast as I used to. Hay-bags is getting low, and yon sweaty mare wants rubbing down. Look lively lad you can do yer explaining later."

Danny set to; he was fond of Abraham. As long as he was working here, then he'd do his share, and as much of Abrahams as he could manage. He had a great respect for him, and never forgot how much he'd learned; and how the old man had looked out for him, when he was young.

Danny worked hard to catch up. He'd worked up a fine sweat, when he looked up and saw Emily coming across the yard towards him, carrying a welcome tankard of cider. As he straightened up with an appreciative smile Emily thrust the cider into his hand.

"Here Danny have this, I brought one out for A'bram not long since. You missed a right carry on inside. It seems taverns along coast, are all being searched. Somewhere between 'ere an' Bridport, a special order of wine from France, went missing. Lord knows who'd of 'ad the nerve."

She winked; "a whole *con- sign- ment* they called it. I hear tell the Customs is going to start watching coast from fast ships they call *Cutters,* I think they said. Anyway I thought 'as 'ow I'd let you in on gossip! See anyone we know down town? Mister was asking where you was, I said you'd be on an errand for A'bram."

"Thanks; but slow down Emily!"

Emily paused for breath, and Danny drained his tankard.

He hesitated, and decided against telling her that he had been with Millie, and what her young brother had been up to. In the light of what Emily had just said, it seemed least said soonest mended. So with a shrug he just mentioned that he had seen Millie, and left it at that.

It took Danny a long time to fall asleep that night. His thoughts went down to the cellar where the liquor was stored. Remembering, how as a lad he watched from the shadows, as strangers carried cases across to where barrels lined the far wall, hiding a low doorway. Once when they left a gap, he had squeezed through, into another small low room, filled with a variety of bottles, and smelling of tobacco. As he grew older he became aware, that only Mister Murkin fetched 'special orders' from the cellar.

He was too young to let it bother him, but old enough to know he should keep his mouth shut! He thought again of Emily's gossip. *So Mister Murkin's hidden room was still safe, but did Emily know about it? What had Jamie seen over at 'The Vaults,' and was Jack implicated? Emily may have more information.*

Danny was determined to probe a bit deeper. Millie could be in for a shock and if she was, he wanted to be in a position to help. His thoughts wandered back to the moment his arm had slipped around her small waist. Her young body pressed against his, had made his heart beat a little faster. *If only, I was earning a bit more and Millie felt the same way about me.*

He was sure they could be happy together. Cottages were hard to come by and probably more rent than he could manage, but if he went on working hard and pursued his dream of going for a groom, it might happen... *didn't they give priority to wedded couples, in the big houses? Millie was a hard worker. They would have a roof over their heads and...* Danny brought himself back to the present.

I'm running away with meself," he said out loud as he turned over and settled down to sleep. *But it was a dream worth following...*

The days passed, and Jack had been home nearly a week before he secured duties for his next sailing, on small vessel called 'Mistral,' bound for the Channel Islands and France.

Fanny was glad it was a small boat, the larger the vessel the further the voyage it seemed. She sometimes felt her whole life would be measured by not wanting

Jack to go, or waiting for Jack to come back. Before he left they decided Jamie would stay on at the Church school for a while longer, just to see if he would knuckle down. There was always work for Fanny, but what of Millie?

Millie had become dissatisfied with her lot. Fanny could see the girl's point of view, and didn't want her to waste her youth in the same way that she had been forced to.

But sometimes she just didn't seem like her Millie at all. Half child, half woman, she seemed to hold a part of herself secret. A fleeting glance, a vacant stare, took her away to a place that Fanny could only wonder about.

On a quiet Sunday afternoon when all the jobs were finished, and Jamie was away searching for curios, Fanny resolved to talk to her daughter about her seemingly unsettled feelings.

Millie had retreated to the small upstairs room that she shared with her young brother. Mounting the stairs, Fanny called, "Millie? Oh there you are. Why you sitting up 'ere all alone? You're not sickening for summat, are you?" Millie hastily placed her hand over material covering a cheap bonnet that she seldom wore, and stared at Fanny.

"I'm alright Ma. For ages I've bin wanting to – well, I mean... Seeing the things Pa brought home, gave me an idea; an' it was quiet up 'ere, an' you didn't need me, so" she hesitated, "Ma I've used the lilac silk and all the purple ribbon, do you want to see? Look I'm so pleased; it's taken me ages to get it right, but I seemed to have a picture in me 'ead of 'ow I wanted it to be."

She uncovered the prettiest bonnet, trimmed with shades of lilac and purple, set off by long satin ribbons.

Thrusting it in front of her Ma, she sat back, searching her face for a reaction. Fanny stared.

"Oh Millie luv, it's beautiful! 'ow did you manage that? You sewed it all yourself? I know you're good with your needle - I've me new cotton dress to prove it, but this– I reckon the folks in London would be 'appy to wear it"

Before Fanny could say any more, Millie practically bubbled over with the thoughts that had been going round and round in her head.

"Ma, if I could get enough together, you know, materials and trims and things, do you think maybe I could *sell* a bonnet like this? You know the Miss Hartnells, those two spinster ladies at top of Broad Street? Well they got a small shop like, and sometimes they put bonnets in the window. Can I go an' talk to them? Or maybe *you* could Ma? Oh say yes, I'll do all me work 'ere, then 'stead of doing harbour work with you, I could do sewing like; I could do repairs and alter folks clothes. Oh I'd really like that. I don't want to waste me life smelling of fish!"

Millie stopped short. "Oh Ma I'm sorry, I know you work so 'ard but I'd work 'ard too... only doing something different. Please say yes, oh *please*. I knew I wanted to do some other kind of work, only I didn't know what, 'til Pa brought home more of these lovely things. The feel of 'em Ma, and the colours, oh please say yes."

She stopped for breath. Fanny smiled and reaching out, hugged Millie to her. If only things had been different, Millie might have had a very different life. How could she deny this strange child anything? Child, what was she thinking? Fifteen years old come autumn. They clung together, each with dreams. Millie's for the future and Fanny's from the past.

"There girl, all I can say is, work 'ard a bit longer. I've got some money put by. We'll give it a few months, and then with what yer Pa brings 'ome and the bits and pieces of material an' ribbons an' lace I got tucked away, we'll see if we can't work something out.

I know the pubs and inns send torn or worn linen, and pillow slips to outworkers for mending. We'll see what we can do. There's no such thing as starting at the top. The only way from there is down. You work hard with your needle, and get yourself known for a good sewing job, and you can work yourself up to yer dresses and bonnets. Who'd of thought it? That bonnet luv, it's certainly something. Aye, an' who knows where it'll lead, I'm real proud of yer!"

With tears in her eyes she hastily left the room. "'urry up now, clear up and come down for yer tea," she called over her shoulder, disappearing down the narrow stairway.

Millie was left with a wonderful warm feeling of knowing just which way she was going. All the other feelings of 'not quite knowing what she wanted,' had been dispelled by her Ma's words. *Yes she would work hard; she would start at the bottom.* She felt glad she had spoken out at last.

For the first time since leaving Mister Lane's classroom, Millie had a vision of her future. Once she got work and experience sewing, she would move on. Already she could see herself making and trimming dresses and bonnets for the shop on Broad Street. It would make her feel so respectable! 'Ladies will say to *each other; Oh Miss Drew trimmed my new bonnet and smile as they pass me in town.'* Millie was walking on air as she descended to the little kitchen to *take tea,* with her *Mama!*

CHAPTER FOUR

Jamie was lost in his favourite pastimes of hunting for curios on west beach, and climbing on the undercliff. The first was harmless, the second highly dangerous. Jamie carefully stowed away his find of two small curios, thinking how much more money could be made from the bigger ones–if only he could carry them.

Placing them beside a marker rock and covering them with his jacket, he surveyed the cliff face. After deciding on a series of footholds, he began to climb. Lost in thought he continued for some time, getting hot and sticky. He rested for a while, and then continued until his arms and fingers began to ache. It didn't seem to be quite as easy here. He glanced over his shoulder, wondering if it would be easier further down the beach. It seemed a shame to quit having come this far.

He could continue going up, or go down the same way. He chose the latter. Trying to negotiate backwards was a bit more difficult. Not one to give up easily, he was slowly but surely retracing his steps when he heard, "Jamie Drew, you bin told *not* to climb the undercliff. You know there's bin rock falls and all, get yerself down here *now*!"

Millie, out for one of her solitary strolls, had seen him from The Cobb. Hurrying back and crossing the beach, she was now standing, hands on hips at the base of the cliff. Jamie risked a glance over his shoulder.

"Keep yer wig on! I ain't in trouble; it'll only take a few more minutes."

"Not in trouble! You might not be up there, but wait till I get you down 'ere". Millie, watching her young brother, couldn't fail to notice how agile he was, until amid a flurry of rock, sand and shale, he landed at her feet.

"Oh Jamie, one day you won't be so lucky," said Millie as he picked himself up and shook the dust from his hair and clothes. "Come on lets get back for supper, you missed yer tea." Jamie grinned, picking up his jacket and the curio's saying, "What yer think o' these then?" thrusting them under her nose, he linked arms with his sister as they started to walk back.

Millie smiled too, his grin was infectious, "Worth a couple o' ha'pennies." she conceded.

Lasurus watched from his perch on the lobster pots. Not much got past him. As the pair waved and walked by, the first rumbles of thunder sounded in the distance.

Slowly standing up, he turned and moved along the Cobb wall until he reached the bend, passing the time of day with several 'old salts' on the way, and slowly selecting a couple more lobster pots to work on from another stack awaiting his attention. He glanced back at the shore and the cliffs, I *reckon more o that cliffs goin' to end up in sea, in non to distant future,* he mumbled. Lasurus was usually right in his predictions. Millie and Jamie disappeared from view and his thoughts turned to Jack at sea, and thinking back to his youth, he remembered when his liking for turning a quick coin had led him into the smuggling lark! *Made a pretty penny I did, aye and spent it! Reckon Jack is in it up to his neck, stands to lose it all too; losing Fanny and his family would do for him.*

Lazurus knew all about that. He remembered his own wife Sarah. They had so many frights and close shaves, that Sarah, who was a sickly soul anyway, had taken off and moved in with her sister over at Axminster. Angry words had kept them apart, and before he knew it she was dead and buried before he had returned from his last sailing. *Aye that bounty stuck in me craw.* He had resolved there and then to give up. He hoped his Sarah would know, and smile fondly down on him. *Lord knows I'll never get up there to smile at thee Sarah me love; fool I bin, aye a right fool...* If he could stop Jack making the same mistakes he would.

As Millie and Jamie reached the door of the cottage the heavens opened. The thunder that had been rumbling in the distance, began getting closer at every roll, but now it was preceded by flashes of sheet lightning.

"My word you were lucky" exclaimed Fanny, pulling them inside. Millie smiled in agreement; glad to be home and dry and much relieved that she had managed once again to get Jamie out of a scrape. She dreaded to think what would have happened if he had still been half way up the cliff. Her Ma didn't know the half of it.

"Yes we just about made it, Ma."

The fire gave out a welcome glow although it wasn't cold. Fanny lit the lamp, as the cottage darkened and rain came down in torrents.

"It's your Pa I feel sorry for, on the open sea. Never fails to turn me stomach when the storms come." After the supper of hot broth, and wedges of newly baked bread, Jamie – with a few grumbles – was dispatched to the scullery to clean up and take himself off to bed. He lay down, yawning and thinking what jolly hard work it was, hunting for curios and climbing cliffs. *No matter how much you liked doing it – it was still jolly hard work!*

The thunder and lightning intensified through the night. Millie lay awake, thinking of her new role as 'would be' seamstress. Fanny lay awake, thinking of Jack at sea, and young Jamie slept through it all.

When day dawned the rock fall on the undercliff, covered the very place where he had been climbing!

Fanny had been true to her word. After asking around, she paved the way for Millie to apply for work. Boarding houses were glad to send out menial repairs jobs, in the form of pillow slips or sheets, to be hemmed or darned. Millie had successfully applied to the housekeeper of a small boarding house at Cobb Gate, and was rewarded with a bundle of coarse towels and pillowcases to mend.

The housekeeper passed them over saying that she would have to, 'prove her stitching,' before being taken on. It wasn't a very exciting job, but as her Ma remarked later, "It'll give you a foot in the door."

"Aye it's a start, an' I can put the word around that I'm available for alterations and repairs." Though the remittance was small, and the hours long, from this small beginning Millie was encouraged to pursue her dream.

Time passed and she worked hard. Once her mind was set on something, she simply had to make it happen. If sewing hems and taking in seams for other folk meant gaining experience for her opportunity when it presented itself, then she would be ready to grasp it.

Her dream of one day working with new materials, and fine ribbons, kept her forging ahead with a determination that Fanny was proud of. In between all of this she still found time to take crabs to The Coaching Inn, and see her old friends, Emily and Danny. Millie had less time to keep an eye on Jamie.

Over on the East side of town, at the top of the main street, the Miss Hartnell sisters turned the sign on the door of their small shop to 'OPEN.'

"We are going to need some extra help with the orders that are coming in," remarked Sybil, "trade seems to be picking up! There are more folks visiting the town, taking the waters, and the sea air, than ever before. That Dr. Richard somebody of other, recommended it as a cure for all ills. It's certainly helped us, but it's going to be difficult to continue accepting all the orders, especially now that your poor hand is so swollen."

"I agree. It was such a shock, it rendered me quite faint and nauseated."

Mabel had allowed her hand to rest for a moment, against the door frame. As she stepped out into the street a sudden gust of wind blew the door, painfully trapping her thumb.

Recovering slowly, she found after a few days, she was still unable to do any fine sewing work. Sybil examined the injury. She was sympathetic but decisive and business like.

"Something has to be done."

"It really is quite painful," agreed Mabel, "the swelling and bruising make it very awkward to work. I can still slowly tack, and press, but the finishing, that requires fine needle work, I am finding just too difficult." Sybil thought for a moment.

"I shall make out a card and put it in the window. Even if this hadn't happened, we would need to take on someone sooner or later." Sybil had made up her mind.

"But what shall we do about wages? We can't pay much, or we'll be out of pocket."

"We will certainly be out of pocket if the shop has to close!" exclaimed Sybil, "and it's not as though we haven't thought about it before, we agreed some time ago; we are much busier than in the past."

The sisters were quite alike in appearance, but in character almost the opposite. Sybil kept a tight rein on things and made most of the decisions, whilst Mabel was content to drift along, always pulling her weight, but never worrying too much about anything. Mabel got on with everyone, and in her world everything always turned out for the best.

The card was duly made out, 'Needle Woman Wanted' and placed in the centre of the small window.

It was a chilly afternoon when Millie left home, to deliver the sheets and pillow cases that she had been working on. Walking to town with her bundle firmly under her arm, she hurried past the butchers, where Ned grinned and raised his hand to her, and on past the entrance to the blacksmith's workshop, giving a wide berth to the horses being led in.

She continued past the fishmongers thinking, *I could walk the street with me eyes shut, an' know where I am by the different smells!* On reaching the Boarding House she walked past the front door, and around to the side entrance to deliver her finished work. Pulling once on the bell, the door was opened by the house keeper. Taking the proffered bundle she beamed, "You're doing a good job dearie, keep it up."

"Yes, yes I will." Millie glowed; it was nice to be appreciated. She thanked the small dumpy woman who retreated into the interior with the bundle, only to reappear a moment later, with a fresh one for her. Millie thanked her again, eyeing the enormous bundle, thinking only of the coins it would earn her.

Walking a little further up the hill, she crossed the busy road to look in the window of the small dress shop. Hardly believing her eyes, she saw a large card hanging there. 'Needle Woman Wanted.'

Millie gasped in amazement. Hastily retracing her steps, she hurried back down to the square, across the beach and home. Dumping the sewing work in the cottage on the way, she carried on down to the harbour. Fanny looked up at her unexpected approach.

"What's up now?"

"Guess what ma?" shouted Millie as she approached the women sorting fish. "Guess what? I've just seen a notice in the shop in Broad Street. You know the dress shop, the one that belongs to the sisters? They want someone to work there. There's a notice on the door. It says needle woman wanted, do you think I could be called a 'needle woman' yet ma?"

"One way to find out maid," said Fanny dryly.

"Oh ma will you ask when you go over the morrow? You could tell them how good I am!"

Millie was oblivious to the smiles on the faces of the other women. They were used to Fanny's girl and her 'bright ideas,' she always seemed to have something on the go. But she was a hard worker and well liked.

In their opinion Fanny had brought her up right. They all knew firsthand how hard it was with their men at sea for the most part. Fanny's girl would do well for herself, and good luck to her, was the general feeling.

"So I'm to tell 'em how good you are, am I? Well there's nothing like blowing your own trumpet is there? Well I suppose I could; sound 'em out like, see if the job's still open."

Millie was so excited, her head buzzed for the rest of the day.

The next day, after calling on Mister Lane, Jamie's school teacher – and finding out just how little work Jamie actually applied himself to, Fanny called at the shop and found that the position was still open. After talking to the Miss Hartnells' she left Millie's details, assuring them a harder working assistant would be difficult to find.

Nearing the midweek there had been three replies. The first was a large fat lady, with good plain sewing experience; the second, a young rather unkempt, and out of work scullery maid, and Fanny Drew, applying for her daughter, well known and well liked in the small community.

At the end of that week Fanny called again. There were no further applicants, and no doubt in the sisters minds, who they would ask to bring in the first sample of sewing skills! Fanny reached home and imparted the news to Millie.

"There are two others after that job. You've to look lively and get some of your work up to the Miss Hartnells now – this morning" Millie looked ecstatic.

"Look at me bonnet and dress Ma, I flat ironed 'em. Well, only the ribbons on the bonnet! I'll take 'em both shall I? Will you come?"

Suddenly Millie looked young and vulnerable, Fanny sat down.

"Millie, this is the chance you bin waiting for. It won't look good, you going after a nice job and yer Ma 'olding yer 'and. I know it's first time you'll 'ave worked 'tother end 'o town. But you got to let 'em know you can do the work, responsible like, and don't need constant watching.

Pack up them things, and get yerself up there before they close for their dinner. My bet is that dress'll pass muster. Then you can show 'em the bonnet. I reckon you don't 'ave too much to worry about. Now get yerself off girl."

Millie had been ready and waiting for more than an hour. Taking great care with her appearance, her mop of curls had been tied up, tucked in, and secured by a narrow ribbon and willpower! The pink dress laundered and pressed, with Fanny's new lace collar attached, ready for an occasion such as this. Millie looked neat and tidy; her shabby boots didn't show too much under her long skirt.

Giving her a quick hug, Fanny pushed her out of the door.

She walked the length of the shingle deep in thought. It seemed that her whole life depended on this morning. As she walked across the square and up the main street, Millie gave herself a good talking to.

I shall be quiet, well mannered, answer all the questions, and show willing. I'll work whatever hours they want me to, an' I'll never complain about the amount of work I do. Oh, and I'll tell 'em, I really want to learn. By this time Millie had convinced herself that she could do anything.

As she pushed the door of the small shop open and stepped inside, she was confronted by a tall thin lady with wrinkled skin, grey wispy hair set high in a bun, and a rather severe expression. Millie nearly lost her nerve and clinging on to her dress and bonnet, she felt rooted to the spot.

"Good morning ma'am" she managed. "I'm Millicent Drew and I've come about the work." She closed the door gently behind her, her eyes still glued to the wrinkled face. From her left, came another voice, a nice voice Millie thought. Turning, she saw another smaller lady, with smiling brown eyes and fading light brown hair. Millie heaved an inward sigh of relief!

"Hello, I heard your name, Millicent."

"You can call me Millie, Ma'am."

"Very well – Millie, I am Miss Mabel Hartnell and this is my sister Miss Sybil."

"How old are you girl?" enquired Miss Sybil, leaning towards Millie and looking her up and down.

"I'll be fifteen come September ma'am," whispered Millie.

"Oh good, you are young enough to be pliable, and old enough to be responsible."

Miss Sybil stared into Millie's wide blue- green eyes and thought she saw a certain degree of mild arrogance there; or was it just strength of character? Mabel hastily interrupted. As the main dressmaker of the establishment, Millie would be under her guidance.

"Well now let's start as we mean to go on. My sister is Miss Sybil I am Miss Mabel. I shall want to talk to you, if you will just come through to the back room." She ushered Millie through into her work room.

The room was covered on every available surface, with coloured ribbons, silks, cottons, velvets and lace. Millie drew in a deep breath and almost whispered, "Oh I never seen anything so lovely. Looks like a rainbow's come in the window! Oh I know I could sew really well with these lovely materials, I could make beautiful dresses. Aye an' bonnets, I can just see 'em. Oh everything's just perfect."

Suddenly aware that she was 'going on a bit,' as her Ma would have put it, she became quiet and subdued. "Oh ma'am I'm sorry. I meant only to speak when I was spoken to, but – *the room,*" Millie spread her arms, encompassing the whole room, as she slowly turned around.

Staring at the girl's reddening face; Miss Mabel reached out and clasped Millie's hands in her own. Then she smiled and tipping back her head, laughed out loud with sheer pleasure.

"Oh I don't know when I last witnessed such enthusiasm. You are like a breath of fresh air Millie! Well now, let's look at your work."

Millie proudly shook out the dress that she had been clutching over one arm. It was pale green figured cotton, and she had spent hours with the pin tucks on the bodice; although Fanny had helped.

She wondered if she should admit to it, but Millie knew that she had taken great care with her stitching and fitting, *and* that it showed in the finished garment. There was silence, Millie's heart almost stopped. Miss Mabel called through to the shop.

"Sybil, can you come in here for a moment?" Millie waited. It seemed an eternity before Sybil appeared.

"Now Millie, show Miss Sybil your work."

After another agonising few minutes whilst the sisters examined the garment closely, they turned to face her.

"Is this your own work girl?" the 'moment of truth,' Millie fought with her conscience.

"Well Miss, I mean ma'am; me Ma helped me with the long seams, but I cut it out and sewed it all together. I made it fit and trimmed it like; I reckon I done a good three quarters of it." Millie stood firm, "I could make another without too much help Miss; I know I could.

Aye an' I'm sorry for going on so, about materials and colours and such, I can work quiet like." Millie cast into the air, as how best to impress the sisters. "Look, look Miss, I trimmed me bonnet an' all!"

With a flourish she pulled the bonnet from the box it was squashed into. The sisters sat down. Millie scanned their faces. Suddenly they both began to laugh.

"Oh Millie, you have enough confidence and enthusiasm to carry off this work. With proper training you'll be perfect for our little business."

"Do you mean I can work for you?"

"You will do very well Millie"

"But have I got the job?" persisted Millie.

"When can you start?" the sisters replied in unison. Millie could hardly believe her ears. She looked first at one and then the other.

"I don't know what to say," she murmured quietly.

"Do you mean you are lost for words?" said Miss Mabel, "I find that hard to believe," and smiling she carried on. "I, well I think I speak for both of us when I say that we are very impressed with your standard of work, and yes, if you want the job it's yours. But there are just one or two things to add. You do realise don't you that the work must be carried out here? That means you arrive for work at six in the morning, and with a short break for your dinner, work though until six 'o clock. Of course when there are any special orders you would have to stay on into the evening to complete them. We shall have to take you on a trial period, and work out your payment and time off." Miss Sybil nodded in agreement.

"You can start on Monday morning at six sharp! Now Miss Millicent Drew, pick up your dress and bonnet and go and share your good news."

Millie found her tongue at last,

"I don't know how to thank you. I shall work *so* hard and love doing it! I'll not be late morning times, an' I won't mind staying late either, if I need to. I won't let you down." "Millie, Millie. Don't bombard us with words all over again. Off you go."

The sisters stood up, Miss Sybil, with a rare smile, showed Millie out of the little shop, and as she closed the door Miss Mabel whispered, "I have a good feeling about that young lady. Come now, we shall have some dinner and make ready to explain that the position has been filled.

Through the shop window Miss Mabel watched curiously, as Millie carefully removed the bonnet from the box. Calling to Miss Sybil she said, "Just look at that, the girl is wearing the bonnet!"

Sure enough she had slipped it on, and tying the ribbons under her chin, proceeded to walk on air!

Millie walked back to the square and across the path over the shingle. Although she really wanted to get home to tell her wonderful news to her Ma, part of her wanted to savour the feeling, at last, of having the chance to 'make good.' Her Ma would be so pleased.

She found a flat dry place on the shingle and sat down. But instead of the feeling of elation, she was consumed with doubts. *What about me other jobs? What about the crabs? What about helping me Ma? What if I can't keep up with the orders and things? What if I'm not any good after all?*

Millie scrambled to her feet. Pulling off the bonnet and dangling it by its ribbons she grabbed the box, and with the dress over her arm, half walking half running, she arrived back at the cottage. It was empty!

Wondering for a moment whether to turn and run down to the harbour, she heard her Ma's voice from the stairway.

"How did you get on luv? Let's hear all about it then." They sat down opposite each other, the dress and bonnet on the table between them, "now start from the beginning," said Fanny "an' don't go embroidering it, just tell me what 'appened."

"Well," began Millie, "I got the job. Oh Ma I really am going to work there. With lovely, lovely colours, you should just see 'em. There was this lovely red velvet, the colour of the raspberries we see in the summer market, and beautiful white satin, like the smooth feathers on the seagull's neck, oh and lots of ribbons Ma. Real wide ribbons, in just every colour you can think of, oh and really narrow ones too, for tiny bows. An' lace, oh you should see the lace ma! Some black as night, an' some pure white; an' all the colours of the rainbow, an' so much material there an' all. Yes and guess what? Threads and cottons all to match, they sew everything in matching colours, just think, if you could only *wear* something like that."

"Stop, Stop, Stop girl," Fanny said, throwing up her hands; their faces glowed, Fanny so proud and Millie so pleased. "Well I take it you're going to enjoy working for 'em then. Now, what are the two old biddies like? You're going to 'ave to get on with 'em. Aye an' what about the hours you'll work? And the pay, those are the important things... I suppose you did ask?"

"Oh yes Ma. Well I didn't exactly ask – but they told me we'd talk about pay, an' time off an' such, when I start on Monday. *Monday* Ma, I've to get over there at six. They'll show me where I'll be working, and tell me about everything then."

Fanny stood up, "Well I think this deserves a good strong cup of tea, aye an' some griddle cakes!"

Millie sat with her chin cupped in her hands, gazing into the fire, and remained deep in thought as Fanny went about making griddle cakes. Fanny cast her glance.

"Come on now maid, look lively, there's a lot to sort out 'afore Monday!" She frowned, suspecting there was something else Millie was keeping from her.

"But Ma, when I was on the beach 'afore I got home, I was thinking all sorts of things, an' what about helping you – how will you get crabs up to – Rosie? Just in time she stopped herself from mentioning The Coaching Inn. Jamie poked his head around the door, and Fanny said, "Well there's yer answer to that! Jamie's left the classroom now. I didn't have chance to tell you 'afore, but I talked with Mister Lane, and he agrees that the lad's got enough writing and reading, and numbers to manage. Jamie's not using his time well enough, for me to go on paying; so he's got to finish there, take over where you leave off! You see luv? Things always work out given time. Pa and me had already agreed about this, so it's all over bar the shouting, isn't it young Jamie?" Fanny reached out and tousled his hair as a grinning, grimy, Jamie, made his way to the table!

"Aye I'm going to be earning too, not wasting me time in the classroom. I'll be able to put me share in the pot!"

Looking at his sister he grinned again. "Ma's already told me about you and yer posh job. You got yer 'ead in the clouds you 'ave, but I'm glad for you our Millie, I am." Jamie stuffed his mouth full of griddle cake, and took a mug from the dresser. "I'll join in the celebration seeing as 'ow I'm going to be a working man too."

Oh Jamie, I'm pleased you're ready to leave schooling, I wouldn't 'ave wanted you to stop on my account." Millie reached out and hugged her young brother. They would always be close.

Fanny sighed; Millie's had done her fair share of bringing up young Jamie. She was proud of the pair of them, and so was Jack, they were lucky compared to some. She looked at the table, "those raisins Jack brought 'ome, come in a treat they 'ave. Griddle cakes with raisins, for just such an occasion as this; an' yer Pa 'ome again in a couple of weeks."

Everything seemed to be going smoothly in Fanny's world.

CHAPTER FIVE

Monday dawned and Millie was up before five; it was darker in the mornings now that August was drawing to a close. She crept downstairs in her shift with a blanket wrapped around her shoulders to find Fanny already coaxing the fire into life.

After washing quickly in warm water, Millie helped with the breakfast. She boiled the kettle and made tea, setting it to brew on the range, whilst her Ma set about toasting bread slices. Spreading them with a liberal amount of pig fat they sat eating in silence, Millie deep in thought.

"Eat up girl; you've got a long time to go 'til one o' clock. I've put up a thick slice of fat ham between bread, an' there's an oat cake for you too. I reckon they'll let you 'ave water, or maybe whatever they're 'aving. Now go an' put on yer pink dress, you want to look presentable on yer first day."

"I always want to look that Ma," said Millie emphatically.

"I know girl, an' I was thinking, happen we can make the green dress fit you given time. It'll need a good bit taken in on the sides, but you'll 'ave more use for it than me."

"Oh no ma, that's yours."

Millie knew just how pleased her Ma had been with the dress and resolved to run up another one for herself, with the material from her grey dress turned inside out and trimmed with the left over green cotton material. That way her Ma could keep the dress they had so painstakingly made for her. By half past five Millie was ready to set off.

"Lots o' luck," whispered Fanny with a last hug."

This was it, her first real job. The butterflies in Millie's stomach began their dance when she left home, and by the time she reached Broad Street they were doing a right old jig.

Stay calm and quiet; remember what you said about not talking too much, she admonished herself. She reached the shop and noticing that the 'Closed' sign was still in place she hesitated. Should she ring the bell or try the door?

As Millie firmly pushed against, it Miss Mabel, who had just drawn the bolts, pulled the door open wide saying, "Welcome to your first day at work Millie. Take no notice of the sign – we don't open for custom until nine." She shepherded Millie through into the back room.

"Take off your shawl, you'll find that we shall be kept busy all day. Our customers come in to select from a wide range of materials, with requests for all styles of dresses or formal gowns. We also make – just a few – matching bonnets for our more select clientele. Where possible we do fittings at their home on request – by appointment of course. So Millie, until you are able to undertake work without supervision, I shall have you working with me. Miss Sybil does all the accounts, takes care of the shop, the stock and the ordering, and we shall be working through here, in the dress making room."

As she spoke Miss Mabel ushered Millie through into what would more usually have been the front sitting room, but had been converted to a work room.

It was a large airy room with lots of natural light from a large window which had been cleverly draped with soft muslin across the lower half, allowing light and later in the day, the sun to flood through; at the same time privacy was ensured from passers-by.

Shelves held a wide selection of materials and two large work tables took up a lot of floor space. Baskets of sewing threads and oddments of material were arranged around the room, with half finished garments on hangers against the walls. On one of the tables a pattern, pinned to dark blue satin was in the process of being cut out.

Millie gazed around in wonder. She'd waited so long to be in a place like this, and now she was really here it felt so right. She wasn't in the least overwhelmed by the thought of all she had to learn and the work facing her; in fact she could hardly wait to begin.

"I expect you have noticed how many more people are coming from the bigger towns. There are far more long stay visitors during the summer months taking the new sea cures that seem to be all the fashion now."

Millie had noticed the occasional stranger, and also knew the ladies from the big houses came to the shops this side of town. Now she gazed around again with a feeling of mounting excitement, mixed with a funny sort of tummy ache. She also noticed Miss Mabel's bandaged hand and secretly hoped she would still have a job when it was better.

"I'm going to work hard and pay attention 'cause I really want to learn. It seems like I've always wanted to work in a place like this! What shall I do first?" Millie's enthusiasm threatened to run away with her all over again.

"I think we must settle you in first, Millie, so just do as I say, and we will get on very well indeed, I'm sure."

Miss Mabel set her to work sorting buttons, tidying cotton spools, and sweeping the floor. Millie also made the sisters their cup of tea – and was rewarded with one herself. Next, she took several pairs of scissors to the knife grinder at the top of the street. In fact Millie did everything asked, except for being let loose on the materials she was itching to get her hands on, and the morning passed in a flash.

At one o'clock Miss Mabel called a halt.

"We shall have a half hour's break now, Millie. Do you have something to eat with you?"

"Oh yes Miss Mabel, I brought me dinner but I 'ave to ask if I could 'ave a cup o' water please?"

"Of course you can. We always eat in the kitchen, so bring your food through. It wouldn't do to get anything on the dresses or –"

"Yes, we should have to subtract it from your wage to compensate," chimed in Miss Sybil, who had closed the shop.

Secretly Millie thought it would probably take near on ten years or more 'to compensate' with the small amount she could expect to earn. Her mind ran riot. She couldn't work without pay, however much she loved the job! She resolved never, ever, to go near anything with food or sticky hands – no, she never would!

Miss Mabel guided her to a stool in the corner of the kitchen to eat, and the sisters fell into deep conversation at the table over their midday meal of cold meat and pickles.

The afternoon followed much the same pattern as the morning, except that Miss Mabel explained they were expecting two fittings. At two 'o clock, the first client arrived, and then another called at three. In turn Millie was required to show them into the curtained alcove, where Miss Mabel helped them off with their day clothes, and into the half finished garments. She called for Millie and bade her pass pins and braid.

Millie looked on in amazement as lilac taffeta was measured, gathered, and pinned, with some discomfort on Miss Mabel's part. Millie did as she was bid and assisted where she could, to help Miss Mabel overcome the difficulties she had with her injured hand. It came easily to Millie, who followed instructions to the letter, and she was surprised and pleased when, at the second fitting Miss Mabel announced, "This is my apprenticed seamstress, Miss Millicent Drew; she will be working here, and will be looking after you on some future occasions, Ma'am."

The elegant young woman slightly inclined her head, and Millie blushed to the roots of her hair. She was an apprenticed seamstress! Things were just getting better and better.

"Well, Millie," said Miss Mabel as the young woman left the shop, "you did very well – I could see you were itching to ask questions of her, but you kept a still tongue in your head – something you will do well to remember when you have to deal with the gentry. I'm pleased with the way that you followed my instructions. Now come and sit here, while I show you exactly what I'm doing, and you can ask any questions you like – I want you to learn as we go along. Now watch carefully: the size of the stitches, the way I match the seams, and place the right sides of the fabric together. This is the way to set a sleeve Millie, it has to be pinned and then tacked."

Millie continued with her sewing lesson, passing pins and cutting lengths of tacking thread, all the time asking questions and absorbing and storing the answers. She was genuinely interested in anything Miss Mabel could teach her.

The afternoon tea break was at four o' clock and Millie was dispatched to the scullery to make a pot of tea in the china teapot, as she had been shown. She was almost afraid to lift it. Leaving time for it to brew, she refilled the kettle and replaced it on the range.

Then she placed two cups on saucers, and one teaspoon, onto a tray, with the sugar bowl filled with neat little rocks of sugar, sugar tongs, and a small jug of milk. This she took through to the shop where the sisters took their afternoon break. Setting the tray down on the counter, she was just about to go back into the dressmaking room, when Miss Sybil spoke.

"Thank you Millie but haven't you forgotten something?" Millie looked at the tray; there was the small bowl of sugar rocks, tongs, a jug of milk, two cups on saucers, and one teaspoon – Miss Mabel didn't take sugar. "I don't think so, have I?" Millie hesitated.

Miss Mabel smiled at her and said, "There are three of us working here, Millie, go and fetch another cup and saucer for yourself. We always agree that anyone we employ has the same needs as we do through the day, and I think we all need – and deserve – a cup of tea. Bring a stool from the work room; we can watch the shop while we drink our tea."

Millie smiled at the sisters. She couldn't believe how kind they were to her, although Miss Sybil looked a bit stern sometimes. On her way back to the kitchen she thought to herself that they both had hearts of gold.

They worked on, until at six o' clock the shop was closed. Everything had been tidied ready for the morning. As Millie was slipping her shawl around her shoulders, she turned to face the sisters and a warm feeling enveloped her.

"I 'ope I did things the way you want, an' I 'ope you think I worked 'ard enough. I've really loved being 'ere – all day – yes I have and the morrow I'll work even 'arder. Then when you think I'm ready, I'll make lovely dresses for you an'..."

"Yes, yes Millie my dear," Miss Mabel stopped her in full flow. "We are both very pleased with your first day at work. Now off you go, and make sure you are on time tomorrow!"

"Yes, yes I will, I will be, good bye Miss Mabel, goodbye Miss Sybil."

Millie left the shop feeling happily pleased with herself. She set off at a swift pace when the thought struck her that she wished she had remembered to say to Miss Mabel, that she hoped her hand would feel better the morrow.

Soon she was hurrying across The Square and along the walk to the harbour end of town. There was so much to think about, and so much to tell her Ma.

As she burst into the cottage she was brimming with the various happenings in the day.

"I'm home" she called out, "It was just the way I expected it to be. I loved it Ma, an' it was nice to be surrounded by all the lovely colours, an' I was able to help Miss Mabel do a fitting, an' on me first day too!"

Fanny looked at her enquiringly,

"I did Ma! I know it was just because Miss Mabel 'ad 'urt 'er 'and, but she said afterwards that I was 'thrown in at the deep end,' and that she was *ex-ex-treme-ly* pleased with me, that means –very- *very*- pleased."

"Yes Millie I know what it means," said Fanny, smiling. "Just go an' get washed up before you grow too big for your boots. That means – she added, giving her a sideways glance, "being too clever for your own good!" She softened it by adding; "An' I'm real proud of you."

Millie disappeared into the scullery to wash her hands and face, before they shared the evening meal and news of their day.

It seemed Millie just had to keep talking, and Fanny listened attentively without interrupting the steady stream of chatter. Millie explained and elaborated on everything, from the layout of her workbench to the fine lawn shifts of her 'clients' underwear.

"It's an achievement in itself, to get work on t' other side of town," said her Ma, smiling. "But perhaps it's time we went to bed; we've got to get up early."

With Jamie gone up an hour since, Fanny banked the fire while Millie lit the candles, before they climbed the narrow stairs to sink thankfully into their beds.

CHAPTER SIX

Jack returned home on the 'Mistral,' after a straight forward voyage to France and the Channel Islands, and found his family in a state of change.

Fanny explained that Millie had secured work sewing. A proper job, she called it – on the other side of town. Jack wondered what made her want to go in that direction, first mending other folk's clothes, and then whatever else she did, working in a dressmaking shop. But she seemed pleased about it. Jack was proud of her, as was Fanny, so he supposed it would all work out for the best.

Fanny continued with her news, "Jamie's left the classroom now – but we talked about that before. Not got 'imself anything but odd jobs though, too busy messing about!"

"Give 'im time to settle, a few months at work'll quieten him down a bit; it's time he helped out, the young scallywag – give 'im less time to get up to mischief an' all! It's a shame 'e don't want to go to sea, but we can't all be alike. Probably not fitted for it! No, on second thoughts it's best he stays on dry land, 'cause if anything's going to 'appen, it usually 'appens to our Jamie." Jack was reminded of himself at that age.

A few days of eating, and taverning, saw Jack getting restless. His love of the sea never lessoned, he was again ready to find work. Although the life of a sailor was hard, as long as Jack could find duties aboard ship while he was young and healthy, he had to make the most of it.

There were no ships wanting hands in Lyme, but Jack heard that the 'Admiral Grey' was making up hands. He would need to make the journey to Bridport to secure work.

Jack always knew a man 'who knew a man' and by agreeing to carry certain illicit goods, was able to accept the offer of a free ride, along with several other assorted travellers.

He secured his sea chest to a spare pack horse and after bidding his family farewell, mounted a second scraggy animal he'd bin provided with, and set off; though he was more used to the rolling of a ship's deck, than the jolting of a horse.

Riding cross country there was safety in numbers, and he knew his borrowed horses would be taken care of at Bridport, where, as an experienced Able Seaman he would almost certainly find duties on a ship making preparation to sail.

Arriving at the busy seaport much later, he parted company with his travelling companions, and feeling hot and tired, located the tavern. There he found an old seadog by the name of 'Scavenger' – aptly named. There was no doubt this was the old salt as described to him, and who seemed to be in the business of collecting packages from certain new arrivals.

Jack made his way over to the old mariner in the corner, and was relieved to hand over the package he carried, guessing it to be either gems or jewellery, by the size; whatever it was he would be pleased to be rid of it. It didn't do to ask too many questions.

His part of the bargain completed, he left the horses at the hostelry yard indicated to him, and moved on down to the quay side.

He shaded his eyes and gazed across the harbour at the big ship anchored there, guessing it to be about eighty tons or so, as it was laid off in deep water. Jack reckoned it would need about fifteen deck hands at least, ruling out first mate, ships bo' sun, and the carpenter.

That still left a dozen or so places for ordinary and able seamen. There may be a couple of hands still needed.

He had no difficulty in finding a small manned boat to row him out to the vessel, in return for a couple of coins. On coming alongside he bid the oarsman wait, whilst he climbed aboard shouting,

"Ahoy there! Where bound, what cargo? Any hands needed?" and found himself face to face with the bo'sun.

"Aye 'tis lucky you are. We've 'ad to take on a couple of green horns to make up numbers. But we're still in need of an able seaman." He paused, grinning. "We got ourselves a volunteer, although he don't know it yet; 'e's sleeping it off below!"

Still grinning, the bo'sun led him to the first mate. After a brief conversation Jack accepted terms and conditions, which had also been agreed by Captain Fawsey, and realised this voyage could be to his advantage.

Talk in Lyme, had made him aware that the owner of the Admiral Grey had long established relations on the opposite shores, and many connections at home, that had taken years to build. The result, a thriving contraband business, under cover of the goods legally imported to Lyme and the neighbouring ports.

It was well known that certain customs officers had agreements with ship owners. In return for taking a small part of the proceeds they allowed the most part to be run ashore, thus ensuring a continuous flow to their personal coffers.

Jack's adrenalin was running high. He hadn't been this excited since his first flirtation with smuggling before wedding Fanny. There was nothing like raising a young family to make you draw your horns in, he had stayed on the edge, and been glad of easy pickings up till now!

Retrieving his sea chest from the boat and paying off the oarsman, he climbed aboard again, to become acquainted with the rest of the crew, soon realising that some of them were familiar faces, he hailed them cheerily.

In the back of his mind he vaguely remembered meeting the captain, although he was sure he had never sailed under him. Confident enough to throw in his lot with them, at least for this voyage, his expectations of bounty along with a legitimate cargo, was too good an opportunity to miss. Things had been going well for him, and he felt ready to chance his arm with the promise of richer pickings.

The recent changes at home, with both Millie and Jamie entering the world of paid work, had nudged him into a change of heart.

Staying on the edge of the smuggling lark was all very well, but the wind of change was blowing. After talking at 'The Vaults' it seemed you had to be either for 'em, or against 'em. If you were against 'em, you had to be on the side of the Revenue!

If you were seen to be for the Revenue, it was as good as cutting your own throat; you'd never get duties aboard ship around here again. Jack had decided which way to jump.

The sea was running high as they set sail under grey skies into a south-easterly; a rough start that caused much trimming of sails. The days were getting shorter, the nights colder. Jack wasn't too worried as to the outcome of this voyage; with a bit of luck, and the excise men open to bribes, the odds against Lyme men getting caught were in their favour.

As far as Jack could make out, about a third of the crew were from Lyme Bay and others from further down the coast. All knew what they were doing; all were willing to take a risk.

Jack's one concern was for the young cabin boy who was about the same age as his Jamie; too young in Jack's opinion. This lad appeared to have been below decks when they sailed, and didn't seem to know where he was. The other youngster, Ernest, had already had the corners knocked off!

Several hours later, when the drink had worn off, Jack heard the Captain bellowing at the younger boy, Lenny, to the effect, that if he'd stayed out of the Taverns and stuck to water, he wouldn't be in this predicament, and would just have to make the best of it! Jack knew he must have been 'pressed' to make up numbers and felt sorry for him.

Day to day work on the sailing vessel was hard, even for experienced sailors. For the couple of young lads it was a nightmare. At the butt end of jokes and pranks, neither one of them was fitted for life at sea.

Ernest – and what sort of a name was that for a seafaring lad? – set on in the galley, had became quite good at working with the ship's cook; if you could call him that! Even so he took every opportunity to disappear.

Young Lenny learning cabin duties, didn't know his 'back from his front.' Although sea sickness laid him low for a time, he was willing but slow. Jack made it his business to keep an eye on the pair of them.

Three days out and a bit of straight talking was needed, *'afore they come up against a deck hand with a short fuse.* Jack decided it was in their interest that he put them straight. After he had finished reading them the 'riot act,' he left them to ponder on the advice any experienced mariner would give to a 'greenhorn.'

"There are two very important things to remember at sea. One is duty. The other is mutiny! The first is doing what you are ordered. The second is NOT doing what you are ordered." He spelled out the possible consequences. "So boys, start taking life on board seriously and you'll all the sooner be home and dry!"

From then onward, each began to shape up in his own way.

Below decks the hammocks were strung only inches apart. There was so little space that by the time the seaman's chests were stowed, there was little room to move. Scrambling over other sailors belongings caused many an angry outburst.

Time between watches and deck duties, was whiled away with sea songs, shanties, and spinning yarns. Cards by candlelight passed many a long watch, but given the foulmouthed, cursing nature of the crew, that ended all too often in fights, inflicting injury with impunity on each other.

The youngster's initiation into the ways of the seafarer was extremely hard – but for as many knocks as they took from one half of the crew, they received help and kind words from the other. All in all, it evened out.

After sixteen days at sea they made ready to sail into the Bay of Biscay, usually the most hazardous part of any voyage. As the sky blackened and the wind rose, worst fears were confirmed; the ship began rolling in the gathering storm.

Everything happened at once. Men, already tired out, were woken and dragged from their hammocks to the cry of '*all hands on deck*'. The cargo, loaded at previous ports along the way, began noisily rattling and clanking where it was stowed, prompting the order '*make fast*'. Noisy, frantic activity and muttered oaths filled the air. Lashing rain and high winds made the most ordinary task a feat of endurance. Goods and chattels were washed overboard causing angry shouts and curses.

Almost impossible orders, and a good many threats were issued by the captain, and punishments were lined up for the 'no good swabs,' as they staggered about their business.

Checking that the boys stayed out of harm's way, Jack vowed that when things calmed down, he would teach them at least some of the skills needed for self preservation at sea. Having a lad of the same age, made him doubly aware of the hazards they faced. Even experienced sailors were fearful of the elements, and their superstitious nature did nothing to allay their fears on the high seas; rough as they were many a prayer was uttered.

Eventually the storm passed; storms in The Bay of Biscay rose dramatically and subsided just as quickly. Slowly, damage was made good; the carpenter proving his worth time and again. Tired deck hands were sent below to rest.

During a storm, days were lost, cargo could be lost, and in the worst instance, lives and ships, could be lost. The calm that followed allowed time for repairs and rest. As order was restored, a fresh course was set and they sailed on, ship, crew, and cargo intact.

The crew settled back into their separate routines, work, watch, and rest; a never ending cycle. The Admiral Gray was dependant on the captain and his crew, for safe passage, and in turn the crew dependant on the vessel, and her officers.

Once a day, the third mate served fresh water to each man. Food was prepared in the starboard galley. The usage of food provided by the ship's cook was finely balanced with the seaman's wage, and there were many rows about quantity, not to mention quality!

Salt beef, pork, bacon and cheese, were balanced with hard dry biscuits and Ernest's speciality, oat biscuits. The further the voyage, the more stinking was the meat.

Crowded into a small space in the hold were a few animals to be slaughtered for food, all adding to the filthy stench of bilge water that filled the low spaces between decks, enough to turn the stomach of the most hardened seafarer.

Jack used any spare time he had, to show the two youngsters 'the ropes.' They learned the difference between stem and stern, larboard and starboard. They studied knots; learned when and where to tie reefs and hitches; and the disaster of getting them wrong. They watched whilst sails were hoisted and lowered, furled and unfurled and best of all they began to understand the importance of working with others, and most important, the division of labour.

As the other crew members watched the boy's progress with interest and growing respect, they became friendlier and more approachable.

Ernest and Lenny realised that the colourful language of the seaman, and short sharp commands, were imperative to getting deck and rope work done in the shortest possible time. And they were for the most part, dependable, and in the face of difficulties, tough and courageous men. They also developed a healthy respect for the forces of nature, and learned vigilance in the face of threat from gales and heavy seas.

Watching all this from a distance, Captain Fawsey, who was a fair and patient man, – unless crossed, – gave instructions for the first mate to initiate the boys in the rudiments of navigation; basic requirements of studying the stars, identifying them by name, and recognising their position in the sky at any given time.

Ernest adopted the ships cat, who was a brilliant mouser and a necessity for keeping them and the rats and cockroaches under control, leaving only the maggots that plagued every sailing vessel. Jack, who was well pleased with the pair of them, felt a just pride in himself for enabling them to fit into life on board ship, and furnishing them with skills that would be useful throughout their lives.

Before being taken on at the start of the voyage, Jack had discussed articles, i.e.-wages, approximate length of voyage and workload with the captain, as was usual, and agreed to conditions and wages earned, 'by the run,' although Masters could withhold their destination or even change it, at will.

Reckoning on a long voyage this time out, Jack had prepared Fanny accordingly. They all seemed 'set fair,' at home, and there was no reason to worry as to how they would manage. On a long voyage he always left more than enough in the old sea chest at home. In an emergency Fanny knew of the 'hush money' under the hearthstone, paid to Jack for turning the occasional blind eye; old Lazurus kept *his* eye on things and could still raise a hearthstone if called on!

Fanny had always been economical and even if he were away longer than expected, all three were working now. He could relax on that score and put his mind at rest, leaving him free for the everyday dramas and crises of ship life. Always expect the unexpected was his maxim. Not often was he disappointed

The ships main cargo this time out consisted of wool and assorted goods bound for Italy. Jack knew that on discharging the cargo at an Italian port – he didn't know which one, but guessed it to be Naples, they would take on wine, Florence oil and fresh citrus fruits, along with other commodities.

Purchased at the Italian price quite legally, they would then sell them on at a higher price, avoiding each country's taxes and import duties. By smuggling *into* an assortment of ports, there was a goodly profit to be made.

Returning via a French port, they would take on fine French brandy, wine and tobacco,

to again outwit Revenue officers, disposing of part of the contraband, by calling at the Channel Islands before finally reaching their home port.

Should they run into trouble off the coast, they would take further action. The easiest way of doing this was to load the small boats, and make preparation for sinking. As long as they were out of the way of prying eyes on other ships, skilled hands would tie the full tubs to planks, which were then weighted down just enough to allow them to float two or three feet above the seabed, in smugglers terms 'sowing the crop.'

Lined up with markers along the coast, the smuggled goods could be retrieved later, allowing them to continue their route via boat, then by carrier overland, until hidden, bought or otherwise disposed of. Contacts up and down the country could be relied upon, with many pack horses involved at each haul.

Jack and his shipmates knew full well that as long as they remained unarmed, and undisguised, if challenged they were in no danger of much more than a heavy financial penalty,

According to the 'Act of Indemnity' of 1736, unless they caused bodily harm to Revenue Officers they were free to carry on their 'trade.'

Free traders, they liked to call themselves. The Revenue had another word for them, *smugglers*. Should they be foolhardy enough to gather together in large numbers and resist when challenged, they became open to transportation, or even the death penalty.

The law had been renewed several times, but each time remained basically the same, and was still of little use!

The voyage proceeded with many incidents of foul temper from cheating at cards, petty pilfering, injury from deck work, and outright clashes between drunken seamen. Captain Fawsey's first mate dished out beatings with a pitch mop, and inflicted injury without second thought, to the common seaman.

Jack passed his time between watches, keeping out of trouble. Staying in one piece became of prime importance for Fanny's sake, and the thought of Jamie and Millie stilled his tongue and stayed his hand on many occasions.

Jack's muscular frame and fearless approach to this way of life stood him in good stead.

After more than three weeks, the second great storm broke. The sea never discriminated between experienced sailors or green horns. When the first mate was taken by a gigantic crashing wave, those on the end of his frequent punishments shed no tears.

But when Ernest suffered the same fate, whilst trying to rescue the ships cat, the sorrow was genuinely felt. For hours the storm raged, the noise so loud as to disallow any form of communication. Cargo was loosened and floated, rolled, or banged about in the hold. Animals tied closely together injured each other in their terror.

Resentments and frustrations became of no consequence in the face of nature at her worst. Any tension or conflict between the Captain and his crew was forgotten and at such times each relied instinctively on the other.

By dawn the storm had blown itself out and order was restored. Jack never ceased to wonder at the sheer grit and determination of the crew. Each knew his own and most others work as well, and stepped in wherever help was needed. Petty differences were forgotten in the face of hardship.

The Admiral Grey sailed on, the crew in comparative unity, calling at various ports en route; each presenting its own difficulties and compensations, in the form of topping up with fresh supplies and water.

Although floggings at sea were common place, physical injury's and empty bellies, made uncomfortable bed fellows. Captain Fawsey's liking, for frequent measures of rum, and subsequent bad temper, made life difficult for the crew,

Continuous four hours on, and four hours off watches, were made bearable by the acquisition of varying amounts of bartered food or tobacco. The promise of riches at the end of the voyage was a fine master. Many weeks had passed with the ever present threat of danger, when the look out in the tops, spied a sail on the horizon. The Captain's sixth sense, developed over many years, told him something was amiss.

Glancing aloft, he decided to send a leading hand to the top most shrouds, and tucking his telescope into the top of his ducks, he climbed nimbly up the rigging. The crew were still awaiting news of the other ship, when the cry of, "English colours sir," was heard and some of the crew visibly relaxed.

Jack and the older seamen were well aware of the threat of privateering vessels in these waters, and knew the ship could be sailing under false colours. *Were they going to loose some or even all of their precious cargo?*

The captain's decision to ignore the English flag was the right one. The ship appeared to be gaining on them. The crew becoming fidgety the atmosphere tense. The Admiral Grey would try to outrun them!

As if proving the captain's judgment, the pursuing vessel now hoisted the flags of the privateer. After a barrage of commands back and forth, setting of more sail, and the passage of the best part of two hours, it was certain their ship was faster than the pursuing vessel and would stay out of trouble; the slower ship eventually giving up the unequal struggle.

Exhilarated, captain and crew resumed a lighter note, congratulating captain, officers and each other. In fact privateers were nothing more than licensed pirates. Obtaining a 'Letter of Marque' meant they could capture and rob any likely looking ship *and* with the blessing of their government on a 'half for us half for you' basis; piracy, made legal!

Several weeks passed, navigating The Admiral Grey onward around the Spanish Portuguese coast, further slowed down by urgent repairs to damage from rough seas. Eventually they sailed through the Straits of Gibraltar.

Far from reaching safety, here there was an ever present threat of crossing swords with pirates from the Barbary Coast; water bandits, wanting not just goods but men too, for sale or ransom. In these waters the crew were certainly jittery, all the time on the lookout for Algerians or Turks, who they knew would show no mercy.

At last the Admiral Grey came within sight of her destination port Naples.

The Mediterranean sun warmed the hearts and bones of the weary crewmen, and Lenny watched in wonder as a new way of life unravelled before him.

He had become a proficient and useful hand on board, and a warm bond existed between him and Jack, who watched in satisfaction as he slowly developed from child to youth. Physical work had strengthened his previously thin frame, and his tousled long hair and tanned skin completed the transformation.

If he had any thoughts of going ashore to 'sample' this new way of life, they were quickly crushed, as the dubious joys of unloading the ship were shown him.

Back breaking work carried out mostly by manpower, with the assistance of block and tackle, hoists and leverage. Not until all cargo was unloaded was best part of the crew allowed ashore.

Jack was among them, and as one, they made for the English equivalent of an ale house, and good *fresh* food.

Jack kept young Lenny at his side with instructions to keep his money well out of sight. They entered an eating house, where the lad was fascinated by the sound of excited voices in strange tongues. The music was loud and the food looked unfamiliar, but smelt appetizing. Jack selected their meals by a series of gestures.

They were seated, and served with food and drink. After quenching their thirst on ruby red wine, Lenny was in high spirits; both of them happier and more relaxed than for weeks past. Whilst many of the crew looked for a bed with a clean woman, Jack and Lenny settled happily for beds with clean linen!

Three whole days turn around, days in which to stroll in the sun, drink the local wine, and enjoy the lazy warm hours. Days to unwind, sleep, eat, and sleep some more.

Jack awoke from one such siesta, propped against the barrels lining the white wall of a trattoria, to find young Lenny missing. He stretched lazily and stared around. From one direction came loud laughter, unmistakeably from some shipmates who had found themselves senoritas to spend some of their half pay on. Dark hair, and sultry brown eyes, to sailors soused in unfamiliar liquor, they must seem like the answer to prayer after so long at sea in rough male company.

Turning, Jack looked the other way, down toward the quay. The captain and bo'sun were deep in conversation, probably doing a deal with the third man, who was jabbering in broken English and gesticulating wildly.

Where was young Lenny? Slowly he stood up and started to walk towards the centre of the town. Shutters were being opened, and people began appearing as siesta time ended, and the place slowly came back to life.

Suddenly he heard loud cursing coming from a balcony above him. He looked up in time to witness an Italian seaman holding Lenny's arms from behind. Another rough looking character rifled through the boy's pockets.

A gag had been placed in his mouth and the cursing issued from the man searching his pockets, for Lenny had successfully aimed a kick where it hurt most!

The more Lenny struggled, the tighter he was held. Although he couldn't understand the foreign tongue, he knew well enough he was about to part company with his hard earned pay. Jack bellowed up at the balcony, but not in time to prevent Lenny receiving a few well aimed punches himself.

Rushing through the street door, he took the steps two at a time. Reaching the top, he looked across at the open door in front of him as both men lurched Lenny forward, pushing the boy and Jack backwards down the stairs.

Before they could recover themselves, the two rough necks had climbed over them, and made a hasty exit. By the time Jack and Lenny reached the door they had disappeared into the warren of narrow alley ways.

"Well now, I suppose you've learned a lesson of some sort," Jack said with some irritation, brushing himself down. "What money did you 'ave on yer?"

Lenny was angry with himself – firstly because he knew it to be his own fault. Jack had said not to wander off on his own. Secondly for being taken in by a stranger offering bargain goods which didn't exist; and thirdly because they spoke to him in broken English, which stupidly made him believe that he could trust them. Now he had no money either.

"Damn their eyes" he yelled, "I'll knock 'em flat if I set me eyes on 'em again."

Jack couldn't help but laugh. The boy was less than five feet tall, but the venom came from an angry man.

They brushed themselves down and wandered on in the sunshine, all the while Lenny uttering well learned oaths. It was time to find one last good meal before making their way back, to resume loading the last of the new cargo.

The crew in good spirits, well fed with food that didn't have maggots and actually move by itself, were rested, and ready to put their backs into the next stage, which entailed the back breaking business of stowing, before the turnabout and embarking on the long haul home.

This was the halfway mark, and the return voyage was set to take at least as long again, depending on weather and currents. Hauling anchor they made ready to sail amid the feelings of anticipation and excitement that Jack thrived on. Watching the receding coast line, Jack and Lenny bade a quiet farewell to the sunshine port of Naples.

CHAPTER SEVEN

As summer slipped into autumn, Millie slipped into a daily routine. Rising before five, she crept quietly downstairs to nudge the fire into life, heating water in the large pan and hurrying through to the scullery to wash.

Fanny made a thick gruel from oats and boiled water, brewing a can of tea to wash it down. Breakfast finished, Millie cut two slices of bread, pressed them together with dripping and wrapped the wedge in a clean cloth, to take for her mid-day break.

Millie always managed to be ready to leave the house before her young brother arrived down stairs; it was much the best method of avoiding chaos in the small cottage.

Jamie didn't seem to be settling well, and Fanny knew he knuckled under *only* when he had to, and had a habit of disappearing for long spells. She worried too, that he wouldn't hold down the variety of odd jobs that she secured for him, and would never apply himself long enough to get steady work.

Much chillier in the early mornings now, the damp air and sea spray chilled Millie to the bone. She was relieved to leave the shingle of 'the walk' and head across the square and up the hill to the small shop on Broad Street.

Walking quickly she, pondered on the sheer luck that had brought together the vacancy for a seamstress, and her change of interest and direction, *though it wasn't very lucky for Miss Mabel,* was her immediate afterthought.

The sisters had been kind and patient in their method of teaching their apprentice. Millie was a very willing pupil. Each day she improved and learned something new, becoming proficient at measuring and pinning, and during 'fittings' Miss Mabel was especially pleased with her manner toward the ladies of the big houses.

The measuring was more usually carried out by home appointment, but on some occasions younger ladies found it less time consuming, to call into Miss Mabel's fitting room, whilst they were in town.

It was on one such occasion that an elegant young lady called at the establishment, to choose her material and have her measurements taken; a delicate procedure.

Watched closely by Miss Mabel, Millie put her acquired knowledge into practice proficiently, and without embarrassment to either her client or herself.

She had shown extreme patience in her client's indecision, but together they made a choice of russet silk. Completing the measuring procedure, Millie, assured her of further help should she need it. Stepping from the tiny fitting room she slid the curtain back into place ensuring privacy, and allowing her client to slip into her outer garments and tidy her hair.

Millie could see that Miss Mabel was pleased with the way she handled her first fitting.

As the young lady left the shop with a further appointment, Miss Mabel enquired, "Is there anything you want to ask Millie?"

"Oh yes there's a lot I'd like to ask, but first, who is the young lady?" Miss Mabel looked at Millie's expectant face, "so I can put the name on the work ticket I meant."

"*I meant* was there anything about the *measuring* that you found difficult? She paused; but her name is Clara Elliot, from the Manor House, above Uplyme. A much valued customer!"

Millie froze for a moment, rendered speechless. She thought quickly, *Emily said the young gentleman up at The Coaching Inn was from the Manor House. It must be – but it can't; she didn't say he was wed!* Now Miss Mabel was asking, "Is there anything you need to know about the measurements, Millie?" Millie bent to gather up the material, and her work ticket, saying, "I think I remembered everything, I'll fill this in," and assured Miss Mabel that she would be glad to accept help, when it came to altering the pattern to fit.

The thoughts tumbled around in Millie's head. She felt as though a horse had kicked her in the stomach. Suddenly she realised that Miss Mabel was watching her.

"Is there anything wrong Millie?"

"Oh no-no, it's alright, I was just wishing I could look as pretty as her, that's all."

Well Millie I can assure you that character is far more important than looks, but I dare say you have more than your fair share of both, so don't waste any time on envy, it doesn't become you!"

Much chastened Millie hung up the dress, and brought all of her attention back to the work bench. She listened intently as the finer points of transferring measurements to patterns, and pinning patterns to material, was explained to her. By closing time the procedure was completed.

"First thing tomorrow we begin cutting," Miss Mabel declared, and with a certain satisfaction, they shut up shop.

At intervals throughout that evening, Millie's thoughts returned to the possibility of 'her gentleman' already being spoken for; and if he was, why did he look at her the way he did? Millie's naivety was total.

The next day work was resumed and the material smoothed out onto the work bench. When it came to placing the pattern pieces on the cloth, the enormity of getting it wrong never failed to bring on a feeling of dread. Next came the even trickier part, the only part Millie feared; once past the cutting stage, it would be plain sailing, with enjoyment woven into each stitch. As long as cutting was in progress Millie ensured Miss Mabel was never far from her side.

She stole another look at the cream silk dress hanging on the back of the door. It was the first 'made up' garment Millie had been allowed to put the final touches to.

It was trimmed with tiny pink rosebuds around the bodice, which she had fashioned entirely by herself, from narrow satin ribbon. The pink lace that edged the sleeves and hem felt crisp, setting off the style, making it look, and feel, expensive. She reached out and again felt the smooth cool silk between her fingers. How many times had Millie stopped work to look at it? Miss Mabel broke into her thoughts,

"I know you are quite taken with the dress Millie, but I'm sure the young Brading sisters will be back. It was made for the elder of the two, but there seems to be a slight problem in collecting it. However she asked especially, that we keep that particular dress on one side for her. I'm certain it won't be long before it finds a good home!"

"Yes I am sure she'll be back soon." Wistfully Millie nodded her agreement.

Miss Mabel smiled, and walked through to Miss Sybil in the shop, to collect a new reel of thread, saying quietly, "Bless the child; she has perfect taste, that's what makes her so good at the work, the primrose taffeta, ordered by Clara Elliot; it was Millie who suggested pale coffee ribbon for the bows. And wasn't it she, who secured a second order, in the russet silk? Yes, Millie is an asset, and it was a good day for us the day she applied for work."

Miss Sybil agreed wholeheartedly.

"She learns quickly, she will soon be ready to go with you to appointments, in fact why not ask her now, it's all good experience?"

"I'll do that Sybil; in fact I'll ask her right away." Miss Mabel went back to the sewing room with the thread, and seated herself at the long table again.

"Millie, I shall want you to accompany me up to the Manor house, one day next week. I shall let you know when, a bit nearer the time" Millie's heart missed a beat.

"The Manor House?" she whispered.

Since that day when she had almost bumped into Master Gerard, she had not set eyes on him. That, however had not stopped her dreaming of him, she still remembered the way he had smiled at her; on *two* occasions!

For the rest of the morning Millie had to rein in her thoughts, setting her mind to concentrate on work. When it was time to take a well earned break, the 'closed' sign was turned on the door, and the three of them went through to the small kitchen. Mabel and Sybil ate their dinner at the table, whilst Millie brewed tea for them all, before retiring to the corner window seat to eat and dream.

"Don't you think so Millie?" She was suddenly aware that Miss Mabel had been addressing her and had spoken more than once.

"Oh I'm sorry; I was lost in me thoughts! Did you ask me something Miss Mabel? I didn't mean to be rude."

"Of course you didn't dear. I was asking if you would consider moving into the attic room. With the weather on the change, and a long winter ahead, we don't like to think of you coming to

work and walking home again in the dark" For a moment Millie couldn't grasp the sense of what Miss Mabel had just said, *surely workers didn't live with their employers? Not unless they were in service.*

"What do you think dear?" Miss Mabel pressed her. "Do you really mean that I should move here; have a room of me own?" Millie gaped in amazement, lost for words. Miss Mabel waited a moment before saying,

"Well you still haven't said whether that would be acceptable to you. Of course you would have to talk to your mother about it, but it would seem the sensible things to do, don't you think?"

"Yes – yes I do, and I will, talk to me Ma, I mean, I would like that, I really would, and I am sure she will agree. Ma often worries when it's dark, an 'I'm a bit late 'ome!"

"Of course," Miss Sybil interrupted, "it's not so much a room as the attic space above the bedrooms. It has a door that locks, so it would be quite private, and it would be your own.

Once you leave the workroom at the end of the day, we wouldn't expect anything more of you." Millie began to get hold of the idea at last.

"It sounds wonderful, and I could 'ave me own things there. I'm sure me Ma will be agreeable, yes I'm sure of it."

"Well now, you must talk to her this evening, and we'll see what can be done before the shorter days are here." Now Millie had something else to think about!

The afternoon dragged on, usually Millie was lost in the garment they were working on, but at last the clock showed six o' clock. Millie's glanced around; her workbench was tidy with everything in its place ready for the morrow, just as she had been shown.

"Off you go then, wrap that shawl around you, it's blowing well out there, remember to talk to your mother when you get in, and we'll see you in the morning."

The sisters waved her off as she left the shop. Her dreams were coming true one by one. She ticked them off in her mind. *First I leave the Cobb and go sewing; clean and warm and best of all not smelly. Then, I get taken on at the shop – with all the lovely materials and things; An' now the chance of a room of me very own.*

Millie's head was spinning; she could hardly wait to reach home, although a nagging doubt about leaving her Ma, niggled somewhere at the back of her mind.

What about Clara Elliot? She pushed the thought from her, it had never entered her head that any of the young gentlemen could be wed, especially him. *The way he looked at me an' all.* Sadness stole over her, but on reaching the cottage, and in the excitement and anticipation of relating the happenings of the day, it was again pushed to the far corners of her mind.

Millie pushed the door open and hung her shawl on the peg, noting that her Ma's shawl already hung there. Millie was never one to keep anything to herself for long, and rushing through to the scullery, found her Ma preparing vegetables from the market.

"'Ello Millie luv, 'ad a good day?" enquired Fanny "I'm just putting a stew together; there's plenty of tatties and carrots. Jamie'll be back soon."

"Ma, guess what Miss Sybil and Miss Mabel want me to do?"

"Work harder and talk less I shouldn't wonder," said Fanny wiping her hands on her apron. Millie tried a different approach.

"You know how you worry when I'm late home an' it's dark Ma; well they worry an' all. You wouldn't think so would you?"

Millie wasn't sure now how her Ma would take the news. She tried again. "Ma, they want me to move in! 'ave the attic room like, make it into me own, so as not to 'ave the long walk morning an' night. But Ma I would still come over every opportunity, an' give you the same money; oh but I'd 'ave to pay them something wouldn't I? I would really *miss* you an' Jamie, an' when Pa comes home I'd make sure of seeing him." Fanny sat down at the table and stared at Millie who pulled out a chair and sat opposite, "do you think it selfish Ma? I won't do anything unless it's alright with you."

Fanny gazed into the enquiring eyes of her firstborn.

"Oh Millie luv, I knew this day would come, an' I'm glad it's something you want for yourself, cause it won't 'urt me, although I'll miss you too. I will, and that's a fact.

But you know, when the blackberries are ripe, that's when I 'ad you, and that will be fifteen Septembers ago. You're all but grown up, an' of *course* you have to do what's best, aye and sensible, an' I reckon that idea's both."

She reached out and patted Millie's hand, "Aye I will miss you. But you'll go with my blessing; an' like you said, you can come over 'ere anytime; More often after winter's come and gone. Now I reckon that's Jamie kicking 'is boots off, we'll 'ave a bite, an' later there'll be lots to sort out." Jamie burst into the scullery.

"You know what Ma?" he stepped past Millie and reached out to the open door of the range, where the fire gave a warm and welcome glow. Looking over his shoulder and grinning at Millie, he continued, "I took crabs to Coaching Inn, delivered mackerel to fish stalls, an' tarred the gaffer's boots. That was all 'afore noon. *Then* I 'ad to learn the nets again! I *hate* 'em. I'm not going for a fisherman, *never,* can't see the point of earning a living from the sea, when I can do it from dry land."

Fanny smiled and shook her head. He was going to take time settling. Everything had to fit into his plan, and that included leaving time for hunting his curios, and whatever else he did in his long absences. Fanny sighed; he wasn't a bit like his hard working Pa.

"Sit to the table now, the both of you, an' get this inside you."

Later after the meal, they sat exchanging ideas about all the things Millie would need to set herself up, befitting her new station in life. Fanny turned things over in her head.

"You'll need a bed and blankets – they can be got cheap from the second 'and stall, an' a floor pallet won't do, not in a house on Broad Street."

"I'll need a proper bed then, aye, an' a chest to keep my clothes in!"

Fanny planned to go through the cottage to see what she could spare, then with a jolt she thought of the stash of coins behind the hearthstone.

Their emergency fund! It was for a rainy day, but what's the use of keeping it when it's needed now?" Millie was on the way to making something of herself, and Fanny was going to give her all the help she could.

"That'll show 'im whether we're good enough or not!" She murmured to herself.

Fanny stopped short. *Oh my Lord what's wrong wi' me? I've not thought on Millie's blood father in years, aye an' I'll not think on 'im again; Millie'll get on, by 'er own efforts an' with my 'elp.* She quickly pushed the thought of her first love to the back of her mind, as she slowly climbed the stairs, intent on checking through the contents of the old chest in the back room.

Jack was the one who had brought Millie up as his own, he was a real father to her and she loved him and knew no different. But Fanny couldn't help thinking how alike Millie and her blood father were. Her red gold curls, the toss of her head, her longing for nice things. She did have some of the gentry in her!

Her mind returned to Jack; an over whelming wave of love and gratitude enveloped her. If it hadn't been for him it would have been the workhouse for her and the infant, when the gold coins ran out.

With the passing years, Fanny had come to realise that what in her youth had seemed the consuming passion of her life, had been just another episode in the life of her colourful Gentleman Sea Captain! Her silence bought with a handful of gold sovereigns. *My, she had been gullible and no mistake!*

Fanny came back to earth with a thud, as the bedroom door opened behind her pushing her unceremoniously across the bed.

"My stars, Jamie, you're nought but a young whirlwind," she spluttered, "when you going to calm down?" Jamie, amid apologies, grabbed his jacket and shouting over his shoulder, "I'll be back 'afore dark," rushed down the stairs and left the cottage.

Fanny sat down; sometimes she wondered what life would throw at her next. She hoped he wouldn't get into bad company, but she had her doubts on that score, knowing how easily her young son was led.

Jamie arrived at the Cobb, to meet up with a couple of young scallywags he was in the habit of spending any spare time with, also -on occasions- time when he should have been working.

Freddie Parkin was several years older than Jamie and a bit of a hero in his eyes. He was a gangly youth with a pallid, spotty complexion, and cold grey eyes that missed nothing and in the habit of 'lifting' anything that wasn't nailed down. In fact Jamie had been prevailed upon on more than one occasion to assist him.

Having already been brought up before the justices and got off with a warning, he escaped the house of correction by the skin of his teeth; avoiding the poor house, by earning enough money to keep his mother and sister, clothed and fed. It wouldn't do to enquire too closely just how he came by it. The fisher folk around about kept a wary eye on Freddie and his 'goings on'.

Now having got the two younger boys interested in his latest lark, Jamie and another timid lad – Freddie, assumed the role of leader. Quick of eye, and fleet of foot, he seemed to know in advance any messages to be run, or where the Riding Officers were stationed along the cliffs. The trio moved quickly along West beach.

It was early evening, and Freddie paid particular attention to putting distance between themselves and the Cobb, coming to a halt just past a rocky outcrop. Unwilling to divulge exactly what he was up to, he was intent on setting a small fire on the beach near the shoreline, in the small secluded bay.

Jamie swelled with pride at being included in the group. He was certain the information they had gleaned at 'The Vaults' would be used to warn and safeguard smugglers. Freddie was so sure of himself. The whole idea pleased Jamie's romantic streak, and as he had grown older, he had many times witnessed the odd group of smugglers intent on their business. He was nobody's fool when it came to accepting money in return for helping them, and his lips were sealed.

As they waited as the dull, late September evening closed around them. The grey sky merged into the grey sea. There was a chill in the air. Jamie became restless, and would much rather have filled this waiting time searching for more curios to sell.

At last Freddie decided the time was right, when peering out to sea they spied a sailing craft. It gradually increased in size, making it easier to recognise it was rigged as a Lugger.

On deck, the crew guided by the Cobb, and knowing the waters like the back of their hand, prepared to lay off to the west, quickly lowering a rowing boat. Arrangements for tub-men on shore to meet their small boat, had been put in place and all seemed well.

Back on the shingle after what seemed an almost endless wait, the watchers recognised a small boat pulling towards them. When it was well past the halfway point between ship and shore, Freddie became agitated.

His instructions from 'The Vaults' were clear, his cut depended on the smugglers being *caught*. If he alerted the riders too soon, they would simply row back to their ship; if not soon enough, they would make shore, and be away with their spoils.

The small pile of driftwood had been kept dry by Ben's coat. Now Jamie produced the paper handbill he had managed to procure, and thrust it under the dry wood, igniting it by means of the flint that he always carried.

"Get it going, wait - now blow," Freddie hissed orders at them. In a short time a steady blaze was going, "now, put some seaweed on it and watch the smoke go up!"

Making sure the plume of smoke was well established he stood back in satisfaction, *"right now run"* he hissed, turning and sprinting off the way they had come.

Jamie and Ben stared at Freddie's retreating back for a moment; Ben turned and ran after him. Jamie perplexed, yelled after Freddie, "Can't we stay and help 'em now we guided 'em in?"

"Shut it stupid," snarled Fred, pausing in mid flight, "scarper." With that he was gone, leaping over the rocks and across the shingle, intent on reaching the headland before the incoming tide cut him off.

Jamie began to run after the retreating figures, there wasn't much to be gained by hanging around. Although he didn't understand what Freddie was up to, he instinctively knew *something was wrong*.

In the small boat sudden panic set in.

"Look smoke! summat's wrong. Aye, an' look at top 'o cliff."

Peering through the failing light the crew spotted swaying lights, and what looked to be a couple of horsemen silhouetted at the top of the cliff. Suddenly amid much cursing, they recognised them to be Riding Officers.

Still in deep water the men began ditching their cargo of half a dozen brandy barrels. The boat emptied as if by magic and the 'would be' smugglers swam for their lives. It was unlikely the Officers, landlubbers as they were, would risk their lives trying to retrieve the bounty, and they were still too far away to identify the men in the half light.

Even if they could be identified there was now no evidence, or rather it was at the bottom of the sea, and nothing to 'tie' them to it!

As soon as foot set on shingle they were away, putting as much distance as possible between themselves and the yelling officers, who had dismounted to find the path down the cliff.

The smugglers, knowing every inch of the beach, had no fear of being caught. It would take the 'gobblers' all their time to find the path down, let alone make the decent! If only they hadn't been disturbed! *Who were the three figures hot- footing it along the beach? And that smoke! By the stars, they were nought but young un's, giving them away to the Revenue.*

Looking back out to sea in the failing light, they could make out a Revenue Cutter appearing around the point. Quick off the mark, once the sign it had been waiting for materialised in the form of the spiral of thick smoke.

No trouble for their Lugger, still manned, to outrun it. the Lugger, being a much faster boat, would soon be out of harm's way; but the Riding Officers on the cliff path had certainly been tipped off. Ahead they caught a glimpse of three disappearing figures.

Almost exhausted, stumbling their way amid much cursing, they came within sight of the harbour. It was the luck of the draw to the small wet group, that not for the first time, nor the last, they were thwarted. The carriers on land would have smelt a rat and disappeared, or maybe not even turned up in the first place. But by the law of averages they reckoned on better luck next time, and there would be a next time.

For now they were more interested in reaching the first safe house. No questions asked, a hot toddy and dry clothes would be the greeting! Of course if they cared to relate the evening's events, sighs and chuckles would be the order of the day.

Outside the cottage, never a word would be breathed, they'd go 'creeping' - dragging the seabed - to retrieve their spoils, at the first opportunity.

But who were those young 'uns? The frustrated smugglers vowed to do a bit of snooping of their own, and they'd begin by asking around in the right circles. 'The Vaults' seemed a good place to start.

Fanny looked at James's flushed cheeks, as he came into the cottage after running all the way back from West beach. He slipped past her into the warm kitchen. Fanny would have been interested to know what he had been up to, but instead of answering her question he countered it with one of his own.

"Got anything to eat Ma? I'm starving." Fanny brought out bread, and cut and toasted a thick slice. He cleverly side stepped any further inquiries, and after munching his way through his wedge, bid his Ma goodnight and made his way up to bed.

Now he felt bad about the way things had turned out, he'd meant no harm, how was he to know that Freddie was on 'the other side'? He would go over to 'The Vaults' first thing the morrow, on the quiet like – just to see if there was any talk of the nights happenings.

As soon as he finished his jobs he made his way over to the bawdy tavern. Sitting on the steps he kept his ears open and his mouth shut. Soon he recognised a couple of mean looking characters approaching, remembering he had seen them talking to Freddie. He was just about to slip away, when Freddie appeared from inside and stepped towards them. The greeting he got was obviously not what he expected.

"So you think you're clever," said one, grabbing him by the shoulder and pushing him up against the tavern wall.

"An' you wants to be one o' us?" growled the other, giving him a shove in the chest. Freddie took a sharp slap on the cheek from the first man, all his bravado seemed to have left him. Jamie cowered down beside a drunken sailor and his dog, doing his best to become invisible; pulling his jacket collar up to his ears in an effort to hide.

No one had spotted him, and he would draw attention to himself if he stood up to leave now. Besides, he wanted to know more. The first man looked like getting rough.

"You know what 'appens to lad's as mess up," he snarled, his broken yellow teeth inches from Fred's face. "We ties 'em 'and an' foot, an' takes 'em on board ship, an' lash's 'em to bowsprit. Or we could lower 'em *down into the deep green sea. You've 'eard o' keel'auling?* An' we keeps on till they choke's an' drowns. Or gets ripped about wi' the barnacles, *an' that's after we tar's 'em*!" He leaned even closer- the second man took over. Pushing his face close to Freddie's, he continued.

"Aye we tars 'em wi' *'ot* tar. That's if they can't get things right. We got no use for lad's what mess up." Jamie had heard enough, a quick glance in Freddie's direction showed that the lad had turned ashen, and was visibly shaking in his boots. Suddenly the men gripped his arms one each side, forcibly quashing him against the wall.

All Jamie's admiration had evaporated. *If I leave 'ere in one piece, I'll stay clear; 'ot tar, keel'auling?* The words conjured up unimaginable agony.

He waited until all three had disappeared inside, and under cover of a brewers dray made a break for it, not stopping until safely back at the harbour. He was hard put to keep his mind on his next job. He'd had a lucky escape this time; but would Freddie be as lucky? Would they stop at just scaring him, before letting him go?

It took a long time for the scene Jamie had witnessed, to fade, and his nightmares were a source of concern. His changed attitude to work surprised Fanny, but he remained silent on both subjects. *Would Freddie name him, or say where to find him?*

As time passed, Freddie was nowhere to be seen. Jamie had visions of him being keelhauled, or worse. Would they come knocking on *his* door? It had all swelled to unmanageable proportions in his head.

He had to stop looking everywhere for signs of trouble, stop imagining the worst. But if Freddie didn't turn up soon he knew he would have to tell his Pa just as soon as he returned from sea.

CHAPTER EIGHT

When dawn broke Millie had already been awake a good hour; Jamie had been restless all night. She had explored the idea of moving to the other side of town, to a room of her own, and her first misgivings had been dispelled by Fanny's acceptance of it as a natural progression of things.

The more she thought of it, the more excited she became at the prospect. Never one to do things by halves, she gladly accepted the coverlet that her Ma had stitched in her younger days as there was still plenty of wear and warmth left in it.

Millie decided to ask the sisters if she could save the leftover lengths of coloured thread for her own use. Already in her mind's eye, she had embroidered, and embellished, the pretty coverlet that would drape the second hand bed. *It'll look just perfect when it's finished! Then I'll make a runner for the small chest. I'll need that for me clothes. Ma will help me sort that out, an' then....*

Millie's thoughts were interrupted by Fanny's voice calling up the stairs, "Come on Millie, look lively, wake yerself up an' get down 'ere, it's a new day not started yet, an' us with Lord knows what to fit into it" Millie hastened from her bed and hurtled down the stairs.

The fire that had been banked up overnight, was picking up again, as Fanny stirred it into life.

"I've got such ideas for me new room Ma." Millie bounced into the kitchen. "It will be so tidy; not 'aveing to share with anyone."

"That'll be a change then," replied Fanny.

Totally undaunted Millie carried on, "Then when I start on me bonnets, I can work as long as I like in the evenings; oh, but then I s'pose I might 'ave to buy me own candles."

"Yes, well never mind that now, let's set about getting a good breakfast inside you, a bowl of oats an' honey should set you up.

Old man over the market tried his 'and at keeping bees this summer. I was lucky to get the last of 'is honeycomb, not much, but it rings the changes."

Millie was barely listening, and took the steaming bowl across to sit down on the hearthstone, and with a full mouth muttered, "Ma, *honey!*" she savoured a mouthful of the sweet, hot oats.

"Yes, well, seems as 'ow I won't be able to spoil you for long, but eat up, then 'urry an' get yerself washed and dressed."

Millie glanced around wondering if her Ma was having second thoughts about letting her go; but no, Fanny continued to talk whilst they ate breakfast.

"I 'bin thinking. You ought to ask one of 'em if there'll be anything in that attic room; 'afore we go buying. It makes more sense. When you go in today, put it to 'em.. Ask what you'll need then we'll know where we are. Hurry up now maid, you're cutting it fine this morning."

Millie finished her breakfast, dressed quickly and collected all she needed, before hurrying from the cottage. *How many more mornings will I wake to see the waves an' 'ear the gulls, an' tell the weather by the clouds? Things change so quick.*

Watching her girl, stepping out to get on with the new life she was carving out for herself, tugged at Fanny's heart strings. She was well aware of just how much Millie would be missed, but making decisions in Jacks absence wasn't always easy. In this case she knew it was the right one, and Jack would be proud...

Millie arrived at the shop and stared intently in the window, drinking in every fold of the russet gown displayed there, and the pale fawn silk bonnet and kid gloves, which lay softly on the swathe of pale green taffeta.

She stepped back and looked up at the names above the door. Misses S. and M. Hartnell. Underneath in smaller letters, Haberdashery and Dressmaking.

She was on the threshold of a new life, and knew that as soon as she said yes to the move, she would be miss Millicent Drew, who lived and worked on Broad Street! How grand that sounded.

She pushed open the door. As usual the bolts had been pulled back just before six, pending her arrival, just as promptly Millie shot them again behind her. Moving through the shop and across the hall, then down the step into the workroom, she could hear Miss Mabel and Miss Sybil talking. They looked up as she entered.

"Hello dear" greeted Miss Mabel, "was it a chilly walk this morning?"

"Yes, oh yes, there's a sea mist but it will be sunny later in the day," Millie hung her shawl on the back of the door and smiled at the sisters. "I put it to me Ma, about staying here, having me own room like, and she thought it was a good idea and very nice of you to ask me." Mabel clapped her hands together,

"I knew it, it's the very best solution, and didn't I say as much Sybil?"

"Many times, dear many times, in fact you would have been most disappointed if Millie's mother needed her to be at home." Miss Sybil couldn't help the ghost of a smile touching her lips. She often appeared to be rather stern, but her bark was always much worse than her bite.

"Well that's settled now," beamed Mabel. Millie felt a fresh surge of excitement.

"There's lots of things that I want to ask you, but I'll wait till me dinner break."

Millie wanted to ask about the bed, and chest of drawers, but not in working time. Her Ma would say it would be, taking advantage, to stay gossiping when she should be working, Millie hurried to her worktable, with Miss Mabel close on her heels.

"Indeed, we will talk of it again later on. We would like to go together to see Mr Matthews, the accountant who keeps an eye on our books. Miss Sybil does as much as she can, but there are certain things that we need help with.

Our appointment isn't until half past eleven, so until we are ready to leave I would like you to continue stitching the lilac taffeta, and then you will be on your own for a short while."

Millie had been at the Broad Street shop for now some time now and due to the kindness, and encouragement shown her, was becoming confident as well as proficient.

"Will you be leaving the shop open?" she enquired, "I could take some work through and keep an eye on things while you are gone."

"Well" began Miss Sybil, "we were going to close up, but if you think you can manage, we'll be happy to leave you in charge. It won't be for long, an hour and a half at most. If there's any problem, then just close the shop, lock up, and carry on working in the sewing room."

At ten past eleven the sisters made ready to leave for their appointment. As they crossed the street and continued on their way, Millie, who was watching their departure through the shop window, recognised the elder of the two Brading sisters approaching from the opposite direction. She appeared to be in a hurry as she pushed open the door and entered, looking startled to see Millie behind the counter. She hesitantly asked, "May I speak with one of the proprietors, please."

"I'm sorry miss; they had to go out for a short while. I'm here on me own, but I can help you, or take a message." Millie paused.

"I'm disinclined to discuss the matter with anyone else." Eliza Brading looked uncomfortable. Millie should have left it at that and suggested that she call back later, but inexperience made her pursue the matter.

"Is it to do with the cream silk dress that we have put aside for you Miss?" pressed Millie in her best shop voice.

"Yes, I, well it seems... No, I shall call again and speak to your employer, good day to you." In a moment the shop was empty. *She's not going to collect it!* The thought hit Millie, *how could she bear not to?*

Millie thought of the beautiful silk dress and in a second she was across the shop, bolting the door and turning the sign to closed! She hurried through to the workroom where the dress hung on the back of the door, covered by a length of white linen. As she uncovered it she glanced at the time on the workroom clock.

It was just after half past eleven, the time of the appointment, so they would be a while yet. *Dare I?* She lifted the dress off its hanger and held it up in front of her. If anything, Miss Brading was slightly bigger than she was; *I won't split it or anything. I'll just try it on...*

Quickly she moved to the fitting room. There a free standing mirror showed just how well it suited her. She held it against herself and stared in the mirror. It was perfect with her creamy skin and red gold curls.

Holding her breath, she nimbly unbuttoned, and stepped out of her pink dress. Millie stood in her shift and listened, all was quiet! Gently she undid the small covered buttons and slipped the cool dress over her head.

Drawing in a deep breath she listened again. As she found the sleeves and pushed her arms through, she thought she would faint from the sheer feel of the dress, it was so soft and smelled so fresh and new. In another moment it was on, and the tiny buttons on the bodice fastened! Millie couldn't believe her eyes. She had never, *ever* seen anything so lovely.

She did a twirl, looking first over one shoulder, and then the other at the neat back view. Then facing herself again and smiling at the reflection. *'If only he could see me in this.'* Suddenly she remembered, *'but he's wed'*!

As quickly as she had become elated she was deflated. Slowly Millie removed the dress, looking closely at the tiny rosebuds and the pink lace, all of which she had taken such care with, it was beautiful.

Glancing at the clock again, she gently hung up the dress and replaced the linen cloth. Dressing hurriedly, smoothing her hair, and casting a last glance in the mirror she went quickly to unbolt the front door, and resume her place on Miss Sybil's stool. Several customers came and went... Millie had been carefully stitching a lace inset, for the neckline of the lilac dress, when the door opened again. There was Miss Mabel, followed closely by Miss Sybil. Millie put down her sewing and stood up, smiling at them.

"Has everything been alright whilst we have been gone dear? How did you get on?" Slipping off their gloves, and removing hats and capes, they hung them in the hall before returning to continue the conversation. Millie, feeling slightly uncomfortable replied.

"Very well I think. I've sold a length of wide green ribbon and a lace collar...some buttons, oh and two hat pins. I've written them up, an' the money's in the drawer. Oh and Miss Brading came in too, about the dress I expect. She didn't say, but she's coming back another time. I'm sure it will be to collect it."

Millie sounded more relaxed than she felt; inside she felt more than a little guilty! The sisters seemed pleased with her ability to accept responsibility, for it *was* a responsibility, being in sole charge of their business, even if it was only for a little over an hour.

"Well now, there's still a little while before we close for our luncheon. Meanwhile come back into the workroom and show me what you have been working on." Millie gathered up the lilac dress and followed behind Miss Mabel.

As she pushed the door, the dress hanging on the other side, was shaken off its hanger, becoming caught under the bottom edge. Millie gasped and held her breath. After a few minutes Miss Mabel extricated it, only to find that the sleeve had become hitched and torn, caught somehow between the splintered floor board and the door.

She examined it, exclaiming, "Oh my goodness, how on earth could that happen? Miss Brading will be coming back to collect it soon." She turned to a shocked

Millie, "did she say when? How much time do we have?" Miss Mabel became agitated, "how can we repair it without it showing?"

Millie stared guiltily, first at the dress, and then at Miss Mabel's concerned face, and almost heard her thoughts, shouted into the following silence. *It's all my fault! It wouldn't 'ave happened if I 'adn't got too big for me boots. Ma would say I should 'ave known me place and stayed in it. Shall I tell?* There was nothing to be gained at that moment, by making matters worse. Reaching out she took the dress from Miss Mabel.

"I'll look at it, there may be enough left over material to make another sleeve." Putting it on her work table Millie went to look in the oddments bag. Miss Mabel followed her.

"So many times we have been in and out. I suppose it must have been slipping from the hanger for a while, we just didn't notice. Oh well that will teach me to be more careful in future." Miss Mabel shouldering all the blame was almost more than Millie could bear. Words formed themselves in her head saying; *Let this be a lesson to you Millicent Drew! Pride really does go before a fall.* She admonished herself inwardly and set about trying to put things right; but alas the oddment bag held no cream silk!

"Put the dress to one side, we will have to see what can be done, if anything." Miss Mabel sounded matter of fact, but Millie knew her well enough to know she was upset. They set about their respective tasks, whilst she racked her brains to come up with a solution.

When they stopped for dinner Millie brewed the usual pot of tea and fetching her food, took her seat in the corner and watched as Miss Mabel sliced into a home baked meat pie, and her sister joined them after locking the shop and turning the sign to 'closed.'

"Half an hour to ourselves, bliss," she breathed.

They finished eating, but Millie decided it still wasn't the right time to ask about the attic room; not with the disaster of the dress fresh in her mind!

They talked only of the accounts in quiet voices. Later as they all settled back to work, Millie, made the dress a priority, putting all her energies into exploring an idea regarding the repair. Turning it over in her own mind, until she was clear on what she intended to do.

Searching the oddment box once more, she found the half reel of wide lace she was looking for. Exactly the same colour as the narrow lace trim she had so painstaking stitched in place. With a clear picture in her mind now of the alteration intended, she approached Miss Mabel.

"I've bin thinking," she began lace in hand, "what if I was to shorten both the sleeves by three inches? That would take it above the tear, and I could make up the length in wide ruffled lace. It would match the pink that's already on it. Then with both sleeves finished, no one would ever know."

Suspecting as she did that Miss Brading would only be coming back to say that she *didn't* want it, it seemed to be the perfect solution.

"Well now, I think it would be a very good idea Millie," agreed Mabel, "leave the other dress, and work on that one, maybe we can save the situation yet!" Millie heaved a sigh of relief; she could go some way to making good the trouble that she had caused. She set to work with a will.

By half past six the dress was completed. Both Miss Sybil and Miss Mabel were pleased with the result and Millie felt great satisfaction and relief that the situation had been resolved.

"Well hang it up now and off you go, you have done an excellent job on it." Millie was relieved to have completed the task, she wouldn't have wanted to lie awake thinking about it all night, *and* have to face it again in the morning.

She waved goodbye and stepped out onto Broad Street; the evening air was chilly. As she walked, Millie couldn't help thinking how nice it would be not to have the long trek home, and made a mental note of things she would need for the room. She hoped everything would be settled before October came to an end, knowing that November heralded dark drizzly nights.

She shivered, feeling bad about the dress, and decided to confide in her Ma. Maybe if she talked about it, the guilt would ease. But she knew to expect the sharp edge of her Ma's tongue. She wondered why she always seemed to have such hare brained ideas, and knew that Fanny would tell her to think things through before jumping in!

Millie pushed open the cottage door. Her Ma was usually home before her, so she went straight through to the scullery where Fanny was once again preparing the evening meal. She decided to get her confessions over as quickly as possible.

When the large stew pot was set over the flames, and a mug of tea in their hands, Millie judged the time to be right; or as right as it ever could be.

"Ma, I did something today that I shouldn't have done, an' it caused a dress to be spoiled. I let Miss Mabel think it was 'er fault, 'cos I was too scared to own up!" Millie stared into Fanny's face and waited. After a few seconds Fanny said,

"Well go on girl, it seems to me that's only half a story." Millie carried on; "I know I *deserve* to get into trouble, but Ma don't think too bad of me. When I 'ad this idea, it seemed like it couldn't 'urt anyone!" Fanny stayed quiet for a few minutes, until at last she said, "Millie tell me exactly what it is that you have done."

"Oh Ma, I tried on a lovely silk dress, one we 'ad put by for a customer. They, that is the Miss Hartnells 'ad to leave the shop to go to an appointment in town, an' they left me in charge. Well I offered really, an' then the young Miss came about the dress, and I didn't think she wanted it anymore, so I closed the shop an' tried it on." Millie stopped for breath, but couldn't resist adding, "it did look good on me though Ma!"

"Go on," said Fanny guessing the worst was yet to come.

"Well, 'anging it up was the trouble; when I put it back on its hanger I thought it was safely back on the peg be'ind the door, but it must 'ave slipped, 'cos when Miss Mabel pushed the door open it fell on the floor and got caught underneath." Millie paused again. Still her Ma was staring at her; *if only she'd say something, say it wasn't her fault!*

Millie was at the end of her confession and the tears ran down her face. She surveyed Fanny's straight face. After a moment Fanny stood up.

"Temptation usually leads to trouble, haven't I always tried to make you remember that? The guilt you feel now is your just reward for doing something I see as under'and." Millie felt even worse.

"But Ma," she began.

"But Ma nothing," Fanny was cross. "You'd best ask yourself if there is anything you can do to make amends, put things right like. Better still ask Miss Mabel."

"Oh I did Ma, I did. I worked all afternoon on altering the sleeves so the dress wouldn't be spoilt, an'

Miss Mabel was pleased with it." Millie paused before saying quietly, "do you think I should tell her everything? Oh I couldn't bear it, I'll lose me job an' me room, an' I'll lose the way they feel about me an' all." At this point Fanny decided that Millie had learned a very valuable lesson, and eased up on her.

"Well there's nothing to be gained now, by telling all. The dress *may* not 'ave fallen down by your carelessness, so the whole thing may not 'ave bin your fault anyway.

On the other 'and, it most probably *was*. So wash yer face, an' try an' put the 'ole thing be'ind yer; an' let that be a lesson to you for the future! Oh, an' by the way, the 'nice way' folks feel about you, is called their 'good opinion' of you, an' if you care about that, it's as good a reason as any, not to do anything be'ind their back, that you wouldn't do in front of 'em, so think on !"

Much chastened, Millie felt she had deserved the ticking off from her Ma, and was only too glad to put it behind her. She did value people's good opinion of her, and vowed to keep her bright ideas in check, especially if they involved anyone else.

When Jamie came in, Fanny simply couldn't bring herself to ask what he had been doing, afraid she wouldn't like the answer. It seemed Jamie was always late for everything, or missed it altogether. Jack would have to have a talk with him when he came back.

For now it was enough that they were all home, food was on the table and the bulk of the day's work at an end.

Millie had a lot to think about, mulling over her Ma's words as she preceded Jamie up to bed. Quickly slipping into the pallet bed in her shift, and shivering as she waited for sleep to come, she realised that the attic room had been completely forgotten, with the dreadful business of the dress and even worse, the confession that followed. *I'll never do anything like that again,* she vowed, *no I never will.* Millie fell asleep at last savouring the thoughts of asking the sisters, at the first opportunity, if there was anything in the attic room; and say again how grateful she an' her Ma was...

As Fanny lay waiting for sleep that night, she remembered her own Ma laying down the law. Poor Millie, trouble just seemed to find her, whereas *Jamie*, he just seemed to go looking for it. The next day at lunchtime, Millie decided to open the conversation regarding the attic. As they finished she said casually, "When I talked to Ma yesterday, we though it best to ask what I'll need in the room?" She wasn't sure how to go on, and looked at Miss Mabel.

"Well there's no time like the present, we still have ten minutes, let me show it to you now."

"Oh yes please." Millie jumped up in excitement

Miss Mabel led the way out into the hallway, up a flight of stairs, across a small landing, with several doors leading off, and up yet more stairs.

At the top, another door stood. Turning the brass knob and bending her head a little, Miss Mabel, followed closely by Millie and then Miss Sybil, stepped into a low attic room with a tiny high window set in the eves at one end. Against one wall was an iron bedstead. Against the other, stood a rickety old table with a small china jug and bowl. Millie gasped, "There's so much space, it will be wonderful to 'ave it as my own room. Oh you're so kind; I don't know 'ow to repay you."

"Well I do," said Miss Mabel dryly. "Just continue the way that you have started. As we said, we are more than pleased with your sewing skills, and the willing way you tackle other things too. You are a hard worker Millie, just keep it up and we will all help each other."

Millie glowed, their confidence in her made her determined that it would never be misplaced! Miss Sybil stepped past them.

"Of course we shall have to make a small deduction from your pay, but it won't be much. Through that door," she pointed to a door that Millie hadn't noticed, "is another room used for storage." Miss Mabel crossed the room saying, "there should be a rag rug in there which will cover the floor boards beside the bed; but of course I'd forgotten, it will be locked. Miss Sybil will find the key later. You'll have no need to worry, as it is always kept locked and seldom used. The window in here is too high to need a curtain." Miss Mabel stopped and looked at Millie gazing around in wonder, her eyes wide.

"A room of me own!" she almost wanted to start cleaning, and moving things around there and then, but she contented herself by visualising for a moment the finished effect.

"Yes dear, well you can see what you will need, although there are one or two spare blankets in the chest on the landing that you can use. Other than that, if you have any difficulties let us know and we will see what we can do. Come along, it's time we started work again."

Millie cast a last glance over her shoulder, *I'll make it cosy and keep it clean, and...* At the bottom of the stairs, Millie slipped into the kitchen to clear away, and wash up, before taking her place at her work bench, making a mental note of all the things in the attic already. *A bed, a table, a rug,* there wouldn't be much left for them to get. Millie was going to put all her efforts into working hard, and helping in the house to make them glad they had given her this chance. *Oh an' two blankets an' all,* she remembered.

CHAPTER NINE

Gerard Elliot stood outside The Coaching Inn, waiting for his horse to be brought around from the stable yard. The drinking down here was more convivial, he also relished the food.

It was far too stuffy to relax up at The Manor House, and he was now in the habit of spending several evenings a week with the other 'young blades' that met here.

Rowdy drinking parties were a pleasant interlude from the world of work that his father inhabited, and into which he was being slowly initiated since finishing his education.

He propped himself against the stone mounting steps and continued his train of thought.

As young children, he and Clara remembered fun and laughter in the house, but his father, always a ladies' man and comfortable to be known as such, had been more absent than present, leaving his Mama feeling undervalued and lonely.

As the years passed she had slipped into a decline, her escape from the pressures of her husband's lavish entertaining, and the duties as wife of a successful business man. London trips to the shipping company in which he was part owner, were a regular feature of his working life, and also where he found solace in the charms of the 'London Ladies.'

Then there was Clara. He sometimes wondered if his Mama knew her daughter as well as she thought she did.

There was something about the look in Clara's eyes, the quickly changing expression, the subtle way she was able to change a subject...

Tall and slender, with pale skin and dark eyes, hair lavishly coiled at the nape of her neck, she cultured a demure look, but in essence her personality was anything but.

Clara could be fun; a year younger than himself, she got quickly bored and on some occasions Gerard helped her fabricate an excuse to accompany him on selected outings. This pleased both her and his new friends, *and* added to his own popularity. He brought himself back from his reverie with a start.

As he stared down the hill, he saw again the lad who seemed to have taken over delivery of the crabs. Since almost bumping into the young girl down on the town square, he had only set eyes on her twice, both times on Broad Street. As the boy approached he hailed him.

"A coin for some information if you please," Jamie stopped, the toffs were always good for a coin or two if you played your cards right. "Do you know the whereabouts of the young girl that used to deliver the crabs?" Gerard jingled the coins in his pocket.

"Who's asking?" replied Jamie with a grin.

"Never mind your lip, do you know or not?"

"Yeh, I know," grinned Jamie. The toff would have to prize it out of him. Gerard tossed him a coin, "Well?" Jamie was becoming interested.

"Why do yer want to know?" he ventured. Gerard was becoming impatient. He shrugged his shoulders and turned away; immediately Jamie called after him, "Tell you 'er name Mister," Gerard turned back, took another coin from his pocket and held it up.

"Name *and* where she's gone," he said. With a wide grin Jamie passed on the information.

"Moved in with the old biddies over on Broad Street; sewing stuff!" Gerard threw another coin at the boy, which he deftly caught only just saving the crabs from sliding from the tray, "An' 'er name's Millie. Thanks Mister,"

Jamie, thinking he was on to a good thing disappeared around the corner, hoping that by keeping quiet the fact that she was his sister; he might just reap the benefit of another reward at a later date.

"So the young miss has left the harbour and moved to the other side of town...well, well." Gerard muttered this to himself, feeling the need for Clara's assistance. He would probably have to put her in the picture before he could rely on her support. But she may come up with an idea. *Nothing ventured, nothing gained*

Danny rounded the corner of the yard. He led the horse to the stone steps, holding him close, before giving over the reins, doffing his cap and returning to his work. Gerard quickly mounted and moved off up the hill. Danny watched as he rode away. A fine rider he noticed, and a fine cut to his clothes too.

He slipped across the yard and into the kitchen to find Emily, who was rolling out a pastry cover, for the large apple pie that she was in the process of making.

"Emily, when I'm finished here, I'm going down to the quay. Fanny Drew should still be there, and I want to ask her about Millie, she hardly ever comes over now."

"It won't do no good Danny, she'll come when she's ready. It's been a big up'eaval for 'er, what with 'er new job in the dress shop, an' moving over there. I met 'er in the market; she was full of it, like as not we'll see 'er again when she settles.

Give Millie 'er due, she did tell us she was going to move; excited she was! A bit worried though, 'bout leaving her Ma on 'er own, with that young scallywag brother of 'ers."

"Aye 'appen you're right. Shame she seems to 'ave forgot 'er old friends, but I still want to talk to 'er Ma. I want to ask Millie to walk out with me; I know I've said it 'afore, but this time I'll see Fanny first as Jack's away. Then I'm going over to find Millie!"

Danny was resolute; he was convinced Millie needed taking care of, even more now that she had left home. Little did Millie know she now had two prospective suitors...

Finishing his main jobs for the day, he was soon making his way down to the harbour. At his approach Fanny looked up from the small group of women that she was deep in conversation with. If she wasn't mistaken, he had something on his mind.

"Danny, what brings you 'ere?" Danny looked uncomfortable.

"Can I walk along 'o you, when you're ready for 'ome? There's sommat I want to talk about." Danny was embarrassed in the presence of the other women.

"Course you can Danny; nothing wrong is there, or is it our Jamie again?" For a moment Fanny expected trouble, but Danny reassured her.

"No, no nothing like that, I'll just wait over there." he pointed to the Cobb wall. After a few minutes Fanny left the group, to walk over to where he was leaning.

"Well now what's on yer mind?" They started to walk back to the cottage; Danny tried to sort out the thoughts going round in his head. After a short silence he began.

"Well, you know don't you, that I've always 'ad a soft spot for Millie? I wanted to tell you, no, *ask* you, if you 'ad any objection like, to me walking out with 'er serious like! You know I would ask Jack, but as 'e isn't 'ere, I thought it only right to talk to you first." Fanny sighed,

"Well Danny, there's none I'd rather she settled with, that's for sure. But I'm afraid our Millie's a long way from settling with anyone! She's got 'er 'ead filled with dream's, an' she's reaching for the stars; no 'arm in that, if you don't mind getting 'urt, but I reckon our Millie's in for a shock if 'er dreams comes to pass.

She thinks I don't know what goes on in 'er 'ead but it don't' take a mind reader to see she's in love with love; an' all 'er fine ideas are going to come back an' haunt her! Well now Danny, I've said me piece, an' anything you can do to save our Millie from 'erself, will be more than welcome, aye more than welcome."

Danny was taken aback; he thought he was the only one to suspect Millie's aspirations toward the gentry. It was a shock to see her go ahead with the move to Broad Street, it seemed she had set herself apart from those who loved her; but he had to try.

They reached the cottage and bidding Fanny goodbye, he walked on across the shingle with her words ringing in his ears. Reaching Town Square he crossed and turned onto Broad Street. It was less busy now, and being early evening surely meant that Millie would have finished her work.

Danny was apprehensive as he walked toward the small shop. He'd had no opportunity to talk to Millie, since she had taken up her new employment, and was disappointed that she had changed course so drastically, putting herself even further out of reach. He hoped if they were wed, she could be a maid and him a groom, employed in a big house. Both young, he hoped she would get it out of her system, meanwhile, he intended to do all he could to keep her from the likes of Squire Elliot's son. The dream would not be laid to rest, not without at least trying to shape it to reality.

With these thoughts he reached the door of the dress shop. Hesitating for a moment he walked past, but knowing that unless he spoke out nothing would change, he summoned all his courage, turned and walked back.

Just as he was peering through the window about to pull on the bell, he saw movement inside. Suddenly the door opened and a forbidding looking woman demanded to know just what he wanted and what he was doing, loitering there after the shop had closed.

Danny smiled, and disarmingly enquired if Miss Millicent Drew was inside, and if so could she please step out for a minute. He realised it wouldn't be proper to ask if he might visit her inside. Miss Sybil was startled by the sight of a handsome young man calling, but always fair, she decided to call Millie to the door, whilst she stayed firmly put.

Millie was surprised to see Danny, to say the least, but assured Miss Sybil, that this was an especially dear friend, and she would be happy to stroll down the street and back with him, as there was still some daylight left.

Danny was pleased to see Millie looking well and happy, and even more pleased with her description of him. They stepped into the street and Danny began to explain the reason for his unexpected visit. He began, sounding more confident than he felt.

"Well Millie, I have to say we all miss you, but you've done well. I know you must be surprised to see me 'ere, but there's something I've bin meaning to ask for some time now." Danny took Millie's elbow and turned to search her face. Millie was smiling up at him in such an innocent way, it made his heart turn over.

"What is it Danny? Everything's alright at 'ome isn't it?"

"Yes, yes 'course it is." He glanced around to see that Miss Sybil had stepped quietly back into the doorway.

Taking Millie's arm, Danny steered her down toward the square, and after some initial small talk, tentatively began again.

"Well I 'ave to tell you, I 'ave feelings for you Millie. I want us to walk out together, proper like; you must know I feel something very special for you, an' you know I would do anything for you." Danny watched as the smile left Millie's face. She looked quite sad.

"Oh Danny, you're my dear friend and always will be; but I don't think of you in the same way. I'm so sorry *I am.*" Millie reached out her hand in an effort to soften the blow. She'd really had no idea that his feelings for her were anything more than friendship.

They reached the square, and now continuing in silence, turned slowly to walk back up the hill, Millie was lost for words and could only squeeze Danny's hand. He stared down at her earnest face, her enquiring eyes.

"If you can't return my feelings now, will you always remember that I'll be close by if ever you should need me?" He lifted his hand to touch her face, but let it fall again.

"Of course I will. I really wish I felt the same. There's no one nicer than you, yes I'll always feel like I can turn to you, an' I'll always want you for my friend."

Danny felt as though he had been kicked by one of the horses he tended, the stuffing had been knocked out of him. Summoning up every last bit of his courage he had put into words the way he felt, and now they were said, he began to wish that he was still in a state of ignorance regarding her true feelings.

His eyes welled up and a lump came to his throat; his world of dreams had crumbled. It seemed as though he had always loved her without truly recognising it, but lately his feelings had become more intense; just looking at her, stirred strange and unfamiliar emotions and sensations. Why would she reject him? Was it the clumsy way he had put it to her? Was it too soon – or too late? His lack of experience made him feel inadequate and sad. He could imagine no one else but Millie at his side.

They walked on up the hill in relative silence, reaching the shop door where, Miss Sybil was still hovering. Impulsively Millie stood on tiptoe, gently and quickly, brushing Danny's cheek with her lips. Catching Miss Sybil's eye, she said defensively, "I know that wasn't ladylike, but Danny really *is* a particular dear friend," and with that, she turned and rushed through the shop, and up the stairs to her room. Throwing herself on the bed, she collapsed in tears of despair.

What on earth am I waiting for? Any young woman my age would be happy to have Danny speak out for her; it's not as if I don't care for him. Why is it I always seem to react to things in a different way from anyone else? Why do I always feel different? At times she just puzzled herself.

Danny continued on his way deep in thought, turning into the lane that led across the top of town to The Coaching Inn.

Head bent, hands deep in his pockets, he could still feel the light touch on his cheek where her lips had brushed him. Although filled with sadness he felt a warm glow, as he remembered the warm squeeze of her soft and gentle hand.

As he made his way into the stable yard, he tried to clear his mind, and hoped he could avoid Emily's questioning looks, until he was ready to talk. Abraham too, would be sure to ask where he had been, but he could handle Abraham's questions.

As he expected, Emily was watching out for him.

"Hey Danny, you look as though you lost a sovereign and found a silver sixpence." Danny looked at her concerned face. The lump in his throat threatened to choke him.

"Aye Emily, well that's about the way of it; I asked an' I got told. So now you know." He brushed past her, and throwing off his jacket onto a hay bale, he made off to fetch pails to fill with oats. Seeing Abraham approach, he changed his mind and climbed the ladder to the hayloft, where his pallet bed and few possessions lined the end of the loft. His thoughts jabbed at him. *Well now I know.* Now I know just which way the wind blows. So much for me aiming high; Thinking of becoming a groom. To think she's bettered herself, and now I'm not good enough!

The future he had imagined had seeped away on the long walk back, he thumped the hay bale, muttering, "I'll leave here, I'll go to London, or go to sea, what does it matter?"

Danny lay on his back staring at the rafters, the cobwebs swaying in the draughty loft. How long he lay there he didn't know, but was roused by Emily's voice in the darkness.

"Danny, Danny, come down. Come across to the kitchen, I'm making drinks an' there's a side o' bacon wants cutting into. I know you're upset, but it don't do no good to stay up there on yer own; not without eating or anything. Danny come on down 'ere."

He listened; Emily's voice was urgent and concerned. Slowly he sat up, with no idea of time. Abraham had seen him climb the ladder and said nothing. He knew the late stage would soon be in, if he'd not already missed it. He should get himself together, and go down and see to things. He listened again. Emily must have gone back in, no one else would care and that was for sure.

Danny climbed down the ladder, and grabbing his jacket made for the horse's water trough, where he sluiced his face and ran his fingers through his hair.

Pushing the back door, he went into the warm kitchen and saw Emily preparing to take food through to the bar. As he watched she pushed open the door and he caught the sound of voices and laughter. A little closer and he smelled the smoke and beer. He marvelled to himself; though his whole world had crumbled, nothing else seemed to have changed.

He pulled out his accustomed chair, and as Emily came back, for the first time he noticed her wide smile. She was so reliable was Emily, so easy to get along with, he was never tongue tied when he was with Emily.

Millie had little sleep that night; could *her* dreams ever become reality? She was closer to finding out than she realised.

Up and dressed far earlier than need be, she was in the habit of arriving first in the kitchen. The kitchen range, a larger version of the one at home, had the fire banked up last thing at night so there was always warmth downstairs. It was no hardship to leave the attic room and come down into the warm kitchen each morning.

Gradually a routine had been established. Millie laid breakfast for three, the sisters insisted she ate with them at mealtimes, and in return for her food and room Millie supplemented the small amount taken from her pay, with extra help whenever and wherever it was needed, in addition to her long day in the sewing room.

So grateful were the sisters in finding such a willing employee, that Millie was also allowed a little time off every other Sunday, after attending the early service at the church in their company. Busy with her tasks she didn't hear anyone enter the kitchen, until Miss Mabel spoke.

"Miss Sybil tells me you have a 'would be' suitor Millie, she also says that he seemed to be a very respectable young man." Millie looked up quickly.

"Danny is an old friend, and a very dear friend Miss Mabel, but that's all he is. I don't have any thoughts in that direction. I just want to concentrate on me work!"

"Of course dear" replied Miss Mabel. Just then Miss Sybil entered the kitchen, and the kettle came to the boil. Millie busied herself brewing tea and bringing the bread to the table. Changing the subject back to work, they sat down to start the day.

Time passed pleasantly and days merged into weeks. Lost in her sea of colours and materials, Millie remained happily occupied; her expert teacher Miss Mabel, used Millie's flare for colour and design to full advantage. Encouragement and praise was gradually turning her into a proficient dressmaker.

One afternoon, Miss Mabel gathered up several samples of satins and taffetas. Taking them to where Millie was working, she placed them on the work table saying, "I would like you to select an assortment of ribbons and lace, to match or contrast, with these colours Millie. We are to go up to the Manor House at Uplyme, tomorrow.

At three o' clock we have an appointment with Clara Elliot. I shall need you to accompany me. We will take measurements and discuss her ideas, regarding choice of colour and design. It will advance your knowledge and also help me. We stand to gain more orders if the finished gowns are admired in wider circles!" Miss Mabel was too busy to notice the colour creeping into Millie's cheeks, her less than usual enthusiasm.

"But do you think I will be alright, ready like, to go up to the big house. I don't want to let you down." Pulling herself together quickly Millie managed a rather half hearted smile.

"Of course you're ready, I wouldn't have suggested it otherwise, and the lady particularly asked for you. Your flare for colour is already getting talked about; it's time we showed you off."

"Yes of course, I'd like that" murmured Millie. Unknown to her, the scene had been set the previous week, to ensure her attendance!

In the Manor House at Uplyme, Clara had listened to Gerard as he told her of his intentions regarding the new assistant, at her favoured dressmaking establishment.

"Really Gerard, father would have forty fits if he knew what you've planned. Well I must say it will brighten up a dull day *and* I'll get a new gown into the bargain. You will have to catch the girl either on the way in here, or on the way out. I will try to engage the old biddy in conversation, or maybe you could slip the girl a note - I suppose she can read?"

"You don't need to worry your head about that; I just need to speak to her for a moment. You will have done your bit by wringing a new gown out of father. That gives me a golden opportunity. As sisters go I reckon you are not that bad!"

Clara, who was extremely fond of her handsome elder brother, glowed. It had been her idea to beg a new gown from her indulgent father, and purposefully order from the Lyme shop. She was willing to enter into any lark just to relieve the boredom, and this one promised some excitement.

Now the day had arrived. As the grandfather clock in the hallway began to chime three o'clock, the front door bell rang.

Gerard was standing near the drawing room door, whilst Clara hung over the banisters on the next landing. Stokes the manservant appeared from nowhere and strode toward the front door, and opening it, muttered a few curt words, closing it again almost immediately. *What had gone wrong?* Clara could contain herself no longer.

"Stokes, who was that. Why have you sent them away?" Stokes looked up the stairway to where Miss Clara was standing.

"Why Miss, it was the dressmakers, from the shop in Lyme. I have sent them around the tradesmen's entrance, which, with respect Miss, they should have used in the first place.

"Quite right Stokes; trades people at the front door, whatever next!" Gerard spoke from the hallway, hiding a smile, and took himself off to waylay the girl at the side door.

As Lily, the downstairs maid appeared the side door bell rang; Clara rushed past, intent on separating the two needle women, by pushing herself in front of Lily, who was busy taking their cloaks to hang up. Gerard positioned himself between Miss Mabel Hartnell and Millie, excusing himself saying, "A word if you please."

Clara deftly greeted Miss Mabel and ushered her into the drawing room, brushing away a surprised Lily in the process. Gerard smiled into Millie's confused face.

"Sir, the carrier cart will return for us at four o'clock." She spluttered.

"Never mind that, I think you know of my interest. You attract me, and it is my intention to get to know you." He smiled his special smile and Millie's heart turned over; lost for words she stared at the floor whilst he continued,

"What time, do your employers give you, for yourself?"

"Every other Sunday sir, after church that is." was all that Millie could quietly manage.

"When you come again, I will have arranged a meeting, what do you say?"

"Oh sir, I, I don't know." Millie backed away, conscious that Miss Mabel had come to the drawing room door and was awaiting the measuring tape, and samples of satin and taffeta.

"Well, until next time." He walked away.

Looking at Miss Mabel's face, Millie felt an explanation was required, desperate but plausible.

"The gentleman wanted to be sure we had return transport, it was kind of him don't you think?" It was clear that Miss Mabel's only thought was *how very strange that a gentleman should concern himself at all, with such matters,* but saying quickly, "Yes, yes of course."

Miss Mabel hurried Millie into the drawing room, saying rather curtly, "Miss Clara is waiting." Proceeding to explain styles, choose materials and trimmings, and with Millie's help, steer Miss Clara toward the colours most suited to her pale colouring. Next came the most important part; the taking of measurements.

Suddenly it hit Millie, she needn't have been so upset, MISS Clara. She was his sister not his wife. *It wouldn't be so bad to meet him, would it?* Miss Mabel was busy with the tape measure.

"Hold this end Millie and don't let it slip," Millie wondered if Miss Mabel would notice how her hands were shaking, but everything appeared normal, and she continued, "We are agreed that the apricot satin is right for Miss Clara's final choice, that's the one *you* thought would suit, Millie".

Millie glanced at Miss Clara, who was watching her with a smile on her lips. She looked quickly away, *did she know?* She pushed the thought away and tried to concentrate on the job in hand. At last four o'clock came, and Lily poked her head around the door to announce the arrival of the carrier cart, at the side entrance.

With everything gathered up, and Miss Clara obviously well pleased with the choice of material, the care and attention, and herself too,- it seemed; they collected their cloaks from Lily and boarded the carrier-cart.

Safely stowing their sewing baskets, they left the Manor House and made the return journey back to the shop.

Miss Sybil greeted them anxiously enquiring how the consultation had gone. Following them into the workroom, the sisters conversed in whispers about the grand Manor House and how lucky they were to secure an order there.

Millie was left to lay out the apricot satin on the cleared work bench. She kept pushing the thought of Master Gerard to the back of her mind. *Did he really want to meet her, get to know her?* Miss Mabel came over to her... "An experience for you Millie, what did you think?" Millie agreed readily that it was indeed an experience, but whether they were referring to the same thing was debatable.

"Miss Sybil had the foresight to boil the kettle for tea; we'll take a few moments, before we begin. Just lay out the large scissors and the notes on measurements, and we'll pin the pattern while there is still some daylight left."

Following the familiar routine and drinking a cup of hot strong tea, went some way towards calming the turmoil in Millie's mind – for the moment. But he had said he would be waiting next time for her answer. What was she to do? Her Ma's words went round and round in her head. *'Folk's good opinion of you'* Millie tried hard not to dwell on it.

She decided that she might not go next time, or he might not be there; or she might just say No to him! *Pigs might fly*, she thought. Gathering up the cups and saucers she quickly washed them up. Millie had reached her decision; all she had to do now was sleep on it; if she felt the same way the next day she knew exactly what her answer would be.

On Millie's next visit to her old home and right in the middle of Sunday dinner, mutton, potatoes and turnips resplendent on the plates, Jamie dropped his bombshell.

"I told the toff I knew you, our Millie; 'e paid me three coins; one to say where you'd moved too, cause 'e 'adn't seen yer delivering crabs; an' then another to say what yer doing there. An' then to tell 'im your name." He grinned at her and then at his Ma. Millie nearly choked on her dinner.

"What do you mean? I don't know no toffs, as you call 'em." Millie's face was a picture. She stared at her Ma, as Jamie sat back to watch the fun.

"What's this then?" said Fanny, what does 'e mean?"

"I *said* I don't' know, an' I don't." Millie blushed to the roots of her hair. Fanny put down her knife and looked first at one and then the other.

"Millie I *hope* there's nothing to worry about, because you should be very careful if you *do* know what Jamie means."

It was a very angry look that Millie gave her young brother. Trust him to talk out of turn, he certainly picked his moments; if you wanted him to say something you wouldn't get a word out of him. But Jamie just couldn't leave it there.

"She does know Ma, she does, Flyn told me." It was obvious that Jamie had no intention of backing down, so a reluctant Millie quietly said,

"Ma there is a - a so called toff, that looks at me; but I know how to be'ave, not like some." She shot Jamie another withering glare. Fanny, fearing the worst said quickly, "It's not *your* be'aviour that worries me girl, but we'll talk some more, when this young troublemaker leaves the table."

Eventually stilted conversation resumed, and Jamie left them.

"Now young lady, is there anything you want to say, 'cause I'll tell you this much. No good can come of getting out of your depth."

"Ma I said you've no need to worry. I can't say more 'cause there's nothing more to say! Jamie gets thing's wrong all the time." Having endured a lecture from her worried Ma, the rest of the afternoon passed without incident. Millie took her leave, thanking her Ma for her Sunday dinner, and much subdued, made her way back to the peace and quiet of her own attic sanctuary.

A week passed quite quickly for they were very busy. On the due date Millie and Miss Mabel arrived at the Manor House for their second visit. Miss Mabel, noticing how nervous Millie had become, put it down to the fact that she was in awe of her surroundings in general, and Miss Clara in particular.

The carrier cart pulled up at the side entrance, and they collected together materials and sewing baskets and walked across to the side door. Mounting the two steps Millie pulled on the bell. The door was opened by Lily, who, taking their outdoor garments showed them through to the drawing room. Miss Clara was awaiting them.

Millie cast a glance around the passageway and to the front hall. Seeing no one else around, she began to visibly relax, thinking that he had tired of his game.

The first fitting of the carefully tacked bodice, went fairly well, although further pinned alterations needed to be made. Miss Clara seemed quite an agreeable young lady, asking Millie all sorts of questions, and showing interest in her home, family and work.

Miss Mabel thought it unbecoming of a lady, to show so much interest in a mere worker, although she did join in the general conversation.

At four 'o clock they packed up their work, and Lily appeared at the drawing room door to announce the arrival of their transport. The next appointment was to be arranged again at Miss Clara's convenience. They walked to the lobby and with Lily's help, cloaked and loaded, they were ready to depart. Millie wasn't sure whether to be relieved or disappointed.

Lily opened the door to find Master Gerard on the steps. He seemed to be trying to remove some of the mud from his boots by way of the scraper.

"Begging your pardon sir," ventured Lily, "but the dressmakers are just leaving" Gerard looked up.

"Dressmakers? Oh yes." He shuffled aside.

"I'm sorry sir, I didn't expect to see you at the side entrance," continued Lily, feeling slightly flustered. She wasn't the only one! Millie stopped dead in her tracks.

Smiling he stood aside as Miss Mabel passed, then Lily, carrying a sewing basket to place on the cart. Gerard, catching Millie's eye, deftly and discreetly, dropped a small folded piece of paper into the corner of her basket, which she carried herself.

Retrieving it quickly she placed it in her pocket, before following close on Miss Mabel's heels. They settled into their seats and the cart set in motion. Millie could hardly lift her eyes to Miss Mabel's face, feeling all the while that the paper may somehow burst into flames and betray her.

The ride home was not a comfortable one, mainly due to Millie's feelings of unease. Arriving at the shop Miss Mabel was soon telling her sister all about the second visit! Disciplining herself not to touch the folded paper in her pocket, Millie was glad when the time came to pack away her work.

At last the endless afternoon stretched into the evening meal, and finally Millie was climbing the stairs to her own room. She hardly dared to unfold the paper, fingering it and turning it over and over in her hand. At last she smoothed it flat and slowly began to read.

I shall wait at Horn Bridge on Sunday next,
From Two o'clock until a quarter past the hour.

That was all. Millie read and reread it to make sure she wasn't dreaming. *What shall I do? Now that I know for sure he's not wed. Dare I?* Millie spent another restless night, eventually falling into a deep sleep.

Next morning as she dreamily remembered the previous day's happenings, she quickly withdrew the note from beneath her makeshift pillow, read it again, and casting around for a place to keep it, lifted the lid of her old chest and tucked it safely away. Chasing the wide smile from her face, she descended to the kitchen.

CHAPTER TEN

Fanny was lonely after Millie left to live on Broad Street, she missed their cosy chats. Millie had always been a companionable sort of girl, and not knowing how long Jack would be away didn't help either.

Jamie's choice of friends left a lot to be desired. As for the gossip about Freddie's last escapade, she thought it a wonder he came through it in one piece.

Fanny was sure Freddie was only one step ahead of trouble, and Jamie only one step behind him. She sensed an unrest in him that had nothing to do with Millie's absence. Sometimes she could talk sense into him, but he seemed hell bent on a course that would lead to self destruction. *Oh Jack the boy needs you,* she sighed for the umpteenth time.

Millie would be over for her dinner the next day, Sunday, and Fanny really looked forward to the company of her clever daughter, knowing there would be lots of tales to tell. Funny anecdotes and town gossip would be a welcome relief from wet days, work, and worry.

It was with a start that Fanny heard a sharp rap on the door. Thinking that most folks roundabout would usually knock, shout, and walk in, she brushed down her dress and smoothing her hair crossed the room to open it. "Clive?" A gasp escaped her.

Her instinct was to slam the door shut, but she was forestalled by the tall colourful frame filling the doorway...

"So my dear... the seas have brought me back to you."
He smiled that same smile that had melted her heart all
those years before; but Fanny's life had been hard since
then.

"Aye, an' you're about sixteen years too late!" Her
voice had an edge to it that she hadn't intended.

"So my fair lady, won't you ask me inside? I made it
my business to enquire about you, and find I have a
beautiful daughter too! I also found out that your new
man is at sea!" Fanny could hardly contain herself.

"My new *man*, as you call 'im, is my 'usband! Truly
wed we are; aye an' 'im twice the man you'll ever be. As
for *your* daughter, *your daughter!* You don't 'ave a
daughter! You gave 'er up the day you left me waiting.
Never a word; why you didn't even care to know she
existed. How *dare* you come 'ere an' say *your* daughter.
She's mine, mine an' Jacks. He's been a true father to her,
all these years."

Fanny stopped for breath. Clive De la Hart took the
opportunity to pass her and move into the small cottage,
noting that Frances had lost none of her fire!

He glanced around; neat, clean and warm. He looked
again at Fanny's angry face, how could he ever have
thought that she might forgive him? In sixteen years of
sailing in and out of different ports, in different
countries, no one had ever come near to the way he had
felt about Frances.

But that was all in the past, clearly there was no way
back. But maybe if he handled the situation more
sensitively, she would let him meet his child.

They stared across the table sizing each other up.
Fanny saw again the tall, tanned young adventurer, who
had stolen her heart. The years fell away as the twinkling

eyes, the arrogant look, took her down memory lane. Flashes of shared laughter, presents and pretty dresses, warmth from strong encircling arms. She brought herself back with a start.

Clive in turn was watching the change in Fanny's face.

"Frances my dear, you must believe I never meant to hurt you. By way of explanation, not excuses but reasons, I have to tell you that my uncle who owned the ship I was on, took exception to the way I conducted myself; I was young. Before I knew what was happening I was bound for 'The Americas,' then given command of my own ship and life took a different turn.

As time passed, I really did think of you often. Not a night went by when I didn't miss your soft warmth. But unable to do anything about it, I used liquor to dull the senses."

Clive sat down, his head in his hands, "Frances, believe me, if I could have changed anything I would have." He continued his story. "In the Americas I met the daughter of a very rich man; a man rich enough to buy and sell my uncle's business of seagoing vessels, and hardly notice that he was doing it. But to keep a foot on both ships I had to agree marriage - to his daughter.

I was land bound for several years, trying always to satisfy the whims and fortunes of her greedy family. We lost our only child, a son, soon after his birth, and Isabella never recovered her health. On her death I vowed to return full time to the sea, to lose myself in its depths, or find fresh courage to seek you out; my first and only true love.

Fanny was quiet and still, Clive could only guess at what she was she thinking. Would his words temper the anger that had greeted him?

"And so my dear, at last I sailed for England and the Dorset coast. Putting into a Guernsey port, by pure chance, I met the bo'sun and a couple of hands from a small ship, not long out of Lyme Bay. We started talking and I asked for any news of Frances Pearce.

They were unfamiliar with the name, but I gave a vivid description of you, and they got to thinking it could be young Fanny Drew who had a child, nearly sixteen years ago, unwed. They went on to tell me of your subsequent wedding to Jack Drew, and the birth of your son... Frances, Frances, forgive me," Clive ended quietly.

Fanny was pale, and as her hands rested on the table so her eyes rested on his face, taking in the remembered blue-green, of his eyes, and shock of fading red gold curls; all the time thinking how Millie, was the image of her father. Her heart was beating faster. Was it just the shock of seeing him again or something more? Clive reached across the table, and just for a moment Fanny ached for his touch. Then quickly, so quickly that the stool fell from under her, she jumped up saying,

"Please, please leave. Please go now."

Clive De la Hart, Sea Captain, stood up and for a moment thought he saw a chink in her armour. He decided that another meeting, after she had chance to think things over, may go his way, but he would have to tread carefully. He had to find out about the child, but that *child* was now a young woman.

"I will leave now Francis. I know this has been a shock to you. But please think favourably about allowing, he paused, allowing *your* daughter to meet her natural father." He crossed to the door, Fanny staring after him. Slowly she stood up and taking a few steps watched as he stepped out into the cool evening. Clive turned, saying, "May I return, say one week from today, for news of our daughter?"

Fanny couldn't answer, couldn't wrench her gaze from his face, slowly and gently she shut the door and closing her eyes leaned back against it, staying there for several minutes. Her mind was in turmoil. Why now, when everything was going so well, why come back at all? Out loud she muttered, "'E's only thinking about doing the best for one person an' that's 'imself!

Knowing that she was in no fit state to make any decisions, Fanny tried in vain to close her mind to his visit. Exploring old feelings only led to trouble. She decided to sleep on it. Almost sixteen years had gone by without Millie knowing who her real father was; a few more days wouldn't change anything. She stopped short, *Days? Millie will be here the morrow.* Only one thing was certain. Millie would have to know, and sooner rather than later, *an' I've got to tell 'er.* The all consuming thought filled Fanny's head, as she mechanically went about her chores.

As the door banged, Fanny quickly looked up, half afraid of whom she might see, but no, it was only Jamie, looking particularly red in the face.

"Where have you been young man?" demanded Fanny, at the same time knowing how glad she was that he hadn't been there a few minutes earlier.

"Oh just kicking around," said James nonchalantly, he didn't want to be questioned too closely, so changed the subject quickly. "Our Millie's coming the morrow, aint she? I'll be around for me dinner, but I'm going collecting me curio's again straight after. Millie won't mind; you'll only be talking about 'er sewing stuff. I'll be out of yer way!"

James stopped, aware that his Ma didn't look her usual self. Fanny quickly turned away from him.

"'Ere, get yer supper down yer, an' don't cause any upset the night, I'm not in the mood."

Fanny was sharper than she meant to be, and quickly carried on. "Come on lad, let's enjoy an 'ot meal. I've got some flat cakes made, ready for griddle, they won't take long. We'll sit by the fire an' enjoy 'em before bed. Like you say Millie's 'ere the morrow, an' I can do with a good night's sleep."

She stared at James, now happily spooning up the last of his stew. Thoughts still running round in her head...

I'll 'ave to tell 'er, an' it'll 'ave to be the morrow. Best when Jamie's not 'ere. Though 'e'll 'ave to know an' all. She didn't know if she was sorry that Jack was away, or glad he wasn't at home. Whichever way she turned it Millie *would* have to know, and the sooner the better or *he* might take it into his head to enlighten her!

The day started as any other Sunday. At half past nine Millie and the sisters were dressed and ready for church. Sybil and Mabel were waiting at the bottom of the stairs, wearing their best bonnets and cloaks against the bitter November wind.

Millie, clad in her one and only thin, worn, cloak, pulled closely over her shawl, hurried down the stairs to join them in the hall.

"It strikes me," began Miss Sybil "that you, young lady, could really do with something a little warmer and more befitting a dressmaking establishment. First thing tomorrow you can start work on the blue serge material. It's put to one side because of the flaws we found in it. We were going to complain to the supplier, but I am sure that with Mabel's help and skilful cutting, they could be camouflaged and the material put to good use after all."

Millie glowed; she had been worrying about looking dowdy, especially now that... but she wasn't going to think about that, not now! They let themselves out and walked down Broad Street, crossed the square and on into Church Street.

As a small child Millie had enjoyed Sunday school, the Church had many steps, and she remembered how she felt, it was somehow a stepladder to heaven. They climbed them, and entered the cold church, taking their usual places. The service progressed and at last drew to a close. Millie was free for the rest of the day. Taking her leave of Miss Mabel and Miss Sybil, knowing they would take time to shake hands and talk with the vicar, and speak with clients, friends and acquaintances, she hurried off across the square, anxious to cross the shingle and get home to see her Ma.

Although she loved her attic room, she really missed the warmth and company of her Ma's chatter. Strangely enough she missed Jamie too, and her Pa, who was away at sea on a regular basis, but that seemed different. She hurried on, and reaching the cottage, almost burst in.

"Ma, Ma, I'm 'ere she called; oh dinner smells good, I'm that 'ungry I could eat a mouldy pig!" She stopped as her Ma appeared from the scullery.

"I'm really pleased to see you maid, come and give me an 'ug" Fanny held out her arms, and threw them around Millie, wondering just how she was going to tell her of the visit.

Although worried, Fanny knew that the bond they shared could not easily be severed, but still there was always a chance that Millie would be more hurt by the secret being kept from her for so long, than by the revelation itself. *Why oh why had she not prepared the girl for it?*

They talked about Millie's room, about Miss Sybil; about how Millie had settled in and what she had learned, even about the sermon at Church that morning; anything to put off the moment of truth. When dinner was finished, Fanny dropped several hints to Jamie about making good use of the fine weather, and at last he left the house.

Clearing away and taking their mugs of tea to the fireside, Fanny knew it could be put off no longer. Knowing what she had to say couldn't be hurried; she looked at Millie and felt again the bond between them. Would what she had to say alter anything? The only way forward was to tell her everything as it happened, all those years ago. Millie gazed into the fire, as Fanny sat down trying to ignore the knot in her stomach.

"Are you alright Ma?" slowly looking up into Fanny's face, Millie saw that her Ma was far from alright. Quietly reaching out she squeezed her Ma's hand." What's wrong?"

Quickly grasping both of Millie's hands in her own, Fanny took a deep breath. The moment was here.

"Millie" she began hesitantly, "you *know* how much your Pa and I love you, but there's something more you should know." Millie stared into Fanny's concerned face as she continued, "I 'ad a visitor 'ere yesterday, someone from way back in me past, someone I once 'ad very strong feelings for. It was long 'afore your Pa Jack came on the scene. I need to tell you something now that I should 'ave told you a long time ago."

Fanny paused, and Millie made as if to speak, but hushing her with a squeeze of her hand, she pressed on with tears in her eyes. Whatever her Ma had to say, Millie knew it was going to be serious.

"Millie, the person that came 'ere, was the man who fathered you when I was but a young woman, just a year older than you are now." She waited.

The colour drained from Millie's face as she jumped to her feet.

"*No* Ma, what are you saying? How could Pa, – Jack, I mean, how can 'e *not* be my father? 'e is, 'e is, 'e's my Pa".

Millie sank down onto her knees, hands clasped to her chin, tears now coursing down her face. Fanny reached out, half afraid of being pushed away, but Millie allowed herself to be encircled in Fanny's comforting arms, but only for a moment, "If Jack's not me Pa, who is? - Ma, didn't you want me?" Millie's face was so pale and questioning.

"Oh my lovely, don't you ever go thinking that; from the minute you were born you were the best thing in me young life. But back then, I thought me 'ole world would end, when Clive, - *that's* yer blood father- left and never came back for me. An' me not even knowing of me condition before 'e went." Fanny paused and pushed a damp curl from Millie's cheek.

"Times were 'ard then. I suppose I thought 'e would offer some sort of escape. But I did love 'im, aye I did; or as much as an innocent seventeen year old could love; I 'ad to face me shame, an' yer' grandmother's anger. But we managed." Millie still couldn't speak, and Fanny continued.

"Coming from a line of nonconformists, - what I 'ad done brought the wrath of the chapel down on 'er. It went against everything she believed in. But then, witnessing my misery, she turned a deaf ear to the gossips, aye, an' a blind eye to the pointing fingers.

I couldn't 'ave gone on without 'er 'elp. I waited and waited for his return, but 'e just never came back. Me Ma looked after me when me time came, an' then, with me lovely daughter and with your granny's help, I picked up the pieces of me life, an' just kept on managing... Until Jack came along that is!

Millie, your Pa Jack, was and *is* the best thing that ever 'appened to me, the only man I've ever wanted since, and 'e loves us all, and is strong for us. Millie, Jack loves you so much an' is so proud of you, there's never a moment goes by, 'e don't think of you as 'is own." Fanny paused again, this time willing her to speak, but still afraid of what she might say.

Rising to her feet Millie walked across to the window, and a silence followed; a silence in which both Fanny and Millie relived the revelations of the last emotional twenty minutes.

Then, quickly brushing away the last tears, and turning to face her Ma with a faint smile, Millie began,

"It must 'ave bin awful for you. All these years Ma, wondering whether to tell me or not. You didn't know if I'd understand Ma, but I do, I do and nothing's changed 'as it? Pa, I mean Jack, I mean me Pa is still Pa, and it's still just the four of us, isn't it?" Fanny heaved a sigh of relief.

"Yes, yes luv, 'an I'm sorry, really sorry that I stayed quiet for so long, an' now it's all come out in a rush with no warning like. But I 'ave to tell you that Clive de la Hart, who by the way was a sea captain an' I thought a gentleman, will be calling again next Saturday morning, to find out if you will agree to see 'im."

"But why didn't 'e come back before Ma, or didn't 'e care about us, where's 'e been, an' why 'as 'e come back now? What does 'e want Ma?"

"Slow down maid. Well he's only now explained to me that family pressure was used to keep us apart; and yes he did love me, but 'e didn't know about you. Then not long ago 'e met up with some sailors fresh out o' Lyme. I'm sure if 'e 'ad known, things would 'ave bin different – but then we wouldn't 'ave Jack." Again Millie interrupted.

"But what does 'e *want* Ma?"

"You'll find that out if you agree to meet 'im"

"But Ma," continued Millie, "you won't leave Pa will you, even if 'e, this Clive man, offers you nice things?"

"Millie luv, I almost wish you could 'ave bin 'ere when 'e called. I was that shocked that 'e got the raw edge of me tongue. I told 'im straight what I thought of 'im an' 'is excuses. That Jack's a proper father to you, an as 'ow 'e - Clive - lost all rights to call you 'is daughter, an' knows that any feelings we shared were dead and buried long ago!"

"But Ma, what about Jamie? Will we 'ave to tell 'im? An' what will Pa say when 'e knows?" Fanny tried to calm Millie.

"I promise nothing will change, an' we'll tell everything in good time".

"What about the Miss Hartnells an' me job, will I need to tell *them*?" Poor Millie was becoming agitated again."

"No, we needn't say anything yet" soothed Fanny. Millie looked at her Ma with wide eyes and the tears threatened again, as quietly she whispered,

"Does it mean - I'm a bastard?"

"Oh hush Millie. I luv you and Pa luvs you. You are *our* daughter; aye an' all the 'arbour folks know you, an' no one would ever breathe that word to you. Put it from your mind. Now be still. We'll talk again, but for now, that's enough for anyone to take in. I Promise nothing will change."

With her arm around Millie's shoulders they walked through to the scullery, where with a shaky smile, Millie straightened up and said, "Clive de la Hart. So I would have been Miss Millicent De la Hart; that sounds..." Fanny cut in quickly,

"Sounds very unlikely, Miss!"

After her outburst, Millie recovered herself to the extent of feeling secretly pleased with the fact that she had 'Gentleman's blood in her veins. Fanny was satisfied that there would be no lasting damage and that Millie's unquellable spirit actually relished the circumstances of her birth, just as long as nothing changed - *unless she wanted it to;* there was always that!

It was time to change the subject. Fanny brought out the dough cake that she had baked that morning.

"There was just enough currants and flour left to make this," she said, "so we'll cut ourselves a good chunk, an' with another mug o' tea, we'll sit by the fire and you can tell me 'ow you're getting on with the old bedspread you started to embroider. Let's enjoy the rest of the afternoon, and sit quiet like 'til you 'ave to go back. You can let me know your answer when you've 'ad time to think about it. I'll walk over for flour mid week and call in, just see 'ow you are."

When Fanny was satisfied that Millie had regained her usual 'bounce' and the clock hands pointed to five, Millie pulled her cloak around her and made ready for the walk back. Her concern now was not for herself, but for her Ma.

"Will you be alright Ma?" she whispered, as she was leaving.

"Aye luv, just as long as I know you are." Fanny felt that a heavy weight had been lifted from her shoulders, but hated the idea that she had just transferred it to her daughter. *No good meeting trouble half way. Time enough to worry, if or when Millie wants to meet her father, aye time enough.* As she closed the cottage door, it crossed her mind that Jamie should be back by now, and *he* still had to be told.

CHAPTER ELEVEN

By half past eight Jamie still hadn't appeared. Fanny was beginning to get decidedly edgy. Thinking she might encounter someone who had seen him, she pulled on her cloak and let herself out into the darkening night, and walked towards the harbour. After an hour or so of calling and searching, with the help of old Lasurus, who was leaving the tavern, Fanny returned to the cottage, grateful for the old man's company. *What now!* A sinking feeling filled her stomach; her vivid imagination did the rest.

As the hour of eleven approached Fanny and Lasurus, made the decision to knock up the Cobb warden. Maybe he would organise a search. Jamie had been gone since two that afternoon. Nine hours. Far longer than ever before; and whilst Fanny wasn't given to worrying unduly, she felt deep inside, that something was really wrong.

Old Thomas the Cobb Warden, listening to their story gladly agreed to knock up a small group of helpers who in their turn enlisted further help. All were willing to join in the search for Fanny's lad.

Splitting up, they started a search that was to take them through a cold wet night, into first light of a cold wet morning. Not for the first time Fanny's intuition was to be proved right.

After the last encounter with Freddie, Jamie had decided to 'go it alone.' He was used to the odd stranger or someone from the local community willing to pass over a few coins, even a packet of tea for him to sell on, in exchange for some help or information.

He had to be careful and quick, two things Jamie was good at. His romantic view of helping the smugglers outwit Riders and Revenue men alike caused him many an inward chuckle. He was also good at being in the wrong place, at the right time! Eaves dropping, led to important information being passed on, which Jamie relished and was also rewarded for.

He knew of barns, mills and cottages, all with their special hiding places. Cellars in taverns, concealed store rooms, even secret passages leading down to the shore. Even more worrying Jamie could name magistrates, preventive men, and also some clergy. All receiving smuggled goods enhancing their lifestyle, while living under their cloak of respectability.

The information Jamie held, could bring many an otherwise respectable man to his knees; although *he* was totally unaware of the mayhem he could cause. It was no wonder Jamie had little time for genuine work.

Fanny had every right to be worried about him. She was unaware of his longing for adventure, his affinity with the smuggling community, and his thirst for excitement.

Jamie's only concern was what should he do with the coins he received? So he simply put some in the pot on the mantelpiece and the rest went into his own secret hiding place. Most boys helped fathers and brothers, earning coins gleaned by slightly suspect means.

Keeping things simple, there was just enough to ease their daily lives, but not enough to be obvious. It was wise to stash the surplus; most family's dreamed of a time when they would own their own small boat, or make their humble dwelling more comfortable. As these things gradually materialised, none of the locals batted an eyelid, let alone asked questions.

As Jamie moved down to the shore, and headed west along the beach, instead of indulging in rock climbing, he decided to see if any contraband had been left in a certain cave. He had discovered it fairly recently, by listening to snippets of conversation he had no right to hear.

The day was heavy with cloud and threatened rain. As he wandered on, his thoughts turned to Freddie. He couldn't believe how anyone could turn on friends. His feelings of contempt for someone who at first had seemed to him to be a hero, was heightened, when he heard how the

other young lad, had been hauled before the Justices. Let off with a severe warning, the youngster had learned his lesson. James now thought it prudent to 'work' alone. But this was the way he liked it.

After walking for some time, and judging the distance to be about right, he began moving up the beach toward the foot of the cliffs, scrutinising them as he did so. Walking quite slowly, he soon located the craggy rock face, where half way up a wide rent partially showed.

Half covered by stubby bushes and a young sapling, it was just visible; providing you knew roughly the area to search, and were well aware of the tides.

Scaling the cliff was no hardship, and after a few false starts he began to climb steadily upward. Grey shale and granite scraped his hand and knees, grassy tufts came away in his hands. It was a long arduous climb, and he dared not look down. He reached an opening, and edging carefully into the slit, saw it opened out into a fair sized cave. He peered in; it appeared to stretch well back into the stony cliff.

It was darker in here, but Jamie's precious flint which he always carried with him, was soon sparking enough, to set light to some dry grass which he fuelled with dry twigs, sending a faint light into the darkness.

He gazed around and knowing that the small blaze wouldn't last many minutes, fumbled for the small tallow candle stub in his pocket, and set the wick flickering. At the back of the cave there were stacked many packages, some large, some small, many of which were tied up in oilskin. Along one wall, stood assorted boxes and several tubs, opposite them against the other wall, stood a chest. *This was a stash indeed.*

Moving to a small tin box, set aside from the others, he was intrigued to find it much heavier than it looked. Shaking it, and judging by the noise, he visualised gold coins or jewellery. His curiosity aroused, he cast around for something to use to smash the fastening. Reaching for a narrow flat stone, he jabbed at the thin clasp. A few more stabs at it, and it bent and loosened. One more blow, this time with a larger, heavier piece of rock, allowed him to force the tin box open causing some of the contents to fall to the cave floor.

He raised his candle, and by the glow of the flickering flame could just make out the contents of the box. Drawing in a sharp breath he saw it was half filled with pieces of jewellery, and many gold coins just as he had hoped, glinting in the faint light.

He snapped it shut, realising the old oilskin bag perched precariously on the pile of boxes had split down one edge, allowing this particular box to fall where he found it. Further investigation showed more tin boxes inside.

Jamie whistled softly to himself. The candle was flickering now, smoking slightly and casting strange shadows. Realising that quite some time had passed, he decided to make the descent again, but knowing he couldn't carry all of the contents of the box, he helped himself to several pieces of jewellery and a handful of gold coins.

Tucking them away into his pockets, he quickly snapped the lid shut, sliding it behind the others inside the oilskin bag. Satisfied that all was more or less as he found it, apart from the box that he had opened, he began moving towards the cave mouth, pinching out the small flame of his precious candle stub.

As he approached the front of the cave, a sudden noise of falling stones and shale made him jump, and his heart thump. The noise was followed by low mumbling voices. Jamie jumped back, pressing himself to the side of the cave.

"I tell 'ee we'm to stay 'ere till dark," growled one deep voice, "don' 'e argue. Small boat'll be coming off the 'Merry Belle' on late tide."

"Aye, an' like as not we'm the ones'll get caught," whimpered a second voice.

"Well you'm getting' well paid for priv'lige. Got the ropes?"

A scrawny brown hand came level with the cave. Jamie's heart skipped a beat. On seeing it, he almost fell over backwards in his hurry to keep out of sight.

Where could he go? He was trapped. Who's to say how friendly or otherwise they would be on his discovery. The first was unlikely, and the second didn't bear thinking about. He moved slowly to the back of the cave, and crouched in an awkward position, just slightly behind the boxes and barrels.

The space between them and the oilskin packages, just about allowed him to squeeze though, under cover of the two men's cursing. They were trying to gain a foot hold and pull themselves into the cave.

The small fire that Jamie had set had gone out moments after it was lit. Luckily he had pinched the candle out too, and his eyes had become accustomed to the failing light. After a moment or two, both men stood almost upright just inside the entrance. Pausing to get their breath back and tune into the semi darkness, Jamie could see their silhouettes against the sky, and heard the taller man begin to sniff loudly.

"Can smell summat" he announced. The other man started to sniff.

"Naa! Nothin' but dry moss an' bird droppings," he snorted. They moved toward the back of the cave; Jamie held his breath. Closer and closer they came, examining the haul. Muttered oaths, exclamations and excited whispers were hanging on the still air.

"Reckon they'm gonn'a sink what they bring in on this trip; an' shift this 'ere lot first.

"I 'ere tell, there's close on a dozen carriers wi' pack 'orses'll be waitin' atop the night."

Jamie started to shiver; the cave was cold and damp. He couldn't guess what time it was, but his stomach knew it to be past supper time. The last of the grey day was fading, when with a surprising noise, the smaller man struck a spark with his flint, and ignited a paper spill which he produced from his pocket.

Reaching down beside the chest, he fetched up an old lantern; they had obviously been here before.Lighting this, he placed it on the ground with a large rock directly in front of it, shielding the light from the cave entrance.

Jamie began to feel his limbs stiffen, and feared that cramp would set in from having to keep so still, in such an awkward position. As the discomfort gradually subsided, he was quite suddenly gripped again by a vice like pain in his calf muscle.

Unable to stop himself, he jumped up, uttering an oath and knocking over all the packets to his left...He almost scared the two men to death. Leaping to their feet they fell over each other in sheer terror.

To the smugglers, fear of the revenue men was bad enough, but they were primarily seafaring men, and riddled with the old superstitions and folklore. *Didn't the rebels joining the Monmouth Rebellion meet their dreadful end here, hanged on this very beach? Their earth bound souls still trapped here, maybe in this very cave!*

It took a few minutes to assure themselves that the leaping, yelling, thing that came at them out of the darkness, was indeed flesh and blood; a living being.

Luckily for Jamie, cramped muscles can recover just as quickly, and scrabbling out into the open, he had the advantage of surprise and the speed of youth on his side. He lost no time beating the men to the entrance. But manoeuvring out and down, was trickier.

Collecting their thoughts, and with some relief that it was a force that they could probably deal with, they made after the intruder.

"Tis a lad, e'll 'ave to be silenced," the larger of the two mumbled,

"Aye, if us can catch 'im" agreed the other, "grab 'im, get 'old of the lil' bugger."

Jamie lost his footing, and began descending far more quickly than he had intended. The two men negotiated the edge of the cave, and began their decent, also with great difficulty. Suddenly below them there was a flurry and a muffled scream.

When rocks and shale settled, they guessed the cliff had done their work for them. Jamie had indeed descended faster than he had anticipated, and was aware of rocks tearing and jabbing at him. Suddenly there was excruciating pain, first his leg, then his head, before the darkness enveloped him.

Slipping and sliding to the foot of the cliff, they found Jamie's slight form lying motionless. Approaching cautiously, fearing there may be others in the vicinity - for they were no ordinary smugglers - the 'wanted' men, stared down at the still and twisted body. Totally without compassion they began to drag him to somewhere less conspicuous. Unluckily for Jamie, this time he had truly been in the wrong place at the wrong time.

"Look sharp, we'll 'ide 'im away from cave, further down beach, tide'll take 'im, an' 'tis going on dark."

The first man half lifted Jamie's unconscious form, the second man grabbed his legs. They began to move as swiftly as possible over the shifting shale. Some fifty yards along the beach, they made their way down to the shoreline.

Laying his inert body down, half concealed by a rocky outcrop and wet through, battered and bleeding, they left him to the mercy of the elements.

As they were about to move away, a last sharp kick to the hip produced a faint chink of coins. On further investigation, and hardly believing their luck, pieces of jewellery too, spilled from the boy's pocket. In the semi darkness they began fumbling around trying to drag out the rest.

"Look 'ere, look at this!"

"Aye, grab what us can, an' let's get out of 'ere," growled the other one. Making off in haste they left the boy to his fate.

Stirring slightly Jamie was aware of the sound of a rough sea, heavy waves breaking close, too close; of dark clouds in the black night sky, and fierce stabbing pains in his leg. His head throbbed and he was numb with cold. Again the darkness overtook him.

Several of the men had gone to the tavern, thinking perhaps the boy may have fallen asleep there earlier, and got locked inside. They woke Rosie, only to find that she had not seen him all day.

"He could 'ave walked up to Coaching Inn to see Danny, an' fallen asleep in the stables." Anything was worth a try. From the Tavern they made their way up the hill to the Inn, and knocked hard on the door. Combined with much shouting they soon woke Mister Murkin, whose head, complete with nightcap, appeared as he threw open an upper window demanding to know what all the noise was about.

On hearing the news he hurried down, and minutes later produced keys to open up the yard doors. Letting them in, he sent one man to wake Danny and Abraham above the stables explaining to them what the rumpus was about, and beginning a thorough search of the outside premises.

Emily and one or two others searched the inside. Danny, knowing Jamie's haunts and habits better than most, was concerned for his safety, and worried about the effect his disappearance would have on Millie and her Ma.

After exhausting all possibilities, Danny took the half flagon of rum that Mister Murkin thrust at him, with the words "warm 'em up with this lad." Danny took it gratefully, and hoisting it onto his broad shoulder, thanked him and made his long, dark way, down to West beach, there to link up with the others.

It was nearly two in the morning when he arrived, bringing rum to warm the bellies of the searchers. Having drawn a blank and after a welcome tot, they split into two groups.

The first group searched the foreshore and the remaining men, searched close to the foot of the cliffs. Danny immediately sought out Fanny, to offer what comfort he could, knowing Jamie frequented this area in his searches for curios.

"Don't worry we'll find 'im," he tried to reassure her, whilst with a sinking feeling in his stomach, what he really thought was, *it seems like Jamie's really done it this time.*

Another half hour brought them to a halt by a large rocky outcrop. Breaking into the sound of the waves, the leading group sent up a yell that echoed the length of the beach; waving their lanterns to gain the attention of the others, the leader shouted above the waves and wind;

"The lad's 'ere, looks bad it do." Danny, who was right up front with them, knelt down beside the limp form of a small twisted body, the sea already swirling round him.

"Jamie, Jamie lad, can you ere' me? It's Danny, Jamie, can you speak to me?"

Fanny came hurrying up to them her face pale as the waning moon. Her hands shook as she grasped Jamie's cold limp hand in hers, and crouched low beside him.

"Jamie, son, its Ma, can you speak? Oh my Lord, tell me you're all right. We got you lad, you're safe now." There was no response.

Rubbing the cold flesh she whimpered like a whipped puppy. Under her breath she murmured, "How many more shocks must I endure? First it's Clive appearing out the blue, then explaining everything to Millie, now this; all while Jack's away an' all. It's more than flesh and blood can stand." Danny, kneeling close beside her, cast her a puzzled look; shock could do strange things.

"Fanny, lad's found now; e'll be alright."

She gazed around at the concerned faces; tears streaming down her cheeks. Slipping a kindly arm around her shoulders, he gently helped her to her feet. Two burly seamen, well known to her, took over.

"Look lively lads, let's get boy 'ome in warm an' dry." A volunteer was sent on ahead to waken old Doc Bird, meanwhile four willing pairs of hands lifted and supported the boy's limp body, trying to keep him as straight as possible. Making their way slowly over the ever shifting shingle, back past the Cobb, and eventually into the small warm cottage, it seemed a never ending walk. The remaining searchers drifted away calling their offers of ongoing help, amid Fanny's grateful thanks.

Fanny could take over now, directing that Jamie be laid gently down on the rough cut clippie mat in front of the fire, the easier to move him later. Heaving a sigh of relief to be home at last, Fanny slipped upstairs to collect a warm blanket, a small pillow, and cotton cloths for cleaning his obvious wounds.

She busied herself making Jamie comfortable, supporting his leg, which lay at an unnatural angle. The message came back that the doctor would come at first light. Danny and Lasurus had volunteered to stay with Fanny, one banking the fire, the other brewing tea.

As Fanny was peeling and cutting Jamie's wet, stained and ragged clothes from him, she jabbed her finger on a sharp object. As she quickly pulled her finger away a large jewelled brooch and a coin, fell from his trouser pocket into Fanny's crumpled lap. She let out a small gasp and quickly looked up.

Danny was feeding the range fire with dry wood, making the flames dance, and giving out a welcome heat, and Lazurus was coming through from the scullery with steaming mugs. Neither of them appeared to have seen anything.

Fanny quickly gathered up the objects and on the pretence of fetching fresh cloths, quickly disappeared upstairs to hide the unexpected find, until she could deal with it. This was adding insult to injury. She paused at the top of the stairs before descending.

Jamie, Jamie what in the Lords name 'ave you bin up to now? She was filled with a mixture of anger, guilt and sorrow. Had she left him to his own devices too much, since he finished in the classroom?

Hurrying back down to the kitchen, she finished tucking warm blankets around him on the makeshift bed, all the while murmuring comforting words; although she was pretty sure he couldn't hear her. She worked quickly, disturbing his limbs as little as possible in the confined space, her momentary anger forgotten.

Danny had opted to stay until the doctor arrived and when Fanny was certain that Jamie was as comfortable as he could be in the circumstances, and the hot drinks had gradually warmed them through, she asked Danny, "Will you be the one to go across to Broad Street and fetch Millie? She'll take it better from you, than from anyone." Danny agreed to go; the whole dreadful night had seemed endless, and soon after five, he set off again into the cold wet morning, not relishing the job of breaking the bad news.

Most of that same night Millie had lain awake, tossing and turning, eventually she reached a decision. Knowing her curiosity would never rest until she had met her blood father, she made her choice. She went over it in her mind.

I am Miss Millicent Drew; Ma and Pa are Fanny and Jack Drew. That's me real family. I will meet Clive de la Hart, but only cause I'm curious. Aye an' I'll go an' meet Master Gerard too! For good or ill I'll meet the pair of 'em; at least I won't be left wishing I'd done it when it's too late! Millie at last drifted into a heavy sleep.

Waking before it was time to rise; she continued her train of thought from the previous night. Content with her lot, after being taken under the wings of Miss Mabel and Miss Sybil, she considered herself more than fortunate. Now she knew which way she was going.

Already the sisters had agreed it would be a wonderful idea to offer matching dress *and* bonnet, to their higher class clientele. It was agreed Millie certainly had a flair for millinery. Having seen the example of her work, they were only awaiting basic supplies, before putting plans in motion. Millie sighed, there was such a lot to think about. But at the moment she must think about getting up - just two more minutes in the warm!

Turning her mind to Master Gerard - her whole train of thought softened. Gerard! His smile, his handsome face, and that black curling hair. It made her feel warm and content, just to think of him.

She carried his note in her pocket; she fingered it. The plan was to meet on the next Sunday, close to Horn Bridge, which was about half way to Uplyme, following the river bank.

Millie went through it in her mind. She planned to tell her Ma she was needed back in the sewing room, to finish an important order.

I'll 'ave to leave Ma's early, oh and tell 'er I will see Clive what's it, too. Why must everything come at once?

Millie hated telling untruths, but could see no other way, and simply *had* to meet Master Gerard. She planned to wear her dusky pink dress. Washed and pressed it looked quite presentable, and was the best she had.

Millie would dearly have loved to wear something as grand as the cream silk dress hanging in the workroom! It was still waiting to be collected. *If only I could have something like that, I would want to take it home the minute it was finished.* She came out of her reverie, and jumped out of bed, splashing her face and hands with water from the jug and bowl on her dressing table. Dressing hurriedly, to arrive downstairs ahead of the sisters, she was already preparing breakfast as Miss Sybil came into the kitchen. "Good morning Millie, Miss Mabel is on her way down." Just then came a loud knocking on the door. Looking at each other - for it was still only half past the hour of five 'o clock, Miss Sybil, rose from her seat and walked slowly to the front door.

Seconds later she returned with Danny of all people.

As they arrived in the kitchen Millie stood up quickly, the colour draining from her face. It had to be bad news to bring him across in the dark this time of the morning.

"Danny! Oh Danny what is it. Is it Ma?"

Turning to Miss Sybil, saying in a respectful tone, "Begging yer pardon Ma'am," he strode across the kitchen to reach out and take Millie's outstretched hands.

"No, not yer Ma Millie, it's Jamie, 'e's 'ad an' accident, you're to come over as quick as you can. They've brought 'im back from the beach. He's 'urt bad, don't worry yet, just come an' 'elp yer Ma." He turned again to Miss Sybil, "she can come, ma'am, can't she?"

"Of course she can go with you, of course she can. Oh poor Millie, put on your shawl and your cloak and go to your poor mother right away. It may not be as bad as you think, but your mother will be glad of your support. If there's anything we can do, send word."

Miss Sybil led the way to the door and Miss Mabel arrived downstairs in time to hear what had taken place. Giving Millie an affectionate pat on the shoulder, she added, "Try not to worry dear," and then to Danny, "look after her." The sisters, genuinely fond of Millie, gladly gave reassurance about absence from her work.

Danny led the way as Millie tied her shawl, and quickly took her cloak from the door. Pulling it around her, they stepped out into the black morning. Millie's mind was still in turmoil from Fanny's revelations about Clive, and now this.

She dearly wished her Pa Jack would get home soon. They hurried on across the shingle, Millie glad of

Danny's strength and presence. Reaching the cottage, Millie was panic stricken. Although Danny had broken the news gently she was shocked that something she had feared for so long had come to pass.

She knew Jamie must be badly hurt, and her poor Ma in a state, for Danny to fetch her so early. Pushing the door she almost fell into Fanny's arms.

"Oh thank the Lord you're here Millie, Oh thank you Danny, thank you."

"Ma, is 'e really bad, what will we do? Where's the doctor, isn't 'e 'ere yet?

Fanny led her to Jamie's side and related the story as it had happened, whilst Millie could only stare at her young brother.

Kneeling beside him holding his hand, and trying to take in all her Ma told her. Fanny deliberately left out the bit about the jewellery, one thing at a time!

After a lengthy discussion about the best way to manage the situation, they were now in agreement. Millie would stay at least for the first week, just to see how things went.

At last Doctor Bird arrived. A small, stocky man, his good natured face and air of authority, inspired confidence. Also the fact that the poor, as well as the rich, were assured the best of care, with time and money tailored to their needs.

Millie led him to Jamie's side. The atmosphere lightened as they all looked to him to shoulder the responsibility of what to do next. Their trust in him was implicit, hadn't he brought Jamie into the world when the midwife was unable to help?

"Make way, let's look at the damage. Now, what have we got here?" He examined him thoroughly, taking his time. After turning the boys head to the side, he pulled the blanket back up over Jamie's still form, and tucking it under his chin, he turned to Fanny. "The boy's in a bad way Fanny, I'll pull no punches. If the cold hasn't already done its damage, the injuries have! He's unconscious, and there's no telling how long he will be that way, but while he is, I must set the leg."

The Doctor shook his head, "I can't understand how he got down on the shoreline. His injuries are more likely sustained from falling down a cliff, and the gash on his head would have caused him to lose consciousness. I don't think the skull is cracked."

The Doctor stood back all eyes on him, "I've got to straighten that leg, and push the bone back, can't move him again yet, so we'll have to do everything that needs doing, here." He glanced at Fanny's ashen face. "Don't you worry, nature provides its own anaesthetic, and he's still unconscious, so I'll get on with it! Then it's over to you Fanny. With constant care, and attention to keeping the wounds clean, he's got a fifty- fifty chance." Fanny stifled a cry.

"I'll do everything you say Doctor, I can pay for anything that will help, just get 'im on 'is feet again."

The Doctor took off his jacket and opened his bag. Bidding Danny hold Jamie firmly by the shoulders; whilst taking a good grip on his feet, he proceeded to pull the leg straight, securing the injured limb with wide bands of calico to a makeshift splint.

Calling for a bowl of warm water, he dropped some strong smelling liquid into it, and soaking a clean muslin cloth which he wrung out, began to clean Jamie's wounds again. They were then covered, and padded with clean rags from Fanny supply.

At last ready to leave, the Doctor turned to Fanny again, saying, "The next twenty four hours will decide which way it's going, meanwhile keep his head on one side and don't let anything get in the way of his breathing.

Dissolve these powders in some warm milk and try to spoon it into him. Be careful that he doesn't choke. He must have liquid if nothing else, so when you've got that in, keep on with plain water. There are herbs in the miller's garden that will help him. Joshua's good lady will show you what to do, send Millie up there later today. I'll call again tomorrow."

Fanny thanked him warmly with tears in her eyes, as he took his leave. She returned to Jamie's side, where Millie gazed down at her young brother.

"So white Ma, and look at the black rings under 'is eyes."

"Poor little lad, in pain, an' cold an' wet all night. Sea was lapping round ' im when 'e was found."

Doctor Bird called again the next morning, and was pleased to see that the instructions he left were being followed.

"Avail yourself of the Valerian herbal remedy Fanny; it will relieve your anxiety and tension. Jamie's sudden fever is dramatic, and worrying I know, but sweating will help rid him of the poisons in his body; then it can start to heal. I don't want to bleed the boy, he's lost enough I fear. Just get fluids into him, and sponge him down to cool him."

Fanny listened attentively, and vowed to do all in her power for her helpless son; his moments of delirium were frightening for both her and Millie.

The first forty eight hours passed in a haze of tending to his unconscious needs, and spoon feeding him liquids.

Raising Jamie's head was difficult, without disturbing the dressings covering his head wounds; and cool sponging Jamie's hot dry body with tepid water every half hour was another time consuming task.

Millie visited Josh the miller and talked to his wife about herbs. Maisie willingly made up potions to reduce fever, but insisted on continuing to do it herself, as to be truly effective it must be accurate.

She agreed to teach Millie how to do it, but not while Jamie's life depended on it. Millie was only too happy to walk up to the mill each day to collect the freshly made up herbal potion, and the Valerian remedy for her Ma.

The week moved on, Doctor Bird came every other day, and Fanny kept an almost night and day vigil, tending to his needs.

She couldn't have managed without Millie to lean on, helping with whatever needed doing, her presence allowing Fanny to snatch short periods of sleep. Between them, they kept Jamie and his dressing's fresh, and laundered a daily supply of fresh linen. Millie continued to collect the herbal remedies, bread, milk and anything else needed from the town.

When she at last walked up to the shop at Broad Street to let her employers know the situation, she was relieved by their concern and reassurance.

"I'm sorry I 'ad to let Danny come back to tell you what was happening, Miss Sybil, but I couldn't be spared once we got 'im 'ome!"

"There's no need to worry about details dear when you have so much else to think of. How is your brother now, and your poor mother?"

"Well the doctor's visiting, and Jamie is still not come out of 'is sleep yet, but we're doing everything Doctor

Bird says. I'm sorry I can't stay more than a few minutes, but I 'ave to get back again."

Prevailing on Millie to at least have a short rest and a drink, the sisters packed a few eggs and some cheese, to further aid Jamie's recovery, if and when he began to eat.

Millie returned home with a sense of relief that her lovely room and her work, would still be there as soon as she was able to return.

She fervently hoped she would still be able to meet Master Gerard on Sunday? *I won't stay long, a few minutes, I must meet 'im!* But even the thought made her feel guilty, with Jamie still so poorly. The busy week passed until at last, Sunday dawned.

CHAPTER TWELVE

Clive de la Hart had been forgotten in the dramatic happenings since his last visit. As Fanny opened the door to the sharp knock, she again took his breath away, but this time in a different way.

"I forgot you was coming back." she said, by way of greeting.

Through the open door, the cottage smelled hot and fetid. Fanny's face was pale and drawn as she barred his way. Clive stared at the woman he had loved. Tired face, grubby apron, red sore hands, he could hardly believe how much she had changed from the young Frances he had been close to all those years before.

"Things 'ave 'appened 'ere, since you came 'afore; me son's 'ad an accident. An' no, I've not got Millie's answer. We've 'ad more important things to think about. You'll 'ave to wait, or call again. But give us time to sort ourselves out."

Fanny stared at Clive; he stared back; she even spoke now in the rough dialect of the Dorset fisher folk. He took a step backwards, "I can see it's not a good time, and I'll be willing to postpone my visit, but I *will* see my daughter!"

"Aye, but only if she agrees, we've not talked of it since you forced me to give 'er background. I've got a sick child to tend, so leave it be a while." Saying this Fanny banged the door shut.

Clive walked back towards the Town Square deep in thought, he didn't have much time before his ship sailed, and he had made up his mind to see young Millie. He hoped Fanny wasn't going to be difficult, although she had every right to be. If only he had stayed all those years ago, or taken her with him. But that had been out of the question, there was no going back. *I still want to see my only child, what man wouldn't? By Jove I will see her, one way or another.*

On re- entering the sick room, Fanny too became aware of the warm stench. Wrapping Jamie close in another blanket, and placing her shawl over him, she opened the window and breathed deeply.

It wasn't until she had smelled the fresh air when talking to Clive, that she became aware of the state of the room that she was nursing Jamie in, her only thoughts to keep him warm. She was so tired, and wished fervently that he had not caught her at such a bad time.

She looked down at her apron and pulled it undone, throwing it on the pile of washing waiting to be attended to.

Finding her clean apron, she tidied her hair. Fanny's pride was hurt. She wished again that he had not called just when he did. *Isn't that always the way of things?*

Leaving the window open she banked up the fire, cleared up, and burned the last of the used dressings. She glanced down at Jamie. Did he move? No she must have imagined it. Looking closely, Fanny was sure his eyelids were moving; but he remained quiet.

No delirious mumblings. This had happened before, when he had appeared to stare for a moment with unseeing eyes; *dare she hope that this time he would wake?*

Millie reached the door of the cottage, and Fanny rushed to greet her.

"He's moved, our Jamie's stirred," she grabbed Millie's arm and pulled her down beside the makeshift bed. Quickly Millie pushed her precious bottles of herbal cures safely to one side, and stared closely into his face.

For a moment – nothing; she was beginning to think that her Ma was seeing what she wanted to see, but then his eyelids flickered, and his eyes opened for a second. She moved closer and waited.

"There, I told you." Fanny was beside herself, Millie couldn't believe her own eyes.

"Jamie it's me Millie, and Ma too, Jamie can you hear me?"

Fanny took his hand, "Jamie my son..." The tears ran down Fanny's face. Jamie spoke in a dry whisper.

"Aye, I can 'ere you, what you crying for Ma? It's my leg that's 'urting." He tried to lift his head, but let it fall back on the pillow, "by the stars, 'ave I 'ad a kicking, or what? An' me mouths that dry."

Fanny was overcome with relief, and without thinking, said, "I told you about climbing them cliffs, you've 'ad a bad fall. But never mind that now. I'll get you a cool drink. Oh Jamie it's good to 'ear yer voice, you'll be alright now, just rest"

Millie cut in, "Jamie can you remember what happened?"

"In a minute sis, after I've 'ad me drink." Jamie drank long and deep, from the proffered mug of cool water, and then looked blankly into his sister's face. "I'm 'oping you'll tell me; I know you came over for yer dinner." He looked down at the makeshift bed and his mother and sister on their knees. "What's up Ma?" He began to look a bit scared, "I can't move me leg, an' it 'urts bad,"

Pushing his hand down under the covers, he encountered the rough splint. "What's wrong with me, why am I on floor, in 'ere?"

"Like I said son, we're pretty sure you were climbing cliffs again," began Fanny, "you 'ad an accident, an' you must 'ave fallen, and dragged yerself down to the shore. That's were we found you. But you were way over along West beach. We 'ad the search parties out looking for you. Gone all afternoon an' all night you were. We thought we'd lost you for good."

Fanny bent down and kissed his cheek.

"Aw get off Ma." Fanny and Millie looked at each other and broke into smiles of relief.

"He'll be alright now," murmured Fanny, taking herself off to the scullery to bring broth from the range, "we'll fill 'is stomach, an' let doctor know boys woke up, first thing the morrow... Aye I reckon 'e'll be alright now."

"Oh Jamie, it's good to 'ere you talk again, an' I *never* thought I'd say that!

Millie was relieved, and for her Ma too.

But Fanny knew that even if careful bathing and clean bandages brought the wound under control, it would still be many weeks before he could stand, and only then with the help of a crutch. The outcome was far from sure; the leg may yet be permanently crooked.

The effort of talking and trying to remember, and having a full stomach again, left Jamie exhausted, and he went off into a deep sleep. Fanny proceeded to tell Millie of the last visit from Clive, who had called whilst she was at the mill.

"You only just missed 'im" she ended, "but 'e will call again. What you going to say to 'im?" Millie paused only long enough to let this news filter through.

"I don't know Ma, but I'll meet 'im, but only if you're sure it won't upset you." She lifted her eyes, Clive's eyes – to her Ma's face.

Fanny reached out and patted her hand. Millie had been her salvation on more than one occasion, and deserved to be allowed to make up her own mind.

"It won't hurt me maid, and sometimes it's good to get things over with. Meet 'im an' take it from there. Now, let's check Jamie's comfortable an' we can rest for a while."

After reassuring themselves that he was still sleeping peacefully, they cleared away, to spend time quietly and sleepily, examining their own thoughts.

Millie, comfortable on the settle, in that hazy place between waking and sleeping, almost gasped out loud as an unbidden thought slipped into her mind; the colour rushed to her face.

Sunday, Sunday - she had forgotten all about her meeting with Master Gerard. *How could so much happen in a week?* She glanced at her Ma, exhausted, and sleeping in the chair opposite. She looked at the mantle clock; it was just five minutes before the hour of one o' clock. *Should she leave now, with just enough time to make herself ready? Yes, she need not stay long with him, but at least he would know of her interest.*

She quietly stood up went through to the scullery, where she washed her face and hands. Going up the stairs to her old room, she took off her apron, changed into her clean grey dress, and finding the broken mirror stared at herself, before brushing her hair and tying it back with the green velvet ribbon from the old chest of draws. She crept downstairs and stared across at her Ma's cloak which hung on the back of the door, it was newer than her own. *Would she mind if she borrowed it?*

Millie smoothed her dress and looked down, she'd pass. At least she would be able to explain things to Master Gerard. She knew she couldn't spend time with him, but maybe they could arrange to meet on another occasion. She tip-toed across the room, her Ma looked relaxed, still sleeping. She glanced at Jamie who began to stir. Just as she reached his side, to pass quietly by, he held out his hand and caught at her dress.

"Millie, my leg's on fire, will you cool it for me, with those wet cloths? An' Millie, I know how you're taking care of me, an' I'm glad you're 'ere. I always feel better when you're around." Jamie reached for her hand, "I know I've done some dumb things, but I'm go'nna make it up to you and Ma, you see if I don't." He slumped back exhausted, but still clutching her hand.

What should she do, he might fall into a deep sleep again; Millie wrestled with the thought. Should she slip away? The clock showed twenty minutes past one o' clock. Gerard would wait until a quarter past two. Millie could just make it, across the town, past the mill and along the river bank to Horn Bridge. She'd have to hurry. She looked at James's flushed face, hesitating, looking at the clock.

Slowly Millie pulled the ribbon from her hair, tears filled her eyes. Slowly she went upstairs to change back into her other dress and retrieve the apron that she had discarded not fifteen minutes since. Tying it around her she walked slowly down to the scullery where she filled the bowl with cold water, and placing the cloth in it, took it to Jamie's side. Forcing a smile into her voice she said brightly, "Here we are then, lets put a cooling cloth on that leg; we must get you well again, but first we'll get you comfortable." Jamie opened his eyes; Millie saw something of the old cheeky grin, as he allowed her to change his dressing and cool his wound.

Much as she loved her brother, she'd had to make some hard choices on his account, she immediately felt guilty worrying about her own life at a time like this, what was she thinking?

Glancing in Fanny's direction, she realised that her Ma was just waking, and watching them both. Fanny closed her eyes again and thanked God for her little family.

Making Jamie comfortable and clearing away, Millie resumed her seat. She glanced at the clock again. Fifteen minutes before two. She imagined herself hurrying across the shingle, the square, and Broad Street, into Coombe Street, on past the Mill. She would probably have been waylaid by old Joshua and Masie.

In her imagination she went on to follow the leat up to Gosling Bridge and then to Jordan Flats, the outer limits of town. On past the dipping steps, how many times had she played there as a child? In trouble for wandering too far! Joining the pack horse path, and past the stretch of river that the Baptists used for baptisms. She reigned in her thoughts and tried not to dwell on her disappointment.

She glanced at the clock, the time was running away with her, and she knew that she wouldn't have arrived by two, or even by fifteen minutes past. She heaved a deep sigh; Master Gerard would have left by the time she'd reached Horn Bridge. *Likely he will have disappeared inside Horn Tavern by now!* Tears came to her eyes again. At last a quarter past the hour, it was too late now – she could relax, and pray that he would try to contact her again. *I will meet him; -sometime – somehow, yes I will!*

Gerard paced up and down on the deserted river bank, his mare contentedly munching the lush grass beneath the hedgerow. Reaching for his pocket watch, he checked the time yet again. In the distance he heard the stage coach up on the turn-pike road, announcing its arrival by the sounding of the horn. He turned, making his way down beneath the bridge.

Walking up and down by the river he had to admit at last that the girl had actually decided not to turn up! It was a new experience for Gerard and one he didn't care for. He checked his pocket watch again, a quarter past the hour of two o' clock. *Well Miss, you had your chance!* he muttered, now decidedly put out. Nestling in his saddle bag was a silk crochet shawl. Even Clara had to admit his good taste. Palest green, it would have matched her colouring perfectly! He strode toward his patient chestnut mare and mounted. Swinging her head around none to gently, he began to retrace his steps back to Uplyme.

On reaching the house he felt disinclined to face Clara, who would be expecting a blow by blow account of the meeting. Instead he walked the horse around to the stables. The stable lad immediately came over, taking the reigns as Gerard dismounted, leading the horse away. Gerard tried desperately not to admit to himself, his disappointment.

There was something about that young girl that totally fascinated him. But could there be a genuine explanation for her absence? Pondering, he made his way quickly to the library, there to lounge in peace and contemplation, safe for the moment from Clara's inquisition.

After lounging deep in thought for some time, he stood up and strolled over to the drinks table. There he poured himself a large brandy and contemplated what to do next. His first thought was to shrug off his disappointment and put it down to experience, but somehow he could not let it go. Gerard thought back to the first time he had noticed the girl. Gold- red curls caught in the breeze as she walked by Rosie's Tavern. Her skin glowing, her bare arms lightly tanned by the sun. He'd wanted to touch her skin, just to feel if it was as soft as he imagined; but she was young then, it must have been nearly eighteen months ago!

What a change in her now. Walking through The Coaching Inn as if she owned it, and well aware of the eyes on her! He knew she had delivered crabs, but something told him that she would hate to know that *he* was aware of it. She aspired to playing the lady.

He smiled to himself and took a gulp of brandy, remembering too, how he had nearly knocked her over outside a shop on Town Square. Yes, he knew from that moment that she was truly aware of him, and shared the same feelings. Then she had disappeared.

Well he hadn't given up that easily, and decided to pursue this new interest to its conclusion Sure enough she had reappeared as a dressmaker, ladies' gowns and bonnets! *I take my hat off to her.* He smiled at his unintentional pun. *That's where Clara will come in useful. Well, I set out to get to know the girl, and by George get to know her I will.*

Chapter Thirteen

Fanny had partly resumed her own work at the harbour, sorting, salting and packing the first landed catch of the day. At least she could lose herself for a time in the noise and activity, amid the loud cries of fishwives shouting their prices, vying with each other to be heard, for fish were sold by number, not weight.

Buyers from the nearest towns were pushing and shoving to get first choice for their shops, the undersized fish being sold for a pittance, to the locals, Above all the other sounds, could be heard the constant shriek of hungry seagulls. This was Fanny's world, how could she have thought otherwise?

Finishing for the day, she walked back to the cottage, a succession of jumbled thoughts filling her head. Why did Jamie have to have an accident? And poor Millie, just as her life was taking a turn for the better, why did HE have to show himself? She tried to toss the thoughts to one side. Knowing that Jamie may be permanently crippled made her heart turn over.

Immersing herself in work had been a brief respite from the constant care and worry of looking after the needs of her family. Millie too, was able to return to her own work, for a few hours each day, pleasing the sisters, and allowing her to continue sharing Jamie's care. A routine was established, and Jamie was making slow progress.

Today was Saturday, Clive would be calling again, and Millie was as ready as she ever would be.

"Ma please stay; at least until he arrives," she begged, suddenly feeling vulnerable. But as Fanny pointed out, "You both need privacy, especially for your first meeting. If it gets awkward you can always send 'im on 'is way."

In due course the knock came on the door. Millie's heart turned over; she thought she had prepared herself, but realised she didn't know in the least what to expect. For a split second, the thought of shooting the bolt and pretending that none of it had ever happened, tempted her. Just as quickly, her curiosity took over. She pulled the door open and stood quite still.

They stared at each other. Millie was transfixed by the hair, the same as her own, though not as vibrant, the eyes too, the fading good looks, the colourful clothes, the tall stranger, her blood father!

Taking in the image in front of him, Clive de la Hart drew in a breath, and swallowed hard; thinking of what he had lost. The beautiful young girl standing there was his flesh and blood. Not as tall, thinner too, than he had imagined. With Fanny's perfect complexion – at least how he remembered it, all those years before. There too, were the red gold curls of his youth.

Extending his hands, he breathed one word, "Millie." Instead of the greeting he had visualised, Millie took a step back.

Quietly she whispered, "So you are the man that left me Ma to fend for 'erself. Why didn't you come back for 'er? Ma said you gave 'er money, an' then left 'er. It was hard for 'er she told me all about it."

She hadn't meant to greet him like this, where had the words come from?

Clive was thrown off balance for a moment, but deciding to ignore her initial reaction, he reached out to take her hand. Millie stepped back again; unperturbed he took a step towards her.

"So you are my beautiful daughter, at last we meet, may I come inside? We have so much to talk about" Millie glanced back at Jamie by the hearth.

"No you can't come in, but I'll walk with you a while." Curiosity forbade her sending him away. She reached for her cloak and stepped out beside him, quietly closing the door behind her.

"I s'pose you might be ashamed of me, – people seeing us I mean."

"No never, Millie – what a lovely name, I would indeed be honoured to walk with you. I have waited a long time for this moment, and wondered if your mother would allow this meeting. But the Francis I knew had a kind and gentle nature, and I am sure you would have been brought up to have an open mind. Also I had hoped that you may have inherited my own curiosity for new people, new places and change. If that was the case then I knew that you would quite likely, want us to become acquainted."

He paused and in spite of herself Millie found that she was warming to this gentleman.

"You're right about me Ma, she is known for bein' kind, an' I suppose you're right about me an 'all. I like change, an' meeting people." Clive nodded.

"I don't have long, three days until my ship sails out of Bridport, but if it is possible may we meet again; maybe for a few hours? There is so much I want to know about you."

Millie hesitated but only for a moment.

"I 'ave to go now, but yes, yes, tomorrow is Sunday. It's me afternoon off; we could meet about two o' clock. I've to check Jamie now, an' give 'im some dinner before I go to me work. I've got a proper job you know! I'd better get back now." Clive looked genuinely pleased.

"Well that sounds good Millie. I am staying at 'The Lion Inn' on Broad Street. If you could walk along there tomorrow, we could talk in warmth and comfort in the small snug, there will be lots of other people around, it will be quite in order for you to be there."

Millie thought quickly, she would love to see inside... She frequently walked past The Lion; it looked posh! And it would be better to be in the warm, the November chill and rain would make it unpleasant to go walking, and what else was there? And there would be other people there.

"I'll be there soon after two o'clock." She smiled and bid him farewell, hoping her Ma wouldn't be too troubled by it. Clive was about to take his leave when a thought struck him.

"Could you not meet me at - midday say, for a meal at the Inn? It would be pleasant, and give us a little more time." Millie was taken aback; she wasn't used to eating meals anywhere but at home, or with the sisters. She thought for a moment, a new experience, why shouldn't she?

"Twelve o'clock? Well yes, I'm sure I can be there by twelve. " Clive took his leave saying with a smile, "Until tomorrow then Millie," and turning, strode back the way he had come.

Millie reached the cottage door and almost fell inside. *A meal at the Inn!* A smile spread across her face, she was thinking what good practice it would be, getting used to nice things before she met Master Gerard. *There I go again!* But it all felt so right. She warmed her hands at the range and set about making Jamie his dinner, stirring the fire into a blaze, knowing first hand just how cold her Ma would be.

When Fanny arrived, her first thought was to find out how the meeting between Millie and Clive had gone. Millie was in the scullery humming softly.

"You sound pleased with yourself," she smiled as Millie turned to face her.

"Oh Ma I can see why you fell for 'im! Would you be 'urt if I was to meet 'im again? We talked a bit about me an' a bit about you too. But I want to know more about 'im. It don't mean I love you any less."

"I can understand your feelings maid, an' I said it was up to you. I'm not about to go back on that; you must do what feels right for you. When do you think you'll see 'im again?"

"The morrow Ma, if it's alright, I'm going to walk over to The Lion Inn, 'es staying there, an' wants me to 'ave me dinner with 'im at midday. Will it be alright?"

"'Course it will, I knew it might 'appen one day, but you've got yer 'ead screwed on I 'ope, Go on an' meet 'im again. But you just come right back 'ere if it don't go according to plan."

Millie gave Fanny a quick hug, as she rushed past her to get over to Broad Street in time to start her work. How would she last through the afternoon without telling anyone her exciting news?

Miss Sybil and Miss Mabel greeted her warmly. She started sewing a seam, but her mind was on what she should wear the next day. She looked around for the blue serge cloak which had been cut out in readiness for her attention.

Miss Mabel had helped her start it, now Millie noted that she had it on her lap, still working on it. Both sisters felt sorry for Millie, being torn between caring for her brother, and keeping up with her work. This was their way of showing her how much they had missed her.

Since Millie returned to work in the afternoons, it had served only to make the contrast more noticeable between her presence and absence. The house was definitely darker and quieter without her.

As the clock reached the hour of six, MissMabel walked across to where Millie was tidying her work bench. Holding up the blue serge cloak, she called Millie's name. Quickly looking up, Millie couldn't believe her eyes.

"There now, we are all finished!" Miss Mabel placed the cloak around Millie's shoulders. "It will be warm, much warmer than your old one; the flaw is across the bottom, just above the hemline on the back panel, and doesn't show at all." Miss Mabel looked at Millie's happy face; that was all the reward that she needed.

"Oh Miss Mabel it feels so warm and the clasp is so pretty, thank you, oh thank you." she darted over to the long mirror to admire herself. Miss Sybil came through after closing the shop, and Millie exclaimed, after doing a twirl, "Look, oh look it's finished." Miss Sybil smiled, casting a glance at Miss Mabel.

"Well, that was a good idea that paid off, and here's another one! Miss Brading has sent word that she is unable to purchase the dress due to unforeseen circumstances. Turning to Miss Mabel she said more quietly, "we all know what that means, I suspect her father has been gambling again, the poor child must be so embarrassed. Her Mama won't come near the place, except when he is on a winning streak."

Then to Millie, "But that suits us very well, for we shan't have to explain the alterations; I have to say Millie, it will suit *you* very well indeed, so consider it yours – by default." Millie could see no 'fault' in it and could hardly believe what she was hearing.

"Suit me? Do you mean I can *wear* it?"

"Yes you can wear it, but not until you have time to remove the trimmings. Make it plainer, more suitable. You are going through a difficult time at the moment and we think the cloak, and dress, will be useful additions to your wardrobe. Not to mention that new attire will indirectly benefit the image of our dress shop."

Millie gasped, "Thank you both so much. I'll alter it any way you think best, oh *thank* you." Miss Sybil cut her short, a little embarrassed at Millie's show of emotion.

"Well, off home with you, back to that young brother of yours. Take these eggs and a pat of butter with you, Miss Mabel has them ready, on the hall table. Put them in the small shopping basket and bring it back with you next time you come." Millie was pleased and gratefully thanked them accordingly, but hesitated, "Do you think I could wear?"…she smoothed the material of her new cloak.

"Yes, yes wear it home dear and leave the other one behind, it may benefit from some attention."

After saying their goodbyes, the shop door closed after Millie, and she began the long walk home, proudly swishing her cloak as she walked deep in thought. She pondered on how kind the Miss Hartnells were and *real ladies*; she would try to be more like them. Not talk too fast, nor drop her aiches, that would be a good start.

Already she thought that she was looking the part. Millie, had an idea; Mister Lane the school master might help. If there was anything he could do, she knew he would be glad to help. He hadn't wánted her to leave the classroom. Yes, she would go and see Mister Lane.

Millie felt she was well on her way to becoming a 'lady'.

Back at home after making Jamie comfortable, and setting the evening meal, Fanny waited for Millie's arrival, noting again the grey dress hung up in the scullery. Millie had certainly reworked it; the time watching over her brother had been well spent.

Stitching green banding around neck sleeves and hem, made the grey, turned material, seem much fresher. Fanny thought she might as well set the flat iron on the fire. Millie would be sure to press the dress; tomorrow would be a big day for her. It was funny how things turned out Fanny mused, 'The Lion Inn' to eat a mid-day meal with 'er father! *Well 'e must 'ave some money be'ind 'im.*

Millie interrupted her Ma's line of thought, as she pushed open the door, pausing for a moment to see if she would notice her new cloak. Fanny was tired, tired and preoccupied.

Raising Jamie into a half sitting position, the easier to eat a little supper, she eventually glanced up.

"What's up Millie?" she was aware that Millie was still just inside the door, beaming at her, rather than rushing straight through as was her usual practice. Throwing open the cloak she did a twirl, sending mugs and spoons flying from the table.

"Oh Millie can't you see I'm on me last legs, I'm that tired. Why can't you just say 'look at me new cloak' like anybody else? Pick up those things and give me an 'and with Jamie."

Fanny was sharper than she meant to be, it seemed it was happening more and more, but truth to tell, the extra work entailed with nursing, washing, and returning to work at the harbour, was taking its toll. Millie, immediately contrite, hung up the cloak and kneeled beside her.

"Sorry Ma, I don't' know what comes over me sometimes. I get sort of carried away."

"You can say that again! But I didn't mean to squash you, an' I did notice the cloak. The old one needed replacing; 'ow much 'ave you got to pay?"

"Nothing, Ma nothing at all. Miss Mabel made it up for me. I was going to help, but with the accident an' all, I didn't get a chance. They are good to me." Millie's gratitude was genuine. Fanny continued in a softer tone.

"Lazurus got us an old flock mattress from the market for this young man, an' e's going to set it under the window, on top the pallet; get 'im off the floor. When doctor comes on Monday it's likely it'll be 'is last visit, so if 'e agrees to moving 'im it'll make things easier. We'll 'ave more room 'ere, an' won't 'ave to keep stepping round 'im. It's not doing my back any good, neither!"

"I'm gonna try to sit up for a bit longer," Jamie piped up, " I'll get me legs out over the side, it'll be easier to move now I'm feeling stronger. I can catch 'old the window sill an' pull meself up!" He looked pleased, till Fanny chimed in.

"You'll do no such thing, you've got a lot of healing to do yet; we don't want you opening up that wound again, Lord knows it took long enough to start knitting together." Jamie had an afterthought,

"I do get to keep it after I'm well, don't I? The new bed I mean, not me leg!"

They all laughed.

"You say some funny things Jamie. I can tell you're feeling better." remarked Millie with a grin.

"Course you get to keep the bed." said Fanny quickly. Knowing it was paid for with the coins she found from Jamie's pocket, on the night of the accident; it seemed only fair to put them to good use. She struggled to her feet, and with Millie went into the scullery.

"I was looking at the dress you washed out; it's an improvement on 'ow it looked before. I've put the flat iron on to heat, but suppers ready now. I'll take this to Jamie; you go on an 'ave yours then we can rest up. It's your big day the morrow."

After supper was finished Millie cleared the table. She set too with the flat iron, stopping at intervals to reheat it on the fire. Finished at last she joined Fanny by the hearth, and the evening passed peacefully.

It was Sunday morning and Millie got up late. Rushing downstairs she asked Fanny, "Why did you let me sleep in?"

"Because I wanted to meself I suppose," came her Ma's honest answer. "Jamie's had a really good night an' the extra rest 'as done us good. I can't remember the last time we did that."

At eleven o' clock, Millie decided to get ready for her visit to The Lion Inn. Brushing her hair till it shone, she tied it back with the green ribbon, and donned her clean dress. Twenty minutes to mid-day, and she was ready.

As she was leaving, Jamie's question, "where you off to Millie?" was met by a passing look between Fanny and the excited Millie. Fanny hastily said, "you go on luv, now's as good a time as any to explain, an' I'll 'ave it sorted, time you gets back."

She waved Millie off and turned back inside, approaching James with a 'here goes' expression. Her edited explanation to him was received far better than she expected, and owed more to the fact that Clive del a Hart was a sea captain, than compassion for their dilemma.

Arriving at the square just before five minutes to twelve o' clock, Millie dreaded to think what she would do if her – if Clive de la Hart, wasn't there to meet her.

The Lion Inn looked quite busy. Millie didn't relish the thought of entering alone. As she reached the door, she heaved a sigh of relief as Clive, *her father* walked out to greet her. They entered together, and despite the heat of the establishment she declined his offer to take her cloak, which she felt, looked quite respectable. Her father, she noted was well dressed and in an affable mood.

"Welcome, welcome, come through, have a warming glass of — what?" he realised that he knew nothing about this young lady, and should start to rectify that right away... "What would you like Millie my dear, a glass of warm mead, or ginger wine? Choose anything you wish anything at all." Millie didn't know anything other than ginger wine, which they sometimes had at Christmas, so that's what she asked for. Gin or ale didn't seem quite acceptable for a young lady!

Clive guided her to a table near the window and motioned her to the padded window seat. As they sat down Millie was aware that a few faces were familiar to her. She recognised several of the womenfolk, who had purchased from the shop, and one or two wealthier shopkeepers.

As she caught their eye she smiled and nodded, hoping fervently that none would make it their business to inform the sisters, that this was where she came on a Sunday!

The serving wench took their order after reciting what was available.

"I would like steak and ale pie with pease-pudding, please." She glanced at Clive,

"A good choice indeed Millie, I'll have the same."

When it came, Millie stared at the steaming hot lumps of rich brown meat oozing from beneath a golden pastry crust, in thick fat marbled gravy. All with a generous helping of pease pudding, which, looking at the size, she hoped she could finish. She needn't have worried, it was delicious enough to linger over and savour to the very last mouthful

Clive smiled at her obvious enjoyment, and encouraged her to choose a delectable desert, made with fruit, honey and marzipan. Millie began to slow down even more, but was determined not to leave anything.

Halfway through the meal she had discarded her cloak, the warmth of the log fire and good food, not to mention lively conversation and ginger wine, made her glow.

Clive beckoned the serving wench to bring more wine, and they continued their conversation. Millie, realising that she had asked a lot of questions, and answered just as many, felt that she and Clive de la Hart were getting on extremely well. Lots of the strange ideas and fancies that passed through her head were echoed by the man who was, until yesterday, an unknown part of her.

They talked at length and laughed at leisure, until Millie began to feel slightly guilty about the time. On the first count she was getting on so well with him; and on the second, for leaving her Ma alone for so long.

At intervals strangers hailed her father in a friendly manner, and she realised that he was remembered and quite well thought of in these parts.

When the time crept toward three o'clock Millie made the decision to leave. She hadn't meant to stay so long, but had enjoyed herself so much; the hands on the clock seemed to have wings. Millie voiced her thoughts.

"My dear Millie, it has done my heart good to find you and begin to know you. It has been my deepest pleasure, and I thank you. I sincerely hope that we will meet again the next time I return to these waters.

Clive de la Hart rose to his feet, pulling a velvet pouch from his waistcoat.

"In the meanwhile, from what you have told me, your family could make good use of these sovereigns. I want you to take them with you. Please accept them. Say nothing if you choose, but they may make the difference between your brother walking again or remaining a cripple.

I want you to know that I realise your, er Pa, has done you proud, it is he and your mother, who have shaped your character. You are a credit to them, they have given you roots to grow and wings to fly, use them Millie. They have moulded you into the kind, gentle but strong young woman you are today. While I can take none of that credit, I see a lot of myself in you."

Millie glowed; he certainly had a way with words. Crossing the room Clive brought Millie's cloak and slipped it around her shoulders. Reaching for her hand, he gently kissed it. Millie felt slightly embarrassed.

"Thank you for me dinner- the meal- and I am pleased to have met you." Millie still felt a bit awkward, but stepping to the door beside her he said, "I'll walk with you after I have settled up inside."

"Oh no, I'd rather walk h-home on me – my own, I really would, if you don't mind. But I've enjoyed it, I have and thank you again." she couldn't bring herself to say father, *that would be overdoing it* she thought.

Impulsively Millie stood on tip toe to kiss his cheek, and immediately felt embarrassed all over again. She quickly hurried off clutching two gold sovereigns in her hand, for she had none of Fanny's inhibitions about accepting money.

It was a present from father to daughter she told herself. Thinking only of the good it may do them, she just couldn't refuse. Her mother need never know. It may help them all to get back on their feet, not just Jamie!

As Clive watched Millie's receding figure, a lump came to his throat, thinking of all the wasted years.

Millie, while hurrying home, was trying to decide whether to suppress her excitement, and brush him off to save her Ma's feelings; or to be honest and tell her how nice she found him. But one thing she did know for sure; the sovereigns must stay her secret! Millie's intuition told her that it would be akin to being bought a second time if her Ma found out where they came from. No, her Ma need never know, and she would find some excuse if the need arose.

As she walked home Millie decided to take the middle road. Whilst admitting to having enjoyed the meal, and to having her curiosity satisfied, she thought it would be wise to leave it at that, and await any further questions from her Ma. That way she could judge just how much information to give out. She was wise enough to know it would serve no useful purpose to go overboard in her description of the meeting. She was also aware of how easily she embroidered and embellished the way she related things; especially things that had an impact on her. It might open old wounds, and she really did understand now how her Ma's head was turned all those years ago!

It suddenly hit her that she was putting herself in the same position!

Gerard. But with Gerard things would be different. She was still determined they would meet again. There would be another chance... Pushing the door open, Millie called out,

"I'm back."

"Aye so I see" said Fanny, greeting her daughter with a slightly questioning look, as she walked from the scullery. "We've not got much water, I was just about to go to the pump; I won't be a tick." It would give both of them time to think.

Walking back a few minutes later, she heard Jamie animatedly questioning Millie. Moving to a position where she could see both their faces, she was surprised to see them staring at each other, Jamie with a strange questioning look on his face. Millie hesitated, and then putting her arms around Jamie said gently, "Of course you are still me real brother, I never wanted it to be any other way, an' I love Pa and Ma *an'* you; He's just an extra, like."

Although Millie could see both her Ma and Jamie were burning with curiosity, she said in an offhand manner, "I enjoyed me dinner, an' it was nice to meet 'im, but now that I 'ave, we can all get back to normal."

"Aye it's to be 'oped we can maid," Fanny doubted it.

Just as she had expected, she found *herself* on the end of a questions and answers quiz, from both of them. The subject of Clive de la Hart was debated at some length. At last the discussion was closed, at least for now. But that nothing had changed, or would change, was a figment of Millie's imagination!

CHAPTER FOURTEEN

Squire Elliot had been talking to his son about the new venture that he wished him to become involved in. They were in the study and the squire had previously noticed that Gerard seemed to be at a loose end on many occasions.

His mood changes, and recent arguments with Clara, had further drawn his attention to the boy. *Young man,* I suppose, he acknowledged.

Continuing his line of thought, he arrived at the conclusion that the 'young man' should be given more responsibility on the business side. The conversation that followed was rather one sided, Gerard being much in favour of more travelling.

Time spent in France and Germany, had given him a taste for the good life, with little spare time to think of his Father's business, which had always taken second place. He had therefore been rather peeved, when it had expanded, and he was denied a further trip.

"If it's travel you want boy, then you will accompany me on my next business trip to London." Not exactly what Gerard had in mind.

He suspected his father wanted him to eventually learn the shipping business from top to bottom and both sides; ashore and at sea! London? Well he supposed he had to do something, and intended to vehemently resist all persuasion that he becomes familiar with life at sea.

Travelling to London by stagecoach had become one of the squire's pleasures; not the actual journey but his club in London, which was made up of other likeminded business men and a haven when paperwork and a sick wife became overwhelming.

Having just celebrated Gerard's twenty first birthday, it seemed fitting to take the boy with him on his next trip. Likely he would not enjoy the long journey either, or the idea that he was to be steered into taking more responsibility in the family business, but he had to start somewhere.

His education had been completed, or rather come to a halt, some two years before, and it had been fitting that he travelled a bit to broaden his mind. He had also worked for a friend of his father, a solicitor in Bristol, on a very 'part of the time' basis, gaining more experience in the world of work; that hadn't gone too well either.

Squire Elliott was ready to glean back some of the money spent on education and travel, and to initiate the boy into some real work in the family firm of shipping.

"If you show some initiative and you're not afraid of hard work, you can make the most of your time getting to grips with the business of earning a living. You will find that I am a fair man, and given time you can work your way up."

Gerard was slightly taken aback at the thought of 'working his way up,' he had thought that as the only son, he would start at the top; but his father was continuing, "by the time you are ready to take a wife, you will be in a position to keep both her and yourself, in the way that you are accustomed.

Meanwhile keep your nose clean and to the grind stone and you will come to see that the rewards merit your hard work. Always remembering that as my only son, *all* will one day be yours." Gerard was in no danger of forgetting.

On thinking things over he had warmed to the idea of going to London, and when the time came had agreed with alacrity. The prospect of meeting other young men in that setting, some of whom may have sisters, delighted him. The situation promised rewards for both Gerard *and* the Squire.

As Christmas drew nearer, the promise of London faded into the New Year; partly because of pressure of work, and partly due to the worsening weather conditions. Time passed and preparations for the festive season were under way, celebrated in different ways, in different places.

On Christmas Eve Church bells celebrated the birth of Christ, simple nativity scenes were displayed inside, along with festive greenery. Christmas morning saw most families attending the Christmas sermon. Later in the day the Squire, a generous and convivial host, presided, whist his wife surveyed the celebrations from her chaise lounge.

Parties at the Manor House were flowing with a plenteous supply of liquor, and tables were laden with good food. When dinner was served, a glass was raised to absent friends. Millie remained disturbingly in Gerard's thoughts.

Music and dancing continued into the small hours. Gerard and Clara made the most of it, relishing the company of other young people, enjoying the excuse for ladies to wear new gowns, and the gentleman colourful attire.

Down at the harbour cottages, Christmas was much shortened. Stopping only for Christmas day, the poorer families in general, celebrated each in their own way. Fanny, Millie and James, entertained Lazurus, and a friend of Fanny's - with her daughter, who would otherwise have spent the time alone.

Fanny's family indulged in a rare treat, of a small bacon joint, with onions and parsnips. A deliciously rich pudding followed. Made up with flour, rough shredded suet and any dried fruits saved up over the preceding weeks. With the addition of eggs, all was stirred well, and with a small quantity of brown ale, steamed for hours over the fire.

They exchanged small gifts of ribbon, lavender bags and handkerchiefs. A red neckerchief for Jamie, and a clay pipe for Lazurus, who brought driftwood to keep the fire dancing. He also produced a beautifully carved box that Jack had left with him for this occasion.

Jack had acquired the cherry wood box and for his part, Lazurus had painstakingly carved it, presenting it to Fanny on Christmas day, a present from both of them. Jack was sorely missed on this special day and a mug of ginger wine was raised for his safe return *'To absent friends, both near and far.'* And in Millie's case *not that far.*

Up the hill The Coaching Inn was bursting at the seams with merrymakers. Yuletide greetings were loudly exchanged above the sound of even louder music, which filled the air.

Young Danny and Old Abraham, were always included in the celebrations, and joined wholeheartedly in the festive spirit. Emily had gone as usual to visit her family. In the midst of food, drink, and a rowdy crowd, Danny felt alone, his thoughts lingering on Millie; he quietly lifted a mug of ale *'to her health and happiness.'*

On the other side of town, Miss Mabel and Miss Sybil entertained four close friends, to a Christmas dinner of roast duck, with an assortment of winter vegetables, filling the small rooms with an appetising aroma. When full justice was done to the main course, it was followed by a rich dark plum pudding. After their meal they exchanged gifts, and took turns to sing and recite poetry. Miss Mabel and Miss Sybil raised their glasses of port wine, 'to all our friends, and to Millie's speedy return.'

Jack and his company of shipmates could have been on the other side of the moon; so far from home, and loved ones, did they feel. The only deference to Christmas was a few extra rations, purloined while in the last port; a good increase in liquor; and raucous singing from those not on watch. Lenny, who was the youngest crew member, avoided another bout of home sickness by over indulging in the good Italian wine that had somehow found its way on board.

Captain Fawsey turned a blind eye to many things that would have earned a flogging the day before, or in deed the day after. Another couple of weeks and The Admiral Grey would reach its furthest port of call, before the turn around that would herald its return voyage. This thought was uppermost in Jack's mind, as he joined in the drinking of toasts, raising his mug for the umpteenth time. Seagoing men needed no excuse, nor any special occasion, to indulge in this their favourite pastime.

As Christmas slipped into the New Year, Fanny returned full time to her work. Millie moved back to Broad Street, glad to be in her own room at last; but Jamie's leg again gave cause for concern. Another visit from doctor Bird was called for.

On examination, further attention was needed. With constant care and herbal remedies, they had reduced the fever and his head was healing well. The main concern now was to reduce the inflammation around the leg wound, which refused to completely heal.

Doctor Bird explained, "This may mean surgery, threatening the loss of the limb! But there is one other thing I suggest you try. I advise you to contact a bonesetter and healer. I recommend Mistress Beattie York. She lives at Axminster, and may be the only hope of saving the leg... at a price."

Unwilling to saddle Millie with anymore worries, Fanny sought out Lazurus, who although old, could be relied on to give his own brand of good advice.

To Fanny's surprise he immediately named Ada York. Scratching his head, he sighed, "I don't know as 'ow she's still alive, but if she *is*, there's a chance we can get 'old of 'er sister, Beattie.

Ada lives in a rundown old cottage on outskirts of Charmouth. I'll put word out, find out if she's still there, an' if old Beattie still visits 'er. It wouldn't be beyond realms of possibility, to get Jamie over to 'er when she's there."

Fanny, listening to him, felt a wave of hope mingled with warmth and gratitude for the old man.

Millie immersed herself in work; the sister's were relieved and happy to have their source of sunshine restored to them. Working hard through the day, in the evenings, she gradually began filling her time with cutting, stitching, and sewing the bonnets that were her first love.

Working late into the evening and by the light of two candles, heeding the warnings of Miss Sybil for extreme care, she moved to the chest to find a certain piece of lace.

Moving the contents she came across the note from Gerard, which she had carefully secreted away and which she now read again. With all that had happened she was still surprised, when the fast beating of her heart, reminded her that those strange feelings she had toward him, hadn't lessoned.

Feeling sure he must have lost interest, and afraid she would never get the chance to explain her reason for not turning up, she tucked the note back into its hiding place, and walked back to her stool beside the fire. Gazing for a short while into the glow, she stirred it into life, and by the light of flame and candle again became engrossed in her work.

In the process of making a bonnet, Millie was working with colour and material from the latest gown they were completing downstairs. Both were to take pride of place, displayed in the centre of the shop window.

The dressmaking establishment was becoming ever more popular, and based on an idea of Millie's, the sisters found that besides orders for more elaborate gowns, plainer and more modest dresses, of cheaper fabric, were enabling them to sell to a wider clientele.

Business was booming, and the expected influx of visitors in the spring had widened their horizons considerably. The notable doctor's advice of taking the 'seawater cures' had benefits for everyone.

It was on a crisp sunny day in February that Clara, who was staring out of the library window, settled on a clever plan to relieve her boredom. She was envious of

Gerard's planned trip to London the following week, and ringing for Lily, bid her find Master Gerard and send him to her.

As she waited, her plan took shape, and as soon as Gerard entered the room she swiftly moved across to meet him. With outstretched hands and a wide smile, she proceeded to entreat him to accompany her on a drive down to Lyme to take the air and stroll through the town. Gerard was delighted with the idea, seeing an opportunity present itself.

"No time like the present, if the coach is not in use, we shall go this very day" Ringing in turn for Stokes, Gerard enquired after his father's whereabouts, and satisfied that the coach was not in use, sent him to Bigson their coachman, who was duly instructed accordingly. At two o' clock all was made ready and the coach set off.

"The Town Square, Bigson," called Gerard as they settled themselves for the short journey into Lyme.

"Why Gerard, I thought you would alight at the first ale house" Clara teased, "you know I am quite prepared to stroll down Broad Street on my own."

"Not at all fitting for a young lady," returned Gerard, "I must accompany you, especially as you have to walk past a certain dressmaking establishment. Who knows? You may see something that takes your fancy,- *and so might I.*" Their eyes met and a knowing look passed between them.

Having now reached the square, Gerard and Clara alighted. Bigson took the coach to the yard of the George Inn, with instructions to pick them up in one hour.

Strolling up the street, Gerard's first call was to the tobacconist. Leaving Clara to look in the window, he disappeared inside, returning a few moments later they continued to stroll up the hill, crossing the busy road, they arrived outside the small dressmaking shop. Clara looked in the window and sighed.

"I really think that I should have a new bonnet, perhaps to match the gown I'm wearing. I should go inside, don't you think?" She turned to Gerard who was grinning.

"Well thought out, sis," he murmured as he pushed the door open.

Millie was in the workroom, intent on choosing materials and ribbon. She simply loved the part of her work that necessitated her browsing through the stock. The feel of satin and velvet set her dreaming, and each gown that she helped Miss Mabel create, or bonnet that she designed, allowed her to feel that she was a lady choosing anything that she desired.

Looking up at the sound of her name, she became aware that Miss Sybil was addressing her.

"Come through to the shop dear, there is a customer waiting to place an order for a bonnet. Her gown was made by us, so we will be able to match to her requirements."

Millie rose quickly and walked through to where Miss Sybil was now in conversation with a young lady. Not just *any* young lady. Millie realised immediately that she was looking at the back of Miss Clara, from the Manor House at Uplyme.

"Take over here Millie, will you? Our client needs assistance, and this is more your domain than mine."

"Yes of course, how can I help you Miss?" Clara turned to explain her requirements, and at the same time a young gentleman faced her, from his position just inside the door. Millie's heart skipped a beat, *it was him.*

Her eyes darted back to Clara's face and she listened intently, trying to block out Gerard's dark good looks.

Explaining that she must fetch samples of ribbons, lace and material, she hurried back to the workroom. She could hear Miss Sybil, and Miss Clara, in quiet conversation.

On completing her task of searching for - and finding - all she needed, she returned, and proceeded to acquaint herself with Clara's requirements. Colours, style, shape and size, and transferred them to a work sheet.

All the while Gerard stood in the background.

When Millie had all the information she needed, and they were on the point of leaving, Gerard turned to Clara saying, "As the weather is so inclement at this time of year, would it not be wise to ask that the order be delivered? And if the young person, who designed it, were to deliver it herself, any slight adjustments could be carried out there and then, saving a journey back to the shop. What do you think Clara?"

"Why I think that is an excellent idea." Turning to Miss Sybil and Millie, she asked, "Would that be possible?" Miss Sybil answered while Millie was still thinking of the implications.

"Of course; it would be no trouble at all." Looking at Millie, Miss Sybil asked, "How long would you need to complete?" Millie stared, "At least five, maybe seven days; if everything goes well." Miss Sybil addressed Miss Clara, who in turn looked at Millie. "Then that's settled, shall we say this time next week?"

"Of course Miss, please send down to arrange an appointment time to suit."

Clara agreed that would be most acceptable and accompanied by Gerard, who briefly met Millie's eye, left the shop.

"Well Millie you are becoming indispensable, I mean, we couldn't do without you!"

Millie's already pink cheeks glowed even more, *another visit, another chance!*

"Thank you Miss Sybil." Days passed as Millie put most of her energies into planning how she would react to Gerard's much hoped for invitation, and what she would wear to the appointment with Miss Clara at the Manor House. The rest she put into creating a very special bonnet, in the chosen colours

Many hours of stitching were spent getting it just right, and on showing the finished article to her employers, Millie knew she had achieved her aim. There was no doubting she had a real feel for this part of her work. The bonnet was duly packed into a hat box to await the summons from the Manor.

Early the following week, Mabel received word.

"In the morning Millie, you will board the carrier cart at half past the hour of nine, and deliver the order. You can manage that on your own, can't you?"

"On me own? I can't do that. Won't you come too Miss Mabel? What if"...

"There are no 'what ifs' Millie; Sybil can't leave the shop, and I have outstanding orders to complete, there simply isn't the time to allow both of us to be away. You will do admirably; I have every faith in you." There was no further debate; Millie knew that this time she was really on her own.

At the appropriate time she left the shop, and walked to the spot were the carrier cart stopped. A few minutes later she was boarding the cart with her precious box.

"The Manor House at Uplyme, please." Millie really enjoyed saying that; she paid the fare and sat back to enjoy the ride. It was really serving two very useful purposes. Enabling her to further her dreams of creating bonnets for the gentry, and also realise her hopes of another meeting with Master Gerard. At least she felt that *he* would make it possible.

When the cart arrived at the fork in the lane, just fifty yards from the drive, she chose to alight. *The walk will clear me head* she thought, or was she just putting off the moment? Knowing she had plenty of time, and was expecting to wait in the side porch anyway, Millie slowly walked up the drive taking the fork that would bring her to the side door.

At last she rang on the bell; Lily opened the door, remembering her from previous visits and with a bright smile said,

"Hello Miss Millie. Miss Clara, said to show you straight through to the drawing room."

"Good morning Lily, thank you," Taking Millie's cloak to hang up, she led her down the passage into the hallway. Millie stared ahead to the front hall, and at the front door; no sign of anyone.

Lily glanced at the tall clock, and tapped on the drawing room door. Listening, and then opening it, she announced her to Miss Clara, who was standing by the window.

"Do come in, I can't wait to see my new bonnet, I'm quite sure that it will please me."

Millie crossed the room, taking in the wide, gold brocade, drapes, and noting several comfortable settees and armchairs. Setting the hat box on a small table, she did a quick bob as she replied, "Good morning Miss. I hope it will be as you wanted. If not, I can change things, there's still lots I could alter, to get it just right for you!"

Millie, gently and with great pride, reached inside to lift the bonnet aloft for Miss Clara's inspection.

"It is exactly as I hoped; it is beautiful." Clara reached out to take it, but Millie quickly pulled back, saying in a respectful tone, "Please Miss may I? I mean, I would like to place it on you, and arrange the ribbons."

"Yes of course, but I must look in the mirror, hurry I must see it on." Millie recognised the excitement and impatience, as traits of her own, and was further drawn to this young woman.

With the bonnet in place, Clara quickly walked towards the large guilt edged mirror which hung above the ornate fire place, admiring herself from all angles. The smile on Clara's face was matched only by the pleasure and pride on Millie's.

Stepping forward Millie explained various ways of tying the bow, first on one side and then the other, arranging curls to peep out, or changing the tilt to achieve a different look. They were thus engrossed, when the door opened and Master Gerard stepped just inside.

"Clara, I'm sorry to interrupt, but Mama is asking for you; would you go up to her for a moment please." A knowing look passed between them and carefully removing the bonnet and handing it to Millie, she said, "Of course Gerard." And with a nod in Millie's direction, "Please excuse me, Mama is unwell, I must go to her." Millie took the bonnet from her, and placed it on the small table.

As the door closed behind Clara, Gerard lost no time in crossing the room. Taking a surprised Millie's hand in his own, he found that all his disgruntled feelings of, *you had your chance Miss,* were washed away, as he gazed into her wide blue- green eyes.

"What happened, why did you not keep our rendezvous, did you lose my note, did your employers see it?"

Millie had fervently hoped to see him, *but not alone! Not in the drawing room.* She was speechless – but only for a moment. As Gerard reached out to touch her red gold curls, lowering her eyes she quickly murmured, "I really wanted to meet you, but my brother had a 'haccident." Millie was trying too hard not to drop her 'aitches'! "I had to help- me- my Ma – mother, an' my brother was"...

"Well never mind that now." Gerard moved closer, "I have to leave for London in a day or two, but when I return we shall meet again."

Pulling her gently but firmly to him, Millie's heart began to thump; she could feel his warm breath against her cheek, and knew that she should pull away. But she also knew that she wanted this, wanted his hands to clasp hers, his lips to touch...

Gently he tipped back her head and kissed her full on the lips, his arms now around her, his body pressed to hers, his own heart racing.

She was soft and warm, young, pretty and so innocent; he felt her tremble in his embrace. Millie was lost, in her own sea of emotions; *this is the dark haired young man, this is Master Gerard of the Manor House, and this is my own special dream.*

Suddenly a noise outside the door made them spring apart. Aware again of their surroundings, reality took over. Millie busily bent over the hat box, taking out an assortment of hat pins, which Clara had asked to view.

Gerard slowly crossed to the door, giving Clara a slight nod as she entered. Without a backward glance he casually left the room. He had said nothing, about a meeting!

Clara in turn glanced at Millie, who was looking slightly flushed, and she thought, rather embarrassed. She smiled, wondering just what had taken place in the short time since she left them together.

Walking over to where Millie was still sorting through hat pins, Clara continued brightly, and as though no interruption had taken place, "I am so pleased with my bonnet and it needs no alteration, none whatsoever." She stepped up to Millie, holding out her hand, "I would love to include one, maybe two, of those very pretty pins," she spent a few moments deciding which to choose and finally selected two.

"I agree your choice of pins Miss, they are most fitting. The bonnet suits your colouring very well, and I am pleased it is to your liking. If there is anything more I can help you with, at anytime, please send word. Millie replaced the bonnet in the hat box, she knew better than to broach the subject of the account, and prepared to take her leave.

Clara rang for Lily, who appeared almost immediately to show her out. As the drawing room door closed, Lily looked knowingly at Millie, and made bold by youth, muttered, "'e went out the front door Miss!"

Millie felt her colour rising, but could think of nothing to say for once. So she *had* noticed how quickly Gerard left the room. Reaching out for the proffered cloak she placed it around her shoulders and swished past Lily with a curt goodbye, heading down the passage and through the side door; well ahead of her.

Setting off toward the front drive, she almost bumped into Master Gerard, as he rounded the corner of the house.

"Well timed," he whispered, reaching out to steady her, while at the same time pressing a piece of paper into her hand, and continuing on his way. Millie stopped in her tracks, *I knew it; I knew he wouldn't just leave me wondering.* She'd had no chance to answer, and Gerard was already turning the corner and almost out of sight.

Millie slowly walked down the drive fighting the over whelming need to read his note. She felt warm, and her lips still felt the strong pressure of his. Walking on air, she lingered at the gate for the carrier cart, which she guessed would be another fifteen minutes or so. Glancing back up the drive behind her, and then each way along the lane, she made quite sure all was clear.

She *must* read his note. Quickly ascertaining again, that there really was *no-one* in sight, she drew it from her pocket. It read...*The first Sunday in March. Time and place as arranged before.*

Millie would have liked the note to start with, 'my dearest Millie' and end with, 'warmest thoughts.' She'd seen that written down once, and thought it a beautiful ending.

She told herself not to be silly; anyway there wasn't time for him to write more. How could she wait until the first Sunday in March? It seemed like forever!

At that moment the cart came trundling around the corner, and pulled up beside her. Millie climbed aboard and settled herself for the drive back to town, knowing that she had handled the appointment with Miss Clara, in a way that would make the sisters proud or her.

Words tumbled in her head; *they must never know about the other thing. Not 'til I'm ready to tell people; when Gerard agrees - when we're together!*

CHAPTER FIFTEEN

Squire Elliot was as good as his word. The trip to London was arranged for the second week in February, during an unseasonable mild spell. The Squire preferred to split the journey by way of the Stage to Winchester, enabling him to rest overnight, continuing to London early on the following day.

The journey was endured, rather than enjoyed, for it was not the most comfortable undertaking. Progress had been slow but steady, the road rough; at last the coach drew to a halt outside The Wykeham Arms.

The weary travellers glad to alight, were welcomed into a large comfortable looking establishment where rooms were readily available. The promise of food had been uppermost in their minds, but the roaring log fire was immediately the focal point for the ladies. Although warmly dressed for the journey, they were none the less chilled to the bone.

Centre of attention for the gentlemen it seemed, were the voluptuous charms of the welcoming serving wenches... The smoky atmosphere, and smell of dripping tallow candles, yellowing walls and rough benches alongside even rougher tables, completed their first impression. Noisy conversation and raucous laughter, did nothing to dim the relief felt at the longed for break in the journey.

The business of rooms and payment completed, the party moved to the comparative comfort of the upholstered snug, and the overall feeling of warmth and comfort.

After consuming a more than adequate supper, the company drifted off to their beds, and Gerard and his father, sinking a last double whisky retired also.

An early start and a hearty breakfast awaited them, and feeling much refreshed, those bound for London boarded Winchester's own stage coach, and the long tedious journey resumed, eventually reaching the outskirts of London town.

In contrast to the clean fresh air on the journey through open countryside, the first thing to hit them as they entered the busy main street was the stench. The ladies covered their noses with delicately perfumed handkerchiefs; the gentlemen put a brave face on things. All were glad to be dropped at their respective destinations, to retire into pomaded or otherwise relatively freshened accommodation.

Gerard had thought Bristol a big smelly place, especially in the hovels leading down to the river, and quay. The stench that came from the trading ships, with the slave trade in full swing, had made him heave on more than one occasion; this was at least as bad, and in all probability worse!

Breaking into his thoughts, the coachman announced in a loud voice,

"Gen'lemen an' ladies, we 'ave reached our destination, this is as far as I'm bound."

They were about to turn into another hostelry yard, the coach slowed to a standstill. The passengers alighted, each to go about their own business. Straitening up and stretching aching limbs, the Squire stated in a loud voice,

"Well now, a good stiff walk will do us good," and nodding to the coachman, "send the trunk on to 'The Golden Galleon, Thames Walk," he passed a half sovereign over, for which generous amount, the tired coachman was only too happy to find someone to oblige for coppers, whilst he pocketed the lions share.

"Just for one night my boy," He had noted his son's expression. Making their way to the 'The Golden Galleon' just about two hundred yards further on, Gerard engaged his father in conversation.

"I intend to work father, but I also feel intrigued at the possibility of some light entertainment. Theatre visits perhaps? or social events, even the sights of London Town? Very different to anything I am used to!"

"Work first my son, then we'll see about other things, but for now, look forward to a fine meal, and a good night's sleep. The morrow will be soon enough to engage in business, and secure rooms and get the trunk moved on to my club later in the evening, if time allows."

Gerard, looking forward to spending time at the gentlemen's club, but was instead, about to learn some useful lessons in the shipping industry. The first was, that 'time allowed' was very little, in the Squire's book.

At the premises of Squire Elliot's contact, the shipping firm of Goddard and Son, Gerard began his initiation into business affairs. He was kept busy working late into the evenings, leaving him far less free time than he had expected. Even *less* time for socialising.

It seemed the most that he could expect, was acceptance of several dreary invitations to supper dances, issued by boring young men's mothers, to meet their even more boring daughters.

His thoughts strayed to his home in Dorset, the freedom he enjoyed there, and of course his attraction to a certain young girl.

'Young Lady' he corrected himself with a smile, knowing that was how Millie thought of herself. Not *one* of the fashionably wigged, and powdered, new female acquaintances, could compete with his affections for the youthful and fresh faced Millie, with her swinging copper curls.

He decided to apply his mind to the recreational pastimes of drinking with other young blades at the club, on the rare occasions he was able to put in an appearance. Unfortunately this often led to blunders in business, bringing the wrath of Squire Elliot, down on the head of his unfortunate son.

Time was dragging and much to his surprise Gerard conceded, London didn't seem to agree with him at all. He remained bored and preoccupied, he hadn't visualised it like this at all, and was actually glad, when his father finalised his business deal.

Squire Elliot, satisfied with what he had accomplished in London, and Gerard, content with ideas of what he *might* accomplish in Lyme, boarded the stagecoach, and prepared for the long haul back to Dorset.

Involving an overnight stay at The Wykeham Arms again, it proved just as comfortable on the return journey, and the new mix of passengers more interesting.

The second half of the journey resumed, with several new passengers. Atop the coach, were the two young men from London, who had become louder and more jovial than the rest of the company, and not averse to sharing the vacated 'up top,' space with assorted chests and trunks for a reduction in fares.

Two brothers joined the party, accountants by profession; more to Gerard's liking, being closer to his age. Also sharing the coach, were two younger ladies, travelling with a Clergyman and his wife.

Around midday a change of horses, and a short break to slake their thirst and assuage their hunger, made it bearable. Eventually passing through Dorchester and well on the road to Bridport, they rounded a bend and were amazed to see a young tree lying across their path.

Pulling the horses abruptly to a halt, the coachman dismounted to inspect the obstacle more closely. It was clear there was no room to go around it, and scratching his head whilst thinking of the best way to tackle this unexpected turn of events, he returned to inform the passengers, requesting help from the younger men.

Quite without warning, a group of five horsemen appeared from the nearby copse. Amid shouting men, weeping women, and neighing horses, they made clear their business was to relieve the coach party of any possessions they may be carrying.

With shouts and threats ringing in their ears, everyone who hadn't already done so, was made to leave the coach and held at gunpoint. Systematically searched, jewellery and purses were wrenched from the now near hysterical ladies. To the squire's outrage, his silver snuff box, engraved with the family crest, along with his gold pocket watch, and a good deal of money, were wrested from him.

Gerard was also relieved of his fob watch, along with his winnings from a successful game of cards. A Further mix of gold half sovereigns, and other coins and valuables, were wrested from the other gentlemen.

Amid merriment, silver hip flasks were drained, and added to the spoils. Lastly, the younger of the ladies, being comforted by the Clergy's wife, was pulled ungallantly around, and a necklace torn from her person.

Leaping to her defence one of the young men, who had ridden atop the coach, was shot in the shoulder, and stepping forward to pull him back, his companion was hit across the cheek with the butt end of a pistol, but not before pulling away the red spotted kerchief covering the face of their assailant.

At this point, events were about to take an even more unfortunate twist. The driver, getting a sideways glance at the leader of the group, thought the robber looked uncannily like Jack Drew of Lyme. It was definitely his build, the same black curly hair and red neckerchief.

But was he sure enough to report it? Surely the man wouldn't risk everything? As far as he remembered Jack had a wife and a couple of kids. But, he mused, times were hard and it was well known he used to keep company with all sorts at The Vaults. *It might just be...*

The kerchief had been quickly replaced, and the leader yelled to the others who were engaged in rifling through the forced-open trunks, "Make ready to ride men," and in another moment with shouts of self satisfaction, and a cheery grin, their leader called, "Good- day to one and all, I thank you for your generosity," and leaving them to clear their path as best they may, the plundering gang made off, leaving the unfortunate travellers to recover as best they could.

"The law shall hear of this," yelled the crimson faced squire amid general rumblings of anger. But no doubt the marauders would have little trouble disposing of the spoils.

With help, the coachman tried in vain to drag the tree from their path, until Gerard suggested, "Why don't you un-harness one of the horses and rope it to the obstacle? The horse will easily drag it clear."

"I were just goin' to do that young sir," a sour look was cast in his direction...

With much muttering, they eventually made ready to resume their journey, tired cold, and the ladies much distressed. All were now unfortunately much poorer than when they started out. It was unbelievable, considering the distance they had covered, that this should happen so close to home.

Pondering on the identity of the robbers, the coachman thought again of Jack Drew, it was several years since they had shared a few jars together. The Vaults was a known den of thieves, the Drew fellow definitely into other free trading. The coachman wasn't the only one interested. Gerard was still smarting from the loss of his winnings.

"My first significant win and this happens!"

The Squire, angry at the thefts and indignities, not to mention the injury to a fellow traveller, rashly vowed, "I *will* get to the bottom of it. See if I don't."

Reaching home ground and journeys end, the Town Watch was duly informed of the thefts, and the whole sorry business brought to the notice of the Parish magistrate. He, acting on information given, saw fit to send a thief taker to check on the whereabouts of Jack Drew.

The very next day he called at the cottage, to be met with anger and disbelief by Fanny. Her insistence that Jack was at sea, made no difference to the common thief taker, whose only interest anyway, was the payment he could expect on apprehending another felon. The house was searched and the area combed, and on more than one occasion.

Jack's name had been mentioned, and it would be only a matter of time, before he was run to ground. Fanny called them a few choice names, but knowing as she did, that what she had told them was the truth - as far as she knew it - she didn't spend too much time worrying about it, there was far too much going on in her household at the moment!

At last the first Sunday in March dawned, and with it the promise of a warm spring. Millie had been over the sequence of events in her mind, until she knew them off by heart. First she would accompany Miss Sybil and Miss Mabel to Church as usual, and afterwards make her way over to the cottage, for dinner with her Ma and Jamie. Later, claiming a need to return to the shop to help with an urgent order, she would make her way back through the town, and walk along the river as far as Horn Bridge. It would be quite a walk.

Her heart beat faster just thinking about it, and wondering what would happen when she got there. Would he be waiting? Or would he stay away; just to pay her back for letting him down the first time?

She arrived at her Ma's with a slightly anxious look on her face. Fanny noticed, and was also aware of how Millie kept glancing at the old mantle clock.

Venturing to enquire just how important this order was, that required her to work on her day off, Millie brushed off her Ma's concern, guiltily setting her mind at rest. After dinner, Fanny, having no reason to disbelieve her story, waved her off.

Millie felt uncomfortable, *an' so I should* she thought, but it didn't stop her.

Following the river after leaving the town, she was surprised at how few folks were about. She walked quickly past the mill, thankful that Joshua and his good lady were nowhere in sight. They would, she knew, slow her progress with their pleasant chatter.

A chill wind sprang up, and Millie was glad of her new warm cloak, pulling it closely around her.

Finally reaching Horn Bridge, Millie was dismayed to find she was alone. But after a few moments of glancing up and down the river bank, a familiar figure leading his chestnut horse emerged from the tow- path running under the bridge. He slapped the horse's rump and it wandered on a few paces, grazing on rich green grass.

Quickly walking toward each other, Millie's smile told Gerard just how pleased she was to see him. Neither spoke, but catching her by the hand, he pulled her quickly to him and leaned against the wall under the bridge. For a moment she wasn't sure how to react, but Gerard took her hands in his saying, "I am so glad that you have come, Millie, I hoped you would,"

He casually raised her hands and slipped her arms around his neck as he pressed his lips to hers, holding her gently and then more firmly, around her slim waist. "Quickly, come with me" he breathed, "We'll move further along under the bridge."

She moved behind him, her hand clasped in his, excitement making her reckless. Pulling her to him again, his words came in deep breaths.

"Mille, Millie, how I have waited for this moment," his hands gradually moved up her body, and around her bodice. She covered his hands with her own and looked into his face.

Looking into her eyes, he saw a strange quizzical look.

Thinking quickly he continued, "But this is no place for us, I just needed to know that you felt the same way as I do! There is an empty cottage on my father's estate. Next time we meet, and there will be a next time, it will be in comfort, warm and dry; you deserve better than this." He gestured at the damp wall above and behind them.

Millie relaxed as he whispered in her ear, his kisses gentle, but as Millie felt the warmth of his lips, she responded in a way that was new to her. Slowly his kisses became more demanding, more urgent. As his eager hand's sought to undo the buttons on her bodice she pushed him from her, exclaiming, "No, no, not like this, I don't know you properly, we 'ave to walk out together."

Innocent she may be, but Millie knew exactly what he had in mind. After a few moments, she took a deep shuddering breath and without looking at him whispered, in a voice Gerard had difficulty hearing, "We must get to know one another. I need more time. No one has ever got this close to me 'afore!"

Millie was thrown well and truly off balance. It was true, nobody had ever got inside her head the way he had. Her thoughts spun. She did need time; time to be the sort of lady that he deserved. And a lady, she was quite sure, wouldn't be expected to behave like this.

She pulled her bodice together, and with tears in her eyes, half walking, half running from the dim light under the bridge, stumbled up the bank. Quickly he followed her.

"Don't be upset Millie, I won't hurt you. It's just that you are so beautiful; you have such an effect on me. I have waited so long to kiss you again, to hold you. I promise to arrange a proper meeting place; I *will* manage it, for next time. The cottage – you will love the cottage on my fathers' estate. We can get to know one another properly, just as you say. I can see you are different from other young ladies, and I am glad of it. Please say we can meet again, and don't be upset, I'm truly sorry. I will never take you for granted again."

Gerard caught up with her and turning her to face him, traced a tear down her cheek with his finger.

"Please smile again for me." The look in Gerard's eyes, made Millie feel that she must have misjudged him. Of course she would give him another chance. Fastening her cloak against the cold wind she nodded gently.

"If you still want to, of course I'll come and meet you again." Smiling her gentle smile, Gerard relaxed, and immediately began to look forward to their next rendezvous.

"Next Sunday? I'll show you the cottage." Gerard was eager to get it settled, but for Millie it wasn't that easy.

"No, I mean, well, I have to tell Ma, an' I won't see her again 'til next Sunday. I can tell her then, that the following week I can't be there for me dinner."

"That's wonderful; I knew we were meant to meet again,"

Millie regained her composure; "it'll give me all day free. I can excuse me - myself from Church, and be up by the cross roads beyond The Coaching Inn, at whatever time you say."

She wondered if she had been a bit bold, but Gerard immediately agreed.

"Wonderful, shall we say eleven o'clock then?"

"Yes, eleven," she whispered, pushing any apprehension to the back of her mind.

"Very well, next Sunday week. Walk to where the packhorse track meets the coach road, walk on in the direction of Uplyme, and I will ride down to pick you up.

Have you ridden on a horse before?" Millie thought for a moment before saying with a smile,

"Only the donkeys, and pack mules, when I was little."

"There's nothing to it. You'll ride behind me. Try to be there Millie, do try." Millie gave a little nod and turned away. When she looked back to wave, Gerard was already mounting his horse.

Millie faced the long walk back to Broad Street, hoping she didn't look as guilty as she felt, but what she did know for certain was that it wouldn't stop her. *An empty cottage*! Maybe Master Gerard already had plans for their future.

Millie visualized herself standing in the doorway of a pretty cottage, the door surrounded by roses. Dreams of welcoming him home with a gentle kiss.

Pictures of domestic bliss passed before her eyes; of being the very best wife a gentleman ever had. *I've got gentleman's blood in me veins*. Mille was sure Gerard couldn't fail to be impressed, when she enlightened him.

There would be no need to mention the circumstances of her birth, and who's to say whether her Ma and blood father were married or not? Who would know? Gerard would know only that her real father was a gentleman sea captain, and no one could ever tell him different could they? It was the truth. But things could be complicated, and the more you thought about them the more complicated they became.

She reached Broad Street, letting herself in quickly and quietly, and slipping up the stairs to her room. Glad that her lessons with Mister Lane began at the end of the week, Millie could hardly wait for the next step, which she felt would bring her closer to becoming a 'lady'.

The week slipped by until Friday evening arrived, and with it Millie's first lesson. She was pleased that he had agreed to help her. Miss Mabel and Miss Sybil thought it 'very commendable' to better herself in this way.

Millie's first lesson was used to acquaint Mister Lane with how much she already knew. He agreed that her reading was more advanced than her writing, but her speech left much to be desired, explaining that Millie's way of talking was the lazy speech of three counties.

On the borders of Devon and Dorset, in close proximity to Somerset, the local folk spoke with a lazy drawl. Millie's main problem area showed most when she became angry, or excited. The aitches were the first thing to go. The other thing she could do to help herself, he explained, was to slow down her speech, and remembers to substitute 'my' for the mis-use of 'me'.

"For example 'me book' becomes '*my* book,' 'me 'ouse is *my house,* do you get the idea Millie?" Millie nodded vigorously.

"So if I talk slower, and don't forget me- *my* '*haiches*,' it will sound better? Every one always tells me to slow down; I will pay *particlar* attention to it."

Mister Lane looked slightly amused.

"Well done yes; those and a few other changes as we go along. The way you pronounced, par-tic-lar for instance; it should in fact be *par-tic- u- lar*, also when you say 'talk slower' it sounds much more lady like if you say, 'speak more slowly' But as I say, if we correct as we go along we will make headway."

Mr Lane was pleased to help. Millie, not yet seventeen had none of the hard dialect of the old, born and bred fisher folk, it should be easier for her. After practising her writing for some time, Millie's concentration was broken, as Mr Lane cleared his throat.

"Finish the sentence you are writing Millie, it is time we packed up. I shall correct it before your next lesson." As Millie was preparing to leave, the subject of Jamie's accident came up.

Everyone seemed to know the circumstances of his fall, and Mister Lane bade Millie convey his sympathy to her mother, adding, "At school the lad had potential Millie, but just could not apply himself. His mind was always on other things. You were both bright scholars, and it saddens me to hear of the company he keeps."

"Why, whatever do you mean, Mister Lane?" His statement had stopped Millie in her tracks, "I don't understand, he's not yet nine years old"

Quite obviously the girl hadn't heard the rumours circulating. Deciding he didn't want to be the one to enlighten her, he quickly changed the subject. Millie couldn't bring herself to ask further questions, so she paid for her lesson, and thanking him, made ready to leave.

"I'm glad to have you back, you have done well Millie. Shall we say the same time next week?" Millie agreed, feeling pleased with her efforts. Hurrying off, she was still deep in thought when she reached the shop door. Fitting her key in the large keyhole, and entering, she looked up to see Miss Mabel in the hall.

"Oh it's you Millie, how did you get on?" Millie assured her that she had enjoyed it, and would be going again. With Miss Mabel muttering, "Very commendable," she made her way up to her room. Taking of her cloak and hanging it on the hook behind the door, Mister Lane's words again rang in her ears. Was there more to Jamie's accident than met the eye? Did Danny know more than he let on? Her Ma too - was there something she wasn't saying? Millie sat down on her bed; wishing things were as straightforward as they were in her childhood. Sixteen didn't seem an easy age to be. One moment she felt like a confident young woman, embarking on an exciting life and the next she felt as undecided and vulnerable as a child. Nothing seemed easy anymore.

CHAPTER SIXTEEN

The Admiral Grey was making ready to sail out of Naples. Captain Fawsey completed his business allowing for last minute deals to be struck. Now the crew were concerned only with making good time loading fresh cargo and putting to sea again within three days, after which their seamen's pay was stopped.

Duties completed, the men figured they deserved the good times that they most certainly had enjoyed ashore. Well rested, filled with good food and satisfaction, they awaited the tide and further orders. This was the halfway mark; the return voyage set to take as long again, depending on weather and currents.

Hauling anchor they made ready to sail amid feelings of anticipation and excitement. The hold was stacked with dried fruits, Florence oil, wine and other commodities acquired through various means.

Proving to be a successful trip, the crew's provisions were stowed in every available space along with fresh water, and their rum rations. Keeping time to the beat of sea shanties, Jack and his shipmates prepared to cast off.

A heat haze dimmed the receding coastline, as Jack and Lenny bade a quiet farewell to the sunshine port of Naples, though the hot humid air did nothing to improve the stench of their living quarters.

Captain and crew were set fair.

Leaving the safe harbour of Naples they prepared to embark on the long haul back to Gibraltar, the first leg of the homeward voyage.

Soon after setting sail into the hot rising wind, the lookout in the rigging spied what appeared to be a Spanish Galleon further down the coast. With shouts of 'ship ahoy,' and after observing it for some time, he noted that it seemed to be drifting aimlessly. A short deliberation followed between captain and bo'sun and it was decided to stand off and run with the wind, in her direction. The situation must be ascertained.

Changing course to get closer to the sailing ship, and with the majority of the crew in agreement, the promise of spoils for anyone brave enough or foolish enough to board her, drew the ship and her crew, precious hours out of their way.

This was indeed the most foolhardy choice of the voyage. Jack and several others, outvoted by all who counted, were forced to go along with this seemingly chaotic change of plan, which in turn would lead them into an unexpected, and indeed unwanted, turn of events.

Eventually coming alongside the vessel, which appeared to be abandoned, four crewmen were volunteered to investigate. The inky black sea between the two vessels was choppy. Slinging and securing a grappling iron over the bulwark, with rope attached, enabled the first of the crewmen, with the help of eager mates to swing easily across the gap between the vessels.

Dropping quickly and cautiously to the deck before beckoning the others to follow, they thoroughly searched the upper deck from stem to stern; all was quiet.

The crew left aboard the Admiral Grey watched and waited, as it quickly became apparent there was no other movement anywhere on the Spanish ship.

It was unnatural, eerie. Then, disappearing into the bowels of the ship, an old deckhand reappeared moments later, yelling that she was abandoned, and bodies strewn below decks. The atmosphere changed noticeably.

Superstition reared its head and the crew became jittery. Reporting back, the small search party, pistols still cocked, told a tale of murder and plunder! Counting six or seven bodies, it became increasingly obvious the rest of the crew must have been taken prisoner.

It seemed most likely that Algerians or Turks had already visited the stricken vessel stripping her of anything worthwhile. Carrying off the remaining unfortunate Spaniards to offer for sale to the highest bidder they had murdered anyone who resisted.

Keeping look-outs posted, several more of the crew were ordered to make the transfer, to double check for any remaining booty, and search specifically for Spanish gold, or 'pieces of eight.' Keeping their nerve, they eventually came across a couple of small, flat, Moroccan leather pouches, which had been well hidden.

Searching a small room below decks used as the bread room, and lined with tin against the rats, further spoils were found. Spanish gold! It had been slipped between the linings which had then been beaten back into place. Now, duly prised back, the gold was brought up amid cheers and shouts of excitement.

Jack was as happy as the next man with the ill gotten gains, but couldn't understand why Captain Fawsey didn't quit while they were ahead.

It was still possible that a Barbary pirate ship would appear on the horizon at any moment. If that should happen, they would more than likely suffer the same fate as the unfortunate Spaniards.

After what had seemed an age of scurrying and searching, the crew swung precariously back onto the deck of The Admiral Grey and safety, the spoils given over to their captain.

The order was given for all hands on deck, and Lenny, who had been keeping a low profile, was relieved when the further order was given to stand by. The helmsman made ready to sail; the intervening width of inky blue water widening by the minute.

Watching the bawdy seamen congratulate themselves, and each other, Lenny breathed a sigh of relief. He had been on Jack's side when it came to voting for a home run. With the Admiral Grey well in profit, each man now had only one thing on his mind; home to England.

The captain gave the order to 'turn about and proceed on course,' the frantic activity that ensued, meant they were well on their way to at last starting on the delayed homeward run.

Meanwhile down below Captain Fawsey's celebrations were in the form of hard liquor, and the more coins he counted, the more liquor he took. Jack and the bo'sun were alarmed that in such a situation, given the dangerous waters they were sailing, his behaviour appeared unwise at best, and downright irresponsible at worst.

Taking orders now from the bo'sun, they set sail across the Tyrrhenian Sea, on course for the Mediterranean, and the straits of Gibraltar.

After several uneventful days, it seemed that their ship may yet go unhindered, but the hazardous voyage off the North coast of Africa, lay ahead.

The heat made tempers short, along with the rations. They were yet many days from Gibraltar when a fight broke out. It was discovered that an ordinary seaman had stolen and hidden his presumed share of gold.

Sober, the captain was a fair man, but two floggings and a hanging from the yard-arm, gave credence to his state of mind, befuddled as he was by drink and heat.

Jack's intervention earned him a flogging of his own, and he vowed to watch his back for the remainder of the voyage. The mood on deck was black, when again the cry went up from the rigging, 'sail ho' and with a feeling of foreboding all eyes searched the horizon. With their sense of danger heightened, instincts of self preservation were brought to the fore.

Away to their starboard, just appearing in the distance the lookout had spied two sailing vessels. The captain, who had been roused from sleep, had at least a couple of hours in which the drink had started to wear off, but the threat of water bandits quickly brought him to his senses.

Fearing the loss of his precious cargo, and with the Spanish Galleon's fate still fresh in his mind, he gave orders that The Admiral Grey should try to outrun them.

Playing cat and mouse with sailing vessels, before plundering, murdering, or taking prisoners, was the fate of any smaller vessel. Captain Fawsey relied on his bigger ship and skilled hands, to outrun any threat, and hoped they could keep out of trouble long enough for the now pursuing vessels to lose interest.

Alas they were slowed by the sheer bulk of cargo and the inept making of sail, due to the crews liking for their own rum ration, consumed as the captain slept. Slowly but surely the pursuing ships gained on them, eventually putting a shot across their bows.

Heaving - to, in an effort to prevent damage to the ship or injury to the crew, a second shot followed, killing a seaman and injuring two more. Damage enough to bring men to their senses.

The Captain, sober now, bellowed, "Repel all boarders; Make more sail."

"Aye aye cap'n," a rousing chorus greeted this order.

Should the pirates manage to come alongside The Admiral Grey, then each crewman, armed with pistol, sword, knife, or any other likely weapon, was on his mettle.

The second order to make yet more sail was obeyed with alacrity, and slowly they put distance between the vessels.

Once out of range and under full sail, they at last looked as though they might yet out-run the marauders. If they could only make it to within sight of Gibraltar, it was certain the ships of the King's Navy would deter any further attack from their pursuers.

But ideally The Admiral Grey needed to stay out of *their* way too, for fear of confiscation of their own cargo. Or what was worse, being press ganged into the king's service. To Jack's mind the phrase 'between the devil and the deep blue sea' never seemed more apt.

Lady luck was on their side, and after what seemed an eternity, the pursuers lost interest and gave up the chase. It was certainly an encounter to make the adrenalin flow and a sobering one at that.

With the injured taken care of, the body of the unfortunate seaman was then wrapped, and stitched into his hammock by the carpenter. The last stitch traditionally put through the soft tissue between the nostrils, to completely ascertain death. Finally, dispatching the body to the ocean, weighted down with pig iron ballast, a few words were spoken for the deceased.

The routine traditional auction bidding and buying the unfortunate sailor's possessions, - raising cash for his widow- was then completed. Jack and his shipmates had all had enough excitement for one voyage.

Continuing under captain's orders, sailing only into safe ports for essential supplies and fresh water as needed, they continued turning goods into money, further swelling their coffers.

Negotiating the Bay of Biscay, anticipating rough weather, it was with relief that repairs to the ship had been completed in good time, despite all the extra work involved.

The already tired crew and exhausted carpenter were longing for quieter waters, and thankfully encountering no major storms crossing the bay, they made good time.

At last rounding the tip of France, and with no further mishaps, they at last completed their long and eventful voyage into British waters. Calling at the Islands of Jersey and Guernsey, and eventually with England in sight, they sailed safely back into Bridport, amid raucous sea shanties and good humour.

Discharging both legitimate and illicit cargo in time honoured ways, hoodwinking or bribing customs to avoid taxes, they were ready to rest and recuperate. The crew collected their dues, the length and dangers of the voyage taken into account in the reckoning. For now all were content to count their rich pickings and enjoy the benefits of their 'free trading.'

Keeping their heads down, they would go their separate ways until the dust settled yet again!

CHAPTER SEVENTEEN

As events unfolded on the high seas, back home in Lyme Millie's young life was becoming ever more complicated. Arrangements for the day that she was to again meet with Gerard had placed Millie in a dilemma, which had caused her to think long and hard.

Telling untruths to her Ma and deceiving her employers, didn't sit well on her shoulders. She simply *must* have a good excuse for changing her usual Sunday pattern.

Awaking with a feeling of dread and excitement all mixed into one, she took a deep breath. At last this was the day! Half of her wanted to go ahead and see where it would lead, but the other half was reluctant to put herself in an embarrassing position.

Gerard would find out just how naive and ignorant in the ways of the world, she really was. In different circumstances, she was sure his forward behaviour would have been 'tempered with restraint.' That's just the way Mister Lane would have worded it, she thought.

The snatched meetings were surely the reason Gerard expected more from Millie than she was prepared to give on such short acquaintance. Given time and the right setting, they would take things slowly, get to know each other, and walk out as a couple

Fanny had already been forewarned not to expect Millie on that particular Sunday, and had no reason to disbelieve Millie's explanation, claiming extra work.

The day arrived, and the sisters made ready for Sunday morning worship, and pleading a chill, Millie excused herself from sitting in the icy cold Church. Both sisters agreed that it would not be at all wise, to risk making matters worse.

Waving them off, she mentioned that she may visit her Ma later, if she felt better, just to get some fresh air.

The house was quiet, and Millie's thoughts strayed to the cream silk dress, which now had pride of place in the tall, workroom wardrobe. After the unfortunate incident Miss Mabel had hung it there out of harm's way, and with Miss Brading no longer wanting to purchase the dress, and feeling unable to offer it for sale, they had passed it on to a grateful Millie. But both had been adamant. To wear it, it had to be made much plainer.

She had hated removing all the extra trimming that she so lovingly created in the first place. Ribbon, lace and pink rosebuds; her scissors almost refused to work for her, so reluctant had she been to change anything.

Skipping upstairs to change from her work frock into the now simple, but still beautiful, silk dress; she shook it from its linen cover. Now was certainly the right time to wear it! Quickly she discarded her day dress, and stepped into the soft folds of silk, struggling to button up the bodice. Thank goodness the pretty covered buttons have been allowed to remain. How grand she felt.

I suppose it was a *gown*, when complete with it's 'bits and pieces, and now it's a *dress* she reasoned. Brushing her hair she tied it with a length of pink ribbon. Running downstairs to the work room she stood in front of the fitting room mirror and admired herself. She smiled at the image looking back at her.

Now she knew how Gerard would see her; Millie was determined not to disappoint him. Glancing down she noted how worn her boots were, but nearly covered by the hem of her dress they had to do.

Smiling a secret smile, she reached for her cloak and hurried into the hall to make good her exit while Miss Sybil and Miss Mabel were still in church.

Millie quietly closed and locked the door, then making her way to the lane above town, headed toward the main coach road, walking in the direction of The Coaching Inn.

Her mood was light, her imagination working overtime. Passing the inn yard in haste, in the hope of not being seen or recognised was the tricky bit. But being Sunday it was quieter; no sign of Danny or anyone else who might ask awkward questions.

Feeling thankful the rain had held off, she walked quickly, and after covering quite a distance, was relieved to see a rider come into sight. Reining in his horse, he walked it to a small track leading off the main highway, Millie recognised Gerard.

Although her heart beat faster, her pace remained steady. As she drew within a few feet he hailed her with a grin saying, "Now's your chance to ride my lady. Walk to the stile, I will come alongside and hoist you up here with me!" Millie found her tongue.

"Is it safe?" she whispered.

"It certainly is, providing you hold on tight. Climb up on to the stile, and take care." As her cloak fell open, Gerard, with a low whistle and a twinkle in his eye exclaimed, "You look beautiful Millie."

Millie, choosing not to answer, but relishing his words, obeyed his instructions. She eyed the horse with some misgivings, wondering fleetingly if the dress had been the best choice after all. Gerard rode close alongside, bidding her face the same way. Smiling assurance, he gained a firm grip under the pommel with his left hand and reaching down and back with his right arm, slipped it firmly around her slender waist.

Millie hung on to his upper arm and shoulder with both hands. Gripping him tightly, she took a deep breath, while he firmly swung her up and back.

As he touched her, Millie's heart almost stopped. Gerard's own heart beat hard and fast. He was amazed. She was as light as thistledown, the close proximity made them very aware of their now touching bodies.

Wriggling on the horse's broad rump, until she was in a comfortable position, and arranging her skirts, Millie settled herself for the ride.

"Are you feeling safe? Are you sure you are comfortable? Hold on tightly around my waist my lady, and we're ready to go." Excitement, laced with apprehension, crept over her in little warm waves.

"You won't ride too fast will you?"

"Not too fast, but the quicker we get there, the more time we have to ourselves." Millie grasped his jacket.

"That won't do, put your arms around my waist, and hang on tight"

Millie felt bold, but knew it was the only way to keep her seat, and slipping her arms firmly around him, blotted out the thought of what everyone else might think of her.

Gerard turned his horse, and they set off in the direction of his father's estate. Millie, feeling daring and very grown up, was naively blind to the compromising situation she was happily riding into!

Some distance before reaching the main gates of the Manor House, Gerard urged his horse to leave the main track and follow a narrow bridle path through the coppice. Opening out into a clearing, there was revealed, a high stone wall into which was set a wrought iron gate.

Dismounting, and tying the reins to a low branch, he hesitated as he lifted Millie down, judging that a stolen kiss now might be unwise. Leaving his horse to graze on the long grass verge, he reached out and tried to release the iron latch, which was partially covered by a thick overgrowth of Ivy. Clearly the old gateway was little used, and it was with some difficulty that Gerard exerted more force to push his way in.

Reaching back he caught Millie's soft hand in his and she quietly followed him through the gate, Gerard pushing it roughly shut behind them. They stepped onto what was once a main pathway.

Old, overgrown Lavender bushes trespassed from each side. Hebe, Hydrangeas and assorted shrubs, struggled for light, escaping from overgrown borders.

"Where are we Master Gerard?" breathed Millie,"

"We're here Millie, at the cottage. And just call me Gerard."

It didn't seem respectful, but then nothing was as it seemed, and Millie fell quiet again.

Following the path as it bordered on lawns, and rounding a high Yew hedge, Millie was unexpectedly presented with a mellow and in her eyes, large, stone house with gables and mullioned windows, although Gerard had referred to it as a cottage.

Millie drew in a breath of wonder, as they approached.

An age old, twisting, gnarled trunk of Wisteria, climbed the walls. This was a cottage? It was three, maybe four times the size of the harbour cottage that she grew up in. Seeing the amazement in her face Gerard laughed, and pulled her to him.

"Do you like it Millie, is it what you expected?"

"Like it? It's a small palace - not that I've ever seen a palace. But look at the pretty windows, and the solid chimney stacks; Look at the size of the front door, and the pillars." She glanced behind her. "And the garden, it's so lovely." Gerard was delighted that Millie found the place to her liking. It would make things easier, and he so wanted her to be at her ease. She was such a strange mixture.

He stared at her slight form, trying to work out what fascinated him. It wasn't just her looks. Maybe it was her air of trust and vulnerability! Whatever it was, he had the feeling he must tread carefully this time.

The feeling was new to him, he usually took what he wanted and moved on, but somehow this seemed different. He laughed at the look of amazement on Millie's face.

"I've always been fond of this cottage, it's been empty for too long. It needs a family and hopefully that will be the case in the not too distant future"

He looked again into Millie's face, into her eyes. Then, taking her arm he steered her around the side of the cottage, to the back entrance, which he knew to be unlocked.

Stepping inside, they paused for a moment in the large stone area. There was a wooden settle on one side and a long low chest on the other. They moved towards a door on the right, which Gerard pushed open, to reveal a large flagstone kitchen.

Millie looked over his shoulder, wide eyed. A huge kitchen range with copper pans hanging above it stood along one wall, and two large sinks along the far wall beneath the window. An enormous wooden table stood in the centre of the room. She could hardly believe how big everything seemed to be. Pulling the door closed they continued.

Further down the hall, there were three more doors. The first one seemed to be the small drawing room. There was a faded carpet square on the floor, and the window shutters were partly closed. Next to that was another small room. This was the library judging by the array of shelves and books.

On the opposite side of the hallway and central staircase, Gerard threw open the third door for her inspection. It opened on to a large sitting room, and Millie's eyes were drawn to the large stone inglenook fireplace; complete with logs, stacked both sides of a great iron fire basket. Mounted above, was what appeared to be deer antlers.

On the floor in here, was a faded Indian carpet, a couple of well worn armchairs, and beneath the window, a chaise lounge. Still holding tightly to Gerard's hand Millie gazed, wide eyed. Gerard grinned at her amazed expression.

"Come in here Millie, this is the room we shall call ours."

Millie followed, taking in the fact that here too, the windows were partly shuttered. She hesitated for a moment, watching as Gerard moved quickly to the fire place.

Piling dry sticks and logs in a heap in the iron fire basket, and using a flint to ignite it, he soon had the fire crackling merrily.

Millie marvelled at the easy way he kept up a sort of commentary as he worked, not at all lost for words, as she was. Next he dragged the old chaise lounge in front of the fire.

Finally, turning to her, and slowly undoing the ties of her cloak, he let it slip from her shoulders and fall to the ground.

"Millie; Millie you look entrancing, so pretty, your eyes, your hair." He gently touched her cheek and stood back to admire her. Millie glowed, she wasn't used to compliments.

Noting again how handsome Gerard looked standing there in his fine clothes, she wanted him to pull her close, as he had that day under the bridge.

"You are fond of me?" she whispered. He moved to sit on the chaise lounge.

"Of course I am. Now come and sit here with me Millie I promise I won't bite you!" He patted the cushioned seat beside him. His feelings of treading carefully began to disperse, After all, he thought, she's here isn't she? I invited her, not forced her.

Millie smiled and took a step toward him, feeling *not* quite as comfortable with the situation of being alone in the empty cottage with him. Quickly casting aside any doubts, she sat down, allowing him to slip his arm around her shoulders and pull her to him. She reminded herself that she *wanted* this, to sit close beside him.

As she relaxed, and leaned against him, his arms tightened around her. He buried his face in her soft copper curls. His lips moved down her slender neck. Myriad baby kisses, awakened Millie's buried desires. Pressing her soft body against him she returned his kisses, with a passion she didn't know existed in her. Gerard slipped his arm from around her shoulders and gently, so gently, pressed her into a half sitting, half lying position, amid the cushions.

Still kissing her, but now with an urgency that made something deep, deep inside her stir, his fingers expertly released the buttons on her bodice. With hands smooth and warm, his breath hot on her skin, all her thoughts of propriety cast aside... Millie slipped down amongst the cushions, consumed alike with desire, gripped in passion, she returned his kisses.

What was happening to her? His caresses reached a peak and slipping down on her, Millie was lost.... lost in a sea of incoherent thought and emotion. Wanting only for this to continue, her whole body was wracked with wonder and excitement. She couldn't stop this; she didn't *want* to stop this. Gerard must love her as she loved him, she knew this beyond a shadow of doubt, *and this must be the expression of true love.* The feelings they had for each other reached a crescendo; they clung together.

The tears in Millie's eyes, her hot flushed skin, her sudden feelings of vulnerability, brought her back to earth, and to the realisation it was too late for thoughts of remorse or regret.

But he loves me, Gerard loves me! He will look after me... won't he?

They lay still together, Gerard's lips against her neck, hers against his thick smooth hair. Her arms wrapped around him still holding him close.

As Gerard moved away from her, the spell was broken. Helping to smooth her crumpled gown, he set himself straight, and giving her a light kiss on the cheek, picked up his hip flask that had fallen to the floor, saying, "Just what we need, take a sip of brandy Millie, wet your whistle."

He laughed pushing the flask against Millie's lips as she sat up straight beside him. She pushed it away, declining the drink and looked into his handsome face.

"You do love me Gerard, don't you?" The question came out in a low whisper. Gerard was quiet for a moment, then looking away as he fumbled with his clothing, he muttered.

"Well that's a bit strong, but yes I am fond of you." He stood up and moving over to the hearth, kicked the logs apart with the heel of his boot, and stood looking down as the remains of the small fire died in spark and ash.

"Come along my dear, we had better make ourselves decent. I will take you back as far as the woods below Uplyme. That's a good two thirds of the way; you'll be alright from there won't you? It's but a short step from there to the Coaching Inn. You could rest there before walking home."

Millie, shocked, fumbled with her cloak, as he placed it around her shoulders. She felt suddenly that everything was far from alright. She had to ask, she just had to. With a quaver in her voice she tried again.

"Gerard, what are... your intentions toward me now, shall we be married? Is this where we shall live?" She could have asked a dozen more questions, but the look on his face stopped her in mid stream.

"My dear girl, what on earth are you saying? Of course we can't be married; you are surely not that naïve, why my father would never allow it. I have to marry into a well heeled family, with money; keep the old homestead in good repair and all that. I'm not thinking of settling down with anyone for as long as I can avoid it. So you see, we can continue to enjoy our little liaison.

Millie wasn't quite sure she knew what *liaison* meant, but was pretty certain it didn't mean marriage. She sat down quickly. The blood drained from her face and a weakness overcame her, it was as if her heart had stopped pumping; she couldn't stay upright.

Gerard had the grace to look concerned for a moment, but quickly brushed off her distress. He stared at her white face in silence; Millie tried again; "But this cottage? You said we would move in here; you said it wouldn't be empty for much longer; that it needed a family, that it would be our special place; that we could be together." Her voice trailed away. Gerard shifted from one foot to the other.

"Well, we certainly have been together," he said with a wry grin; the irony of his statement was lost on Millie; "I expect I meant it when I said it!" he answered lamely, " But as far as the cottage is concerned, my *meaning* was, we have a new gamekeeper and his family moving here in a few weeks; you know how it is."

Millie didn't 'know how it was' at all. She couldn't believe the words that she was hearing, and could say nothing more. The silence was palpable. She stood up and turned away, tears filling her eyes and spilling down her face, as she stumbled to the door.

Half blinded, she reached it, and wrenching it open stumbled out into the hall. She dragged the heavy front door open. How could he say those things, how could he be so off hand now? After everything that had happened...

Gerard, crossing the room to follow, caught up with her as she reached the front door.

"Millie, don't go like this, I was hasty, I'll take you back; you can't walk *all* the way."

"I've 'ad to walk further 'un this 'afore, an' I can do it again," Millie flung over her shoulder, "I don't want your ride; I don't ever want to see you again, never!" The last thing on Millie's mind now, was her speech. Gerard locked the door behind him, and trying to catch up with Millie called out, "I'm sorry if you misread my intentions."

He felt really bad about the whole situation. The word guilt sprang to mind, but damn it, the girl

must surely know the difference between flirtation, and.....With hind sight, he realised just how much his words must have hurt her, and how far beyond flirtation, were his actions.

Millie reaching the gate in the wall and wrenching it open, ran out onto the track past Gerard's horse. She knew the whole area well, from when she was a small child, and cutting through the coppice ran until she reached the fields. He stared after her disappearing figure... she would be unlikely to relent even if he rode after her. Head bowed in thought, he walked toward his horse.

Why should he be made to feel any worse than he did already? She'd made it perfectly clear how she felt! *But then I've just - very clumsily - told her how it must be? Can I really blame her?* He drew a deep breath, remembering her soft warmth his arms...

A green silk shawl nestled forgotten, in his saddle bag.

When Millie came within sight of the inn, she made her way across the field, towards the hedge bordering the lane. Finding the stile, she quickly climbed over, and with no one in sight continued down the road, praying she may walk past The Coaching Inn, unhindered.

As she came abreast of the yard she heard a cheery voice calling,

"Hey Millie, hold on, what you doing up this far?" The unmistakable voice of Danny brought her to an abrupt halt. As he came across the yard to her, he repeated,

"What *are* you doing, up 'ere? Is it me you want?"

Looking into his kind, familiar eyes, Millie was almost lost. She wanted to blurt out the reason she was here; Wanted to feel clean and whole. How could she ever be the same again? But then she wouldn't would she? She knew that deep down, the dreamy, fresh apple cheeked Millie had been squashed out of her, as surely as the juice from the cider apples that went to press. Tears welled up inside her as she turned to go.

"I'm in an 'urry Danny, on an' errand like, I'll find some time to come by again to see you, an' Emily." With that Millie hurried on before Danny could ask any leading questions, a fresh outbreak of tears, threatening to overtake her.

As Danny turned to walk back across the yard, two things struck him. Millie was clearly in a state about something. And why was she all dressed up in that posh frock he had glimpsed before she drew her cloak closer to cover it?

CHAPTER EIGHTEEN

Millie hurried on, putting distance between her and her shattered dreams. The walk had seemed endless. How could he have used me so? I won't meet 'im again an' that's for sure! I can't believe 'e said those uncaring things? Fancy suggesting we go on meeting; in secret too! What does 'e think I am? Her head whirled with anger and the injustice of it all.

The tears pricked the back of her eyes; she wanted to run to her Ma the way she had always done, when things went wrong. This time she was on her own, she just *couldn't* tell her what a fool she had been.

How will I know? How long must I wait? Sick with worry, and although naive about details, Millie knew the consequences of her actions may influence the rest of her life.

Arriving at the fork in the path, she deliberately chose the one above and behind her home. She knew her Ma would be there, late on a Sunday afternoon, and wanted only to get over to her room on Broad Street as quickly as possible.

Reaching the shop, and slipping quietly inside, she tiptoed up the stairs. Millie pushed her way into her room, and sliding the latch into place threw off her cloak. Tugging at her dress - she couldn't wait to get out of it - and leaving the crumpled heap on the floor, she moved to her wash jug and basin. She felt nauseous; the hurt inside her wouldn't go away. Her thoughts jabbed at her one after the other.

Is that the way men look after their own needs? I'm too green and too stupid... Didn't I love 'im with everything in me? Every breath an' every thought: and now I hate me-self!

She stopped short. But is that love? How will I ever know? Will I ever dare to put me faith in anyone again? I thought 'e loved me back. What if me life is ruined? What if all men are like that? Her shame was total, her fear enveloping.

When Millie had regained her composure, she smoothed down the grey dress that she had changed into, and walked slowly down the stairs wondering if she looked any different... Miss Sybil greeted her, "You are just in time for tea, are you feeling any better?" Continuing slicing and buttering scones, she turned, with the butter knife poised in her hand, and seeing Millie's white face said, "my goodness Millie, you are pale, you really should have stayed in the warm; come here by the fire and have a hot drink, you don't want to go down with anything!

Millie smiled at the irony of her words, and seeing Miss Sybil's concerned face, thought again of her Ma's words, 'folk's good opinion of you.' She moved to the seat by the fire.

She had let everyone down, and herself most of all. She knew now, in a rush, what shame and pain her Ma must have felt, facing an uncertain future. What a fool she was, as if she hadn't already had that route signposted for her...

Millie hid behind her invented chill for several days, finding the only way to deal with her shock and hurt was to shut it from her mind completely. Each time Gerard or the cottage popped into her head, she forced herself to replace it with another image.

Millie needed to tell somebody. Emily would offer sympathy, Rosie could give good advice. But ultimately she knew her Ma would have to be told, no matter how long she put it off.

Millie was drowning in her dilemma.

She resumed walking on the Cobb. Long silences suited her; she held onto her secret until it threatened to eat her up. On a Sunday visit to Fanny, she found she could carry the burden of her shame no longer.

Millie absentmindedly greeted Jamie as she arrived, passing by him to reach the scullery, where Fanny was washing dishes. Looking at her daughter's pale anxious face, and crossing the small space to close the door behind her, she said, "I 'bin worried about you since you were last 'ere maid. I think there's summat you need to unload, an' now's as good a time as any. Sit down, an' sought out yer thoughts, an' if you want to tell me anything I'm 'ere. Jamie's tucked away in the kitchen, the doors closed so we're on our own."

Millie stared at her Ma and the temptation to share her sorrow was too great to resist.

"Ma I do want to - well, to tell you everything, but I'm afraid you won't love or - trust me again - as you do now. How can I spoil it? I've ruined everything."

"Millie, you're halfway between, sixteen an' seventeen. You're allowed to make mistakes, its part of growing up. You won't change me feelings, no more than you can change being me daughter. I might want to shake you, but that's a chance you 'ave to take." She moved closer to sit on the one hard backed settle beside Millie, moving a cleaned hob-pot to the table. "You remember not so long ago, when I 'ad summat to tell you? So go on girl, start at the beginning."

Millie started at the beginning.

"It seems a long time ago now, but back when I was fifteen, I first noticed this nice looking young man, an' I sort of knew 'e 'ad his eye on me." She paused, and without looking up, went on to tell of the visits to The Coaching Inn. "He's a gentleman Ma. I felt strange when 'e spoke to me, when he smiled at me. It was like I needed to keep on seeing 'im." She tried to gauge her Ma's reaction... but Fanny was tracing the grain on the well scrubbed table with her finger, concentrating on Millie's words, and wondering just how much of a gentleman he really was. Millie continued; "Then I met 'im again at The Manor House, she stopped. This time Fanny looked up, clearly disturbed, "when I went there with Miss Mabel, to learn about fittings, remember I said? Miss Clara, was nice, she was friendly"... Fanny shook her head slowly. Millie went on to tell how she wanted nice things, to be a lady both for herself and for him.

Drawing in a breath, she looked at Fanny's face before continuing with her story. When she got to the part about wearing the silk dress, and riding on the back of his horse to the cottage, she broke down.

Her Ma reached out and clasped her hand, and fearing the worst stayed silent, occasionally patting Millie's cold hand and waiting for her to continue; Millie burst out.

"'E fooled me Ma, he sort of promised things, an' I meant only to get closer to 'im. I didn't think things would 'appen like they did. I didn't think I could 'ave let 'em 'appen. I didn't know what *was* happening till it was too late to stop it. And now I'm so scared, what if there's - consequences? Ma what can I do, 'ow will I manage?"

At this point Millie's tears got the better of her, and any attempt to control them, was lost in her sobs.

"Hush now, hush up; things ain't never so bad as they couldn't be worse. You're not the first to be taken in by the gentry an' you won't be the last. Look at me Millie, – I can't throw no stones, so dry your tears. If an' when the time comes we'll think again. In the meantime, like I always say, it's no use meeting trouble 'alf way."

Millie dried her eyes. Her family, and all her friends, were worth a dozen Gerard's. She still had them didn't she? Slowly the weight of carrying her secret shame was lifted. They sat for a moment until both regained some semblance of composure. "Go on maid, take a few minutes to go an' blow the cobwebs away. Millie stood up, thankful that her Ma now knew everything.

"I think I'll walk on the Cobb, an' then come back, an' we'll start again, an' – thanks Ma."

She managed to smile.

"Aye you do that, an' I'll sort Jamie." Fanny gave her a quick hug, before she hurried through the kitchen, swishing quickly past her puzzled brother.

As Fanny walked in, Jamie looked up, "What's up Ma, our Millie bin 'aving one of 'er do's again?"

"Aye, summat like that lad, but we'll let 'er be; she'll be back again later."

Millie wandered along the Cobb. She stared out to sea and felt the breeze on her face. She thought of her Pa – out there somewhere. Walking to the edge of the high wall she watched the waves travelling sideways against the stone, the sea was running high.

She turned to retrace her steps, a deep sadness in her. Feeling she had betrayed everyone who loved her, and betrayed herself too, where did she go from here? The loss of her first love or what she had mistaken for love was almost bereavement.

"No good can come of thinking like this." She realised she had spoken out loud; it was true though her words were lost in the wind.

As she walked back the way she had come, she saw Lazurus busily mending his nets. Glancing up he smiled, his brown crinkly skin becoming even more crinkly. Millie avoided his eye, not knowing what a sad smile she gave him. He'll have to know, everyone will have to know about me if there's a consequence from me bad behaviour. The thoughts jabbed at her. Heaving a shuddering sigh she made her way back to the cottage.

Lazurus was true to his word. Through a network of friends and acquaintances he got word to the public house in Axminster, who's Landlord would pass word to Beattie York regarding Jamie's injuries. It took a while, but eventually word came back. Beattie remembered Lazurus, and would be pleased to be reacquainted with him.

Her sister still lived in an old cottage on the outskirts of the few dwellings that made up Charmouth, about three miles away. She would be staying there, during the last week of March, or as soon as the weather permitted travel. Lazurus conveyed this information to Fanny, and it seemed there was a ray of hope for Jamie.

Although their plan eased her mind, there was still a lot to do to make a visit to Beattie possible. Fanny's immediate concern was to get Jamie to actually accept further treatment. She also wanted to talk with Beattie herself, just to put her own mind at rest before anything further was done.

At first Jamie was not at all in favour of being 'messed about with' again, but Doctor Bird had been consulted and was in agreement. He had done all he could and encouraged them to go ahead, reassuring them that healers and bone setters, seemed to achieve quite remarkable results.

When it was pointed out to Jamie how limited his future might be, in terms of getting about, he gradually came around to Fanny's way of thinking. A future that didn't include climbing cliffs, searching for curio's, or simply adventuring, went a long way to changing his mind. Fanny's train of thought was more in the direction of him earning a decent living.

They had both arrived at the same conclusion in the end, even if it was for different reasons. The next hurdle Fanny had to overcome was how to pay for any treatment that was needed. Here she had in mind a few gold coins, along with a certain piece of jewellery, which had yet to be turned into money. This was another job for Lazurus who always knew someone, who knew someone else!

Eventually Lasurus gave the 'go ahead' for the first visit, after hearing that Beattie had arrived, and was safely settled in with her sister Ada. Fanny wanted both Jamie and Millie sorted out before Jack returned, around the end of May; it couldn't be soon enough for her.

Her thoughts strayed back to the last time there was any light-hearted fun in the cottage. It seemed a long time ago and she realised it was way back at the Christmas gathering.

Just when things seem quiet, life has a habit of jumping out at you. Fanny set much store, by the bonesetter being able to sort Jamie out, and hoped that Millie would overcome her 'high faluting' ideas with no consequences; *Aye, life jumps out all right!*

As the weeks passed Millie went about her work in a dream. More than once either Miss Sybil or Miss Mabel called her to account, albeit in a nice way. The quality of her work wasn't in question, only the length of time it took her to complete some of her tasks. But spring was well on the way, and sunshine would surely put colour back in her cheeks!

Millie awoke early, and feeling slightly strange swung her legs over the side of the bed; no sooner was she upright than a wave of nausea engulfed her. Stumbling over to the jug and basin, she poured some water, splashing her face and sipping some from her hand. She moved back to sit on the edge of the bed. This was what Ma had warned her about, and she was to tell her just as soon as it happened. She had just begun to relax, pushing her worries to the far corners of her mind. Now here it was again, and couldn't be ignored.

Ma had said this was when she had to choose, the back street so called 'midwife'- or the child. Millie had closed her eyes and her mind once; but now it was here again, the decision had to be made.

Millie, being Millie, knew that if there was to be a new life, she simply couldn't be the one to try and end it. It wasn't choosing to allow that life to continue, that was the difficult part for her; it would be living with the difficulties of the choice afterwards! Millie felt the overwhelming need to talk to her Ma again, and take it from there.

With a sinking heart, she slowly dressed and went downstairs to the warm kitchen, to a life that she had grown so fond of. Things were going to change; of that there was no doubt.

Like a pebble thrown into a pond, the changes would be far reaching. She knew beyond a shadow of a doubt, the 'if' had now become a 'when.'

Although Millie felt she already knew the outcome, her Ma must be told. At the first opportunity, she walked slowly down Broad Street, across the square, and onto the shingle. The breeze refreshed her, but did nothing to quiet the turmoil in her head.

In a way she was relieved. Now she could stop wondering and start planning. Didn't her Ma and Pa always say, 'deal with facts' not 'ifs and buts'? Now she was resigned to planning a future, with Fanny's help, support, and encouragement. Such a huge consequence from a single lapse of commonsense!

Millie allowed herself to recall just for a moment, the memory of Gerard, then pushing it quickly from her mind, as the familiar feelings his nearness or memory provoked, washed over her. She quickened her step as the thoughts rushed into her head.

'No I hate 'im I do, 'e fooled me into thinking that...' She left the thoughts unfinished as she reached the door of her home.

After relating the 'facts' to her Ma accompanied with more tears of despair, Millie pulled herself together, and they began talking through the best thing to do in the situation. It turned out to be 'nothing much at the moment;' a breathing space, a wait and see policy. Later on there would be plenty to do.

"What about the father, will 'e be told?" Millie nearly exploded.

"I don't want 'im to know, I *won't* tell 'im," she was adamant. After having his circumstances pointed out in no uncertain terms, she certainly didn't want any further humiliation.

Fanny decided not to press the matter, there was time enough. Working out her dates, Fanny reckoned on the child being born sometime during the early part of December.

"You'll know when the times right to tell your employers an' you've got a while yet to find the right moment. Or you could just leave!"

"I can't do that, they deserve to know the truth even though I won't know 'ow to face 'em"

"Well you'll 'ave to face up to it. There'll be plenty of sorting out to be done in the time between." Fanny softened her tone, "We got to see 'ow first few weeks go afore we start on anything, maid, then later on we'll list things you'll need to make in preparation for the child.

The hardest thing of all would be for her to greet her Pa with the news of her condition

The summer arrived and wore on. Millie, striving to do her utmost to make up to Miss Sybil and Miss Mabel for something they still had no knowledge of. She still had a while yet, before she would have to tell all, and leave her job.

Millie threw all her energies into designing and making up bonnets to match outfits, and to fill special orders. She could still lose herself in the feel and smell of fresh materials, straw bases, and the soft materials of the bonnets that she loved.

She became even more proficient and daring; and indeed, seemed to put her very soul into her creations. The colours inspired her, the trimmings delighted her, and she was able to deftly create the finished articles from the descriptions and feelings of the clients.

She was collecting things together to embark on yet another 'masterpiece,' when Miss Mabel called her to one side, and with a concerned face asked, "Is everything alright Millie?" After the initial shock, this was the opening Millie needed. The time had arrived when she must tell of her predicament. How could she leave all of this? Once they knew, surly they would have no alternative but to ask her to leave!

She saw her dreams of making beautiful gowns and bonnets for the gentry, and 'becoming a lady' herself, slipping through her fingers, and all because of her wanting nice things in the first place. She had ruined everything.

Staring into Miss Mabel's face, Millie slowly put down the material she was holding and said quietly, "No Miss Mabel, thing aren't as they should be, I 'ave to talk to you."

Miss Mabel wondered what was coming, although she knew Millie had not been herself and had *something* on her mind; that much was quite clear, but she wasn't prepared for the following revelation.

Millie decided to make a clean breast of things and tell just enough to explain why she already knew she would have to leave.

"You see I am to have a child," she ended.

Whatever it was that Miss Mabel expected it certainly wasn't that. She was so young. At the very beginning of her life, so talented, such a considerate, gentle girl. Suddenly Miss Mabel was bubbling with inward anger at the man who must have taken advantage of their vulnerable Millie. Far from turning against her, it seemed that she and Miss Sybil must do all in their power to help her.

Millie was surprised; amazed; she had expected a degree of condemnation. Even for them to withdraw their support, and ask her to leave on the spot. Expected their thoughts to be only for the business, and how the gossip would affect it.

Although they had always shown her kindness, and were she knew, fond of her, she wouldn't have blamed them in any way for a change in attitude towards her.

Miss Sybil came through to the workroom, looking astonished, and a bit pale, having roughly worked out the way the conversation was going. She looked first at Miss Mabel and then at Millie.

"How much did you hear?" Miss Mabel enquired.

"Enough. Enough to know that we have to talk,"

"Well now, what is to be done Sybil?" Miss Sybil paused, her index finger tapping her lip.

"What *is* the best way of dealing with this unexpected situation?" Millie felt her world crumbling around her. Always the practical one, Miss Mabel quickly said, "Sybil and I, will need to talk this through, so for now we will carry on as normal." Millie felt anything but normal, but nodded quietly.

The rest of the day dragged on, the evening came and went.

Next morning conversation seemed somehow not to *flow*, as all three strived to pretend that nothing unusual had taken place.

Finally at lunch time, Miss Mabel said, "Millie my dear, we have reached our decision regarding yesterday's conversation." Millie was dreading what she was about to hear, she wanted to run, put her fingers in her ears, give in her notice first. Instead she sat quietly, waiting for the axe to fall. "I'm sorry but it won't be possible for you to continue to work here for much longer. As you say your mother is to help you, we think it best that you return to your home when things become - er- obvious. In the circumstances, it won't be appropriate for you to continue with the present - er- arrangements, when that time comes." Sybil took over,

"Having said all that Millie, We want you to know that if it becomes possible for you to come back to us in the future, then we would welcome that. That's not to say that we are not shocked with your news, but what's done is done. We must think of your wellbeing, and see what the future brings." Millie, eyes downcast, and reddened cheeks, whispered, "I'm sorry I've let you down."

Having delivered their verdict, the sisters softened the effect by sending Millie to the kitchen to make tea.

Millie, thinking she had got off lightly considering the bombshell she had dropped into their ordered lives, thought again of the kindness shown her, and once again a tear trickled down her cheek. Unknown to her, Miss Mabel too, was wiping a tear from her eye.

Millie would be missed. Of that there was no doubt; her time here was to come to a close. It was halfway through May, and she would be leaving for good in September - if she were allowed to continue that long, *and able to keep her secret safe from prying eyes!*

The exposed coast of Lyme Bay took the brunt of the storms but as the year progressed travel, although never an easy option, was made more comfortable by the warmer weather.

Fanny and Lazurus had worked out the best method of getting Jamie over to Beattie at Charmouth, although the cart ride would be difficult for him no matter what. They managed to board the carrier's long low cart, and Jamie was made reasonably comfortable, knowing that once they joined the toll road it would be a smoother ride, and the cottage just a short distance from where they would alight.

Their first sight of 'Clifftops,' was a small run down cottage, nestling amid wild garden and adjoining orchard. On the gentle slope that led down to the bay the land was open, with a few sheep lazily munching the patches of lush green grass. Further down the hill were several more old cottages.

"Just look at the view out across the bay." Fanny breathed in the sweet scent of spring. "Not often I get a change of scenery," she mumbled, more to herself than anyone else.

From left to right were the cliffs that gave the cottage its name, behind them a sweep of wooded hills and lush valleys.

"We get off 'ere son, not too far to 'obble." With some difficulty they got him down off the cart." She turned to the carrier, "Pick us up on yer late afternoon return."

"Sorry I got to lean on you Ma, give us yer arm an' Lazurus can come t'other side an' use me stick to lean on."

It was only a few yards down the track to old Ada's cottage, where she and Beattie were waiting, for them. Jamie was exhausted by the journey, and said as much. On entering the cottage they exchanged introductions over a cool drink.

Taking Jamie to one side, in order to look closely at the still red, shiny and swollen thigh wound, Beattie noted that it appeared to have knitted together in some places, but still gaped in others. The whole of Jamie's leg was swollen and he could bear little weight on it.

She explained to Fanny - Jamie wasn't interested in the details, "I need to draw out the festering. Get the deep wound clean. This first visit is going to be difficult and painful, but with the help of a goodly quantity of cheap gin, that I reckon he'll be quite willing to swig back, I'll be able to clean the depth of the wound."

When she had finished the first treatment, she placed her hand over the dressing and Jamie felt both warmth and comfort; from Beattie's healing hand, *and* the substantial quantity of gin!

Fanny was more than happy that she had placed him in Beattie's care. Her faith was implicit; they had taken to each other immediately and chatted away, totally at ease. Lazurus and Beattie too, had a lot of catching up to do, giving Jamie time to sleep off the gin induced stupor. On waking, Beattie assuring him that he wouldn't have to go through the same again, for which he was much relieved.

Ada brought tea, and the visit came to an end. But not before Fanny was shown the best method to encourage healing with poultices, and gentle movement to improve the wasting muscles. A second visit was arranged. As they left to await the cart ride home Fanny had the feeling that she and Beattie would become firm friends.

A week later Fanny and Jamie were able to manage the journey alone. Jamie, feeling comfortable for the first time in weeks actually looked forward to the treatment. Fanny paid particular attention to her methods, for Beattie had to get back to Axminster as soon as old Ada was put to rights and the cottage cleaned and stocked.

A sort of reciprocal agreement was reached that suited both the women. In return for Fanny's proffered help of checking on Ada once a month, Beattie would come to Lyme for a third treatment, and check on Jamie's progress later in the summer.

In a moment of weakness and gratitude, Fanny confided the bare facts of Millie's circumstances, saying "but I can only promise to help out at 'Clifftops' until such time as the baby arrives." Beattie took the facts in her stride, and Fanny felt at ease telling her the circumstances of Millie's plight.

"She's going to keep the child, is she?" Beattie could have helped in that direction, although finding out how far on she was, it would have been more of a problem.

"Oh yes, never wanted it any other way. But 'er main worry is 'ow to lessen the gossip, an' not let it 'arm the business, you know, where she works like."

"Beattie nodded, smiled, and offered an immediate solution."

"Why not move Millie away from gossip? It won't be as bad at the harbour end of Lyme, I know, but the town will still hand out a degree of condemnation for the unmarried mother! Millie could move to 'Cliff tops' as soon as she leaves her employment."

Fanny gasped; it would be the perfect solution. Millie and her family would be spared, the Miss Hartnells would be spared, and old Ada would be looked after.

She could hardly believe it, overjoyed she accepted quickly, providing Millie was in agreement.

"Oh Beattie, you're a Godsend, I'll talk to 'er the first opportunity I get."

The last treatment was arranged at Fanny's home, enabling Millie and Beattie to meet.

When the time arrived, Fanny threw open the door almost immediately, thanking Lazurus who had met her and accompanied her, and chatted awhile before he disappeared back to his work, their shared fondness for the old man yet another bond.

Fanny insisted she make herself comfortable with a cup of tea and a griddle cake, before even thinking of starting on Jamie.

With the treatment completed they sat talking and waiting for Millie. It wasn't long before she arrived. Pushing open the door and calling, "It's only me," she sighed as she crossed to a chair and sat down heavily.

Smiling at her Ma and saying to Beattie, "'ello it's nice to meet you I've 'eard a lot about you"

"Aye an' you maid," and to Fanny "so this is your girl Fanny, bonny she is." She bobbed her head, grey wisps of hair escaping from the mob cap she wore, and continued, "Well dearie, yer Ma an' me, 'ave something to put to you. Will I tell 'er Fanny or will you?"

Millie's looked startled, and Fanny took over, "I've not 'ad chance to tell you yet, but Beattie's 'ad an idea."

She nodded, as Millie looked intrigued, "You know as 'ow I've talked about Clifftops, the cottage over at Charmouth?" Millie nodded. "Well, Beattie's sister- oh I'll let Beattie tell you." Millie looked from one to the other.

"Well maid, I thought, - we wondered- if you would like to move over to Charmouth later on when you leave your job. Maybe you could do with moving away for a bit?

You could keep an eye on me sister and things over there. Ada's getting on a bit now, an' if you could take on doing a bit around the house, an' see she's alright, well we thought it might be better for you to 'ave your babby over there. I'll tend you both, you an' the babby, 'til you work out the best thing for you all. What do you think?"

Beattie stopped, and looking at Millie's tired and pale complexion added, "Seems like you could do with someone keeping an eye on *you* dearie." Fanny hoped against hope that Millie would see it in the same light as she did; it was a wonderful answer to their situation.

Millie, watching both women's faces, and taking it all in with a great feeling of relief, settled on Beattie, saying "It's very kind of you, an' Ma speaks well of you an' your sister. I would be right glad to accept your offer. I've bin worrying about what people will say. I'm that ashamed, but I would feel better for meself an' me Ma. An' for Miss Sybil an' Miss Mabel an' all - they're me employers. I'd be glad to move away for a time, an' it's not that far, just far enough."

"Aye an' I'll only be a cart ride away, an' in the good weather I could probably walk over,"

chimed in Fanny; Millie heaved a sigh," I'm that relieved, I feel like a ton weight's been took off me shoulders, thank you, Beattie thank you."

"Glad you said yes dearie, an' I'll not be that far neither, I'll still call over every four or five weeks. Ada's getting on now. So shall we say, when you're ready to leave work, old Lazurus bless 'im, will send word?"

"Yes, yes please." Millie and Fanny looked at each other. Beattie stood up to go.

"It won't do to miss the last ride 'ome." They walked to where the cart did its turnabout, and saw her safely settled. Then waved their goodbyes amid much heartfelt thanks and watched as the cart disappeared up the hill.

"I'm that glad girl, Beattie'll look after you. An' I'll not be far away. She's got 'er own cottage, an' 'usband, to look after too. An' lots more folks needing 'er care, just like Jamie did.

She's a walking miracle that one.

Millie echoed every word in her thoughts; the future didn't seem quite as frightening as it had an hour ago. She listened quietly as her Ma chatted on.

"I'm that pleased Lazurus remembered 'er. An' it was nice for the both of 'em, meeting up again. It's got us out of a tight spot an' all. All we 'ave to do now is set things to rights with yer Pa when 'e gets back! An' that's any time soon I reckon."

CHAPTER NINETEEN

The day Jack arrived home, a great weight lifted from Fanny's shoulders. He pushed his way into the cottage, pockets stuffed full, sea chest dragging behind him, and a huge tarpaulin bag slung over his shoulder; he seemed to fill the small room.

After long sea voyage and sleepless nights in an uncomfortable hammock, Jack had dreamed of this moment.

Slinging everything down, he called out, "Fanny me luv, I'm 'ome..." a delighted Fanny appeared from the kitchen and he immediately encircled her in strong bronzed arms. "You're right pleasing to come home to Fanny me luv. Now I got you in me arms at last, an' all the welcoming 'ugs a man could want."

"Oh Jack it's so good to hear yer voice, so good to see you. I've missed you I have."

Tears welled up in Fanny's eyes, her own arms clasped tightly around his neck.

"Aye an' I missed you, an' all."

Looking over her shoulder, Jack saw a small pale Jamie, struggling to get up. He was still sleeping downstairs, and it was little past seven in the morning. Releasing Fanny from his their embrace Jack stepped towards him; Jamie all smiles, cheeky grin, just as Jack always pictured him.

"What's wrong with yer leg son? What's 'e done Fanny?" Concerned he stood scrutinizing his young son for a moment a slight frown on his sun tanned face, before covering the remaining distance between them.

"Good to see you back Pa, an' it's nothing, almost good as new." Jamie beamed at his Pa and hugged him in turn. All smiles, Fanny stood back looking at the pair of them, knowing Jamie needed to be accounted for now, his crutches ensuring that. But at least he was up and about again.

He's 'ad an accident Jack, but 'es well on the mend, I'll explain everything later."

Fanny made her man comfortable in the big chair. "You tell us 'ow its bin for you, first. My word Jack, I'm that glad to see you. You won't believe what's been going on 'ere."

So glad to have his solid presence to lean on, she was aware of just how much she had needed him over the last few months. Quietly Fanny made her decision to 'bide her time' before telling of Millie's situation.

Bringing them all steaming mugs of strong tea, with a wedge of scone dough spread with the last of the butter, for Jack, she settled down to listen to his account of the long sea voyage.

He told about the storms in the Bay of Biscay, and about Lenny, laughing as he related the lad's antics, and his confrontation with the thieves in Italy.

When he came to the bit about the Barbary Coast bandits, Jamie's eyes were wide in awe and wonder. Fanny couldn't help thinking that in a weird way Jack had enjoyed it - the excitement and all that - but she also had the feeling that he was piling on the drama a bit!

This was exactly what he wanted her to think, it took the sting out of it so to speak. Maybe she would worry less next time out. He still sweated when he thought of the possible consequences of being caught, but judged it best to keep these particular thoughts to himself.

After relating his adventures, Jack turned his attention to Fanny. If he wasn't mistaken, there was a lot she had to tell and he said as much.

"What you been up to then? Looks like you got summat to say." His glance rested on Jamie, then back to Fanny's face.

"Aye I 'ave that, but not till we've 'ad a meal, an' then," she continued with a smile, "you'll wish you never asked me."

As they finished their meal, Jack braced himself for the onslaught. Fanny didn't disappoint. She related in great detail everything that had happened in his absence. She explained about the accident, and the events leading up to it. Went into great detail regarding the search, how much help she'd had, and the eventual discovery of Jamie's small, helpless body, *and* her feelings on finding him.

Jamie's face was a picture, he was revelling in the limelight as he watched the expressions on the faces of first his Ma, and then his Pa. Jack was a good listener.

Fanny went on to tell of the discovery of the brooch, and the gold coins that had paid for Doctor Bird's care. Of the first visit to Beattie York, and how she had taught Fanny to do the gentle, daily stretching exercises, and massage, which she was continuing.

Jamie's great improvement showed that it was money well spent, albeit ill come by.

Here Jack slowly nodded his head.

"The boy's visits to the healer woman seemed to have made a big difference." "Aye an 'e gets around now with the crutches. Fashioned and padded at the armpit by Lazurus they were."

Jack inhaled deeply, shifting position and saying in a heartfelt tone, "It seems I got much to thank the old man for, *and* this Beattie York too. I'd like to make her acquaintance that I would, thank her me-self like."

"You will Jack you'll meet 'er. Lovely she is!"

Whilst Jack was feeling relieved about Jamie's recovery, Fanny decided to plough straight in with Millie's story, waiting only for him to relight his clay pipe, and watching as he deftly tossed the still lighted taper back into the fire.

With misgivings and a dry mouth, she wondered how best to begin. But there was no wrapping it up.

"Now don't go off the deep, Jack, but... about our Millie. She's got 'erself... in the family way."

Jack nearly leapt out of his chair exclaiming, "What?" His voice was both loud and angry. Fanny confirmed that the girl had missed her second course, and together with her established morning sickness Millie's condition had become certain beyond a shadow of doubt. The anxious look on Fanny's face, made him decide to withhold further judgement until she finished her story.

She came to the end looking slightly flustered, and Jack took a few moments to assimilate all the facts, fighting an inward battle to stay calm for her sake. But a few choice oaths escaped him, regarding the stupidity and naivety of his daughter, and a few more expletives describing the rat that took advantage her

"No amount of wishing, cussing or cursing can change things now!" Fanny soothed.

It took some time and effort to calm and quieten him. After his first fury at the man who got his girl into trouble, combined with his barely veiled disappointment with Millie, Jack had run the gauntlet of emotions, but it did little to alter his view that she had certainly been taken advantage of. Fanny knew how much Millie dreaded her Pa knowing, and was glad to have paved the way, considering the explosion it had caused!

Inside, Jack seethed. But it seemed that according to her Ma, young Millie had accepted and absorbed the fact that she was to face a life changing event.

With Jamie on the right road, the biggest thing to sort out was Millie's situation, and her Ma seemed to have that in hand. Fanny had resigned herself to the news that would make her child a mother, and herself a grandmother.

The circumstances of Millie's own birth made Fanny particularly aware of her daughter's dilemma, and thus very accepting. But she had to admit to herself a certain amount of anticipation and excitement. This she deemed prudent to keep quiet for the time being, saying instead, "You would have thought that giving the facts about Millie's own birth father, might have stopped 'er from making the same mistake. I only wish I'd listened, when you said to tell 'er sooner." Jack agreed whole heartedly with this last statement,

"Aye well, if it 'ad bin left to me, she would 'ave known from an early age. It's too late wishing now."

Fanny looked into his face and saw only a strong protective father. She marvelled again at how lucky she was to have him home after that long, and what appeared to have been dangerous voyage, given the number of widows there are in seafaring communities.

After listening at length, Jack felt that even his adventures seemed to pale in comparison with what had been happening on his own doorstep.

The time had been eaten up more quickly than they realised, and it was noon already. Hunger drove Fanny to the kitchen to prepare food. She was glad of the break, *knowing there was more.* They ate their meal, talked small talk and Jack dosed in his favourite chair, and wakened refreshed....But Fanny hadn't finished yet.

The next thing Jack needed to know, was perhaps the hardest for Fanny to tell. Jamie was sitting outside in the sunshine. So very hesitantly, without looking in his eyes, she said quietly, "Clive turned up... after all these years Jack, almost demanding to see 'is daughter."

Jack stared, anger again showing on his normally placid countenance. What a homecoming this had turned out to be! Fanny went on to explain.

"I 'ad to tell 'er that 'e called; an' I 'ad to give 'er the choice. She wanted to meet 'im. What could I do? I left 'im in no doubt as to 'ow *I* felt after all this time. At least she's seen 'im now. Met 'im, just for a few minute, an' then again, when 'e took her for 'er dinner at the pub. She's said nothing about 'im since."

"What the devil? After all this time, wheedling 'is way back, when I'm at sea. I'll find 'im an' knock 'is block off. An' another thing; is this Clive going to try an' mess up our lives now? Well I'll be blowed if I'll let 'im." Fanny's obvious aversion to Clive as he presented himself now, and the one she loved sixteen years ago, mollified Jack, and with peace restored she hastily changed the subject.

Remembering too late what she was about to say was just another 'happening' for Jack to digest; Fanny said matter of factly, "By the way Jack. Back along, nearing end of February, two men came 'ere asking for you. They searched the house. Pushed their way in they did. They wouldn't 'ave it when I said you was at sea. One of 'em was from Guildhall, the thief taker it was; t'other one was a big chap, wouldn't take no for an answer. They went off to search for you, an' come back again *weeks* later. Do you know what that 'ud be about? " Jack stood up and strode over to the mantle, where he knocked out his pipe in the hearth. "Is there no end to the 'appenings' round 'ere, while I bin gone woman?" His touch on Fanny's cheek belied his rough words. In a quieter tone and with some resignation, he said "I've no idea, but if I was at sea they'll know it 'ad nothing to do with me, *whatever* it was."

Moving back to his seat, Jack stretched out, and leaned back in his chair to mull over Fanny's version of events. He closed his eyes and his thoughts took over. Tells a colourful tale does Fanny. And doesn't our Millie take after 'er? Poor little maid, if ever I discover just who's the father of 'er child, I won't be responsible for me actions. What a homecoming – but at least I didn't arrive home to be presented with a grandchild in the flesh! At least I got time to get used to the idea!

His thoughts wandered back over the years, Millie as a young child, Jamie, a babe in arms. He'd missed a good deal of their childhood, but he was a seafaring man; that was their life. He roused himself and stared at Fanny, dozing now in the chair opposite; realizing just how much she meant to him. *All that going on 'ere when I was facing me own demons, you never know what's going to 'appen next!*

Jamie was sleeping peacefully. Well there was another day the morrow and it was late. He stood up and walked over to Fanny gently rousing her.

She opened sleepy eyes, and smiled as memories of Jack's homecoming flooded back. Reaching for his outstretched hand, she rose from her chair and glancing around, ascertained that the fire was banked up, and taking the one candle they slipped quietly up the stairs.

Fanny left Jack to sleep in the next morning, deciding to go to town for fresh food. There was money now, and Millie would be over for her dinner on Sunday.

It was amazing how quickly life reverted to its old comfortable pattern, Jamie continued to improve, Millie seemed more settled, and for Fanny, the pace of life slowed.

She walked over to Town Square and on to the mill for flour. Meat she would buy from butcher Samuels on the way back. Money ceased to be a problem for a while, and they considered they were well due for some good living, before putting money and goods away for the next 'rainy day'.

Fanny hummed a little tune to herself as she walked along. She felt lighter than air, thinking that it was about time too. All the happenings chased themselves around in her head, but the fact that Jack knew everything, was the biggest relief of all.

She walked on up to the mill and bought flour from Joshua, and after a lively conversation with the miller and his wife concerning Jacks homecoming, and Jamie's continued progress, walked back to buy suet, for a large meatloaf she intended to bake.

Deciding to look in a few shop windows before walking home, she set off up Broad Street; she might even see Millie for a few moments, tell her that Pa was safely home.

As she passed the pawnbroker's shop she glanced up. The brooch that she had given to Lazurus to pawn, sat in the front of the window gleaming.

As it caught Fanny's eye, she stopped to look. It had indirectly been responsible for the extra help afforded for Jamie's recovery. Lazurus had raised money on it, and Beattie had been paid; although her continuing care was born of the new friendship with Fanny and her old one with Lazurus.

Fanny stared at the brooch; it meant so many different things to her. She hesitated for just another moment, before pushing the shop door open. Jack had come home well paid, and had put most of his pay back in the bedroom chest. Wasn't he still turning goods into money?

She slipped inside to enquire about the brooch, and to ascertain whether she could afford to retrieve it. It was still within reach. Satisfied, she asked the old man take it from the window, whilst she returned home for the money, and the pawn ticket.

The pawnbroker knew it wasn't for him to question, but did wonder how Fanny Drew came by it in the first place. Old Lasurus had said he was pawning it for a friend, but gossip had it that it was her boy that had come by it. He shook his head, she was asking for trouble. But trade was trade.

As Fanny hurried home, thoughts to justify her action whirled in her head. She had worked hard to keep things together with Jack away. And nursing Jamie was all extra work. Then there was the traipsing over to Charmouth at intervals. She felt she deserved a little something, and if the brooch was put safely away, it may again prove useful for a money fund in the future.

Fanny knew exactly where the pawn ticket was, Lazurus had insisted on it when he returned with the money it had raised.

Pushing the door of her cottage open, she called out to see who was at home. Placing her purchases on the kitchen table, she called again. There was no answer. Guessing that Jack was probably down by the quay, yarning, and that Jamie would be with him, she knew they would make slow progress.

Rushing upstairs she went straight to the chest hidden under the bed. Dragging it out she reached inside for the small box, where she kept her own private bits and pieces. Opening it, she gently moved a curl from each child's baby hair. She smiled as she looked through her other treasures. There was the blue glass bead necklace, worn only on special occasions, handed down from her grandmother and her own mother, who had passed it to her... There was the ticket! Clasping it in her hand, she started back downstairs to return with it before she could change her mind. Hurrying along, she reached the shop quite out of breath.

Looking up and down, checking no one else was close, Fanny slipped inside to retrieve the brooch; still feeling slightly guilty. She was, after all, carrying out her transaction without Jack's knowledge.

Fanny believed in fate, and fate had placed it back in the window where she could see it. The old man gave her a quizzical look, as he passed over the sparkling brooch. Then it was in her hand, soon to be tucked away safely with her other treasures, and who was to know?

It took only a few moments to complete her transaction, and she was once again in the road, clutching her prize.

Chapter Twenty

Through all that had happened Millie and Fanny had continued to work, apart from the first two weeks after Jamie's accident, when he needed almost constant care. Jack marvelled at how tough the womenfolk were. You only had to look down on the quay to see them doing men's jobs; and they were always the ones to sort out problems and hardships, whatever life threw at them.

Jack had been home nearly a week, unusually longer than he liked, without earning. He renewed friendships, and spent time yarning in the sun, swapping sea tales with other mariners, and catching up on local gossip. Most importantly he had thanked those involved in searching for his son, and was generally swinging back into life on dry land.

In Rosie's tavern he chanced to overhear a remark aimed, if not exactly at him, then in a voice loud enough for him to hear. Turning, he recognised the burly form of the cellar man from 'The Vaults.'

"You got something to say, you want me to 'ear?" Jack enquired.

"Aye," replied the surly faced man, "seems like you're listening."

"Spit it out then." Jack placed his tankard purposefully on the table. Rosie looked worried, not wanting trouble.

"Only saying there's some that should keep account of their lad's whereabouts when it comes to poking round! Your lad bin over to cellars, seen things not intended for 'is eyes. Though I 'ere tell as' 'ow 'e's bin stopped in 'is tracks, snooping over west beach. Lucky they Gulliver brothers din' finish 'im off."

"That a fact?" Jack stood up, "you saying them Gulliver's did 'im over?" Jack's usual good humoured countenance was replaced by a grim expression, matched equally by that of the cellar man.

"Aye, I am that; ask 'im what 'twas 'e found, that upset 'em"

"I'll do that." Jack drained his tankard, banging it down on the table. Much to Rosie's relief he left the tavern. Young Jamie has some explaining to do, and Jack needed both sides of the story.

As he walked back, his thoughts were on the events that had led up to Jamie's accident. Fanny had told all she knew, and already said that he had gold coins and jewellery on him when he was found. Jamie was about to be asked to account *in detail* for his movements.

His heart lurched; his son could have died from his injuries, or equally could have been drowned before they reached him. Either way they were lucky to have him in one piece. But it looked as though it was no accident, as the lad had been found just above the tide line.

Jack was convinced now that he'd been up to no good. He should have questioned him more closely, but as they had already used the money and pawned the brooch, Fanny had persuaded him to let it pass, so far.

When Jack arrived back from Rosie's tavern he was clearly ruffled about something.

"What's wrong Jack?" Fanny was surprised when her usually placid Jack, spoke angrily about the Gulliver brothers.

"Known thieves and trouble makers, they are, that's what's wrong. An' they were probably, aye more 'un likely - responsible for Jamie's injuries between 'em." The implications in the tavern, had made Jack furious, and though Fanny had never heard their names before, the story, in the telling, angered her too.

"Calm down Jack," entreated Fanny, "'e probably won't remember anymore anyway."

Knowing how Jamie's stomach dictated his movements they decided to wait for him to appear, and hopefully Jack would be the calmer for it. Sure enough, around midday Jamie arrived home bringing with him some herrings, sewn together through the mouth and looped over one crutch. His cheeky grin, which had returned in full, made Fanny plead his case again - but Jack was adamant.

"Come in and sit down. We need to talk son; you 'ave to *try* an' remember more of what 'appened, before you were 'urt. I know it's a long time ago, but try. You set out to go somewhere special didn't you?" He looked into Jamie's face, the grin had now disappeared. "You saw two men didn't you? I'm not interested in what you were up to, but I want to know if you seen 'em afore."

Jamie looked sheepish; he couldn't answer his Pa's question without admitting to more wrong doing. *Still, might as well get it over.* He took a deep breath.

"I seen 'em over 'The Vaults' first time. They was 'coining it' Pa, filing off the edges of gold and silver coins; Going to send 'em for smelting. It was a real good lark. They get to keep the money, and make more from selling the coin edges."

Jamie was getting excited. Jack could see that he would have to somehow frighten the lad onto the straight and narrow. It was a bit late for punishment, besides he'd had that already.

"Son, do you realise that those two roughnecks that attacked you - an' I *know* they did - they're wanted men. They are *dangerous* and they *recognised* you. They knew you could tell what you'd seen at *anytime*. They tried to *kill* you Jamie. It was meant to look like an accident.

You know son, *I* used to go drinking at 'The Vaults.' It just got too dangerous. Smuggling goods is all right, it's a 'lark' as you call it, to pit your wits against customs an' the like. But the minute violence enters into it, that's when you're done for. You understand? You got to mind the company you keep. You got to watch yer back an' not go meddling. The Gulliver brothers won't be messed with! They could still get to you!"

Not only had Jack frightened Jamie, the lad's face told him that; but he had also succeeded in frightening Fanny.

"I didn't know they'd be over West beach Pa. I was listening at 'Vaults.' I heard 'em on about the cave, before I got chucked out. They were going to stash jewellery there. An' then 'elp others bring more stuff ashore when the boat came in. The cave was full of smuggled stuff. Then I found this tin like. I bashed it open but I only 'ad time to pinch a couple of things."

Fanny felt the blood rush from her head, "I took a brooch from your pocket, along with gold coins, where did that come from?"

"Like I said Ma, it must 'ave been some of their stuff."

"Oh my Lord, Jack, I bin an' got the brooch back! It was lovely, I never 'ad anything like it 'afore. I put it in me tin."

It was Jack's turn to change colour.

"Whatever possessed you Fanny? Getting rid of it once was the best thing you did, but to go an' buy it back! I can't believe you would do such a thing. Well, it can't be pawned a second time, it would 'rouse suspicion. Where is it now?" Fanny looked at Jack, and Jamie looked from one to the other, this seemed to be getting serious.

"I put it up wi' me treasures, in me tin, inside the chest under our bed."

"Well best it stays there, 'til we think what to do with it; we could 'ave done without this Fanny! It's got to be sorted out, afore I go back to sea proper. I've got a short trip lined up, to Channel Islands, an' when I come back in a couple of days, I'll 'ave worked out best way of 'andling it. No, better still I'll take it with me; drop it in sea. Davy Jones' locker, that's best place for it!"

"Oh Jack must you, can't we just keep it in me tin? I won't try an' wear it or anything."

"No. Davy Jones it is. I made me mind up." She knew there would be no shifting Jack now and was resigned to his solution.

Next day Fanny left the house, and Jack followed. They usually only got as far as Rosie's Tavern with the crabs now, what with Millie moving on, and Jamie not able to do much in the way of carrying. But Rosie only paid a pittance, and seeing Fanny empty the catch from her wicker pot, Jack called out to her, "'ow about if I was to take this lot up to 'The Coaching Inn?' I could do wi' the walk, an' get to see Danny an' old Abraham too?"

"Aye, it don't matter where they go, long as they're paid for."

She passed the catch over to Jack, who took the longer walk up the hill, and on reaching the Inn was welcomed in the yard by Abraham. After greeting the old man, he called Danny to one side, saying "I'll take these crabs to Fred Murkin, and come back to talk after I've got me self a pint o' cider. See you in a while Dan lad." Danny was anxious for news of Millie, and nodded agreement.

Moments later, crabs dealt with, and cider in hand, Jack stepped again into the sunshine of the yard. Danny was greeting the coachman, who had just pulled in for a change of horses.

Jack sat on the steps drinking thirstily from his tankard, idly watching as Danny quickly and expertly un-harnessed the team.

The coach's passengers had already alighted at the front of the Inn and disappeared inside to refresh themselves. Jack watched as the coachman fell into deep conversation with Danny, at intervals glancing his way. Jack raised his hand, the coachman seemed vaguely familiar.

As the changeover was completed and the weary team led into the shade to be rubbed down, fed, and watered, the driver disappeared inside, for his own rest and refreshment. Jack walked over to where Danny was busily rubbing down the sweaty mares.

"What was all that about Dan?" Danny looked up, "Looks like this 'un needs a visit to blacksmith, she's loosed a shoe!"

"Dan," said Jack again,

"Oh sorry Jack, did you know the coachman? Only he seemed fair interested in you; wanted to know your name." Danny straightened up, "so I said you was Mister Jack Drew, seaman extraordinary!" Danny laughed at the look on Jack's face. "Don't worry Jack, 'e knew I was being funny, what's up?"

"Nothing, nothing lad, I'm just trying to remember if I seen 'im 'afore. But never mind that, it was you I wanted a word with. Look here now, I know you always 'ad a soft spot for young Millie. Anyway I wanted you to know that our Millie is – well she's to 'ave a babby."

He paused at the look on Danny's face. "Sorry I can't wrap it up like, but she denies it's yours, and forbids me to speak of it to you... But me an' Fanny, well we wanted to be sure like, you know?"

Jack paused and Danny paled.

"You can rest on that score Jack. I wouldn't go messing with your Millie, an' that's the truth. I got a lot o' respect for Millie, aye an' you an' all."

Danny looked angry and was quite aggrieved as well as shocked, before adding; "but I sure as hell reckon I know who *is* responsible."

"Sorry Dan lad, we 'alf wished it was you." Jack touched his shoulder. "Aye Fanny thinks she knows an' all. But our Millie, she won't say. She's that stubborn. I'm all for speaking out an' making 'im pay but between the two of 'em I'm ham tied. They reckon they got it sorted, but I wanted you to know the situation."

Anger, sadness, and frustration flooded through Danny, and there was silence as he struggled to come to terms with the unwelcome news. There was a lot he could say, but not to Jack, not now. So he just said, "I thought she acted a bit strange the last time I saw 'er. She's stopped coming over to see me an' Emily. Am I to talk of it to 'er, if I see 'er? What do you reckon Jack?"

"Best leave things be for the time being, you're not likely to see 'er for a while, she's going to take 'erself off over Charmouth way later on, 'fore it shows. She's staying with 'er Ma's new friend, 'til babby's born. Aye best leave things for time being." Jack rested his hand on Danny's shoulder, "shame," he muttered as he walked away.

As Jack prepared to leave for his short trip to the Channel Islands, he stared out of the cottage door. Fanny had left for work a couple of hours since.

It was a beautiful morning nearing the end of June; the sky was blue, the sea reflecting colour in the gentle calm surface. *Aye the summer's the sailors friend right enough,* he thought as he breathed in the sea air, and took in the scene before him.

Jack's bag was packed; the trip was too short to warrant his sea chest. In a few minutes he was due to leave, and join the small sailing ship that had discharged its incoming cargo. As fresh crew, it would fall to Jack and his shipmates to load the new cargo at present standing on the quay, before setting sail on the late afternoon tide.

The brooch safely stowed in his bag, he heaved it up onto his shoulder and stepped out into the sunshine, pulling the door shut after him. Turning to walk the short distance down to the harbour, he instead walked straight into the path of three men. Two of them were strangers, but the third Jack recognised as the coachman from the previous day. He doffed his cap and made to step around them.

"Not so fast my friend, we've bin looking for you for many a long week." The tallest of them turned to the coachman, "Is this the man?"

"Aye that's him, that's Jack Drew; he was named for me yesterday. Aye that's the one; I recognise his black curly hair. Same build, same red spotted neckerchief, that's him alright."

Jack took a step towards him, "You again, I swear I don't know 'e from Adam. But I'll land 'e one if you're causing trouble!" The coachman quickly took his leave, while Jack, puzzled, surveyed the other two. One grasped his arm, which Jack immediately shook off. The bigger man, drawing a scroll from the deep pocket of his shabby frock coat, held it with dirty hands and, Jack noted, even dirtier finger nails.

He started reading haltingly from the warrant; Jack quickly brought his mind back to the present and focused on him as he droned on.

"Jack Drew, you are being taken up on suspicion of robbery with violence, the taking of goods, money and jewellery, and use of a fire arm. Therefore, in connection with the Stage coach robbery on the London to Exeter highway, on Twenty sixth day of February seventeen sixty seven. You are to accompany us to Bridport Gaol, where you will be held before trial at the assizes, for the said, suspected robbery with violence, and the shooting, and injury, of one Percy Michael Granger."

Jack stood his ground and surveyed the two men and the so called 'warrant.'

"Well now, I have to ask you to come along 'o us."

"What gives you the right to take me anywhere?"

"We are paid as thief takers. Sent out by the justices to detect an' apprehend the likes o' you. Make our living fair 'un square; unlike some!" He gripped Jack firmly by the arm.

Getting caught for something he had done was a risk he lived with, but arrest for something he had no knowledge of, was quite another matter. However much

Jack protested his innocence, it seemed he was to be taken to Bridport Gaol, there to await a hearing before local magistrates, charged with a crime he hadn't committed. The outcome looked bleak. If he was found guilty he could be sentenced to deportation, or even a public hanging.

His unwanted escort eyed his kit bag and scowled, "You won't want that where you're going." Thankfully flinging it back inside the cottage, knowing the brooch nestled inside, Jack slammed the door shut. *That would surely 'ave sealed me fate!* He started to walk, a man either side of him. He was angry. It *was* a mistake and he would endeavour to get it sorted quickly. There was plenty that could surface if the water was muddied too much.

It was left to a curious Lazurus to relay the events to a distraught Fanny. Observing from his perch on the Cobb, he watched as the group made their way around the corner to the waiting cart. For now Jack was filled with barely suppressed rage at his wrongful 'arrest.' He figured that on reaching the gaol and speaking to the governor, it wouldn't take too long to set the record straight.

They only had to ask around, find Captain Fawsey, or a shipmate, to be assured of the truth. If he was at sea, he couldn't be anywhere else, by any stretch of the imagination!

Chapter Twenty One

After a hot and uncomfortable journey, the cart reached the main street of Bridport town. How different from his last visit, when he had been filled with confidence and anticipation for his next voyage. The cart drew to a halt outside the old grey stone building. After some considerable hammering on the part of the taller of his captors, the large doors opened.

Jack's insistence that he be allowed to speak to the governor, fell on deaf ears. He was taken to a room where a clerk took details of his name, and much to his annoyance, his alleged 'crime.' He was then marched down a long dank passage to the cells.

Here, after much protestation of his innocence, and anger at his wrongful arrest, Jack was left to cool off. He found himself in a small stone cell along with four other miscreants, and a handful of rats.

It was a hot day and well into the afternoon. Jack had swapped the fresh sea air, for the stench of foul breath and unwashed bodies.

He felt in the pockets of his ducks and fingered several loose coins, small change by the feel of it, but maybe enough to bribe a poorly paid gaoler. Banging on the cell door and squinting through the small aperture, he saw no one in the dark passage beyond.

Turning back to survey the other inhabitants, he noted two ragged young men apathetically slumped in a corner. As his glance took in the other cell mates, he saw only a pathetically thin, wrinkled old man, and one other, the only one standing; a sturdy man of about his own age.

"No use banging door, nor yet shouting my friend. The only time you see a soul is when they push water, an' stale bread or gruel in twice a day. Or like now, when some other poor bugger is thrown in to join us."

Jack sized up the other man and grunted. Staring around, he took in the fact that there was only a small high window, and nothing but a filthy slop pail in the corner. He covered his face with his hands, running them back through his hair.

"But I've done nothing; I don't know why I'm 'ere." He angrily scuffed the floor.

"Aye, that's what we all say mate, it was some other bugger; *not me m'lud!*"

"But it's true." Jack sighed, "'ow long 'ave you bin 'ere?" He enquired as an afterthought.

"Day afore yesterday it was, but these poor buggers so far as I can tell, the lads bin 'eld for several months without charge, an' the oldie bin 'ere for all o' that time, an' more besides. Don't believe in 'urrying things 'ere abouts!"

Jack sank down the wall, onto the filthy floor. The other man towering over him and thrusting out his hand introduced himself as 'Big Barney.'

"Jack Drew" said Jack reaching up to the proffered hand, "what you in 'ere for?"

"Well it's like this," began Barney joining Jack on his hunkers against the wall. "I'm landlord of a public 'ouse an' eating place. Good pies an' pease pudding, that sort of thing. I work 'ard, to keep a good, law abiding establishment. So when I gets robbed of me takings I tends to lash out.

Caught the bugger fair an' square I did. Unfortunate for 'im, an' even more unfortunate for me, 'e hit 'is 'ead on door frame going down. Didn't mean to do for 'im, I didn't. It were just unfortunate, like I say. *They* don't see it like that. I'm to go to the assizes, probably Dorchester. What about you?"

Jack mulled this over before answering

"You've 'ad a raw deal an' no mistake. S'pose whichever way you turn it, the buggers still dead. Me? I'm accused but not guilty, of robbery using violence; shooting with the intention of killing. The chap was wounded. Thing is, I don't know nothing about it, other 'un what they said when they arrested me - cause I never bin near a stagecoach in me life, nor used a pistol!"

Barney let out a low whistle; Jack finished, "Trouble is they got a witness that identified me like. Says 'e seen me do it"

"Seems like we both got a raw deal. I had neither the intention, nor the stomach for it. An' you seem to 'ave been picked up on false identification... in the absence of anyone else to pin it on! Not good my friend, but what *you* got to do, is get word to someone outside, someone who can *prove* you were somewhere else!"

"Aye, easier said than done I reckon, not that it can't *be* proved, if I can only get word out, seeing as 'ow I *was* at sea at the time."

They lapsed into silence, the youths staring at the newcomer but quickly losing interest, the old man unmoved by the intrusion.

They sat there in silence, each examining their own circumstances. Jack's thoughts returned to his waking moments at the start of the day, when Fanny had left the house after kissing him goodbye, and expecting to see him briefly on the quay before he sailed for Jersey.

He wondered how Fanny would react when she found his kit bag inside the door on her return. How long would she wait before realising that he wasn't coming back? She would know that he would never go aboard ship without it.

And would she take the brooch from his bag? Hide it somewhere, as she had before? He hoped so. What of Millie and Jamie? Jack's mind was in a whirl. The day had dawned bright and ordinary, the events that followed somehow unreal to him, even now.

He looked up to re-establish his whereabouts, and slipped back to the world inside his head. It was easy to see how the others – apart from Barney – had lost any sense of time or hope. Jack determined that he wouldn't be there long enough to go the same way.

By the passage of time, something that Jack was used to judging in four hour bites, he reckoned it to be about seven o' the clock, when he and Barney were roused by the muffled sound of footsteps outside the door and the clunking of a heavy key in the lock.

Slowly the door opened just enough for a bowl of, what appeared to be food, to be pushed across the floor, followed by a large jug of stale tepid water, placed just inside. As Jack leapt to his feet the door was quickly slammed shut again. He was unprepared for the scrabble of bodies, as the youths and the old man began fighting over the meagre rations.

Jack and Barney looked on. They were both big well nourished men, and couldn't bring themselves to partake; happily giving their share to the more needy occupants. They watched as gruel was greedily scooped up with filthy hands. Jack and Barney made do with a slurp of the foul tasting water. They looked at their fellow inmates, and at each other, doubtless wondering if they were to walk the same route.

"No one else will come this side o' morning," announced Barney "best try an' sleep some 'o the time away, that's what I bin' doing... or" with a grin on his face " better still, think of summat' to get us out of 'ere."

Jack agreed, but didn't hold out much hope. Half waking, half sleeping, the hours dragged slowly by, conversation was limited to the occasional remark from either Jack or Barney between fitful snatches of sleep, from which Jack emerged only to renew again the horror of his predicament. Eventually the cell started to lighten to a new day.

"They got to tell us, eventual like, when the case - if they got one- will be 'eard. Surely they will." he muttered already wide awake.

"Don't bet on it," whispered Barney, stirring, "if it's anything like t'others we could be in for a long wait."

"No. No." Jack jumped to his feet. "I'll not take it quiet like. I'll insist on seeing someone. I can pay for advice, an' I know you can get someone in law to speak for you." He thumped his fist into his cupped hand. "I'm not guilty of robbing no stagecoach. I wasn't there. I'll swear an oath. I *got* to get out of 'ere."

As Barney eyed him, somewhat surprised by his further outburst, there was a slight noise outside, followed by the murmur of voices; among them that of a woman. The key turned in the lock. Jack lunged for the door, as it was pushed open.

Mistaking his headlong rush, for an attack, a baton came crashing down, glancing off his head and biting into his shoulder. The blood oozed down his face, and with some choice oaths, the cell door quickly slammed shut.

It was Jack's turn to be surprised. They were left in no doubt that neither food nor water would be proffered for the rest of that day. He nursed his bruised body as his cellmates looked on, cursing him for his stupidity that would deprive them of their already meagre rations.

In two strides Barney was across the cell listening and trying to peer through the door. Alas the voices started to recede, but not before Barney's acute hearing picked up the woman's voice.

Suddenly there seemed to be a slight hopefulness, about the look that Barney cast Jack.

"You hear that?" he enquired, Jack looked blank. "The woman she's coming back the morrow. One of them do-gooders, she might 'elp"

"That right?" asked Jack "maybe she *can* 'elp in some way." With hope on the horizon, albeit faint, the men talked and planned for a while longer, trying to work out how to talk to *anyone*, with access to the outside. Little did they know that Jacks outburst would result in a ban of all visitors, as long as he remained at Bridport.

CHAPTER TWENTY TWO

Down on the quay Fanny was sorting mackerel into sizes, and exchanging small talk with the other women. The episode of the brooch was still fresh in her mind, but Jack had said to guard her tongue. Lazurus was approaching, and Fanny greeted him with a smile which wasn't returned. Her heart sank.

"Where's Jack? 'is ship 'asn't sailed yet, but neither 'as 'e bin down 'ere loading; 'e'll need to get a move on."

Lazurus took her arm and led her to one side. The other women went on talking together. Everyone's business was their own until they shared it was an unwritten rule.

"Jack's bin took off by two officials an' 'e didn't look too 'appy about it neither! They made 'im get in the parish cart, an' went up the 'ill; so they're not going into Lyme. They'd of gone t'other way. It's my bet they're joining toll road to somewhere." Fanny gasped.

"You're quite sure it was 'im?"

"Oh aye it was 'im alright, I saw the 'ole thing. It was a while, but they took 'im alright."

"Keep an eye on Jamie, will yer? I'm off over to find Millie, an' maybe I can find out something in the town." Fanny set off at a rate of knots across the shingle to Town Square.

She changed her mind; Millie had enough to think about. *Suppose I could go straight to Guildhall.*

She reached the Guildhall and pushed her way into the cool building. The town clerk, sat on a high stool at a high desk, his quill poised over a pile of documents. Fanny closed the door behind her, and walked across the bare boards to stand in front of the old man.

As he raised his eyes to see who was disturbing him, she remembered what a stern and grumpy, old gentleman he was. She almost forgot why she was there. Gathering her thoughts, she began to explain.

"My Jack's been driven away by two men in a cart, me friend saw 'em; I think they might of been from 'ere, they looked official by all accounts; 'is ship's due to sail, an' 'e never turned up on the quay. It's not like 'im; 'e's never last minute like, an 'e was alright this morning! Now 'e's gone"...Midway through her torrent of words, he cut her short.

"I can't help you I'm afraid. You must come back the morrow. If it's anything to do with Lyme Justice System his name will be in the ledger. It's locked away till the magistrate is in attendance. That'll be the morrow."

As Fanny stared blankly, then thanked him and turned to go, he called out, as an afterthought, "are you sure he's not crossed anyone? There are many rogues who like to meet out their own rough justice, and little we can do about it."

"I can't be sure of anything, but thank you, I'll come back again if Jack don't turn up."

Fanny left the Guildhall and looked around; *who else could she ask?* 'The Vaults' housed a motley crew, and although Jack didn't drink there now, someone might know something.

She walked to the notorious public house, pushed her way into the smoky room and yelled out in a voice more confident than she felt, "Anyone 'ere seen my Jack? Jack Drew?"

"What's up Fanny, Jack gone missing?" the landlord called over the bar. Fanny explained again, repeating what Lazurus had told her, and the publican yelled in a voice like thunder. "So, does anyone know the whereabouts of Jack Drew?" The noise ceased for a moment, then some comic shouted, "No but if it's a replacement she's wanting, I volunteer."

This was followed by loud laughter, and the general din resumed. No help to be had here; Fanny made her way to the door, glad to get out onto the street, wondering again if it *was* the law that took him, or just some ruffians he had crossed. She was still no nearer finding out.

Realising she needed more information from Lazurus, - what they looked like, what time he was taken, or if anyone else had seen anything - she slowly made her way back to the harbour and set to questioning him.

"Can't you tell me anything else? What did they look like? Why do you think 'e went with 'em? Did 'e say anything to you that might account for it? Try an' remember please. I 'ave to go back to the Guildhall the morrow, tell 'em what 'appened. That's if anyone'll see me."

Lazurus racked his tired brain and rubbed his chin, staring into the distance.

"They marched 'im like. Oh an' they read from a paper to 'im. I don't think 'e 'ad much choice, he 'ad to go with them. Aye, it *did* look official like."

Fanny thanked him, and wished she'd got more information from him the first time, instead of rushing off 'half cocked'. She smiled as she thought of the expression Jack was fond of using. Then Lazurus came up with another idea.

"Go up an' see Danny - 'e might 'ave seen 'em pass by. It's possible 'e might 'ave some idea what it's about." "Aye, I'll do that, but not till after me works done an' I've rested up. It's the heat of the day now, an' I'm not as young as I was; a couple of hours'll make no difference. I can't do nothing till I go back to Guildhall, the morrow." Fanny could find no one else who had witnessed the scene, and later that day she set off up the hill to find Danny.

Arriving at the Coaching Inn she found him in the yard. Going straight over to him Fanny began immediately, before even greeting him.

"Danny, did you seen an 'orse an' cart with our Jack an' two men, pass by earlier? Lazurus thinks they came this way?"

"Slow down Fanny, an' sit down too, afore you say anymore." She sat down heavily on a hay bale, to catch her breath. "Now then, I 'avn't seen Jack since 'e was up 'ere telling me about Millie. I'm sorry you thought that I - you know - I just wanted you to know that I stands by what I told 'im." Fanny, still sitting, put her hand on Danny's arm.

"I just wish it *had* bin you Danny. Leastways we know she would 'ave bin looked after, seen right, as you might say. Our Millie's been in a right state. But that's life innit?" Fanny sighed deeply, and Danny continued, "Now think back Fanny, 'as anyone bin wanting Jack for anything?" they sank into silence, and then in mid thought Fanny suddenly jumped up.

"Oh Danny, I just remembered. What about the ones that was looking for 'im when 'e was at sea? They didn't believe me when I said 'e wasn't hiding out somewhere." Danny scratched his head.

"Aye an' come to think of it, the coachman that was 'ere a few days ago, was a might interested in who 'e was!" Danny uttered an oath - then another. Fanny stared at him.

"I give 'is name out, I didn't think nothing of it at the time. That stage always stops 'ere for changeover on Fridays. It's usually different drivers every other week, the one we want, won't be back til a week on Friday. I'll tackle 'im when I see 'im again; can't do no more til then".

Fanny thanked him, and got up to walk across the yard to the side door, saying over her shoulder, "I'm sorry too Dan, about t'other matter." He smiled and nodded as he turned away.

Fanny didn't even have to tell him to keep it to himself; she knew their secret would be safe with him. She walked to the back door, and putting her head around, called through into the kitchen.

"Give us a drink of water Emily there's a good maid."

At the same time Fred Murkin walked around the building to the outside cellar. Unlocking the chained doors he disappeared down into the depths. Having checked the empty barrels were stacked ready for collection, he reappeared securing the doors behind him. Reassured all was ready for a fresh delivery of ale next day, he was surprised to see Fanny Drew at the door to the kitchen, looking a bit hot under the collar.

"Fanny, what are you doing 'ere?"

"Jack's disappeared Fred, just trying to track 'im down." He looked at her worried face, and at the water proffered by Emily.

"Leave that, come in the snug an' 'ave a tankard of ale wi' me, tell me all about it!"

"That 'ud be welcome Fred, thanks."

As they sat at a table, Fred's bar help served them both with ale, and Fanny retold the story of Jacks disappearance in as much detail as she could, though it didn't amount to much. When she had finished Fred shook his head.

"I got a feeling they can't be local, 'cos everyone round 'ere knows Jack. An' why would they take 'im away? I can't think what 'es 'bin up to that would warrant being taken from Lyme. That's if 'e 'as bin taken or accused of anything."

Fred took a swig of ale, and rubbed his stubbly chin, "Now let's see. If 'e' as bin taken on to Bridport, as seems likely, they could 'ave bin the law such as it is; weighted against the likes of us; - in my eyes, any'ow." Fanny didn't want to hear that, and her face paled. Seeing her worried expression Fred tried to make light of his slip up. "Maybe it's just a big mistake an' Jack'll be back here soon enough; 'e'll turn up, telling the tale to anyone who'll listen. Aye an' laughing about it too, shouldn't wonder."

Fred realised he had done nothing to allay Fanny's worries, and hastily added, "Now don't you worry none; your Jack's got nine lives. Danny'll make it 'is business to see coachman next time 'e's 'ere, an' I'll be putting a few questions to 'im meself. As I say, Jack might well turn up yet.Now drink up, an' tell me 'ow your Millie's doing. 'Ave you said anything to 'er yet, about 'er Pa's disappearance?"

"She's alright Fred, but no, I 'av'nt told 'er. I'll go an' see 'er the morrow, that's soon enough."

Fanny felt uncomfortable not being straight with Fred about Millie's problems, but the whole idea of Millie moving away, was to keep gossip to a minimum. She wasn't about to spill the beans at this early date. Danny wouldn't say anything. It would be a while yet, but folks weren't daft. The absence of any young girl was enough to set tongues wagging.

They both stood up, and with one last effort to reassure Fanny, Fred said, "Your *best* bet is to go along the morrow, an' find Parish Constable, see if 'e knows anything. If 'e don't, then magistrate won't neither. Like as not it's some mix up." Fanny was grateful.

"Thanks Fred, I'll 'ave to tell Millie, and Jamie too. I'll wait 'til Sunday. They think Jack's sailed for the Channel Islands, so it'll give me time to ask more questions, and 'opefully find answers. I can't do no more till the morrow, then I'll go over to the town again."

At the names Jack Drew, and Millie, one of the young gentlemen patrons drinking in the snug, looked up, idly listening to the rise and fall in conversation.

Fanny was still a good looking woman, and the resemblance to Millie made him take special note; surely she must be Millie's mother. He sank lower in his chair. He didn't like the feeling of loss and guilt that enveloped him. In a second it passed, giving way to anger.

The girl had no right to leave him feeling this way. The colour that had seeped into his cheeks, died as the woman took her leave. Vaguely intrigued by the conversation, he turned it over in his mind ... Jack Drew is Millie's father, and seems to be missing! Whatever's going on, Mapledoram might know of it. Next time he comes around for father's card evening, I'll ask a few discreet questions myself.

Having decided on further investigation, Gerard Elliot left the inn soon after Fanny. Later that week he made some subtle and not so subtle enquiries, into the character of Jack Drew.

It seemed that Jack Drew had more friends than enemies, and was well liked in and around Lyme Regis. Why then was he taken away? Justice Mapledoram, a retired magistrate often visited the Manor. The card evening proved to be the perfect opportunity to steer the conversation his way.

After drinks and small talk, Gerard found his opening to discuss the matter. Mapledoram was quick to inform Gerard that should the 'Drew fellow' have been known as felon, or villain, then with his memory second to none, he would certainly have recognised the name.Full of his own importance, Mapledoram undertook to make inquiries further afield.

Squire Elliot, surprised at his son's interest, made a mental note to see if the name Jack Drew held any significance that could do him good or ill. A foot in both camps - never any harm in that my boy! And the subject changed to a lighter note. Gerard's thoughts were slightly more self serving! His interest had been aroused.

If he could help in any way, it might just clear the slate, of what he recognised as his off hand, no, *disgraceful* treatment of the Drew girl. Once again he felt the familiar feeling that had become associated with the sound of her name; whether in his head or spoken out loud. He uttered quiet oaths. "Damn and Blast it. No one has ever got under my skin the way she has."

By the end of the week his enquiries had led him to Bridport, and he felt unable to let the matter drop. By the time Sunday came, Fanny was none the wiser regarding Jack's whereabouts, except that his arrest seemed to be established, and Bridport the most likely place to have been taken. Fanny was in a state of despair. Neither Millie nor Jamie had taken the news lightly.

Fanny decided to try and make contact with Captain Fawsey, who she knew had captained the ship that Jack had sailed on, to find out if he had been in any sort of trouble while on board ship. Following a long string of questions and answers, eventually led only to the realisation and confirmation that the Captain and crew were again at sea. Who then would speak for him?

Back in Bridport, another restless night and long awaited dawn, saw Jack cursing the fact that he had never learned to write. Barny could have written a few words, if only a scrap of paper or charcoal could be found At least he could have let Fanny know what had happened, providing they could find a way to get it out!

As he pondered on his situation, dawn lightened the cell, and Barny stirred beside him. Suddenly he was wide awake and gripping Jack by the arm recalled the memory of their brief conversation regarding the woman's voice outside the cell.

"Maybe she will come back; she's the only link with outside. How can we get to pass a message? We got to think about it." Jack stretched, stood up, and lowering his voice said, "Aye, an' preferable afore we get to stink, an' look like t'others. He gave a wry laugh, "how fortunes change. Couple o' weeks ago I was thinking I was the luckiest man alive - a comely wife, two young 'uns, an' a roof over me head. Not to mention a successful voyage behind me. Now look at me! Aye an' you're worse off again Barny me lad. You knows your sentence, what to expect like; that's if we ever get to trial."

Jack sat down again, Barny remained silent.

After what seemed an age, dry bread and a bowl of gruel, judged sufficient for five occupants, followed by a large pitcher of water, were placed inside the cell on the floor. Jack stood up again very slowly hands outstretched, anxious to avoid the violence that had greeted his last attempt to speak.

"Hold on there, give us a minute mate." The gaoler stared but said nothing, fingering a large baton that hung by his waist. Jack continued, "Can you get word out? There'll be money in it." For answer the gaoler stepped back and pulled the door shut with a bang.

"Wait, who was the woman? Will she come again the morrow maybe? His face pressed to the slit in the door, Jack sounded desperate. The rough looking gaoler was busy pushing another jug and bowl into the cell opposite.

"Aye an' most days after that," he grunted, "don't know why you don't all get big an' strong, with the goodies she brings in. Right little do-gooder she is, and thankful I am for it!"

His cackling laugh bounced off the damp stone walls, as he shuffled off down the dark passage.

Jack was left in no doubt as to who enjoyed the 'goodies,' and even less of being able to pass a verbal message through her.

Each day was the same. Jack marked the passage of time on the wall, scratched with small pieces of loose gravel picked from between the slabs on the floor.

After the first few days Barny and Jack had been forced to eat their share of the food.

"The very worst of crew rations aboard ship, were a feast compared to this," remarked Jack.

"Aye an' when I think of the smell o' me pies cooking, an' think on me girls serving 'ot meals, it fair makes me stomach 'urt." sighed Barny.

The days ran into weeks with no sign of a trial for anyone. The body of the old man had been removed, having died of starvation, neglect and gaol fever. Barny too, was taken from the cell, wrists manacled and leg irons in place. Jacks heart sank. Conversation with Barny had been a lifeline, now there was nothing!

Expecting more weeks of waiting, and convinced that everyone one had forgotten him; Jack was amazed when two days later it was his turn to be moved on. Complete with manacles and leg irons, he too was pushed out into the bright light of day.

His eyes hurt and the noise smote his ears; across the yard stood a rough open cart, a scraggy looking horse harnessed and ready, and two other prisoners already loaded, sitting on the mucky floor. As he was roughly pushed and shoved forwards, his legs, weak from both lack of food and exercise, he saw the burly form of Barny being hustled from the opposite direction.

His heart leapt. Just to see Barny's familiar face was enough to lift his spirits.

They reached the cart at about the same time, and made every effort to stay close, avoiding giving either of the guards any indication that a friendship had developed between them. That would have been enough to get them split up just for spite!

The cart loaded, the double gates of the gaol opened, and they were off up the main street. Cheers and jibes greeted them, and pieces of rotting vegetable found its mark adding to the filth, and their misery. Where were they bound?

Passing 'The Golden Lion,' Jack couldn't help thinking what he would give for a cold pint and good food. Better still, one of Fanny's good square meals. His heart ached for her. What was happening to them all at home in his absence? He looked at Barny, and the others. Pallid faces, dirty stinking bodies, and weight dropped off them all.

Reaching the outskirts of Bridport and a little way beyond, they were reined in. The guards, checking the chain through the irons on their ankles and mid shouts and threats, ordered them to climb down, quite obviously enjoying their surprise and discomfort.

Prodding them to start walking, they watched as the cart turned back having disgorged half the contents of Bridport gaol beyond the outer limits of the town. The governor's responsibilities had ended. They were now bound for Dorchester Assizes. They stared after the departing cart.

It was to prove a long and uncomfortable journey on foot.

Taking the occasional, exhausted sleep overnight, in barns owned by farmers well paid to shelter convicts on the move, they were marched under the ever watchful eyes of two armed guards, to the assize town; there to await their fate.

At the very least they had been spared 'being stabbed by the 'Bridport Dagger,' the local reference to the hangman's noose. So far anyway!

A bright start to the day found Gerard, for want of a more interesting occupation, offering to deliver business papers on his father's behalf; his was a hidden agenda.

His horse saddled early, he set off for Bridport keeping to bridle paths, and riding roughly as the crow flies. He continued his journey across chalk down and scrubby heath beneath blue skies, until he reached the old town where he located 'The Golden Lion.' Dismounting and delving into his saddle bag for the sheaf of documents, his fingers encountered a softness which he suddenly realised was the silk shawl, the gift he had never given to her. It was still tucked away. *Millie!*

Abruptly withdrawing the documents, he gave his horse into the care of the young stable lad who had stepped forward to catch the coin carelessly tossed at him. After taking refreshment, Gerard walked out into the warm but cloudy day to wander down the wide streets.

He was aware that the area surrounding the town was covered with a thick growth of hemp and flax. The soil was conducive to good cropping, for the all important sail and rope making industry which was prevalent here.

Ropes in varying stages and sizes were strung across the streets and long cottage gardens, used as spinning ways. The port town was alive with activities, men women and children hard at work making a meagre living.

Approaching the grey stone warehouses of Joseph Goendy, 'Est.1665' Gerard noted the small dirty windows, and the date. This was the firm his father did business with. Further along the building, it looked cleaner, and time had polished the old oak door.

He fingered the documents in his care, knowing that they must be delivered first and foremost. Although responsibility and hard work were almost alien to Gerard, he realised the importance of getting them into safe hands at the first opportunity.

After discharging his duty, he left the dusty offices of the old warehouse, and continued on his way to the old Bacardo lockup; or Bucky Doo – as it was called by the locals. Passing an old alehouse he couldn't resist another tankard of ale, but inside, the smoke and smell turned his stomach.

Leaving his drink unfinished, he stepped thankfully out into the harbour breeze. A few more steps, and there across the square stood the old stone lockup.

"Well now, let's see what I can find out about Mister Jack Drew" he muttered, not knowing quite why he was putting himself to the trouble. He quickly crossed the square and banged on the solid door to begin his enquiries. Smoothing his hair and standing tall, he waited.

After some moments the door was opened by a sullen looking character, accompanied by the sound of creaking locks, and who quickly adjusted his attitude on being confronted by a gentleman.

Peering disdainfully at him, Gerard requested grandly, that he wished to speak with the governor. With one hand on the heavy keys at his belt, the man nodded and bade him follow.

Securing the door behind them, he led the way to a small office across the yard, just inside the main building. Knocking on the door, he slowly pushed it open, saying in deferential tones,

"A gen'leman to see you sir," and motioned for Gerard to step past him.

"Well now, what can I do for you young sir?" The governor, short, balding and immaculate, stood as Gerard entered the small office.

"I am Gerard Elliot of the Manor House, at Uplyme." After giving his name somewhat pompously, he surprised the governor by asking outright, "I wish to ascertain sir, if a prisoner, by the name of Jack Drew is being detained here?" continuing, before interruption, "the man interests me, and I have reason to believe him to be innocent of any wrongdoing." Gerard took a deep breath; it wasn't an outright lie, but how else could he gain information?

Staring into the face of the governor, Gerard pondered again on just what had driven him to come here, and why he had made it his business. But as Millie's face flashed into his mind, he knew exactly why he was there. It took only a minute to find out that the man he was looking for was even now on his way to Dorchester Gaol. He had missed him by only twenty four hours.

With strict instructions not to try and approach the prisoner 'en route,' the governor intimated that he may be allowed to speak for him, at his trial. Gerard, thanking him for his time, turned away. After crossing the yard, he waited, as the gateman placed the key back into the lock and allowed him to step out of the gaol yard and into the street. From outside he heard the sound of the heavy key turning in the lock behind him.

The Governor stared after him, *what did Squire Elliot's son want, enquiring about Jack Drew?* Gerard was pleased with the visit; he at least had some positive information. The thought was quickly followed by vaguely wondering what he should do with it!

Making his way back up the main street, the smell of good food and the thought of an evening's relaxation, enticed him to stay over at 'The Golden Lion' and return home the following day. Pondering on his findings, Gerard came to the conclusion that whatever Jack had done, or rather whatever he had been arrested for was almost certainly more than a 'petty' crime.

Trial at the assizes was a serious business, as would be the penalty if found guilty... *but guilty of what?*

CHAPTER TWENTY THREE

August was dry and clear, contrasting strongly with the heat and thunderstorms that had seen out the end of July. Clara, with two other young ladies strolled in the gardens, between herbaceous borders lining the long straight paths behind The Manor House.

The grounds were set out either side of central steps that led down to the ornamental fountains, where it seemed cooler in the hot August sunshine. Here, the paths veered off to right and left around and beyond the fountains, leading directly to the tumbling pergolas covered in a profusion of sweet scented rambling roses. Deepest apricot, where buds were tightly closed, and as flowers opened and turned lighter, they presented small full blown roses of palest peach; beneath, fallen petals carpeted the ground.

As the young ladies made their way to the bower seats, folding their parasols and settling themselves either side of Clara, the conversation turned, for the second time to Clara's gown, much admired by her companions. She continued expounding the talents of her new dressmaker.

"I used to send to Axminster for samples of materials and dress patterns, but having them made up exactly to my liking proved irksome, and involved several trips and lengthy discourse.

The completed garments never quite fitted as I would wish; even after the second fitting one still needed to have alterations made. The journey too, was tedious and time consuming. I'm so relieved to find exactly what I need nearer to home. It really does save so much time. Now, when father invites business colleagues to stay, or announces another dinner party, I have a wonderful excuse for a new gown, knowing it will be ready in plenty of time." The ladies appeared to be quite envious and a little impatient to know her secret, much to Clara's barely veiled delight.

"Do tell us where you find such lovely materials, and who makes them up for you around here?" For a moment Clara wanted to keep Millie's talents to herself, but being the centre of attention got the better of her. She continued, nodding first to one and then the other,

"She's a funny little thing, but she really seems to have a flare for her work. She interprets my descriptions of style and colour, *exactly* as I would wish."

Excitedly begging her name and where to find her, was exactly the reaction Clara had anticipated from the ladies. Having given so much information already, she was pressed to give the name of the establishment where such a 'genius' could be found.

"The little shop in Lyme Regis; you must know it. It is on Broad Street, and used to be just a Haberdashery and Drapers, with only simple gowns offered. Readymade of course, and a few plain dresses made to order; but that's all changed."

She leaned in to them and continued in a conspiratorial tone.

"There is a young girl working there now; I have placed one or two orders, and called into the shop myself, on occasions. She has also been here once or twice, by appointment of course! I find her most helpful.

The Misses Hartnells own the business, and the girl's name is Millicent Drew".

Unknown to Millie, her reputation for fine gowns and bonnet's was spreading fast. Clara smiled to herself.

After exhausting that particular topic, conversation continued; and centred now on theatre visits in London, invitations to balls in the bigger houses, and introductions to eligible young men, which in all amounted to very few.

The appearance of Lily, announcing that afternoon tea was served in the sitting room, brought a temporary lull to conversation.

The ladies moved slowly back past the fountains, and up the steps, amid much swishing of skirts and light hearted banter. Reaching the garden room door, they made their way to the sitting room, where half closed blinds ensured that the room stayed cool. A platter of cucumber sandwiches cut into small triangles were set on a side table, and an assortment of small delicately decorated cakes adorned three tiers of an ornate cake stand.

Lily hovered in attendance, pouring tea into fine bone-china teacups. All was accompanied by happy chatter, until afternoon tea came to an end and the ladies awaited their respective carriages.

Later when the house was quiet, Clara, who had been trying to put her mind to the embroidery that now lay crumpled in her lap, glanced up as the door opened, and was pleasantly surprised to see Gerard enter the room smiling. She knew that smile, and waited expectantly as he came to share the window seat with her.

"I need your help Clara. I know you never let me down, so how do you fancy a visit to the dressmaker's in Lyme?" He placed a folded note on her lap.

"Why, you must have heard us talking on that very subject Gerard. Father would be exasperated to say the least if he knew of your plans involving the Drew girl, especially if he knew just how far they have already gone. But yes, I shall certainly accompany you into the town."

"Well, I shall leave it with you sis, and await the right time to act." Gerard stood up to go, lazily winking at her as he did so. It was enough for Clara to bask in his approval and wait results, thriving on the escapades and attention of her brother.

She had at first asked questions about the liaison, which she viewed as 'helped along' by her involvement. But of late Gerard had said little of the Drew girl, and Clara had stopped questioning him, believing that she would soon be delivering notes to some other fortunate young woman.

She had to admit Millie's station in life did lend some feeling of romance and illicit love, to the whole affair, and as such enhanced the excitement! Secretly she was pleased to think that she could again play a part in the intrigue, which she feared had run its course.

Millie received the story of her Pa's disappearance with horror.

"How can Pa just disappear, Ma? Everyone knows 'im. What will we do now, who else can we ask? we 'ave to find 'im."

"I've already bin to Rosie's Tavern, the Guildhall and even The Vaults; oh an' up to see Danny; 'e told me about the coachman pointing the finger, and said 'e would tackle 'im' the next time 'e saw him. Other than that I don't know what else I can do." She sighed, and seeing how tired her Ma looked Millie went quiet.

Jamie stared at them both, stunned into silence. It could all be his fault. Pa said no good would come of meddling. It wasn't fair! Now he was afraid the Gulliver brothers would come after him again. Was it them that took his Pa? He was keeping his mouth shut, afraid of making matters worse.

"For now," Fanny soothed, "we must all go on as usual. Yer Pa will be alright I'm sure; 'e'll find a way to let us know what 'appened, soon as 'e can; for now we 'ave to go about our business 'til we think what to do next. Cheer up Millie, it won't do no good getting upset, especially in your condition. " Jamie looked at his Ma, and then at Millie, maybe it was her fault his Pa had gone? They had been whispering a lot lately an' changing tack when he came into the room. At the end of a week, Danny walked down to the harbour to seek out Fanny.

"I don't know for sure, but I'm betting that the coach fellow knows more 'un 'e's letting on. After I asked about Jack 'e clammed up an' looked right shifty; mumbling something about a hold-up, a coach robbery like. It don't get us no nearer I know, but I'll keep asking questions. If anything turns up, you'll know quick as I do. I can't hang round now, got to get back; but we'll talk of it again."

As he waved a cheerful farewell, Fanny thanked him, and resigned herself to getting on with life as best she could. Once again they would have to start watching point's money-wise. It wouldn't stretch for ever, and there was no telling how long he would be away.

All that was left for now was to play the waiting game until something turned up. It was something they all knew well, but this seemed different. Fanny felt sick at heart.

August merged into a clear warm September, when on a usual Sunday visit, Millie eagerly rushed into the cottage calling, "Ma, - Ma where are you? I 'eard from 'im - I mean...

"Hush Millie, I'm right 'ere," called Fanny, clattering dishes in the scullery, "you fair made me 'eart turn over, whatever is it?" Fanny turned quickly, wiping her rough hands on her apron, "you 'eard from yer Pa? Millie waved a piece of paper in front of her.

"No, no, not Pa, it's just that I seen someone an' they give me this. But it's news, news of Pa, where 'e is an' that. I can't believe it! Ma 'e's made it 'is business to find out, to track Pa down an' - oh I feel so sick." Millie sat down heavily on a stool.

"For goodness sake girl - get a hold of yerself, you'll do yerself a mischief rushing round like that, getting all fired up, an' you near on six months gone." Fanny caught her by the arm and looked into her flushed face, "what on earth's 'appened? What are you talking about?" Millie took a deep breath.

"Ma, you never pushed me into saying who me babby's father is, but now for Pa's sake, I 'ave to tell you." It was Fanny's turn to gasp.

"Millie, that's good - but why now? What's 'appened?" Fanny noticed that the colour in Millie's face was fast draining away, "don't take on luv, we already knows – or think we knows anyway. Is it the Squire's? ..." she left the sentence unfinished.

Millie almost screeched, the Squire's? 'is SON Ma, Master Gerard! What you saying Ma – *the Squire's?*"

"Oh Millie luv I didn't mean," for a moment the mood lifted while the picture of the large and formidable

Squire Elliott sprang to mind, making them smile. "I *meant* the squire's son. Well we thought as much. He should be made to *pay* you know Millie." There was a pause. Whether with violence *to* him, or money *from* him Millie wasn't quite sure, but she carried on.

"I told 'im I didn't want anything more to do with him, and I meant it. 'e don't know about... Millie patted her belly. Anyway listen to this. His sister Miss Clara, came into the shop. You remember I said about the young lady from the Manor House? Well she came in and passed me this piece of paper, on the quiet like. She made sure she asked for me, she always does when she wants a new dress or anything,"

Millie allowed herself just for a moment to glow with pride; she couldn't resist mentioning other orders, stemming from successful dress fittings. She paused for a moment, correcting herself, "gowns – I should say." Fanny gave her a slight shake.

"Millie get on with it girl, what's it got to do with your Pa?" Fanny was totally puzzled.

"Well like I said, Miss Clara," Millie paused again,

"Yes yes, what about 'er" interrupted Fanny again,

"She gave me this note. It's from 'im." She thrust a folded piece of paper at Fanny, who immediately thrust it back at her.

"Well read it to me girl, read it" Millie took another deep breath and read hesitantly,

Your father - was - held -at- Bridport - goal - then – tran-trans-ferred

to Dor - chester Ass-i-zes. I shall make it my – business to a- a-qu-ire fur-ther

in-form-ation in due course.

G. E.

"That's Gerard Elliott, and it means Pa was taken to Dorchester. Ma he's trying to 'elp us and now I can't refuse his 'elp, but I don't know what to do next." Fanny took a few moments to assimilate this latest revelation, and Jack in Dorchester gaol?

"Oh my Lord we'll 'ave to be patient and stay put, or rather just go on with work. Don't tell anyone anything yet, we must just wait and see what 'appens."

It was all very well telling Millie to be patient, but after a while, having no news from any quarter, it was Fanny who was getting restless. Returning to the subject, she ended by saying,

"No, there's not a lot *you* can do maid, but *I'm* going to make me way to Dorchester!" Fanny told no one outside the family of her plans. Jamie had been left in charge at home, with instructions to go over to Millie if he needed anything, and Lazurus was always close by.

It would have meant saying why she would be away, and *that* would mean answering awkward questions on how she knew where to go, and why!

As she made ready to leave, she remembered the brooch rescued from Jacks kit bag. This she pinned on the underside of her petticoat. A new town! It would be safe to exchange it for coins; anything she could get for it would help.

Several uncomfortable days later, Fanny sat on the steps of Dorchester Jail.

She had saved money by walking, and sleeping rough. The only food she carried was dry bread and cheese, tucked into a towel and stuffed into the small sack slung over her shoulder, along with a change of skirt and a clean blouse in case of any court appearance. If she looked like a down and out, a threat to the parish - she would be in danger of detainment herself.

Sheltering one night of her journey at an isolated cottage, she was taken in by a kindly family who showed sympathy on listening to her story. Another was spent sharing an open barn with chicken, and anything else that moved in the hay. Walking roughly nine miles a day starting at sun up, and wishing she had the strength and stamina of her youth, it had taken the best part of three days to cover the twenty six miles from Lyme.

Arriving at the bustling town of Dorchester in the late afternoon, it appeared to Fanny both big and noisy. When asking directions to the gaol, she had been amazed, when the local innkeeper had laughingly referred to it as St Peter's Palace! Adding, "Anyone unlucky enough to be sent there, man or woman, will like as not, end up in hard labour or worse." This did nothing to lighten Fanny's mood of foreboding.

After cleaning up at the public baths, as best she could, Fanny searched out the local pawn brokers, pawning the brooch for far less than it was worth. Pleased only to be rid of it, she had begun to think that it was jinxed. The money raised, would have to stretch to a couple of nights at the cheapest rooming house, while she gathered all the information she could.

Arriving at the steps of the gaol, Fanny paused. She must first pluck up courage to approach the gate-man. Resting for a moment on the steps to gather her wits, and with a show of confidence she didn't feel, she rapped loudly on the outer doors, much as Gerard had done at Bridport several weeks previously.

After a few minutes, a sliding observation panel was drawn back, to reveal an angry pair of eyes staring at her.

"What you want?"

Fanny screwed up her courage, "I want to see me 'usband Jack Drew." She waited. "I know 'e's bin brought 'ere. When's visiting?"

"When I sez so! Short visits for copper, longer visits for silver, take yer pick. If yer can't pay in money use yer imagination, come back the morrow." The gateman guffawed loudly. The panel slammed shut.

Fanny, who was tired out and hungry, turned to go, all confidence leaving her. She cast a last look over her shoulder, and realising that this was the closest she had been to Jack in many weeks, took what comfort she could from the thought, and set about finding cheap lodgings; "the morrow Jack - I'll see you on the morrow, God willing."

Her first acquaintance with the rooming house owners brought her attention to a large fat woman, who stepped purposefully in front of her. Straw like hair under a dirty mob cap, her clothes better described as rags; smiling broadly she introduced herself as the widow Lewis. Fanny's first thought as she asked about beds, were to 'let the smile make up for the smell'...

"I've not much space to spare dearie," the widow declared, "less you want to double up in a bed!" Realising she was almost certainly filling her dirty beds, with as many bodies as she could get away with, Fanny thanked her and declined.

Around the next corner she noticed the name of the ally; Gallows Lane. She shivered involuntarily. Walking along the row of small rundown dwellings, keeping well out of the muddy effluent in the gutter, she saw a small skinny woman shaking a rag rug from her doorway.

The dust and straw filled the air with choking particles, but slung between the two upper windows hung a freshly washed sheet. Fanny took heart from this and paused,

"Do you have any beds for rent?"

"You've struck lucky, one in me downstairs front 'as come empty. There's only three others in there, two women what share, an' a young lad on the floor. You can 'ave it cheap." Cheap was just what Fanny needed, and quickly accepted as the evening was on her, and the nights beginning to draw in. It was nearing seven o' clock and she wanted to be settled before another hour passed.

"I'll take it" she sighed with some relief, heaving herself and her bundle up the three steps, into the proffered room. The two women in the doorway looked more like ladies of the night, dressed as they were in colourful low cut gowns, with highly rouged cheeks. They nodded as she stepped past.

Fanny was way past caring who her room mates were, and slung her bundle onto the rough bed that had been pointed out to her. The landlady followed her in, clearly glad of another couple of coins.

"I'm Nancy and my man's Noah, we run a clean safe 'ouse. Any 'int of trouble from anyone, an' my Noah sees 'em off sharpish." Fanny smiled a tired smile. Nancy continued, "I expect you could do wi' a drop of ale, aye and some food inside yer by the looks of you. Go along to 'Silver Tavern.' you'll find yer money goes further if you say we sent yer."

Nancy seemed to have taken charge. "Then come back and get yer 'ead down. Yer bed'll be waiting for yer. Looks like you could drop in now, but get that food in yer belly; you'll sleep all the sounder for it."

Fanny decided to accept her advice and thanking her for her kindness set off. 'The Silver Tavern' she found easily enough in the main street, and mentioned the rooming landlady and her man by name, surprised and pleased that it seemed to make a difference. She hungrily devoured a faggot and some pea's pudding – the best meal she'd had in days.

Quenching her thirst with cool ale, she returned to her bed and seeing nobody around, was asleep as soon as her head hit the pillow, her few possessions clasped for safe keeping in bed beside her.

CHAPTER TWENTY FOUR

Gerard felt the need to talk over his findings once again with Justice Mapledoram, and to ask further questions and advice. He sought him out, and over whisky and good cigars they discussed it at length.

Mapledoram nodded his head from time to time as he listened, endorsing Gerard's thoughts on the severity of trial at Dorchester. After a few moments silence, he stood up, hands in pockets and imparted the following information.

It seemed the length of time spent awaiting trial was indeterminable. But should the prisoner be found guilty and sentenced to hang, the execution of that sentence must be carried out within two days - unless the second day fell on a Sunday - in which case they would gain a day. Time was an important factor and Mapledoram's advice was, "Endeavour to gather more information, get the right questions asked in the right places. Most importantly, attempt to get the trial delayed, at all costs."

This struck Gerard as sound advice. If *only* he could find out what Jack was accused of. He applied his mind to determining the approximate time when Jack's so called 'crime' was committed. A visit to the Lyme Guildhall was indicated. Using his standing in the community, allowed him access to records of all warrants issued that year. He wished he had begun here in the first place, before following Jack's trail to Bridport.

Here it was, written in ink. 'Robbery on the King's Highway with use of firearm.'

He read a bit further, looking for a date. Here it was, *February*, I wonder, could it be the same? He sifted through his memory to the last time he and his father went up to London town. The dates fitted, and his purse was the lighter for it. The accused was Jack Drew!

Gerard was astounded. He had Millie's family down as an honest one, give or take the odd smuggling foray. The information made him more determined than ever to pursue the case.

He racked his brains; who else of his further acquaintances might be in a position to help? Suddenly it came to him. At the next opportunity Gerard rode to The Coaching Inn, hoping to meet up and talk things through with his gentleman friends. One especially sprang to mind. He had studied law; though not as yet practised it.

Leaving his horse to be taken care of, and entering the familiar establishment, he was pleasantly surprised to see just the chap he had in mind, deep in conversation with several other friends and drinking companions.

After the back slapping and ribald remarks, Gerard downed the tot of whisky placed in front of him, and engaging in genial banter, shepherded two of the group to a quieter corner.

Placing their glasses on a low table in the snug, they sat down, making themselves comfortable on the high backed settle, with cushions at their backs. Gerard steered the conversation around to the reason for this particular visit, directing his words now to Malcolm Ashworth, who liked nothing better than to expound and share his knowledge. Sitting back in comfort,

Ashworth looked every inch a man of the law, with - eventually - a fine career ahead of him.

"I have an acquaintance who seems to be on the wrong side of the law, Ashworth my friend. Though it seems to be a case of mistaken identity, and riding on the word of one man, I might add. What can you suggest one might do to 'help,' as it were?"

"One should never rely on opinions and conjecture, but always firmly on facts and evidence." Gerard waited for him to savour another mouthful of the golden, malt liquor, and set down his whisky glass, before proceeding to ask a whole series of questions, regarding his enquiries. This opened up a whole new topic of conversation, both general and then more specific, as he warmed to his theme.

On concluding the discussion, his knowledgeable companion reiterated, "Evidence my friend, irrefutable evidence. This is what it all boils down to. Get your hands on evidence to support his case, and he could walk away a free man."

Ashworth hooked his thumbs in his waistcoat and waited for the impact of his words to sink in. He couldn't resist adding, "Though why you should concern yourself with the lower class I simply cannot imagine."

Looking at his pocket watch, he stood up to leave. He couldn't help sounding grand, and full of his own importance. Nevertheless Gerard was glad of any help he could get, and thanked him warmly. Standing up, the small group continued in conversation, walking around to the yard to collect their horses.

Danny, seeing the young men coming brought the horses from the drinking trough and stood patiently holding the reins. Overhearing Jack's name, his attention focused suddenly on their conversation. As far as he could tell, from the snatches he overheard, it seemed that earlier in the year, a stage coach had been held up at gun point, and a villain had seriously injured one of the travellers.

He wondered if it could be the same hold up the coachman had referred to, thinking to recognise Jack. He forgot himself, so far as to interrupt their conversation.

"Sir" he began, "I think I may be able to help. I couldn't help overhearing the name of Jack Drew, but I can say without doubt that he was away at sea. A five month voyage it was, but he sailed the last day of November and didn't return to Bridport till near middle of May."

The group had gone quiet as Danny began to speak; now they all spoke at once.

"Who asked you to intervene?" one young man sneered.

"Who indeed, and how would you know anything?" said the other. Gerard was more than interested in what Danny had to say. Quickly interrupting his ill mannered friends, he enquired if by any chance Danny should know the name of the ship that Jack Drew sailed on.

"Aye I do indeed sir; it was The Admiral Grey, out of Bridport. Her Captain was Nathan Fawsey, bound for Italy I think."

Gerard thanked him saying, "I have an interest. I and my father the Squire may have been on that very coach. We were also robbed about the same time in February." Then dismissing Danny with a nod, turned to the others, but Danny feigning concern over a fetlock, was able to listen further, as Gerard carried on talking with his drinking companions.

"If Drew is innocent, as I have now heard, and I can do anything to *prove* that innocence, it means the real culprit may yet be tracked down and apprehended. I intend speaking to Justice Mapledoram again, and I shall also ride over to Bridport. With luck I may meet up with Captain Fawsey, thus making him aware of the situation and establishing without doubt, Drew's whereabouts at the time in question. If Drew sailed on The Admiral Grey, there should be no trouble securing documents to that effect, and Captain Fawsey as a witness.

"Aye, if he's not gone to sea again," mumbled Danny to himself. If it hadn't been in Danny's own interest to help Jack, Gerard Elliott would not even have got the time of day from him. But Millie's Pa was more important than the suspicions he held of this man.

The three mounted their horses and left. Danny looked after them, detesting their bad manners and behaviour. But if Jack was to get justice, the likes of them and their fine words, carried more weight than anything he could say. *Any port in a storm!*

Gerard was deep in thought regarding Jack Drew's alibi, and a good strong one it was too. He knew Captain Fawsey would be able to prove beyond a shadow of doubt, if the man really was away at sea at the crucial time. He just hoped the captain was on dry land now; all he had to do was track him down.

As Gerard had listened to Danny's account, he vowed to tell his father at the very first opportunity, of the injustice which if carried to conclusion, would allow the real villains to go free and condemn an innocent man to be deported, or hung. Millie's father!

Squire Elliott, on hearing of Danny's story agreed that Gerard must ride again to the shipping offices at

Bridport, this was becoming personal. The Admiral Grey was one of his part owned vessels, and should be sailing into Bridport harbour at any time.

Again Gerard set off; this time with some positive questions, which required positive answers; Answers that would stand up in court. The Squire then set in motion a series of events;

The first of which, was to send a letter to Dorchester Law Court. Mapledoram although retired, had advised on the content and text, bidding him rest assured that any proceedings would be halted on receipt of the said letter - providing the trial hadn't already taken place! The letter was sent poste-haste, by his best rider on the fastest horse from his own stables.

After the conversation with Gerard, Danny awaited his chance to seek out Fanny with this latest information. Failing to find her, he made a decision to go over to Broad Street and find Millie. He was well aware of Jack's last words, and that he had agreed not to try to see her, but this was different, this was important.

He walked over the shingle, the salty breeze stinging his cheeks, weighing up the sequence of events as they had fallen into place. Not least his feelings regarding Millie, since he had been confronted with the uncomfortable truth of her condition. He decided to ignore this, difficult as it would be, and concentrate on his mission.

With this in mind he bravely pushed open the shop door and was greeted by Miss Sybil, who recognised him immediately.

"Well if it isn't young Danny." she smiled, "You will want to speak to Millie; shall I call her for you?"

"That's very kind of you ma'm, an' I'm sorry to bother you I'm sure." Danny glanced over his shoulder as Miss Sybil swished past him heading for the workroom.

"Millie dear, a young man is here to see you." As Millie looked up her heart sank, *which young man?*

She slowly rose, making her way into the shop. It was with some relief she saw Danny, but when her eyes met his, a deep shame enveloped her.

"Danny?" she tried to smile.

"I'm sorry Millie, I 'ad to come." He glanced at Miss Sybil. Millie noticed his hesitance and said, "It's alright Danny, you can talk here. It is alright Miss Sybil isn't it?"

"Of course dear, you stay in here; I shall go into the kitchen and put the kettle on," *that poor girl, I never did see any one, who unknowingly courts trouble the way she does.*

Miss Sybil had a feeling that any news for Millie at the moment may not be good! She left them to it.

Danny had not been able to help looking at Millie's no longer slim waist, but quickly averted his eyes as she spoke.

"What is it Danny?" said Millie softly.

"It's about your Pa's disappearance. I got some news so I wanted to tell you soon as I could. It seems that he's been taken on from Bridport to Dorchester goal," Millie interrupted him.

"Yes I know me Ma's gone there..." Millie couldn't at this time say how she knew, but wondered how Danny had found out. Danny was surprised, but continued anyway.

"I've bin talking; he paused and decided not to name the source, "talking to some chaps who told me about a stage coach robbery way back. Someone got shot, an' it's likely the Squire was among them as were robbed. It seems that's what Jack's been accused of taking part in.

That's why 'es bin taken on to Dorchester. It's serious Millie."

He reached for her hand, as he saw tears welling up in her lovely eyes. Guiding her to the customer's chair, he sat her down before continuing. "I was able to tell these 'people' that Jack was at sea at that partic'lar time. Aye an' I gave 'em the name of the ship an' where she sailed from. They're going to follow it up, soon as the ship comes into Bridport, which is any day now by all accounts. It *can* be proved. It's all been a dreadful mistake. Even a retired magistrate's been involved in 'is case. We'll see Jack home safe and sound yet."

Millie was overcome with relief and gratitude. She was in no doubt *who* it was that was looking for answers. She didn't care. Dear Danny, it seemed he was always there when she needed him. If Gerard were serious about helping, then the squire, if he was robbed at the same time, would be involved too. The magistrate would be working in the squire's interest no doubt, but anything that helped her Pa's case was welcome.

"Thank you – oh thank you Danny. It means so much to me after all that's, well you know, 'appened; Thanks for your'elp, and coming 'ere an' that." Danny managed a smile.

"Wish I could bring you some better news, but at least things are coming clearer now. I'm sure I'll see the 'person' again. Soon as I know more I'll be back." They both knew to whom he was referring, but neither could say his name.

Danny left as Miss Sybil came back into the shop. Millie had already made them aware of events from when her Pa had first been taken. As usual they had been both reassuring and supportive. She relayed some of

Danny's information to them, and decided there was nothing to be done just yet. Agreeing that should it become necessary Millie must take the time off to either go to Dorchester, or do whatever she felt needed doing.

Knowing she must forfeit wages, she reluctantly agreed to wait until Danny had further news, then to make her way somehow to the prison. Quite how she would get there, she hadn't yet worked out. She tried to concentrate on her work, but idly turning events over in her mind, remembered the 'rainy day' money Clive had given her. She still had half a sovereign that she was saving for the babby. It would cover the stagecoach fare, and be much quicker than the cart.

Millie realised with a prick to her conscience, that she had not given her blood father, a thought since their meeting, but as he had said when she accepted the money, 'you never know when it will come in useful.'

Later that evening, Millie was still working up in her room, while downstairs Miss Sybil and Miss Mabel were talking things over. Agreeing there was never a dull moment with Millie around, and just how much they would miss her when it came her time to leave them for good.

Consideration of her father's plight went without saying. It was agreed, that should she really try to get to Dorchester, which seemed highly likely knowing Millie, they would ask her to bring news, on her return, whichever way things went.

Failing to settle at all in the next two days, on the third morning Millie decided, for her peace of mind to leave for Dorchester. Asking her employers permission, and assuring them her plans were sensible, she put together a few essentials in her old hessian bag, and set out with mixed feelings, to board the stagecoach for the long journey.

Lost in thought, the miles slipped by as the stage coach rumbled along the toll road on its way to Dorchester, nearer and nearer to her Ma and Pa. Finally, she was set down in the square of the busy and unfamiliar town.

Feeling at a loss as to what she should do next, Millie decided to go first to the goal. Following directions was the easy bit, but when confronted by the large grey stone building, her nerve almost left her. Ma must be here in the town somewhere, probably close by the goal, or at least somewhere in this area, she reasoned.

Millie approached and apprehensively climbed the old steps. Sinking down on the top step of the formidable front entrance, she shuffled back until she was propped against the old wooden doors, hoping no one would open them from within.

Millie rested there for half an hour or more, feeling unwell after the long coach journey. Finally pangs of hunger and a great thirst pushed her into accepting that she must part with more of her precious coins, in order to give herself fresh strength. She would be no good to anyone in her present state. Slowly standing up, she glanced up the street, and saw a rough looking inn. 'The Silver Tavern,' she read. I'll make me way there to eat an' get me strength back, while I think what to do next.

Walking slowly, she reached the open door, her nerve almost deserting her. There were many rough looking characters swilling ale, and as many old woman tippling cheap gin. 'Mothers ruin,' her granny had called it. Looking across the smoke filled room Millie took her courage in both hands, and made for the young barmaid.

Waiting, with her eyes fixed on the notice board above the bar stating; hot pies, faggots and Pease pudding were all served there, her turn came and she ordered a pie and ale.

The young barmaid looked friendly, and Millie decided to ask some questions, after placing her order.

"Have you seen a stranger, round 'ere in the last day or two? I'm looking for me Ma, I 'ave to find 'er. I think we look a bit alike, only she 'as dark hair done up at the back," she finished lamely.

Millie didn't hold out any hope and was amazed when the barmaid called to the older woman.

"Cissy, this young maid's looking for 'er Ma. Wasn't there a woman in 'ere yesterday, said she was new in these parts? She was asking about the old gaol, we 'adn't seen 'er afore."

"Aye that's right, yesterday it was, said she was going there today. I gave 'er directions, not as 'ow you could really miss it. Rather 'er than me." She shrugged her shoulders and continued serving ale. Turning to Millie the younger woman said, "We talked for a while, she said she's staying at Nancy's, number twenty two Gallows cottages, just off the square. If you can't find 'er there, she'll be at the gaol already I shouldn't wonder." And with a practised eye noting Millie's condition, "you take care o'yerself maid, an' I 'ope you find 'er." With many thanks, Millie found a place by the window to sit and eat her meal, relishing every last mouthful, and draining her glass. Then with renewed energy she stood up and set off to find Nancy, whoever she might be.

She didn't have far to go, before a very familiar figure came into sight. Millie let out a yell, and forgetting herself, hitched up her skirt and covered the remaining yards between them before she cannoned into Fanny. So relieved was she to find her Ma so easily, that she could barely let go of her, and it was a minute before the amazed Fanny could really believe her eyes, and the evidence in her own arms. As they hugged each other, immediately the whole sorry situation began to feel more manageable.

"My stars Millie, you'll never cease to amaze me; my I'm that glad to see you."

"Thank goodness, oh thank goodness I've found you Ma." Clinging on to Fanny's arm, mother and daughter walked together to the square. There they sat under a tree in the shade, and Millie proceeded to tell all the latest news that Danny had brought her.

How a stage coach had been robbed. Who had pointed the finger at her Pa, and eventually- and most importantly, who was now involved in getting at the truth.

"So here I am Ma, and help *is* on the way." Fanny was incredulous

"Well, to think the likes of them, 'ud 'elp us. I can't believe it. Even if there's more to it, I still can't believe they'd go out of their way like that." They sat under the tree in the shade and talked for a while. It hadn't passed Fanny that there would be something in it for them, but for whatever reason, it was none the less welcome help.

Screwing up their courage, they stood up, and began their walk to the gaol. Fanny explained on the way that Millie would not be allowed in, as only one visitor a day was allowed.

Deeply worried as to the eventual outcome, tiredness, combined with relief at seeing Millie, brought tears to her eyes. Quickly brushing them aside, the ever practical

Fanny knew that the very act of visiting Jack, would give him a boost. The fact that she could tell him that Millie too had come bringing good news, would cheer him and lift his spirits further. At least Jack would have some hope to hang on to! They all would now. Fancy Millie making the journey too! Fanny disappeared behind the heavy doors, leaving Millie to her thoughts. Maybe, just maybe, things would begin to look up now.

CHAPTER TWENTY FIVE

Jack had lost all sense of time since his transfer to Dorchester gaol. The days slipped by each merging into the next, when word came that he was to be tried the day after the morrow.

He received the news with dread. If he had thought Bridport grim, then this was hell on earth. His own clothes had been torn from him and burned, along with those of other prisoners, but *still* he was clothed in rags. How had he come to this?

The rotting straw barely covered the damp floor where they slept in grossly overcrowded insanitary conditions. Fresh air and cleanliness were unheard of, and listening to other prisoner's tales he was lucky, not to be housed in subterranean dungeons, where water ran down the walls and covered the floor.

Gaol fever, a sort of deadly infection was all around. Each face he looked on, was either sallow or skeletal, or flushed with the fever. How could he survive?

He had almost prayed for trial to escape, one way or the other. Now he was devastated. Word had it, that since Barney's abrupt assisted exit from the cell, he had been tried and executed, and with him, the hope that had kept Jack going was dying too, filling him with despair.

He slumped against the damp wall. Suddenly the door opened and his name was called. Jack looked up, blinked and blinked again.

"Two minutes, or it'll be more silver," grunted the turnkey, glancing furtively over his shoulder. He was aware the taskmaster would pocket any perks, should he witness the transaction. Fanny was pushed into the large stinking cell where Jack was being held, along with many other unfortunates.

Staring into the half light for a familiar face, what she actually saw shocked her to the core. Her Jack, shrunken, filthy and dejected, huddled against the wall of the cell, a totally changed man. She stepped over and around, the clamouring inmates, making her way toward him. He looked up and held her gaze for a split second, not daring to believe his own eyes, as Fanny could hardly believe hers!

"Fanny?" he breathed.

"Oh my Lord, Jack! Oh my Good Lord, what have they done to you?" Fanny was at his side. They clung together, though Fanny could have retched at the stench. "Jack, listen to me, we're going to get you out." Jack started to interrupt her, mumbling and shaking his head. "No, listen," continued Fanny, grasping his hands. "Gerard and Squire Elliott, aye an' Mapledoram the retired justice, they all know about what's 'appened. Danny put 'em on to it. Aye an' our Millie, she's 'ere an' all, told me everything she did.

A stage coach was robbed. The one that pointed the finger was *wrong*. It can be *proved*. There're waiting on The Admiral Grey sailing into Bridport. Captain Fawsey is to be brought 'ere... The court should 'ave a letter by now, saying to wait trial." She stared into his face, willing him to understand. Jack did interrupt this time.

"But, its day after the morrow. I'll be 'anged for sure. Follow Barney to the gallows I will. It's all too late Fanny."

"Jack, *please* don't give up hope."

Before she could say more, Fanny was caught by the arm and wrenched away from him, propelled to the door, and almost slung out. "Jack," she tearfully yelled over her shoulder, "we *will* get you out."

"Yeh, they all say that, I 'eard it all afore," sneered the turnkey. Fanny again found herself out on the street. Millie stood up quickly, feeling slightly dizzy with the effort, looking at her Ma's tearstained face and noting the stench of the gaol about her.

"What's 'appened Ma, 'ow was 'e, 'ow did Pa look? What did 'e say? Did you tell 'im I was 'ere?"

"Yes, yes of course I told 'im; 'e was that surprised. In a bad way 'e was Millie. Glad to see me, and even more to know you was 'ere too. But trial's set for day after the morrow. Looks just awful 'e does, my poor Jack." Fanny was visibly shaken. "They just *got* to get 'ere in time. I must find someone. Ask about the letter. See what's going on. Yes I'll find someone who *knows*, first thing the morrow. We'll start out early an' I'll try to get to see the governor."

Millie was lost for words. Trying hard to suppress her own tears, they walked back to Fanny's lodgings where, seeing their distress, and listening to the latest turn of events, Nancy took pity on them. Aware of Millie's condition, she agreed they share the bed.

They whispered long into the night, before falling into an exhausted sleep; oblivious of the other occupant and the returning ladies of the night. The next day they slept heavy, and longer than intended, though it was just past seven. After rising and paying Nancy, they found a bakers shop where they purchased day old bread to break their fast, stopping at the town pump to wash it down, as best they could.

Making their way to a market stall they picked over, and then bought a fairly presentable shirt and a pair of ducks, for Jack's court appearance, and began making their way back to the goal. Fanny was determined to find someone in authority to get information from.

This proved easier said than done, but after being sent from pillar to post, they eventually arrived at the courthouse. There, it was confirmed that Jack was to be tried for attempted murder and robbery, the very next day. *So he had been right.*

Fanny did her best to plead his case, using Justice Mapledoram's name, and demanding the letter be found, but it was by no means certain that it had yet been received. The trial would indeed take place, and all they could do was pray and wait.

Another short visit endeavouring to lift Jack' spirits, by delivering the clothes personally into his hands, incurred an additional cost! But it was worth it just to see hope flicker in his eyes. The rest of the day was spent walking and talking, as the morrow drew closer and closer.

As it neared six 'o clock, they ate wedges of bread and cheese at 'The Silver Tavern' and used up part of a long evening, trying to answer questions fired at them by the young barmaid.

Another night in the cheap rooming house had been assured and paid for. Sharing watered ale and another heart to heart with the cheery landlady, amid much sadness and sympathy they retired to their shared bed, falling into a fitful sleep with the help of a bedtime tot of Nancy's Geneva spirit!

Back in Bridport, Gerard strode down to the quay. He called out, tossing a piece of silver to an ever ready oarsman. Pointing out The Admiral Grey where she lay-to, just outside the harbour he instructed, "Alongside her, quick as you like man," and settled himself for the short, choppy boat ride.

Turning things over in his mind he began to realise just what a challenge it was, finding out the truth of this business, which was as much for himself as it was for Millie. Once again he mentally congratulated his father on having friends in high places. Eventually coming along side, he yelled for permission to board.

"I am Gerard Elliot Esq., with urgent information for the Captain." Moments later, with permission granted, Gerard bade the oarsman wait, as he climbed aboard and was conducted to the Captain on the foredeck.

Quickly explaining his business, and after further conversation, he realised that the Captain had a great respect for Jack Drew, remembering that he had sailed with him on several previous occasions.

Nathan Fawsey strode to his cabin bidding Gerard follow. Unlocking the ships log book and muster roll, and consulting it in detail he verified immediately that he would be able to vouch for able seaman Jack Drew, and his whereabouts at that time.

"No question, I shall come with you right away. I've time to spare, and I leave The Admiral Grey in safe hands."

Placing his ship under the authority of the new first mate and the bo'sun, he issued instructions to be carried out in his absence. Leading the way, complete with documented evidence, he hailed two other crew members who had worked closely on the same watch as Jack, issuing an order that they accompany them.

Gerard had taken the liberty of hiring a horse for the Captain, and two other nags were quickly found. But the inability of the other men to master anything other than a donkey, meant they were left to take the wagon, and follow on behind. A rider was sent to Uplyme with a message for Squire Elliot, bidding him make all haste to the Assize Court at Dorchester.

The group set off to ride the fifteen miles or so that would bring them to Dorchester, in the hope they would be in time to stop the trial.

At The Manor House, Squire Elliott and Justice Mapledoram had been discussing their next step, and received the messenger with anticipation. Both thrived on challenge. If they could avert an injustice, they would be seen to be on the side of the common people; Always a good move.

Both he and the Squire were excellent horsemen, although the comfort of carriage travel had appealed in the last few years. The more direct route across open countryside seemed to be the most expedient course to take. Preparations were made, the fastest horses in the stable saddled, and the unlikely riding companions set off at first light.

Jack knew little of the chain of events taking place in his favour. Early on the day of his trial, help was on the way, but would it reach the assize court in time?

Half starved and weak, he was pushed and shoved towards the courthouse. Along with other prisoners, the whole group had tumbled from the open wagon that had brought them. There were many people lining the narrow streets; cheering or jeering as the mood took them. He was all too painfully aware that the short journey after his trial would in all probability be the last one he would make.

The group approached by the rear door and were roughly pushed along a narrow corridor and down steep steps to a holding room. The sound of the key turning was a sound they all knew well. No one had spoken; they knew full well no questions would be answered. Jack wished he had Fanny's faith; hadn't she said help was on the way? But that was yesterday, now things seemed to have gone too far. Where were they, Millie and Fanny? *Will I ever look on them again?*

Time passed and the first three prisoner's names were called. Jack knew, as they all did, that their offences meant deportation or worse. All was quiet again. More time passed. Jack felt sick.

He could expect the death penalty for sure, accused as he would be of Highway Robbery and attempted murder! He just wanted it all to end.

"Amos Hardy, Will Marks, Jack Drew."

The door opened, and all three stumbled from the room, and up the stairs. They were halted at the heavy carved oak doors to the courtroom. When it opened again, Amos Hardy's name was called. The doors swallowed him up, closing behind him with a heavy clang. The remaining two were pushed down onto a wooden bench to await their turn.

Who would be next? They didn't have long to wait. The doors opened again and the usher's loud voice called Jack's name. Will's hand rested momentarily on his shoulder. Jack gave a quick nod and walked through the doors.

The court room seemed big, with high ceilings, lots of wood, benches, rails and the dock! Jack was ushered towards it, hands chained behind him, pushed from behind by the duty officer, to whom he was attached by another short length of chain.

Head down he made his way to the railed dock amid jeers, and grasping, pushing, hands. This was free entertainment for many, and the enjoyment on their faces made Jack sick to the pit of his stomach. What did anyone care that he was an innocent man?

The court was assembled. The Judge seated at his bench, the clerk immediately in front of him. Jack cast a look at his impassive face as the gavel was brought down. The clerk spoke in a loud voice that carried around the courtroom.

"Order; Silence in Court!" The noisy room settled down. Jack raised his eyes. Suddenly, there was Fanny, Millie too, waving franticly to gain his attention. His first thoughts were how beautiful were his wife and lovely daughter. *Aye they're mine, an' a grandchild too if I'm spared! But how did they get in here?* It was strange how trivial things served to overshadow horrendous events. Jack was dragged back by the deep voice of the clerk of the court intoning,

"Let the prisoner state his name."

"Me name's Jack Drew, sir." Duly identified, the clerk continued to read out the charges.

"You are brought to this court charged that on the Twenty Sixth day of February in the year of Seventeen Hundred and Sixty Seven you committed the heinous crimes of robbery and attempted murder, on the King's Highway. How do you plead, guilty or not guilty?"

"Not guilty - sir" *and how did carrying a firearm translate into attempted murder?* They even changed the charge!

The clerk sat down. The prosecuting council took over, standing up slowly and glancing all around. He fixed Jack with a stony stare and began to state his case.

In a bored and droning voice the court proceedings continued. Jack shuffled from one foot to the other. This couldn't be happening.

Fanny too was getting worried. Events were moving too fast, where was the letter? Why were they going on as if nothing had happened? Hadn't she gone to great lengths to find them, tell them, and make them understand? Suddenly Fanny had an idea, and whispered to Millie.

"We got to do something, play for time. Make out you're faint. Fall over like, use yer condition." Millie, taking only a moment to cotton on, sighed and gasped out loud; she clutched wildly at her Ma, and let out a loud groan, before falling forward into the woman in front.

"Watch yerself," the fat woman shrieked, as amid waving arms and legs, they both landed in a heap on the floor.

Millie kept her eyes closed and amid grunts and groans, twitched her arms and legs in imitation of a fit she had once witnessed. She hoped it would cause enough disruption to upset things. Eyes tightly shut; she listened while the Judge called for ushers, and amid the general pandemonium, for everyone joined in – called for the courtroom to be cleared, her to be attended to, and the prisoner to be taken down again.

Jack was pushed roughly from the dock, out of the room and past Will, whose face was a picture of amazement. He too was now dragged close on Jacks heels, down the steps, into a small cell, where the two of them were quickly locked in. They were left with no explanation of what would happen next.

"What now" breathed Jack? Will sank to the floor as they looked at each other, and lapsed into silence. Jack wondered what had happened to Millie, was she really in trouble? But somehow the look on Fanny's face told him that it was staged for his benefit. What did they hope to achieve? His love for them, kept him calm. What on earth was the next move?

It must have been more than an hour later when their names were again called. Jack followed the silent figure back to the courtroom with his heart in his boots, or what was left of them; Will followed. As they approached the court Will was pushed forward, disappearing through the doors. A heavy hand on Jacks shoulder pressed him down hard onto the bench.

"It seems *you* are a special case," the court official broke his silence. "We wait here until you are called." Jack's heart leapt, had Fanny been right, had she really managed to find someone to vouch for him?

When the time came for him to re-enter the court room, he saw that Fanny and Millie had again taken their places, and close by them were.... he strained to make out the figures, could it really be Captain Fawsey and two of the crew he'd sailed with?

Franticly Jack thought, *how in God's name did they know to be here? Surely now I must be pronounced a free man. When the Judge hears what they have to say, surely to God I must be freed.* Casting his eyes along the row, they alighted on none other than Gerard Elliot and his father the Squire, *and* Justice Mapledoram too!

A mixture of emotions swept through him, until he felt quite faint. They must have come for Millie's sake. He hadn't expected to see them *here*. Suddenly Jack was filled with apprehension. Did they think they could help, or had they come to gloat? It never even crossed his mind that they could or would speak for him.

The judge brought down the gavel, again bringing the court to order. He was being handed a letter. It surely couldn't go wrong now could it? Jack held his breath; there was silence in the courtroom. The Judge proceeded to read, then pushing his spectacles up from where they had slipped to the end of his nose; he looked up and cleared his throat.

"This appears to be in order; this letter claims that fresh evidence has come to hand and that witnesses are here in my court. I therefore ask; who speaks for the accused?"

The Squire, the Justice, and Gerard, Captain Fawsey and the crew members, all answered at once. There was a murmur among the front benches of the defence council.

"Call the first witness for the defence." He nodded at the clerk of the court, who in turn stood up and in a loud voice summoned Captain Fawsey to take the stand.

"Moving toward the witness box, the Captain was an imposing and impressive figure, the clerk of the court continued.

"Please state your name."

"Captain Nathan Fawsey, Sir"

He was duly sworn in... Addressing the Judge, he tapped the large book in his hand.

"This your honour, is the ship's log book, and as such, holds all the evidence needed to prove beyond a shadow of a doubt, the whereabouts of able seaman Jack Drew when the crime of which he is accused, was committed."

The log book was duly passed as evidence to the judge, who scrutinised it. The court held its breath. After questioning by the defence counsel, Captain Fawsey stepped down, and the two ordinary seamen were called in turn. Satisfied with their evidence Squire Elliott was then called to the stand.

"It now rests only for me to ask if the accused is the same man that you witnessed at the scene of the said robbery." The Squire paused for a moment, as he peered at Jack. I think that...

"Answer the question," the Judge interjected.

"No m' lord this is not the man I saw."

A cheer went up from Fanny and Millie, hugging each other with relief and emotion. Gerard stole a glance at Millie who was now standing. As she turned away from him he could have sworn... his heart lurched, but no, it couldn't be. His attention centred back on the judge, who continued, saying, "Furthermore, I would like to ask *who* accused this man; and why is he not here in my courtroom today?" The silence was palpable. The Squire was asked to step down. The Judge's summing up began.

"Mister Drew, in view of the last minute evidence, presented to this court, a grave miscarriage of justice has been averted this day. I am satisfied that you are totally innocent of the crime of which you have been accused. I pronounce that you have no case to answer. You are free to go," He brought down the gavel. Proceedings were at an end.

Only the jury looked disappointed, deprived as they were of their participation. The Judge stood up to leave the courtroom, and the clerk called for all to be upstanding. After a moment or two, the room gradually began to empty amid shouts and cheers from Jack's supporters.

Making his way through the crowded room toward Captain Fawsey, Jack felt heady with relief, although unsteady on his feet. He grasped the Captain's hand firmly.

"I thank you indeed Sir, for coming 'ere today, all of you," he glanced round, emotion making his voice unsteady." Glad to be of assistance Drew. The Captain turned.

"This is the man you need to thank," he indicated Gerard. "If it hadn't been for him, I wouldn't even have known of your trouble." Jack turned to Gerard, saying "I do indeed thank you most humbly sir." Gerard nodded, and in turn indicated Mapledoram, and the Squire, who had now reached their side...

"Thanks too, should go to my father and the Justice here. Without his knowledge of law, we might not have got the appropriately worded letter to the court in time." Jack shook them both firmly by the hand, oblivious for the time being of his previous thoughts toward Gerard, before all this had taken place.

Gerard wondered momentarily if he was mistaken about Millie's possible 'condition' and if he wasn't, did Jack know. But the smile on Jack's face couldn't be dimmed by anything at this moment. Amid handshakes all round, he pushed his way towards Fanny. She was standing to one side, savouring the first moments of Jack's freedom, although tears blurred her eyes as she moved towards him. Millie was sitting quietly, regaining her energy whilst waiting for her Ma and Pa to make their way to her.

She was overwhelmed with relief for her Pa, and with gratitude to Gerard for his intervention. If only things had been different...

As the group left the building to go their separate ways, Gerard was convinced that Millie was with child, *his child* and if she was, of the complications facing him - if he chose to acknowledge the fact.

As Jack, Fanny, and Millie, walked from the courthouse returning to Lyme and home, was uppermost in their minds. The others involved, made their way to the smarter local hostelries, before choosing to stay over, return to Lyme, or move on, as the case may be.

Gerard's relief at his perceived exoneration of his shameful words and treatment of Millie, had him almost believing that the slate was wiped clean; that he need think no more of it. He hoped so, but was that the end of it?

Millie grasped her Pa's arm, and in an emotional outburst, left him in no doubt as to how happy she was to have him back. Unusually lost for words Fanny guided the trio to The Silver Tavern, where they found a warm welcome, and Jack's two shipmates already seated there! Jack was convinced that the food and ale, was the best that he had ever or would ever taste.

They parted company with the seafarers to board the last wagon back to the comparative luxury of the little town of Lyme, where a further welcome awaited them.

Jack spared quiet moments thinking of - not so lucky- Barney; and with mounting anger at the prison system that had kept him incarcerated for so long. The only comfort was that if justice *had* been swifter, he too would have gone the same way as Barney a long time ago.

Fanny's main concern now was to restore Jack to his former strong and healthy self, before the devastating chain of events took place.

At the first opportunity Millie visited Broad Street to give the good news of Jack's return as an innocent man, and his start on the slow road to recovery after his ordeal.

Miss Sybil and Miss Mabel received the news with relief for the family, and especially for Millie, in *her* 'delicate' condition!

Making ready for the changes awaiting her in the cottage at Charmouth, Millie daydreamed of the coming child, but viewed with some trepidation the wrench of leaving her family, her work, and her friends...and she definitely included her employers, in the last group.

CHAPTER TWENTY SIX

Fanny was much relieved that Jack was making good progress and able to stroll out again in the fresh air. Answering the door to a sharp rap, to her amazement, there stood Clive Del-a-Hart. Unexpected, unannounced, and totally oblivious of the impact he had on other people's lives; as self assured as ever.

She hesitated for a moment, as thoughts tumbled around in her head. Surely he must know he was no longer welcome! Not for the first time it crossed her mind that Clive's self assurance bordered on arrogance.

"My dear Frances forgive the intrusion, but I find myself again in this area, and thought it would be pleasant to reacquaint myself with Millie... I am of course pleased to see you too. I would be grateful if you would let her know that I would very much like to see her again; and you my dear, are looking as beautiful as ever."

He smiled, looking her up and down, Fanny could hardly believe the audacity of the man, he had certainly slipped from his pedestal in her eyes! She bit back her first retort.

"I'm sure you mean well, but she's not 'ere. She's moved away. But if you're ready for a shock I can tell you, that like 'er mother, she's bin taken in by a smooth tongued gentleman such as yourself! So if you'd like to see 'er, come back again after Christmas, an' you'll be able to see yer grandchild an' all. If not, I'll thank you not to call again."

Clive stared for a moment, as Fanny's words filtered through.

"Well you have somewhat surprised me," he said at last, "this will need careful handling. As she's not here, I will call again after - um - at some point; for now, good day to you Frances."

Fanny knew what Clive's 'careful handling' would be before he knew himself, and retorted,

"I won't have Jack upset, 'es Millie's *real* father in our eyes. You're lucky 'es round at the Tavern now, 'cos there'd be another rumpus; an' I can tell you we've 'ad our fair share o them!"

She closed the door and leaned against it, suspecting her own feelings against Clive coloured her judgement of his intentions. Turning on his heel, Clive strode away deep in thought. It had taken him sixteen years to find out he was a father, it was unthinkable he should become a grandfather too, in such a short space of time.

All his finer feelings left him. He had loved Frances, and wanted to get to know his daughter; but things had become too complicated. He was still a comparatively young man! He raised his head and straightened his shoulders. Family pressures had been blamed before, but deep in his heart he knew that he always had, and always would choose the easier path.

He looked at his fob watch, time enough to have a meal, a good malt whisky. His spirits lifted. Sunshine was what he needed; the damp cold English weather didn't suit him at all! Sunny climes were calling and his ship would take him wherever he to chose to go, given the right cargo. Clive's mind was made up.

As Millie reached the end of her sixth month, knowing the time had now come to take her leave of Miss Sybil and Miss Mabel, her last working days were spent finishing off small sewing jobs and transferring other things back to Miss Mable's care. Millie tidied her work bench and sorted her threads for the last time.

Late afternoon and evening saw her packing up her hessian bag, and collecting together her few extra belongings. She took only what she could easily carry, leaving the rest to be collected the next day. Disappointments and regret lay heavy on her, as she slowly moved about her own special room that was hers, just until the morrow. It was with a heavy heart that Millie made her way down to prepare breakfast in the warm kitchen for the last time. Finally she was standing in the small hallway to say her last goodbyes.

Miss Mabel pressed a package into her arms, interrupting Millie's surprised thanks, by blowing her nose somewhat noisily. And if Millie hadn't known better she would have said the 'cold' that Miss Sybil claimed was akin to the tears that both she and Miss Mabel were struggling to suppress.

Slowly she trudged down Broad Street, her cloak held close, not so much for warmth, but to hide a secret that couldn't be hidden much longer. It seemed a long trudge across the 'walk,' the shifting shingle underfoot make her legs and back ache.

On arrival at her Ma's she sank onto a chair, thankful to put down the paper wrapped package tied with string, and the hessian bag that held her clothes and few possessions. Greeting her brother and her Pa, she was about to ask where her Ma was, when Fanny appeared from the scullery.

Looking at Millie's pale and tired face, she said brightly, "Chin up maid you'll be good as knew after a bite to eat and a hot cuppa." Fanny picked up the package, "What's in 'ere then?"

"I don't know yet, a leaving present I think." Millie took it from Fanny and pulled the string. Falling open, the pure white cotton crib sheets, and a crocheted blanket tumbled onto the table. Tucked inside were two small linen bonnets, and two tiny pin tucked flannelette nightgowns.

Millie's eye welled with tears that came easily in her emotional state. She lovingly fingered the soft materials.

"My child - my babby - to be clothed in *quality* things;" She learned the word from Mister Lane, and was now able to apply it to her child's clothes!

Smoothing the soft material between her fingers, she murmured, "quality, something I always dreamed of, sort of deep inside like." She sighed and looking at Fanny said, "They bin so good to me, I feel sad to be leaving with me 'ead down like. I was lucky to 'ave got the job in the first place. I don't deserve anyone's kindness. I let everyone down and really messed up me chances didn't I?"

"Ah, come on maid, you worked 'ard for 'em; an' no-one knows what's round the corner. You're not the first to be taken in by fine words, an' you won't be the last, neither! Let's go through these lovely things again, an' show 'em to your Pa an' Jamie."

The rest of the evening passed pleasantly and just as Fanny had promised, Millie felt much happier after a hot drink. The pair of them spent time talking in excited voices. Plans were made for their short journey over to 'Clifftops' the next day, accompanied by Lazurus, and in accordance with Beattie's instructions.

First thing the next morning as soon as daylight permitted, they set off to Broad Street to collect Millie's quilt and her remaining possessions which had been left ready. Miss Mabel opened the door quickly and they stepped inside. Both sisters greeted them, and Fanny warmly thanked them for all they had done.

Millie cast a last glance up the stairway to her beloved attic room. Remembering her excitement the first time she was asked if she might consider moving in, and how she felt when it was first shown to her.

The dream she had cherished of stitching for the gentry, had blossomed as she sat on her bed and planned her future. It had been a sanctuary as she wrestled with her shame, a place to hide away when she first realised her 'condition,' and now she felt a deep sadness as she was obliged to leave.

She caught Fanny's eye and gave a weak smile before turning back to the task in hand, that of sharing out the assorted bags and bundles, to carry between the three of them. Picking up their bundles, Lazurus pulled the door open, and followed by Fanny, stepped down onto the road. Miss Mabel and Millie grasped hands for a moment, before Millie followed them out into the crisp morning. As they walked past the window of the shop Miss Sybil raised her hand in final farewell, and Fanny mouthed a last 'thank you.'

They trudged in silence down the hill and across the square. The sun had started its climb, eventually breaking through the early cloud as they reached the cottage. Jack was too weak to be of much help, but watched with mixed feelings as Millie's possessions, along with her childhood, were sorted and bundled ready to carry down to where they would board the mid morning carrier cart.

"Take good care of yerself our Millie." Her pale tired face tugged at Jack's heartstrings.

"You'll bring babby back 'ere when time's right." He gripped her hand for an instant, wanting to pull her back into the warmth and safety of her home, but new better.

Feeling a wrench deep inside her, even though accompanied by her Ma and Lazurus, they made their way to the harbour in time to see the cart doing its usual turnabout, before trundling to a halt. Jamie limped along beside them, having given his big sister a hug, whilst hoping no one else would notice. With Fanny's dire warnings, "Don't get into any sort of trouble through the day, and take care of yer Pa while we're gone," he watched, nodding vigorously as they climbed aboard.

The rest of Millie's worldly goods were tossed on the cart, apart from a supply of freshly whittled pegs which she clutched tightly, her knuckles showing white, a precious gift from her Pa and Lazurus. The coming child would bring an extra washday load, along with joys and responsibilities. Painstakingly old Lazurus climbed aboard, and they set out for Millie's new but temporary home.

Fanny was glad that it was Joe's cart they were using. There would be no sideways glances from Joe, he had known Fanny since they were children together, and was now a family man himself. Joe was a good natured fellow, with a shock of greying hair, a bearded chin, and his cheeks ruddy from his outdoor life. He was proud owner of a carrier cart, and might well have been rich if he had collected all his dues. His easy going nature, and meagre charges or acceptance of goods in lieu, meant folk turned to him first; he was never without work.

As the cart rumbled on Millie sank deep into thought, wishing she could have told Emily everything before anyone else did! But, as only her employers and Danny knew her circumstances, it seemed easier just to get on with her arrangements. As her Ma had said, just be as far along her path as possible before having to explain her shame to anyone.

They were relieved when at last the cottage came into sight. Every bump and sway had Millie clutching at her stomach and the side of the cart. The three miles or so had seemed endless. Millie's back ached, both from the uneven ground and her seventh month of pregnancy. Joe passed down Millie's belongings. This was the next stage of Millie's young life! Waving goodbye, they reminded him that Fanny and Lazurus would make the return journey on foot.

Lazurus knocked on Ada's door, the prospects of a drink and a sit down uppermost in all their minds.

Opening it and ushering them inside Ada greeted them all, immediately waving Millie, her new companion, to a nearby chair!

"Take the weight off maid, while we get to know each other!" They exchanged pleasantries, and spoke of Beattie's kindness, as Lazurus sat down and Fanny followed.

The long awaited tea that Ada brewed was the most welcome of drinks. After a good rest on the old cushioned settle, and a lengthy conversation which was somewhat hindered by the old lady's deafness, Fanny and Lazurus stood up to go. Thanking her warmly they knew they could no longer put off the parting. Watched closely by Ada, they hugged Millie in turn, Fanny issuing last minute instructions with assurance that she would visit quite soon. Lastly Lazurus shook Ada by the hand before taking their leave.

Left alone, Millie surveyed the plain room. A faded curtain hung at the window and a rag rug lay before the small stove. Lime washed walls and flagstones completed the overall look. Millie was aware of the absence of colour, mainly because she was used to working with it.

Ada stepped back into the room, saying, "Come along 'o me then maid, I'll show you where you'll be sleeping. It's a small room under the eaves, but it's warm and cosy."

"Thank you Miss um..."

"Ada; call me Ada, we're going to get along well you an' me, I can feel it in me water."

Millie tried to suppress the urge to laugh but failed, it was going to be alright!

"Look at this maid, all ready for you it is!" A small chest had been emptied, and in the bottom were sprinkled dried Lavender heads.

"Thank you; for going to so much trouble I mean. I'll look after things 'ere for you, and 'elp you all I can, thank you Ada." They unpacked the bags filled with Millie's clothes and those stitched for the baby, Ada commenting on the beautifully made baby gowns. Millie placed the rest of the contents in the chest, as the old lady left her to settle into her small room.

Millie could be forgiven for wondering if she would ever come to rest anywhere for very long. *But I've only meself to blame*, she quietly chided, and set about making the best of things. She began by descending the rickety stairs, allowing Ada to show her around her new home, and offering help preparing the evening meal.

Fanny walked back across the fields and cliff path at Lazarus's slow pace, glad of his company, and that he'd refused to let her make the trip alone with Millie. Glad too, that Jack had supported them in decisions regarding Millie's immediate future; although truth to tell, he had only gone along with them; the actual decisions were cut and dried when presented to him!

Smiling to herself she acknowledged that there would be many a man would have raised the roof in the circumstances, and satisfied that the worry of Jack's trial had done neither him nor Millie any lasting damage, she remained lost in thought.

Lazurus needed all his breath just to keep going, and showed signs of acute discomfort in his old joints. Wending their way back through the gathering dusk, they at last reached the cottage, with Fanny vowing that he would ride the cart both ways in future - or stay at home.

The days passed, and Millie worked hard at Clifftops, awaiting her 'time.' She had wanted the new start. The thought of her condition becoming common knowledge among her friends and acquaintances mortified her. But it was *her* child and she would love it and look after it, facing the world when she could no longer avoid it!

Millie, and Ada, found a solid friendship developing between them. She readily forgave the old lady her grumbles and occasional cross words, suspecting that she knew she couldn't manage alone much longer. This arrangement was only a temporary measure for both of them, a sort of breathing space! Millie's sunny nature stood them both in good stead in the coming weeks;

In the evening, conversation sometimes took an interesting turn when Ada described her childhood. She had little trouble recalling those bygone days. During one of these easy chats, Millie's ears pricked up, when

Ada mentioned the 'Hartnell sisters.' It seemed that in their young days they had lived not too far from Ada's family, although both were considerably younger.

Becoming more interested in Ada's recollections, Millie began to press for more background to the Miss Hartnells, being quietly amazed to learn that Miss Mabel had been married for a short time to the son of a local dignitary in Axminster.

It seemed a child had been born to them, a daughter who had lived only hours after her birth. Faced with the loss of his child, and the grief of his young wife, it was not long before the marriage was on the rocks. The young husband returning to his family home, and a broken hearted Miss Mabel resuming her maiden name, and taking up residence with her sister, where they began to establish a successful dressmaking business.

Millie could hardly believe her ears. Was it any wonder the sisters had been so kind to her, and done all in their power to help? They totally understood mistakes, heartbreak, and despair.

Millie fell into a pattern of work and rest which suited both herself and the old lady, who considered the girl a real treasure. Millie's chatter and her own memories kept them company in the autumn evenings.

With the fire burning brightly and Ada in a good mood, Millie absorbed a wealth of helpful advice, mixed with old wives tales, herbal remedies and recipes gleaned originally from her sister Beattie.

Sometimes she spent autumn afternoons embroidering the quilt, which had lain unfinished whilst she had been industriously occupied creating her bonnets. Millie sorely missed working with Miss Sybil and Miss Mabel. Pondering the way of things, she wandered out into the weak afternoon sunshine, picking up the last of the cooking apples from beneath the old trees in the orchard.

Straightening up to ease her aching back, she caught sight of two figures making their way slowly down the track from the toll road where the carrier cart had set them down. As they drew nearer she was amazed to recognise Miss Mabel and Miss Sybil. Calling out to Ada, she walked excitedly to meet them.

"How did you find me? Why 'ave you come? Oh I'm so pleased to see you."

"Millie my dear we missed you too, you haven't' changed a bit".

"Well just a bit" interrupted Miss Mable with her quizzical smile, eyeing Millie up and down. Laughing, Millie called out again, "Ada we have visitors."

After warmly greeting them, distant memories came flooding back.

Ada declared, "I'd a knowed you two maids anywhere; come in, come in." The group went inside, continuing happy greetings and reminiscing. Finally sitting down, they began their explanation of their unexpected visit.

Millie listened intently to the conversation, and they quickly got down to the reason for their visit. Miss Sybil began, and the story unravelled.

"The help we took on in your place Millie is just not working out at all. She can just about be trusted to sew a straight seam, but that seemed to be the extent of it. Anything else seems completely beyond her, and Miss Mabel ends up having to put right too many silly mistakes." Miss Sybil took up the story.

"Because of the surge in business, due in no small part to you Millie, we are finding it much more difficult to manage. The ladies gowns of course take longer than plain dresses. Not to mention the orders for bonnets, which we are unable to fill at present, but really don't want to continue turning away." They continued talking, until Miss Sybil turned to Ada, "and so you see, our loss is your gain. We have made the journey to see Millie, to try and redress the balance, without upsetting the new arrangement *in any way*."

Millie listened wide eyed, she couldn't believe it, but if she wasn't mistaken, they still needed her. The job would always be hers. It would only be the place of work that changed, and then only until after the birth of her child. She would then be free to bring her baby back to Broad Street and continue as before. In fact Miss Sybil had implied they would be welcomed with open arms.

"What do you think of the plan my dear?" enquired Miss Mabel.

They were both staring at her, awaiting a reply. Old Ada smiled quietly. Happy for the girl who had been so kind to her, and on whom she had come to depend; she'd known from the start that it was only a temporary arrangement, she had hoped... she sighed knowing that Millie had her young life to sort out, and that she on the other hand, - oh well, it was no good thinking along those lines. Ada was failing and knew it. Beattie had helped, but both knew her old body was worn out.

Millie had made Ada's time more bearable, the cottage and the garden now a credit to her. As always, unhindered by her pregnancy Millie always put her heart and soul into anything she took on. She stood up, "Well," she began as she digested all the information, "this calls for a cup of tea."

"Aye put the kettle on to sing maid." Ada, although worried about the outcome, needed to know just what that outcome was going to be.

"A good idea, a nice cup of tea clears the mind," chimed in Miss Sybil.

They all laughed- it was just like old times. Later as they finished their tea and fruit loaf, the conversation was reopened by Millie.

"Well I love the idea of coming back to work for you, but I couldn't think of leaving Ada, after the kindness she and Beattie have shown me." Miss Mabel and Miss Sybil looked at each other and at Ada, noticing that she was visibly relieved. "But if you could find a way to get the bonnets and things I need, over to me, I'm sure Ada wouldn't mind. I could still look after her, and then when the babby comes, well, I would just have to see how much I could manage. But I'm sure we could work something out."

Millie looked around, she was bubbling with excitement - her job- her lovely job, was being offered back to her. She would move heaven and earth to keep everyone happy.

The sisters left Clifftops well pleased with the outcome of their visit. Plans had been laid and arrangements made. Once Miss Sybil, Miss Mabel and Millie, had the bit between their teeth, there would be no stopping them. Even Ada had been encompassed with their excitement.

Initially it was decided everything needed to make bonnets, could be sent once a week on the carrier cart. Joe being the good fellow that he was would go out of his way to help, and of course he would be well paid.

All could be packed in the biggest basket, and would include materials in the desired colours, all the trimmings and an assortment of ribbons, velvet and lace. Millie, being well able to read, and write too, thanks to Mister Lane, could send notes relating to the orders, and follow instructions from Broad Street the same way. For the last seven weeks of her pregnancy, Millie was happily occupied doing what she loved best.

Ada was supportive, Millie still managing to keep things going, using only her quiet time for the work which happily kept them both occupied. Whilst Millie was quietly sewing, Ada watched intently, as nimble fingers created beautiful bonnets from the assorted materials pulled from her work basket. She was continually amazed at the talents of this resourceful young woman, who had a quiet aura about her and an almost ladylike manner.

Ada wished, not for the first time that her wedded state had blessed her with sons or daughters. How she envied Fanny, feeling sad that her girl was unwed. She should be at home with her own family. Ada again quietly cursed the busybodies and trouble makers whose lack of understanding had brought about the need for Millie's temporary move.

Fanny still managed to make the tiring journey every couple of weeks, and on one of her visits, as Ada slept off her midday meal, they chattered until the conversation turned to Millie's silk dress.

"What 'appened to it then, are you still 'anging on to it?" Millie answered her quickly.

"Course I am Ma, it wasn't the dress that was the cause of the trouble, it was me thinking I could live up to it like."

"Oh Millie you deserve more 'un that. You don't need to live up to nothing; but the frock, will you keep it?"

"Well the materials good, an' there's lots of it. I just need to keep it tucked away for now; but I've shook it out from time to time, just to look at it." Fanny gazed into the fire remembering the first time she wore a special frock.

"I 'ad a nice frock once, first time I put it on, me Ma, that's yer grandmother - she fair exploded." Fanny smiled at the distant memories... "Anyway, when we was little yer gran always dressed in grey an' white. Bonnet, collar an' cuffs an' apron all pure white. Prided 'erself on it she did. An' 'er frock - that was always done up tight to the neck.

It was the nonconformist faith we was brought up in see, Ma and Pa were strong nonconformist followers, we 'ad to go with them to worship in secret like, way up in the woods above the undercliff. I remember me an' me brother - 'e was called William, we 'ad to stay quiet during the service, but we used to peep at each other out of one eye an' try not to giggle. Aye, William an' me, we 'ad some good times; But 'e was took from us, didn't see 'is seventh birthday.

Millie knew little of her Ma's childhood and was intrigued to know more.

"Go on Ma don't stop now," she shifted her position and Fanny went on.

"White chapel rocks it was. Well anyone caught worshipping there was in for it, an' no mistake. It was all to do with breaking away from the ways of the Catholic Church. I didn't understand it then an' I don't now. Worship is worship, no matter what name you call it.

Well you can imagine what 'appened back in the town when *I* fell from grace. But me Ma stood by me. Still that's enough of that. The frock, got me thinking as 'ow I never wore any colours till I was growed up."

Fanny fell silent remembering now who had introduced *her* to pretty dresses. "Aye I was a headstrong maid. But they say we learn by our mistakes - I'm not sure what, but mine gave me you Millie an' I'd not be without you for the world I wouldn't." Fanny allowed herself a moment to compose herself - she wasn't given to emotional outbursts, as her daughter was. "I suppose I take after yer grandma. Hard work an' trouble, they make you stronger so they say. Well I certainly got that from her, aye an' passed it on to you by the look of it!"

"I never knew about any of that, it's a lovely story Ma." They fell silent for a moment, and then Millie pulled herself to the edge of the settle and stood up with difficulty. Fanny too rose to her feet.

"Aye well, I'm not sitting 'ere no longer, neither. The dimpsy afternoon'll be fading on me. I got to get meself back 'ome an' tell 'em you're alright."

Ada woke in time to see her off, a bit disappointed to have missed her visit; as they walked to the cottage door she whispered, "I reckon babby won't be long 'fore it puts in an appearance," she looked at Fanny and then at Millie's strained face.

"Didn't you say Beattie comes end o' week?" enquired Fanny, "you'd best 'old on 'til then maid!" she laughed as she threw her shawl around her shoulders, but noticing how Millie had gone quiet said gently, "Beatty will be 'ere in time maid, don't worry."

As they watched Fanny 'til she was out of sight, Millie counted her blessings and tried to push her worrying thoughts to one side. But they wouldn't be pushed away. What if Beattie didn't get to them in time? What if Ada had one of her turns? Or they were snowed in, or everyone else was snowed in? How would they let anyone know when her time came? The thoughts whirled around in her head and Millie knew that she would have little peace of mind before her 'babby' put in an appearance.

Each morning, after the fire was banked and the cottage tidied, reassuring herself that Ada needed nothing more, Millie, who had much less energy now, spent longer with her sewing. She seemed to find comfort and peace, as the soft material slipped between her fingers. She followed drawings and instructions from the papers enclosed with each order, designing and stitching them accordingly. Rarely did any work come back, and Millie stitched and dreamed the hours away; stopping only to get their meals.

The only caller besides Joe was the rag and bone man whose cry of 'rags and bones an' rabbit skins,' brought them both to the door. Pushing his old cart against the wall he accepted the offer of Dandelion wine, in return for news of the hamlet. Although they had no old clothes to give him, he accepted a small coin from Millie, for the soft rabbit skin that was tied to the handle of his cart. A further scraping followed by a good scrub and a few days drying in the hearth, would turn it into a warm cover, placed across the bottom of the basket against draughts, in preparation for the coming babby.

The days passed and November was slowly slipping by. Joe brought assorted provisions, from the shop in Lyme; chosen and packed up by the Miss Hartnells. Beattie as always furnished the money for the 'reckoning up,' adding plenty of dry goods for Ada to supplement her store cupboard.

The cold wet weather prevented both Millie and Ada from walking down the steep slippery slope to

Charmouth hamlet, and its only shop. Millie remarked "if the going down don't get you, then the coming back will." Now that Joe fetched and carried twice a week, there was no need to risk it! At the beginning of the last week in November Beattie arrived, and announced her intention to 'stay for as long as it took'! Millie much relieved settled down in excitement and a certain amount of trepidation, to await the coming event!

CHAPTER TWENTY SEVEN

The cottage was warm and cosy. Beattie had arrived almost a full week before Millie's reckoned time. On finding how close she was to the big day, Beattie was glad to have made the journey when she did; for the safety of Millie, the coming child and Ada's peace of mind.

"This babby's not going to keep us waiting long, mark my words," she joked.

Millie's uncomfortable nights had begun to leave dark circles under her eyes. This one was no different. She wandered the house with her candle; quilt wrapped warmly around her, and in the small hours curled up beside the hearth, fell into a fitful sleep. On stirring, Millie returned to her bed to await the dawn chorus, heralding another uncomfortable day.

Slowly she washed, dressed and crept downstairs, to find that although hungry, she could eat nothing. Her back ached, and the dragging feeling in her belly made her think that her course was due, but that couldn't be. Setting about her daily chores more slowly than usual, she filled the kettle from the large water jug, which she could now hardly lift.

Setting breakfast, again she curled up by the hearth waiting for the kettle to boil. Beattie came down stairs, taking note of Millie's white, drawn, face and declared, "You've started Millie; I bet me boots you'll 'ave yer babby in yer arms by this time the morrow." At first

Millie felt excited, but as the long morning wore on and she could settle to nothing, tired too from running out to the midden several times an hour, she began to feel apprehensive. The dragging backache had changed to a dull intermittent pain and moved forward low down in her belly. Nausea swept over her. Beattie was kind and matter of fact.

"It'll take its course maid, an' now it's started there's nothing to do but be as comfortable as you can and wait. Nature won't be hurried!" As the pains got stronger and closer together, Beattie encouraged her to carry on sipping the raspberry leaf tea which she had made up a day or two earlier from leaves collected and dried during the summer. They were crisp and crumbled easily now.

Beattie rubbed Millie's back and massaged her with her specially blended herbal ointment. Ada collected the clean cloths and towels, making sure there was plenty of hot water bubbling on the range. Soon, Beattie judged, it would be time for Millie to lie down on the straw filled makeshift mattress, which had been placed on the floor and which Ada had now covered with the old but clean towels.

There was nothing left for Millie to do but follow Beattie's instructions. It was another hour before the contractions began to gain full strength, and it took all of Millie's courage to stifle her cries of pain.

"How long, how long will it go on?" she clung to Beattie's hand, her eyes tightly shut. "Get Ma, get me Ma, I can't do this on me own.'' She lay back exhausted as the pain receded, before gathering momentum for the next wave.

"That's just it dearie, it's something every woman 'as to do on her own. We can be with you an' encourage you, but in the end it's down to you. Listen to what yer body's telling you, an' don't fight it. It'll be over 'afore you know it."

Beattie was motherly, and so competent that when the child finally slid into the world, Millie seemed quite surprised, as well as relieved and totally exhausted. When the child let out a loud lusty cry, she didn't know whether to laugh or cry herself. Beattie laid the wrinkled scrap across her tummy for warmth, covering it with a warm towel, and after judging all was well with both of them, explained, "Now we 'ave to wait for the afterbirth," though Millie had no idea what that meant.

In a few more minutes nature completed her miracle. Beattie waited for the cord to stop pulsating and assuring herself the child was breathing freely, expertly tied off and severed it. Lifting the child from the now silent Millie, she looked it over again, and wiping the small rosebud mouth, the child let out another lusty cry as if establishing its arrival.

Well satisfied, Beattie handed the infant to her young mother again, who gazed in awe and wonder as the child was guided to her breast.

"Well you've got a lovely little daughter dearie, you can be proud o' yerself." At this moment Millie *was* proud; such a beautiful child, but so small. No matter what had gone before Millie knew that the feelings of love and protectiveness towards this tiny scrap would last a lifetime.

Beattie allowed them both to sleep awhile, before moving them back into Millie's own fresh bed, whilst she and Ada gathered up the straw pallet, removing all traces of the birth out to the ash pit. When everything was to their satisfaction, and the afterbirth buried deep against rats and vermin, they turned their attention to tea and rest. Taking a mug of strong tea to Millie, laced with honey to revive her, Beattie paused in the doorway surveying the sleeping mother and child.

She felt a great satisfaction, as she did each time the miracle occurred, thanking the Lord again for giving her the skills to carry out her work. Millie stirred, woke, and smiling gratefully accepted the sweet tea. Beattie gently took the babe from her, wrapping it in a clean, almost soft towel, and placing it in the warmly lined and covered apple basket, made ready for its arrival.

Noting Millie's rosy cheeks and bright eyes, with a sigh of satisfaction she knew that all was, and would be well.

As Millie pulled herself up, her only regret was that her Ma had not been there to see her first grandchild come into the world. On voicing this, Beattie soothed, "Aye but we'll get word to Fanny soon as the cart comes. Joe'll take news over. It'll be easy enough for him to spot Fanny or Lazurus down by the harbour. If not, there will always be some kind soul eager to pass the news to her. He can take yer sewing work an all."

"Oh *no*" interrupted Millie, "I want me Ma to know first. Leave me work till next trip, there's nothing a couple of days will make a difference to. Then Joe won't 'ave to see me employers, an' 'e won't feel bad, not telling 'em me babby's come. I *do* want me Ma to be first to know, after Joe that is." Beattie agreed, and when Joe arrived he was given the good news.

"Well I'll be blowed, a little maid eh? 'er Ma an' Pa'll be relieved that they both come through it good." Joe seemed quite glad not to have to go up to the shop first. "Gets dark quick now, an' I couldn't do no other an' tell 'em, 'cause they'd be sure to ask. Will I call again? Collect work end o' week like? They pay's me by the trip - so it won't make no odds."

"Yes, yes, Millie's got a bee in 'er own bonnet about 'er Ma knowing first an' it's only right. Thanks Joe, thank you."

He promised to find Fanny, and set off for Lyme harbour grinning from ear to ear, muttering, "who'd a thought it, an' she's nought but a babby 'erself!"

As it happened Fanny had finished her work for the day, and was walking with the other fishwives ready to make for home. Seeing Joe she broke away to meet him, half guessing the reason for his appearance. Joe reined in his horse, drawing the cart to a halt beside her.

"Good news Fanny. Babby's arrived, a little maid 'tis, an' Beattie says they're both doing nicely."

"Oh Joe, that's the news I bin waiting for; bin on pins I 'ave. Oh I'm that relieved,"

"Well you can stop frettin' now Fanny, I just come from there, an' they're alright. 'Tis too late in day now, but I'll go out o' me way to take you over the morrow; reckon it calls for a free ride to celebrate, what you say?"

"Oh yes, thank you kindly, there's not enough light left to do anything today, early or late cart the morrow Joe?"

"I reckon I'll pick 'e up early, 'tis dark mornings, so give it an hour after sun up, an' I'll see you the morrow." As Joe turned about, he was chuckling, "don't do to keep new grandmothers waiting about," see you the morrow Fanny." As an afterthought Fanny called to him,

"Call in and let Danny know as you pass the Coaching Inn will you Joe? An' thanks again." Joe raised a hand in acknowledgement, and Fanny hurried back to the house to pass the good news to Jack and Jamie.

Suddenly Fanny was struck by the thought that Jo might think Danny was the father. Couldn't be helped – likely half the harbour folk would think it anyway. Reaching home Fanny pushed her way in calling, "Jack, our Millie's alright, she 'ad a little daughter; two or three of hours ago by sound of it." Fanny's smile widened. "She's alright Jack, they're both alright, an' Joe's takin' me over the morrow to see 'em.

"Aye Fanny an' we're Grandparents! Who'd of thought it?" Jack was thrilled, although he wished that he had been able to make the journey over with her.

"Oh an' Jamie, it makes you an uncle, 'ow about that?"

Jamie silently absorbed the news, so that's what had been happening. "I'm pleased they're alright. Our Millie an' that, I guessed why she went away. So I'm, babby's uncle eh?"

Talking it over, knowing it was going to be common knowledge anyway, they chose to 'get in first, by going to Rosie's Tavern and sharing their news. Rosie would be astonished; wouldn't they all? But if anything was to be said, it could be said to their faces.

Making ready, all three walked the short distance to the Tavern. Fanny was first through the door, holding it open for Jack, who pushed his way through the gathering crowd of harbour working folk. At this time of day they could usually be found downing cider.

Going straight to the bar he caught Rosie's eye. Lazurus was already there and half way down his first tankard of cider.

"Three pints of yer best ale Rosie luv, an' 'alf for me lad too. We got sommat to celebrate." His voice was loud and clear.

"What's that then Jack, you're looking fair pleased with yerself. What's 'e up to Fanny?" she enquired, looking from one to the other. Fanny smiled, Jack slapped Lazurus on the back.

"Have one with us," he said pushing the first pint towards him and the other to Fanny, Jamie grabbed his half as Jack turned to the regulars.

Surveying the expectant faces and raising his pint *and* his voice he called, "I'm telling 'e all now. Our Millie's 'ad a little maid... So anyone got anything to say, now's yer chance. We're about to drink health to the pair of 'em; if you join us in a toast we'll be right pleased, if not that's your business, but I'll thank 'e to respect ours."

Jack wasn't about to hide the fact that he was a grandfather, far from it! He and Fanny would let nothing detract from the joy and relief they felt from the arrival of Millie's babby, both mother and child, safe and well, and the secret out in the open at last. He raised his glass to Fanny, who raised hers, as Jamie shouted, "To our Millie and our new babby. Ma says it makes me an uncle!" this was greeted with laughter.

After the first silence, the news was digested, and one by one the harbour folks joined in. The noise levels rose again, the glasses clinked and Fanny was relieved at giving out the news at last. There would be one or two women - those who were not born and bred 'Lymers,' who would look down their noses. Like the one that murmured, '*no wonder girl went away to work*!' Which they'd ignored; Fanny could handle that. There would be slight recriminations from others for keeping it secret. But time would lesson gossip, and as long as it wasn't thrust in their faces, things would settle.

Jack fared better. Several shipmates slapped him on the back. Some shook his hand, and others cared neither one way nor the other. By the time they left the tavern they knew the way had been cleared for Millie to return with her child.

Next morning, filled with anticipation, Fanny rode the cart with Joe. Arriving at last, she climbed down in a hurry, thanking him with a pot of bramble jelly, and quickly ran the few yards down the track to the cottage. As Joe moved off, he saw the door was opened even before she reached it, and a smiling but tired looking Ada, ushered her in.

"They're well, they're both well, come in." Fanny greeted both Ada and Beattie, giving them a hug and murmuring her thanks. She followed them into the small warm room that was Millie's 'lying in' room, although Millie assured them all she wouldn't be 'lying in' for long.

"A few days perhaps, then I want to get back to normal as quick as I can." Fanny kissed her, and Beattie agreed to her statement, providing she got plenty of rest.

"How are you maid, my you look alright, rosy cheeks an' that." Her relief brought tears of joy to her eyes, as she squeezed Millie's hand and stepped over to the basket for her first look at her grandchild.

"She's beautiful," she whispered, bending low for a closer look at the sleeping infant, "such fair skin, 'er eyes will be same colour as yours I'll bet."

"Pick 'er up Ma, go on, pick 'er up, it won't 'urt if she wakes! Go on Ma."

Millie was excited, well pleased with herself and so proud!

"What you going to call 'er then?" said Fanny turning back to Millie. This brought her to a halt; she hadn't been able to think of anything that seemed to fit.

"I'm not going to name her 'til it comes into me head an' sounds right, I'll call 'er babby for now."

"What a lovely Christmas present. You know Christmas day is just over two weeks away don't you?" Fanny murmured, as she gently rocked the tiny mite in her arms, "You could call 'er Mary, or Ivy"

"No Ma," said Millie with a smile, "I'll think of something; something *different* like." Fanny smiled to herself thinking, *let's 'ope it's not too high falutin. One of Millie's specials!* Instead she said, "Yes, I do believe she's going to 'ave your colouring, there's already a soft covering of golden down." Fanny stroked the tiny head with her forefinger. She wished with all her heart that Jack could see the tiny mite. Millie guessed her Ma's thoughts

"Don't worry Ma, I'll 'ave me money from me work. I'm getting paid afore Christmas, an' I got another finished order to go back too, so we can wrap up, and get over to see me Pa before too long. "She smoothed the cheek of her little one who was resting contentedly in her grandmother's arms, closed eyes fringed with golden lashes. Fanny laid her gently in the warm basket, and tucked the covers around her.

They chatted happily for some time, Beattie filling Fanny in on all the details of Millie's labour and straightforward delivery. Millie gazed from one to the other - she couldn't see herself sharing that sort of information with anyone - but she knew how the two of them loved to gossip. It was quite nice being the centre of attention! Things would be back to normal soon enough, but deep inside she knew they would never be the same again.

Millie looked again at her babby, knowing she was dressed in her new nightgown and wrapped in her pure white shawl, tucked warmly under her new bed covers. She felt suddenly overwhelmed with the prospect of having such responsibility, but quickly remembered all the help that was at hand. Looking again at her Ma, she knew that even when Beattie left, her Ma would never be too far away.

Ada called them to the kitchen, though Millie stayed propped up in her bed; it was time for a late meal. They shared a dinner of winter vegetables, with meat from a well covered, well stewed hambone, along with wedges of fresh baked bread. One way or another they had all built up good appetites. The stew was one of Ada's specials and had been simmering since early morning; just the thing to set Fanny up for the rough walk back, and build up the strength of the new mother. Ada remarked amid laughter, "Millie lost her appetite and found a donkey's."

Fanny stayed a while longer, but with the clouds filling in and thickening and the temperature dropping, she took her leave to begin the return journey. She was mindful of telling Jack every detail; going over it all in her head so she would forget nothing. Millie had said it wouldn't be too long into the New Year, before she would make the journey home. She had money, which ensured that she was able to ride the cart with the little one as soon as Beattie gave the go ahead and weather allowed.

In the week before Christmas Ada's cottage was filled with the sound of happy chatter, along with the special warmth a baby brings.

As soon as Millie felt strong enough, she helped Beattie pull dark green Ivy from the garden wall and pick mistletoe from the low branches of the old apple tree.

The holly, with its red berries was gathered from the hedgerow close by, and extra logs stacked in the hearth. It was a slow business with neither Ada nor Millie able to work quickly. Enthusiasm helped the tasks along.

Extra Christmas fare was brought from the storeroom and cellar, in the form of a rich pudding made weeks before, a collection of bottled fruits and chutneys and Ada's favourites, pickled beetroot and shallots. Bread was baked, and a fruit loaf sealed in greased muslin. As they looked over the celebratory fare, and the decorated cottage, Millie felt that the preparations for the child's first Christmas did them credit.

Sadly, Beattie had to leave them several days before Christmas. Returning to Axminster where her own family were waiting to welcome. There a tired Beattie would be drawn into the warmth and celebrations of her own home, and in turn looked after by her husband and married daughter.

Millie took well to motherhood, seeming to know instinctively the child's needs. But Ada's health in the colder weather worried her greatly. She was much relieved when a week into the New Year, Beattie, already concerned for her sister, reappeared.

Between them they reached the conclusion it would be safer for Ada to return to Axminster, and be looked after in Beattie's home for the remaining winter, and possibly beyond. In effect this meant that the proposed 'visit' home for Millie would almost certainly come earlier than at first thought. If the tenancy of Ada's cottage was eventually relinquished Millie knew all her possessions would once more have to be moved on.

In the four months or so that she had spent with Ada, she had become truly fond of her and goodbyes would be tinged with sadness, knowing there was the possibility of not seeing the old lady again. Ada, for her part had become pleasantly used to the kindness and company of the gentle girl with her happy contented babe, and knew just how much she would miss them.

As soon as a mild spell was on them they said their tearful goodbyes, with Beattie's assurance that they would still be renting for a while yet, at least until decisions could be made.

Millie, carrying her child well wrapped up against any chill, her Hessian bag with a change of clothes and her baby's things slung over one shoulder, picked her way carefully up the track to the toll road, to await Joe's morning cart.

Filled with excitement at the thought of seeing her family, and showing off the precious bundle in her arms, she had reached the toll road when the sound of horse's hooves on the stony track made her look in the opposite direction.

Into sight rode a familiar figure. Her first thought was that Danny was coming to see them. As the distance closed, it appeared to be a well dressed rider, on a good horse. *It couldn't be.* She stared as they came closer. She couldn't move. She was rooted to the spot. The rider pulled to a halt beside her. Quickly he dismounted and stepped up to her.

"Millie, I heard... when I saw you at the trial. I thought... and I was right. Are you well? Is this - my child?" Gerard babbled. There was no other word for it. Millie's heart turned over. She searched his face.

"You were the *only* one. I think you know that. You can look on her, this once, and I thank you for what you did for me Pa... Then I don't want to see you again." Gerard reached to take her hand, but instead pulled the cover from the child's face. A lump came to his throat as he stared down into blue eyes, fringed with golden lashes.

"Millie, believe me" – she cut him short, "I did – once," she whispered staring into his brown eyes; eyes that seemed to have lost the twinkle she remembered.

Hearing the rumble of wheels, she turned away before he could answer. The cart drew up and Joe jumped to the ground. Millie was glad to see him and pushed past Gerard, who had taken a step closer to her.

She greeted Joe and paid her fare. Joe took the child and the bag, whilst she scrambled aboard. He cast a glance at the Squire's son and doffed his cap, wondering the while, why he was here, talking to Fanny's girl.

Gerard moved back and watched as the carter returned the sleeping child to Millie's arms. Climbing up to his seat, he took the reins again. She refused to look back as they pulled away. Knowing only that she was glad she thanked him for helping her Pa.

"An' I thank 'im for you too," she whispered quietly into the warm cheek of the child, *but now I'll not think on 'im again!* Gerard stared after them; his was the remorse and regret and now it was too late!

The warmth of the child in her arms, and the assured welcome of her family kept Millie company for the remainder of her ride home.

The cart trundled down to the harbour. Millie, lost in thought, felt that things would 'pan out' as her Ma said, and coming to a standstill, climbed down, calling her thanks to Joe who handed her bag down to her. Adjusting the child in her arms she began walking.

The close proximity of the sea, the sound of the shifting shingle and cry of the gulls, welcomed her home. As she walked, she told herself she need not worry. Her skills as a dressmaker and designer of bonnets would always afford them a living. There was no question; she had no need to worry about looking after her daughter. As long as the sisters had their business she would have a job. With these thoughts in mind, she realised that she must pay a visit to the shop sooner rather than later.

Eagerly approaching her old home, the door flew open and Jack's surprised face quickly gave way to smiles. He gathered them into the warm room. Even Jamie's curiosity was such that he couldn't wait to greet the new babby, and of course his big sister. Fanny had seen Millie alight from the cart and leaving the harbour followed, arriving close on Millie's heels.

"I 'oped you'd come girl, soon as the frost gave over for a bit. Seems set now for a mild spell." Standing in the warm kitchen they were all talking at once, and peeping at the still sleeping mite, Fanny gave them both another welcoming hug.

"Jack, take 'er cloak and settle 'em by the fire, it's still January, even if it 'as got a bit milder." Millie looked around – it was good to be home. The warm room buzzed with chatter as Millie told them all her news. Later, the meal over, the new addition to the family was fed and placed in a small drawer which would double as a cot, and which Fanny had emptied and made ready with her own clean linen, for whenever they turned up.

Millie tucked the child up with her shawl and gazed into the fire. So much had happened since this time last year; she couldn't help but wonder what this time *next* year would bring!

After Joe had delivered the news of the birth of Millie's child, Danny's thoughts of her betrayal were pushed away. He knew he had no right to feel that way, and immediately asked after them. Joe's cheerful attitude made acceptance easier in some ways. Emily would be the one who would be shocked. Danny knew that he should tell her straight away, and gently too. He knew that as Millie's friend, she would be hurt to be last to know. He was right.

She had asked many times after her friend and not been told of Millie's circumstances. It was difficult enough with them both working and Millie over on Broad Street, but then moving even further away without even saying goodbye. How could she have done that?

Although guessing her friend had problems, she was hurt by Millie's lack of confidence in her ability to keep a secret. She had even dared to guess what that secret might be. Danny had simply shrugged and changed the subject. When he eventually told her the truth she was still shocked. Danny held up his hands.

"Don't look at me like that Emily, I'm not to blame."

"No? But I still don't know why she couldn't trust *me*. I can understand why she moved away, an' I think it's brave to come home with her babby. But I still can't quite believe it of her."

She watched as Danny pushed a stone around with the toe of his boot.

"It's hit you 'ard too, 'asn't it?" Emily moved to touch his arm. Danny took a swipe at the stone, sending it skimming across the yard before he turned on his heel.

Moving to the empty stable, he took off his jacket and grabbed a rake. He began strenuously mucking out, losing himself in the job at hand.

It was true; Millie's return with a child had hit Danny hard. As long as he didn't see them he could pretend it hadn't happened. But now she was at home, how long before he was confronted with it? At this moment he didn't even want to think about it.

Emily followed him, but he didn't want Emily's sympathy. He threw the rake to one side as a lump came to his throat. Grabbing his jacket he rushed to the ladder leading up to the hay loft climbing swiftly upward to the eves where he slept. Slinging his jacket onto a straw bale he threw himself down on his pallet and gazed at the rafters.

He must have been there for some time. It was growing dark, he was cold, and the first sound he was aware of, was Emily's voice calling, "Danny, Danny are you awake? Come on down, I've poured cider for us, an' there's a bite to eat." He sat up and listened in the dark. Emily too, listened from her place at the bottom of the ladder.

"Danny." she called again. Still there was silence. She turned away. He reluctantly got up, brushing the straw from his clothes and pulling on his jacket, he slowly descended. Walking to the horse trough he sluiced his face with water, and raked his fingers through his hair. Crossing the yard he made his way to the back door.

Pushing it open he saw Emily disappearing into the bar with a tray of food. Danny sat down at his accustomed place at the kitchen table, and tried to make sense of the thoughts tumbling around in his head.

As the bar door swung open and Emily re- entered the kitchen, the first thing Danny noticed was her wide smile. He never usually felt guilty when Emily was around, and it wasn't her fault that Millie had turned him down.

"Here you are Danny 'ave a slice of me meat pie." Offering him the dish and pushing a tankard of cider towards him, he suddenly realised how hungry he was. Why couldn't every one be as straight forward as Emily?

She rested a hand on his shoulder, saying quietly, "You know I'm 'ere if you want to talk. I know you're feelin' bad about the way things 'ave turned out, but I'm 'ere for you Danny. She smiled again. Danny helped himself to another tankard of cider - and then another...

How long Danny had been with Emily in her small room up in the eaves, it was hard to say. She wouldn't have finished work until mid-night, or even later. He judged it to be around four, when he woke. His heart sank; what on earth had made him fall into her arms? Or more to the point her bed! He thought back through a fuddled brain. *Cider; how many tankards I downed I don't dare think on*. His head ached and his conscience was pricking him.

He turned to see the outline of Emily beside him in the narrow bed. He felt for his clothes. Perhaps he'd passed out! But no, she wouldn't have been able to get him across the yard *and* up the ladder to his own pallet that was for sure. Maybe all was well, maybe not, but he had to make a bolt for it now.

He edged toward the window, where a glimmer of moonlight lit the chair beside it. His clothes and boots were there. Slipping his shirt over his head, pulling on his trousers, and picking up his boots, he tiptoed quietly to the door, down the back stair, and out through the quiet kitchen. Once he was safely outside, he made for the ladder, and swiftly climbed up to the hayloft. Nothing stirred; the only sound was the soft whickering of the horse in the stable immediately below.

Danny threw himself down on his pallet which felt excessively cold after the warmth of Emily's bed. He did his best to keep warm, tugging an old horse blanket over his meagre coverings. He would try to get another couple of hours sleep before his early start in the morning.

Later that day when Emily brought ale, Danny was unable to meet her eye, but Emily was having none of that.

"See you later Danny," she whispered as she took the empty tankards, Abraham watched as Danny coloured up.

"Don't 'e go messing wi' Emily if you'm not gone on 'er," he mumbled.

Danny felt a pang; they were both grown, weren't they? But Abraham putting it into words endorsed his own feelings - if he were honest. He could think of nothing to say, and walked over to where the brewer's wagon was drawing to a halt in the yard.

Mr Murkin came out to oversee the barrels of ale, as the drayman rumbled them off the wagon, and down the planks into the cellar to the waiting cellar man. Then Flynn arrived on one of his errands, delivering sharpened tools and various iron parts back to Abraham, from his work with the blacksmith.

Danny threw himself into work, holding the bridle of the great shiny black horse, talking softly to calm the beast, while watching his childhood friend with renewed interest. Flynn's competent hands checked over the great iron horseshoes, and Danny was glad of the easy chat between them as he stared at the great hooves of the dray horse. He sifted back through early memories, when he and Flynn, just two years older than himself, had watched in awe, as the great horses lifted their feet in turn, to allow the blacksmith to nail the still steaming hot, dull shoe onto their hooves.

Just for a moment he smelled the dense pungent smoke given off as the shoe was seated. Watched the glow from the forge, felt the heat as red hot horse shoes were beaten into shape on the anvil, and heard the hiss of steam as they were quenched in the long bosh, running the length of the forge.

If the truth be told Danny was a little bit envious of Flynn, and always looked forward to his own working visits every three weeks or so. They usually led one or maybe two horses, down to the smithy on Broad Street, where he would hang around as they were shod in the dusty acrid interior of the black smiths shop.

Now the horse stood patiently waiting to be stabled, and Danny selected a fresh horse to be harnessed up to the massive wagon, before they could continue their deliveries. At last he waved off the drayman, and then Flynn. He led the now quiet and comfortable dray horse back to be rested. Horses came and horses went. Later the Stage Coach completed its changeover, and by the evening Danny had put away all thoughts of guilt. Abraham had no right speaking out. He'd wait and see what happened!

He didn't have long to wait. Sure enough in the bar later that night, Emily's extra attention was obvious. Mr Murkin too noticed the change, and heaved a sigh, thinking that either they would get together and make a go of it, or one of them would get hurt and leave, which meant upheaval. Mister Murkin disliked intensely the upheaval of finding fresh help.

CHAPTER TWENTY EIGHT

Millie glanced out of the window of her childhood home, watching as the seagulls swooped and circled over the harbour, she intended to make sure her own child gathered happy childhood memories, as she had been allowed to.

Millie returned to the job in hand and finished getting ready, before turning her attention again to the child. Checking she had layers of warm petticoats under a flannelette nightgown, she tucked a soft muslin sheet closely around her, and wrapped her snugly with the soft, warm shawl; overlaid with the small outdoor blanket, they were ready.

Earlier she had announced her intention to go over to the shop, to show her employers her new daughter. The opportunity to better herself, she hoped would now extend to her child. But that was way into the future.

She felt quite nervous and her Ma noticed. Everything had changed; absolutely nothing could ever be the same again; but as Fanny said, "There's only one thing for it, you just start again from now; an' make the best o' things." Jack looked at them both, realising that his 'little girl' had gone for good. In her place he had a beautiful grown daughter and a lovely grandchild - who still had no name!

"You've to think of a name for her. Child will think 'babby' *is* her name." He smiled. Millie had in fact given it a great deal of thought, and then quite suddenly decided.

It would be one of her very first choices. Now, might be as good a time as any to make her final decision known.

"Amelia," she said, looking straight at her Pa. Turning to Fanny she said again; "Amelia, that's what I'm calling 'er."

"Oh my stars Jack, I knew she'd come up with something fancy." Fanny sat down.

"She's my babby an' I'm giving 'er a nice name," said Millie with a wide smile, I just bin waiting 'til I was sure."

"But where on earth did you get that from luv? It's a bit of a mouthful."

It had made exactly the impact that she had intended. Now she could introduce her child properly.

"No it's not Ma - I'll shorten it to Amy, but her full an' proper name is Amelia. I got it from an old news sheet, about London people an' such. Beattie had it wrapped round something at the cottage, an' I liked the sound of it. So Ma, Pa, this is Amelia Drew."

Fanny quickly recovered herself and taking the child from Millie's arms, kissed her small forehead saying, "Hello little Amy, we best get you christened before your mammy thinks of anything else."

Taking the child from her Ma, she bid them goodbye and set off with her precious bundle in her arms. She was both excited, and yet dreading the moment when she would see her employers after so long. Walking along the shingle as she had done so many times before, she thought it strange that Danny hadn't been down to see them. He must be busy, and Emily too. The thought struck her that she couldn't possibly go up to the Coaching Inn; what if she saw... him? No, Danny would be down soon, and Emily was probably waiting until she came down to market. She would call in soon.

Reaching the square, and about to cross the road, Millie heard her name called. It was a surprise when Ned the butcher's boy came out into the street.

"You're alright then Millie? We 'eard about, well let's 'ave a look at the little un then." Millie paused, she was pleased that Ned had spoken; it was a bit of an ordeal walking out in public this end of town. Ned stepped over to them, pulling the shawl back from the child's face. "As it got a name yet?" he enquired,

"Yes, 'er name's Amelia." There, she had said it, and it sounded exactly right. She was just about to continue when a high pitched voice broke in...

"Ned, get away in 'ere, don't go wasting our time with that bad maid."

Any pleasure that she had felt from Ned's friendly greeting, was quickly washed away. She knew she had to be prepared for unkind, as well as friendly words, and so contented herself by giving old man Samuel's wife a 'look,' holding her head high and crossing over the road.

Drawing level with the shop window she saw a customer inside, and wanting to create a grand solo entrance, strolled on a little further. Slowing her steps she turned to walk back, as the customer left pulling the door closed behind her.

Millie recognised the wife of Mr Lane the school master. Her heart sank as she walked towards her. What reception would she get this time?

"Hello Millie, may I peep at your baby? We heard you were both doing well, and you certainly look it."

"Thank you kindly, Mistress Lane, yes we are well. This is Amelia." Millie turned the shawl back, and Mistress Lane clucked over the gurgling child.

"That's a nice name dear, she's so sweet. I'll tell Mister Lane that I've seen you; Good morning." She proceeded on her way.

Millie's confidence was restored. Pushing against the door, she stepped inside and looked around. It seemed so long since she was here.

She breathed in deeply. Still the special smell of new fabrics and lavender pomade Miss Mabel insisted on, to keep the place fresh for her clientele.

Suddenly Miss Sybil's head came up from behind the counter. The expression on her face was something to behold, as Millie later related to Fanny.

"My dear Millie, come, let me look at you both! Oh my dear, let me see your little one. What a beautiful child. Oh Mabel, come out here and see who it is." Miss Sybil rounded the counter and Miss Mabel came hurrying from the workroom. Stopping in her tracks, she gazed at Millie and her small bundle. By now Millie's arms were aching, and she was relieved that Miss Sybil was now taking the child from her, and she stretched her arms gratefully.

"That's the furthest I've carried 'er, an' she gets 'eavier all the time"

"I'm sure." Mabel smiled. "We are so pleased to see you. I'll turn the key for a few minutes; come into the kitchen and sit down. Oh what a lovely surprise, we wondered if you would – or rather *when* you would come."

Now it was Miss Mabel's turn, reaching out eager arms, "Let me hold her now Sybil," then staring at

Millie, "I can't believe you're really here." The sisters clucked over the baby, firing questions about their wellbeing, and when the child had actually arrived.

"Two weeks before Christmas? Well that would make her birthday the eleventh day of December, you must remember that Millie." Absently Miss Mabel said "put the kettle on dear," and it seemed as though she had never been away.

Settling the child on her lap, conversation continued, until they heard the doorbell. Miss Sybil jumped up and moved toward the door.

"Oh dear, she exclaimed, "we've forgotten that we have a business to run, the door is still locked. You stay here Mabel and I will go through and reopen the shop."

In a slightly anxious tone, Millie enquired "was me work alright? I'm going to get right back into it as soon as I can."

"Yes it has been most satisfactory Millie. That reminds me; there is a fresh order for you. Two bonnets awaiting your attention."

"If the order note and materials are put together, I'll take it with me now. I've got time later this afternoon and evening. Oh but I mustn't keep you from work," Millie stood up to go.

"Nonsense, you haven't been here two minuets, stay a little longer," Miss Mabel smiled. "You're to have that cup of tea before you walk back. Sit down dear, you haven't told us what you have called her yet." Millie welled up with pride.

"I've named her Amelia," she said with a flourish.

"Amelia, what a wonderful name, so unusual, is she to take your name dear? Drew I mean, or?"

"Oh yes, Amelia Drew, I'll 'ave 'er Christened like, that's if, well you know..."

"Quite so dear, I understand. Now, I shall take over from Miss Sybil, I have finished my tea, and she can talk to you again before you go." She passed Amelia back to her young mother and got up to take her cup into the scullery, calling to Sybil as she moved back into the shop.

Millie looked around her. Did they really mean it when they said she could come back to work here? They'd said nothing yet. Miss Sybil came back and seemed quite impressed with the child's name.

"Mabel told me, and I think you have chosen well," she took the baby again. Millie quickly took the teapot from the range where it was keeping hot, and poured her a fresh cup of tea.

"I 'ave to go back to Cifftops soon, but if it's alright I'd like to call again, just for a short while, I may have the order finished."

"We would very much like that, and the order would be a bonus. But you mustn't worry, it's not too urgent. I suppose you will be having Amelia christened soon?" Millie was caught off guard; they both seemed to think it important,

" I don't know if I can get her christened in church, proper like, not being married and that, but we 'ave to think about it yes."

Making ready for the walk back, she took her leave with a light heart. They'd certainly been pleased to see her, but hadn't said a word about her taking up her old job again!

When Millie arrived back at the cottage there was only her Pa, piling wood on the fire, he bid her come in and sit close, to get warm.

"Were they pleased to see you then maid?"

"Oh yes, an' I got another order too. I'll just warm through for a minute, then I 'ave to go upstairs an' feed Amy," she said importantly.

Later with a full tummy, the child became sleepy and Millie returned to the fireside, settling her into the drawer beside the hearth.

"It looks like she'll grow out o' that soon enough; me an' old Lazurus 'ave bin thinking of making 'er a cradle. You know, big enough for 'er to grow into, what do you think?

"I think that's a lovely idea Pa, thank you," Millie moved closer to where he was sitting. Slipping her arm around his neck, she lightly kissed his cheek.

"Pa, you bin so good to us, not going for me an' that. I know I done wrong, an' the worst part of it was bringing shame on you an' Ma; an' there's something else too. I want you to know that even though I met..." she hesitated; it was so hard to say. She tried again and stumbling, said quickly, "even though I met Clive what's 'is name, 'e don't feel like no father, not like you Pa." Jack cut in, "I know, I know girl," he patted her arm.

"No Pa I got to say it. I *got* to say it - to me you *are* me real father, an' I'll always love you an' Ma. I got above meself an' I'm sorry if I caused you pain."

She sat beside him her arm still around his neck as she had done when she was small. She felt small now... Her Pa Jack had never once mentioned to her the incidents of her meetings with her blood father. The near silence was warm and comforting, just Amelia's gentle almost inaudible breathing and the occasional crackle of the fire. Jack patted her hand and said nothing, there was no need, and all was well.

Fanny breezed into the cottage.

"My, it's enough to freeze yer eyes shut down by the sea wall, an' 'ow did *you* get on girl? an' Jack, 'ave you 'ad anything to eat yet? Where's Jamie? Millie, fry up these sprats with some tattie's - in the big pan."

"All 'ands on deck," said Jack jumping to his feet grinning, "Ma's 'ome, look lively! An' no I've not 'ad anything to eat, an' I 'aven't set eyes on Jamie." Fanny smiled, thinking once again how much she would miss them when Jack went back to sea, and Millie moved on again.

While the sprats and potatoes slices were spitting in the pan, and the lovely smell filled the cottage, Millie in answer to her Ma's first question said, "Oh yes, but before I got there I saw Ned. He came out and was talking to me, 'til butcher Samuel's wife called to 'im that I was a bad maid. I think I was supposed to 'ear; still Mistress Lane was kind, and she loved babby's name."

"Then get in the habit of using it luv. Didn't I say there'd be bad remarks, as well as good? Take no notice of 'em, they'll get over it, it'll be someone else the morrow. What about the Miss Hartnells, 'ow did they receive you?"

"Oh they were lovely too, they were so kind and they loved Amelia, an' they loved the name an' all, but they didn't say come back to work."

"Trouble with you girl, is you want it all cut an' dried in five minutes you do." Millie sighed, "You're right, I 'ave to give 'em time, an' if it don't pan out I can always work on me own from 'ere!"

Jack and Fanny stared open-mouthed. That was Millie; close one avenue and she simply altered course, she hadn't changed at all, lost nothing of her spirit, for all that had gone before. They smiled at each other and

Jack said quietly, "Let's get dinner on the plates, I'm starving."

Later on, when the table was cleared and Jamie had breezed in, eaten his barely warm meal and breezed out again, Jack wandered down to the quay, and Millie followed her Ma to the scullery.

"I 'ad a talk with Pa," she began quietly, "an' I decided I won't be wantin' to see the other one again." Fanny heaved a sigh of relief, remembering the last conversation she had with Clive.

Almost two weeks had slipped by since the day Millie came home with the baby. With Jamie in and out of jobs, and Jack home all the time, the cottage began to feel a bit crowded.

Fanny did her best to keep things in order, but with all the washing that Millie had to do, and day after day of rain, the place was always draped with wet clothes.

The piles of drift wood and anything else that would burn was piled in the yard, the old sacking doing a poor job of keeping it dry. The hearth too was piled up with sticks, and planks, and peelings, all set to dry out and feed the hungry much needed fire.

Millie felt that she really must get back again to see the situation at 'Clifftops. Talking it over, it was decided that she would go back as soon as she could make ready and borrow a hand - cart. It would mean going the long way round, but money was getting tight.

Jack seemed to gather strength every day, and it would soon be time to get duties on a suitable vessel, and get back to sea. Fanny's heart sank, but much as she was used to managing on next to nothing, the thought of the return of another income didn't go amiss, even though

James brought in the occasional windfall, about which she asked no questions.

Jack intended his first voyage to be a short run if he could get one, just to settle him back gently. He had already made enquiries, but truth to tell, the call of the sea had been nagging at him these last weeks, and he certainly wasn't ready to take a landlubber's job. He reckoned he had a good few more seagoing years in him yet.

The sea was in his blood, but the smell and the feel of the prison, where he had come near to losing his life, either by the gallows or the prison fever, had not quite left him. Once he could get back to sea, the familiar ship life and distance involved would complete the cure.

Before going back to Clifftops, Millie packed up the finished bonnets and set out to see the sisters again. This time she would tell them about Beattie taking Ada back to Axminster, and that very likely the tenancy of the cottage might not be renewed.

She needed to know how she stood, if only to make her own plans. Sitting in the back room at the shop, Amelia in a shallow box with a cushion for a mattress, Millie talked of her work.

Miss Mabel interrupted, "we hoped you would come back to us. We didn't want to push you to soon after the baby was born. It has been quite hard, managing without your usual amount of input and output, and just look at her; she'll be no trouble at all." They looked at the child gurgling happily, draped in her shawl, the picture of contentment. Suddenly Millie began laughing.

"Look at 'er, my babby's just as happy in a box. She's already bin in an apple basket, an' a drawer, but next she's getting a real cradle. Pa an' Lazurus are finishing it off now."

She looked at Miss Mabel smiling, "Is it really alright for me to come back 'ere? I know we talked about it, but if anything 'appens to change your mind, folks talking or anything, I'll understand."

"Nonsense, nothing will change our minds. Sybil, I'm asking Millie if she's ready to come back to us. What do you say?" Miss Sybil appeared in the doorway.

"I say sooner rather than later, we certainly don't seem to be getting the orders out as promptly, since she left us." Miss Mabel looked back at Millie.

"Why take all your things back to Charmouth? Leave everything here; just go back to see what the situation is, and if there is anything you can do there. You said they might just be packing things up. When you load your own stuff from Ada's cottage it can either go to your mothers, or be brought straight here." Millie was overjoyed.

"I'm sure I can sort everything out in the next few days, after that I can move back here again. But - well Amelia does cry sometimes, what if she bothers you?"

"We'll cross that bridge when we come to it. At the moment it's important that we get the place running at full tilt again."

All three of them were excited about the imminent changes.

Mabel was convinced, "They will keep us young, there's enough revenue from the shop to look after us all. She's the answer to our prayers you know." If Millie had known their thoughts, she might have added that she certainly didn't seem to be the answer to anyone else's!

"They're a couple of surprises those two if you ask me," Fanny remarked, when Millie reached home and related her plans, "but I suppose they can afford to 'cock a snook' at the town what with there being nowhere else to buy nice dresses, or material. You best get back to Ada and Beattie, we'll see you again when everything's sorted out, an' we'll keep yer other things safe till we see you.

Next day Millie tucked Amy into her drawer, and secured her firmly onto the small hand cart that had been borrowed for the occasion.

Packing up the old hessian bag, she left the rest to be fetched later when needed. But first Millie would have to find out if she was still wanted. At Clifftops everything was in turmoil. It had been just on two weeks, but in that time everything had either been packed up or sold on.

Down in Charmouth village, Beattie had arranged for the local junk shop to collect most of the old furniture, which fetched a few coins. Much of Ada's old ragged clothes and unwanted cheap and worn out furnishings, went to the rag and bone man. The few things to be taken to Beattie's home were packed, and piled in the downstairs rooms, leaving them only a bed to share, two chairs and just enough utensils and pots to see them over, until Millie's return.

Millie was never gladder to see Clifftops, her arms ached from pushing the hand cart and wrenching it over uneven ground, and the muscles in her legs threatened to cease up. Whatever had possessed her to try walking? Joe's cart fare would have been money well spent.

She walked into the cottage with the child in her arms, knowing full well she couldn't have made the journey between Lyme and Charmouth many times *that* way, and collapsed onto an upright chair. Beattie greeted her saying, "You look done in maid, give me the babby and get yer breathe back; I'll get you a mug o' water."

She got to her feet with Amy on her shoulder, and went to the scullery calling, "I'm sorry it's like this for you to come back to, but I thought I'd best get it all done quick and take Ada home with me, she's no better. You can stay for another week or so if need be, there's food an' firewood, an' you can use the shaky down. Just leave it behind. Your quilt is still there, don't forget. The wagon's coming for us, and the rest of the things to take back to Axminster day after the morrow." Beattie felt bad, but Millie quickly set her mind at rest.

"I've just come to stay as long as you need me, until you move on Beattie. I'll catch Joe at the first opportunity and take my things back to Broad Street, where I used to work; you remember I told you about my attic room? We can go back it's all arranged. Me an' babby, we're going to be alright." Beattie was relieved.

"Good, good, you've done a good job here. Now, come an' sit by the fire an' feed little one, there's a cushion on the rug there. She looks like she's doing well." Peering at the child with a practised eye, she said "she's thriving, filling out she is. Has she got a name yet?" She looked Millie up and down "Aye an' you are a picture of health an' all; tell me what yer folks said when you got there! An' how's that brother of yours?

Millie proudly told Beattie the name she had chosen, and how she had arrived at it, and answering her other questions they chatted for a while, till Beattie sighed saying, "Now it just remains for me to get Ada 'ome and well again, an' we'll *all* be sorted out. Yes you did a good job looking after old Ada; she's missed both of you this last week or so, she really 'as."

Stepping over to where Ada was dozing in the one comfortable chair, Millie, crouching down on her hunkers, gently wakened the old woman and placed Amy on her lap, still gently holding on to her.

"See Ada - this is Amelia Drew. I said I'd have a name for her by the time I saw you again, now she's got a nice name, an' she's going to be christened too! Do you like the name I gave 'er? The old woman smiled, feeling the warmth of the child on her lap, before she slipped back into a world where her own children played around her, "Papa's in the fields" she murmured as she slipped back into sleep. Millie looked worried, but Beattie took the child saying, "She's back an' forth, back an' forth, that's why I need to get 'er 'ome." Millie nodded, "I'll be ready to leave soon as Joe can take me; an' I want to thank you too, for taking me in an' looking after us both."

"Well now," said Beattie with a slight break in her voice, "everything's worked out for the best an' we done each other a favour, didn't we maid?"

The time was spent making ready to close up the cottage for the move, and the last of the vegetables were rescued from the garden. As soon as the wagon appeared the following day, everything left was piled on, and Ada and Beattie were ready to return to Axminster. All their goodbyes were said amid hugs and handshakes, and Millie watched and waved as they faded into the distance.

The next day Joe would call by, and Millie waited with baby Amy for the noon cart. It would take them and the small hand cart and her few possessions, back to her Ma. She wandered through the rooms again. Already the cottage had taken on a chill, and Millie was relieved when she heard wheels rumbling down the track.

She gathered Amy into her arms, along with the bag that she had brought with her, and picked up the small sack filled with the last of the foodstuffs from the pantry, it was too hard come by to waste.

Her quilt and other possessions were on her hand cart already. Everything else had been consigned to the ash pit. Turning the large key in the old lock she slipped it under the crack beneath the door as she had been told, safe in the knowledge that Beattie had the only other key in her possession.

"Been all right then maid?" Joe called out. You're all of you leaving the old place then?

"Yes Joe, things change all the time," she looked at the old cottage that had been home to her during the biggest upheaval of her young life. A fleeting sadness washed over her, but she fixed her thoughts firmly on their future.

"Aye things change maid that they do." Joe jumped down to help. Millie had been a bit apprehensive about having the small hand cart with her, but Joe called out that it was no bother at all. Dropping the tail of his cart, he loaded it from the back and securing it, stacked her few possessions carefully. Swinging up her last bag, and grinning all over his weathered face, he watched as Millie settled herself with the child on her lap.

It was a comforting ride home, stopping occasionally to pick up or set down others, and eventually they reached the road down to the harbour. Joe reined in and Millie, along with her bags was deposited on the quay sooner than expected. Joe, agreeing to deliver the hand cart back to its rightful owner, would save her going out of her way in the opposite direction.

A cry of protest from Amy made Millie aware again of just how she was to manage a babby and three bags when she only had two hands! Leaving the bags beside the Cobb wall, she called to the women busy at work.

"Do you know where me Ma is?

"It's Fanny's girl" said one to the other.

"Aye maid, bring babby over while you're waiting on 'er, she's down along low wall, 'er won't be many minutes."

They cooed over the child in Millie's arms, exclaiming, "Ah just look at 'er liddle face," and generally fussing over her. Soon a surprised Fanny appeared, "You weren't away long this time," she called, and nodded to the other women, pleased that they had made such a fuss of her grandchild. Picking up the bags, they made their way back to the cottage.

"We won't be staying 'ere long, neither Ma." Fanny glanced at Millie's face and hoped that they were doing the right thing.

Privately Millie knew that she must get settled over at Broad Street before her Pa went back to sea, or Fanny might get to depend on her being at home again. She pushed her selfish thoughts from her, and the thought of returning to her attic room set her glowing.

The next few days were a mix of coming and going. First Fanny minded Amy, while Millie carried her bundles over to the shop, and Jack took the cradle. Then Miss Mabel watched over the child while things were put straight. Miss Sybil seemed to join in the spirit of excitement, and when all was put to rights, they stood back and admired their handiwork. For the first time in many a long day Millie actually felt at peace, and Amy either gurgled happily or slept through it all.

The only thing left to arrange now was her christening. How much of a problem was that going to be, and more importantly, could it be settled before her Pa went back to sea?

Before she knew it March was almost on them, with all the memories that it conjured up of the same time last year. Determined to keep busy, as if she didn't have enough to do, Millie threw herself into organising the christening, and with Fanny's help it was all arranged.

In the face of certain difficulties a retired non conformist preacher, well known to the Drew family, stepped in and agreed to perform the ceremony.

Millie's choice of place was the small stream above the harbour in the wooded undercliff. Once upon a time this would have been quite usual, but it had fallen out of favour. However in the circumstances it seemed to be the best way forward.

The early spring brought warm sunny days and it was on such a day, that Millie and Fanny visited Ely Hembrow with their request. All was arranged for the following Sunday providing it was dry.

There were no schedules to keep to, with Ely being a retired minister, and only the family and Ely's wife would be present, or so Millie thought. But what should she tell her employers? One thing she did know was that after all they had done for her they would have to know her plans, although she didn't think for a moment that they would want to be there.

She deliberately withheld them until the last minute in case she was faced with opposition. Early on Saturday afternoon, after turning the event over in her mind she came straight out with it.

"On the morrow I'm getting Amy christened."

The words fell like pebbles in a still pool. Miss Mabel stopped working, and looked first at Millie, and then at the child kicking happily in her cradle.

"How and where will this take place?" was all she said. Millie set down her work and rather uncomfortably explained the plan.

"We'll call at Ma's, gather the family, and walk up to Ely Hembrow's cottage. He's a retired minister. Ma knows 'im, and 'e'll take us through the woods to a stream, where 'e'll carry out the ceremony. Oh, an' it has to be a dry day. So if it's nice the morrow that's when it will be."

Millie's face was scarlet, she had been dreading this moment, and Miss Mabel was strangely silent.

"I see," she said at last "and Miss Sybil and I weren't to be invited, is that right?"

"Oh no - that's why I'll telling you now, but if I told you before it was all arranged, you might 'ave tried to talk me out of it, an' the Reverent Russell won't do it in the church 'cause I'm a sinner an' 'e wont 'ave me or me babby in 'is church!" She stopped for breath.

"I see," repeated Miss Mabel slowly, thinking just how uncharitable were his beliefs for a man of the cloth. She could only guess at Millie's feelings on being turned away from the Parish Church. No wonder she'd said nothing. "So let me get this right, if Miss Sybil and I would like to attend this, um ceremony, would we be welcome?"

"Oh yes you'd be more 'an welcome, only it will be a bit of a rough walk through the woods to the stream, an' I thought, you know, your nice boots an dresses an' that, but well, I'd really like you to come." she finished lamely.

"Well, now that you have explained the situation, I shall talk to Miss Sybil, and we'll see what she thinks." Later as Sybil came through to enquire the availability of a certain material, Mabel relayed Millie's plans. Her answering smile and agreement set Millie's mind at rest.

"So we are all going to have a very special day tomorrow."

"Oh yes, an' it will be even more special with you an' Miss Mabel along."

"Well, we shall be ready by whatever time you say, although we shall have to take the shorter route above town; I understand that you will call at your Mother's home first?"

"Yes an' we must all be at Ely Hembrow's cottage at the top of Cobb Hill at twelve noon." Miss Mabel assured her they would be on time and make their own way there.

Later, bidding them goodnight, Millie took the child upstairs to sleep, and continue with a certain project. She mounted the stairs, and lay Amy on her bed, whilst she went down again to fetch the cradle. Returning, she tucked her in, and picking up her needle and thread proceeded to sew small bows, made from oddments of white satin ribbon, down the front of Amy's clean nightgown. That finished, she laid it on the bed with her freshly washed shawl, and stepped back to admire it. The child slept peacefully.

Next morning preparations were made, and both Sybil and Mabel agreed that given Reverend Russell's stance, they had made their point by forgoing the usual Sunday morning service, in favour of Amy's day.

They lunched early, and left in good time to stroll across the top of town, meeting up with Millie's family at Ely's cottage. Lazurus was resting there too; having taken half the morning to walk the distance, for he had assured them that he wouldn't be left out.

Introductions were made, and Jack, with Jamie on his best behaviour, shook hands with the Miss Hartnells.

Fanny was especially pleased to see them, and spoke of her gratitude to them regarding Millie and Amy, vowing if there was anything she could ever do for them, they had only to ask.

When all were gathered, they set off into the woods and down a narrow track; walking for a short time they reached a fast flowing stream finding its way down to the sea. In a small clearing they stopped. Ely spread his arms wide, and looked up to the sky.

"Here is where we give thanks, here in the sight of God, surrounded by his handiwork." Ely indicated the woods, the wild flowers just beginning to appear, and again the sky above them. "Pass the child to me, and I shall name her and bless her, in God's own name."

Millie reverently and solemnly passed Amy to the old man, hoping silently that he wouldn't drop her.

"What do you name this child?" he looked at Millie, everyone looked at Millie, who took a deep breath and said, "Amelia-Francis-Ada- Drew"

Jack and Fanny stared at her. Millie beamed all round, and the old man carried on. Bending down with some difficulty, he reached for the water and dripped his wet fingers on to the child's forehead, making the sign of the cross, and clearly repeating her names. Amy let out a loud yell as the cold water dripped onto her face, which Ely ignored, as he continued the service. Uttering a last prayer, he handed the squirming infant back to her mother.

The service seemed to be complete, but the group were surprised and pleased, when Sybil took it on herself to start singing one of the old hymns, which everyone joined in. The first verse seemed to be repeated over and again by most of them, although the sisters were word perfect for all three verses. Everyone was happy, the ceremony ended, and they made their way in the early spring sunshine, back to Ely's cottage, amid thanks and happy chatter.

Millie bid the sisters farewell as they went their separate ways. Turning to go down to the harbour cottage with her family, she called that she would see them later on. Ely and his wife watched as the party left, having been thanked in time honoured fashion with gifts and the promise of a couple of free tankards of cider, when he next came down to the tavern. Ely still liked 'the demon drink'!

As Millie walked back with her family they took it in turns to carry little Amelia Francis Ada, "Whatever possessed you? Said Fanny, what does she need three names for?"

"I just got carried away. I wanted to call her something special, that's Amelia, an' then I wanted to give 'er your name, and well, Ada's sick an' I thought it would be nice to... I really wanted Beattie too but... "

"Yes we might 'ave known it wouldn't stop at one," said Fanny laughing. Jack smiled. He would be leaving for duties aboard ship in three days. He hadn't said as much yet, as he didn't want to spoil the lead up to the big day, but soon he would have to tell Fanny his news.

Home in the cottage Fanny, in answer to Millie's query about the legality of the ceremony, stated that although retired, Ely was still a man of God, and no matter where he prayed, or chose to marry, bury, or christen, it was as good as the unforgiving church any day.

"I just wanted 'er to be as good as anyone else," explained Millie, "an' everything was just perfect."

"It was maid, it was, and I was more than surprised to 'ear the sisters burst into song. I reckon they got good hearts an' souls those two. They've proved as much to you, but they tend to keep it well 'idden. I suppose it's 'cause they're in business, an' two women on their own can't be seen to be a soft touch."

The weeks wore on and they settled well into their routines. Such was the delight of Miss Mabel, who really enjoyed having a little one to tend, that she spent a great deal of her time fussing around the child, and was rewarded with happy smiles. Millie applied herself diligently to her work in order to make up for any distractions, thinking all the time of her providence, in the form of the sisters. Her child wanted for nothing, and their new life ran smoothly.

CHAPTER TWENTY NINE

Danny wandered down the cobbled streets, hands thrust deep into his pockets. He had escaped unnoticed, to spend his half day on his own. What an uncomfortable mess he'd made of things. He cut across to the top of town and walked down the hill, past the open front of the blacksmiths workshop. Wandering on down the hill, he crossed the square and took the path past Joshua's flour mill; raising his hand to the old man who stood at the upper storey door adjusting a pulley. On he walked, along the leat path that joined the river.

After some time he sat down on the river bank in the sunshine, head in hands. His thoughts wandered back over the events of the last year; a year that started out with high hopes of walking out with Millie. She was the only one he had ever felt the stirring of deeper feelings for, but she had not wanted him.

Her head had been filled with thoughts of someone else, someone he could never compete with. He and her family had watched helplessly, as she set her course firmly toward heartbreak. Dear Millie she loved nice things, new things. He knew when she had told him excitedly about her blood father, that her longing for fine things was probably inherited from him. Danny wondered idly if she would ever meet with him again.

He remembered when he had asked Millie to walk out with him. She had called him a 'particular dear friend'; he had wanted more than friendship. His eyes welled up as he visualised what could have been. Instead she was out of reach and with another man's child too! How could she, how could she have chosen a 'toff's' uncontrolled lust, over the security of his own steadfast love for her. He shook his head violently and grabbed a stick lying beside him, sending it flying through the air into the fast flowing river. Bright blue damsel flies hovered over golden celandines. He watched as the stick swirled away, before standing up and moving slowly on.

Then there was Emily, how he ached for the easy going friendship that they shared through their growing up years. He remembered the pranks they had played on each other, no wonder Abraham had tried to warn him off, he knew what was going to happen, even if Danny hadn't seen it coming. He had a feeling Emily had taken advantage of his state of mind, his unhappiness at Millie's plight. How could he have gone along with it? Even Flynn had tried to warn him against getting involved, and Mister Murkin wasn't at all happy now that the situation had worsened. Danny knew deep inside he was on a path to nowhere. His sadness and frustration at the situation he found himself in made the future look bleak.

Emily's demands had become more insistent; they should tell Mister Murkin; they should get wed; they should share Emily's room; they should visit Millie; and horror of horrors, they should tell her 'the good news'.

Danny turned on his heel and retraced his steps, he resolved to get it all sorted out. Hard work was the only thing that blotted out the tangled web that now was threatening to tie him to a life that he simply couldn't bring himself to settle for.

He knew it was impossible for him to seek out Millie in the present situation. He instinctively knew that she would never visit The Coaching Inn to see them. She would avoid at all costs the possibility of bumping into the father of her child. Something or someone would have to give, and in all probability it would be him.

Danny cringed daily, and awoke each morning steadfastly clinging to his independence and his hayloft sanctuary. He had tried many times to explain to Emily, in as kind a way as possible, that the short fling they had enjoyed wasn't meant to be the forerunner of a future together. Emily clung on. How long could he make excuses to avoid her whilst working in the same establishment?

After that one night in her room, when thankfully he had passed out, he'd vowed not to repeat it. But he had foolishly put himself into close proximity, seeking the comfort of her arms several more times. Most of Emily's romancing of their future was in her head, although he knew he hadn't been too reluctant with her kisses and cuddles, at first; He was a red-blooded young man after all.

Danny had tried to put things right, he had sat Emily down to have a chat, and try to clear the air. Now her usual smile had been replaced by a sad or sullen face. Any contact between them was carried out in an abrupt manner or silence. Danny was irritated by her reactions. She really had been the instigator of the so called 'romance' and he truly felt she had taken advantage of his unhappy state.

Mister Murkin eyed the situation from a distance. He had weighed it up and got it exactly right. In his opinion it could only continue to stir up more trouble. Danny knew Emily needed her job to send money home; Danny had no dependants and so decided to keep his eyes and ears open; with a view to moving on.

Help came from an unexpected quarter. Contact between the smithy and the inn stables was regular, and on one of his working visits Flynn's conversation took an unexpected turn.

"May not see you many more times," he mumbled as he joined Danny after delivering some sharpened tools across the yard to Abraham.

"'Ow's that then Flynn?" Danny replied.

"Going over to Seaton to 'elp me granddad. Me family want to keep on 'is farm; Pa's on 'is last legs now, though 'e's not old. Can't get 'is breath proper by all accounts, so farm's suffering. Ma an' me sisters can't manage without 'elp. It's only a pocket 'ankerchief but there's hens an' pigs; an' a pony an' cart to keep on road, I *'ave to* go."

A gleam of hope mixed with compassion for the predicament that Flynn found himself in, fleeted across Danny's face.

"Sorry to 'ear it mate." he mumbled,

"What about you?" continued Flynn, "will you wed Emily?"

"Not likely," Danny was adamant. "I got to leave 'ere, move on meself like! I bin a fool, but nothing's going to change unless I do something about it." Flynn seized on this immediately.

"Well maybe we can work it out between us." His face lit up. Danny was already turning over a possibility, he knew the smith well! Flynn ploughed on, the sooner he was sorted out the sooner he could go.

"Look, I already told 'im I've got to move on, but I got to wait 'til 'e finds somebody to take over like. When

I go back I'll tell 'im that you'll be interested, shall I? Then you can go down and talk to 'im yourself. I can't move on 'til 'e says, or I'll lose me money. An' I rent a couple 'o rooms off 'im. The 'ouse an' smithy go together. It's real cheap providing you puts in the long hours.

The two youths, Danny leaning on a yard brush and Flynn hands in pockets, and scuffing his heel on the ground, stood together for a moment in silence.

Danny drew in a low whistle.

"Flynn, you're a life saver, a chance to learn Blacksmiths trade, a fresh start an' somewhere to live, couldn't be better!

Mister Murkin looked out the back door at the pair of them, thinking they usually had a bit more life in them, when they got together. He wondered what was up.

The horses needed to be checked for loose shoes or provided with new ones. It was quite a responsibility, but one Danny had never had a problem with since he had grown big enough to handle them and relieve Abraham of the job. He would definitely voice the idea the day after the morrow, when he was again due to go down to the blacksmiths. He felt sorry for Flynn, but not so sorry that he couldn't rejoice in the unexpected turn of events.

Leading the great horses down the hill and into the yard, and tying them to the iron rings in the wall, Danny moved further into the dim premises of the smithy. There he found both Flynn and the blacksmith hard at work. Looking up, hammer in mid air, and pincers holding red hot iron on the anvil, the blacksmith passed them carefully over to Flynn to continue working them. Wiping his hands on his leather apron, he eyed Danny and the horses.

"What's all this then; you want to work 'ere along 'o me. What makes you think I want you?" Danny was unperturbed he was used to the smiths curt manner, knowing he could laugh along with the rest of them given the right circumstances.

"Yeah, I reckon I could do everything Flynn does once you showed me the ropes like."

The thought of training up another young lad again, when here was everything he needed and someone well known to him went a long way to making up the smiths mind, there and then. He really did need the strength and competence of a grown man to share his load. Danny he knew was a strong and willing worker, well used to handling the horses.

After a long pause as he deliberated, all the time eyeing Danny up and down, he said,

"Right, well it do seem sensible; so you work it out with old man Murkin, an' you an' Flynn 'ere can come to an agreement. Long as I don't lose time or money I'm easy. Flynn grinned as did Danny, taking the blacksmith's proffered hand which had been duly spat on; they all relaxed and started the business of shoeing the first horse.

On imparting the news back at the inn, Mister Murkin was not so well pleased although he was half expecting it. Secretly he had hoped that if one of them did leave his employ, it would be Emily that moved on. Young girls were cheap to take on, more pliable and easier to set in new ways. Still it looked like the choice had been made for him. Both he and Abraham would sorely miss Danny. Abraham couldn't help thinking about how long it would take to get the yard running smoothly again, with a new young 'un after he'd gone. Just as life was getting easier!

Danny could at last relax, now that he had secured a move he could think straight again. Getting things into perspective, his absence would allow Emily to get over the fantasies that she had built around them.

Agreeing to take over the rooms, Danny knew would take a bite out of his wage, but the work was better paid than the job he was leaving, and he had to live somewhere. Although tight at first, the way would be paved to earn better money as time went on. Flynn had always managed well enough, and often ate a meal with the smith and his good lady. It was a step up, and one that Danny now looked forward to.

On the day he left, Mister Murkin put on a good face and wished him well. The same couldn't be said for Emily who insisted on saying a cold 'goodbye Danny' whilst keeping her eyes firmly on the vegetables that she was peeling. Knowing that he would still be calling at intervals, he warmly shook Abraham's hand. It was in part, the old man's encouragement over the years that had given Danny the confidence to 'better himself.' He gripped the old man's hand knowing he had a lot to thank him for.

Danny heaved a sigh as he slung his bundle over his shoulder, and walked out of the yard for the last time as a stable lad. When he returned it would be in a different capacity entirely. He was all fired up for change.

The move to the smithy was achieved smoothly, and Danny found that although the work was hard, it was far more interesting than the day to day work in a stable yard. He found too that in conversation, the smith was an interesting and very knowledgeable man once he embarked on a subject. Danny found that showing his own interest, enabled him to glean much valuable information, and assisted in the learning process on which he wholeheartedly embarked.

He also found that under the solid working exterior there lurked a man with a good sense of humour. The more Danny worked the more his mentor taught him, it was a good day for Danny, for the blacksmith, and for the business, when they all came together.

As the weeks wore on Millie was dismayed by Danny's distant manner. Although now working in such close proximity, she did wonder how or if ever, she would overcome the barrier between them. It would be deemed just too forward to call on him.

Thinking back over events, she had to admit and agree there was reason for his reluctance to resume their old friendship; but she felt there was something else wrong too. Millie knew how much her dalliance with Gerard must have hurt him. Knowing how he had felt about her, the subsequent birth of her child would have added salt to the wound. But that still didn't answer the question as to why he had left his job at The Coaching Inn.

She suspected there were other reasons, but how was she going to sort through all the loose ends? She ached for the old easy going Danny.

Spring moved on, and any opportunity that presented itself saw Millie with a steadily growing Amy, down on the shingle, or sitting in the sun at Bell cliff. Any outing was a slow business, as walking, holding a heavy child on her hip was punctuated with plenty of rests. But the sisters, aware of how hard Millie worked for them even after the shop was closed, made sure that she and the child got plenty of fresh air and short breaks, by sending her to the shops or on other errands.

Unknown to Millie she was watched many times, and Danny suppressed the strong impulse to cross the road to them. How could he bear it if she again turned away from him? But hadn't she said that she would always want him as a friend, why shouldn't he approach her with just friendship in mind?

Hurt at Millie's gentle rebuff, over a year ago, when he had plucked up courage to make his feelings known, it seemed to Danny the more he thought about it, the greater became his desire to heal the rift between them. Millie's 'reaching for the stars' had ended in her grasping only the unfortunate truths of her short liaison. Her dreams of the gentry had crumbled. Recent changes may yet pave the way for Danny to prove his continuing strong feelings for her.

An unshakable love was still there deep down, although well hidden during the days of despair following the birth of her child, when a sort of madness had overtaken him. Heaving a sigh he hoped Emily hadn't been too hurt by it all. If Danny resumed his longed for friendship with Millie, he would have to admit to her his fling with her best friend. What was he to do? It was the truth regarding him and Emily, which was really holding him back.

With a shudder he realised that Millie would have to know at some stage, and he would rather it came from him than from anyone else. He hoped time would heal, and his love would offer security, and resolved to try at the very least to renew their friendship.

Millie had noted with interest that Danny seemed to be much more in evidence over at the black- smiths. Occasionally she would see him actually leading the horses out, and sending them on their way in the care of another young man. Puzzled she felt the need to ask around regarding the changes. Idle gossip completed the picture and when she spoke to Ned, he confirmed that Danny was indeed working full time at the smithy.

She got used to seeing his smiling face, but longed for his acceptance of her present circumstances. Millie found a pride in Danny's change of direction. Her secret fear of him pursuing his idea of going for a groom in a big house and leaving the area for good, had been laid to rest with his recent move. It seemed that he lived on the premises and taken had over the rooms that Flynn vacated. He had grown tall and broad; his strength managing the great cart horses awed her. Millie had to admit to herself that she still cared, and as the thoughts whirled around in her head, tears sprang to her eyes.

On a warm Sunday afternoon, she made ready for their walk. Picking up Amy and waving goodbye to Miss Mabel, she decided to visit her Ma over at the harbour cottage. It was half way through May and the trees above the town were dressed in bright patches of pink and white blossom. Millie breathed in the fresh air and turning to Amy murmured, "You're a lucky little maid to be born in such a lovely place. We got the sea and the shore in front of us, an' the hills and woods be'ind. I 'ope you appreciate it," she laughed.

The child was fascinated with the seagulls, and on warm days loved it when Millie, bundling up her clothes, and holding her safely under the arms pits, allowed her to dip her toes in the sea, which brought forth shrieks of laughter from them both.

The days and weeks wore on, Amy grew and thrived. When Millie was able, in what was left of her break for dinner, she was in the habit of taking a little walk to the bottom of the hill and back. There was never much time, but quite often now, she would see Danny, and on the pretext of letting Amy watch the horses, she was able to linger. Sometimes he waved to them.

Millie honed her artistic skills, and the orders came steadily in. Miss Sybil, had begun to slow down a bit, but Miss Mabel was filled with renewed energy in her new role as Auntie Mabel. Although gowns for titled ladies were numbered among their orders, Millie noted with satisfaction, the fact that Clara no longer patronized the establishment, which was just as well in the circumstances.

Kind as the sisters were it became increasingly time-consuming, watching out for Amy, once she started to crawl. The days of sitting happily wherever Millie plonked her, were over. An inquisitive baby in a room full of exciting colours and soft fabrics was becoming difficult. Explore she must and Millie, even with Miss Mabel's help, needed all her wits about her to keep Amy's prying fingers from the expensive fabrics, not to mention pins and scissors.

"It looks like I'm going to 'ave to go upstairs with 'er to work. She loves the colours an' cottons as much as I do. But she's on the move now, an' I spend half me time fetching 'er back an' taking things off 'er."

"We do so love having her in here, but I fear you're right. It's no place for her at the moment. It's not fair to keep saying no, everywhere she turns. But I did laugh, when she crawled under the curtain of the fitting room, and brought the whole lot down. The rather large Mistress Stanbury was standing there in her bodice and drawers." Millie remembered the spectacle and laughed out loud; then on a more serious note.

"It's the only thing I can think of doing, work upstairs for a while. She plays happily with tin pots an' spoons an' that. I tried fencing 'er in like; with me bed, 'er cot, and the low chest. It seemed to work alright, you wouldn't 'ear the racket from the attic."

Miss Mabel chuckled at her choice of words.

"I can pile all me work stuff on top the bed, she can't reach that yet, an' I'd still get all the work out, except that I might 'ave to finish it in me own time." Agreeing that it might be the best solution, given that the times between crawling, walking and understanding, was going to be a difficult phase. Millie slipped upstairs to make the room ready, and returned to collect all she would need to complete the work in progress. She then made a third journey with the squirming Amy under her arm.

Millie took the child over to the harbour cottage on her time off, Fanny was glad of the company for Jamie was often missing. With just a heavy limp left to show for his accident, it hadn't taken him long to slip back into his old ways.

Changes had gradually taken place and Lazurus, finding it increasingly difficult to look after himself, gave up his one room home and on Fanny's suggestion, moved into the cottage on a permanent basis. He was both relieved and grateful. It was Fanny's turn to keep an eye on him and she was more than happy with the arrangement.

It seemed a very long walk to her Ma's these days, needing frequent stops along the way, as Amy was growing ever heavier. Because of this Millie only chanced the walk if it seemed set fair.

Occasionally they met Danny, who now seemed more ready to stop for a few words. Millie realised that she had begun to look out for him, and was disappointed if they didn't see him. In fact Danny was in her thoughts more often than she cared to admit.

Millie had been working extra hard and had little time of late, but had made time to walk as far as Bell Cliff. She sat there holding Amy on her lap turning events over in her mind and wondering why Emily had never been to see her, when she heard her name called.

"Millie. It's been a long time since we talked together, can I sit with you for a while?" Millie turned at the sound of the familiar voice, her stomach turned over.

"Oh, 'ello Danny; Yes, come and sit here with us..." Millie's voice trailed off. She turned her attention to the child who was examining a pebble. Danny watched her face as she continued quickly. "Her proper name's Amelia you know, but me Ma says it's a bit of a mouthful, so she's just Amy." Danny nodded, "Nice," he said and tentatively reached out to the child, who promptly grabbed his finger and tried to stuff it in her mouth. "Hey, are you 'ungry then?" He retracted his finger and wiped it on his shirt. Millie laughed.

"She puts everything in 'er mouth now, she can sit by herself and crawl." Danny stared down at the busy child, "we see you sometimes; she likes to watch the horses." Millie looked into Danny's smiling eyes. "She's a pretty little maid, but 'ow are *you* Millie, are you managing alright?" Leaning forward he picked Amy up beneath the armpits and swung her into the air, the child chuckled, which brought a bright smile to Millie's face.

"Yes, I'm managing, I love me work an' I've got a nice room; everyone's been so kind to me, and Danny, I 'ave missed you," she said softly.

"Not so much as I've missed you Millie," he smiled his warm smile, and passing the child back, stood up thinking, maybe Millie could feel the same way...

Moving to stand up awkwardly with Amy on one hip, Danny grasped Millie's arm as he pulled her to her feet, slipping her shawl back into place around her shoulders.

"Maybe we should meet up again, take a walk together in the sunshine, I could 'elp you carry little'un. I can get out most days when it's me break, around midday. Long as I pick me time when we're not in middle of anything, he's a good sort Smithy is. I can work hard for 'im an' no mistake."

"Yes it would be really nice to walk together. Just watch out for me and if you're free, come with us. We'd like that wouldn't we Amy?" She hugged the child to her. Danny turned to hurry back to work. It was all he could do not to leap in the air or try a cartwheel. His heart felt lighter than for many a day. Entering the smithy he went to work with a will, and at the end of his working day, applied himself to cleaning every inch of his small rooms.

Over the next few days he bought a few extra pieces of crockery, another knife, and a couple of spoons. Warm blankets from the market stall cheap, because it was the middle of summer. He resolved each week to add something to the comfort of his new home. It was strange the effect the prospect of getting closer to Millie had on him.

Chapter Thirty

Danny's work pleased the blacksmith, and his natural ability under accomplished guidance, cemented their working relationship. The blacksmith's jolly wife Dora watched and approved of the new work- hand.

She had known Danny over a number of years from when he was a child, watching the smith in awe and mainly silence, struggling to help pull on the giant bellows with skinny arms. Her man had enjoyed the company of the two urchins, who in turn had enjoyed every moment of their spare time spent at the smithy. Later, when Flynn was taken on, she had lost track of Danny who had begun his working life up at The Coaching Inn. He appeared again, grown big enough to lead the horses down to be shod.

Knowing that his Ma died when he was quite young, meant she always had a soft spot for him. Dora lost count of how many times she had wished she and Walter had been blest with family and in particular with a son like Danny. It was with great happiness that she welcomed him back into their lives, when he applied for the job that Flynn vacated.

From afar the smith and his good lady watched the blossoming romance between Danny, and Fanny Drew's girl. Dora was all in favour.

"The little 'un's a credit to young Millie, though there's not many this side of town accept her unwed state so easily. But she's a hard little worker an' keeps the child proper nice. Fanny's a good woman too, but talk about history repeating itself."

"Aye but don't go letting 'er 'ear you say so." Walter retired back behind his pipe.

"I speak as I find," replied Dora, "it'll 'elp young Danny settle, an' reinforce 'is interest in the business." Walter stayed quiet, puffing clouds of tobacco smoke in the air, and then said,

"'ow will it?" He didn't always follow Dora's train of thought.

"Won't 'e be more likely to stay put with a family of his own?"

"Arr," was the only agreement she wrested from him. Her big strong husband was growing older and with no family, they could do worse. On a purely selfish note she knew she would love the opportunity to take them all under her wing, and help care for the child.

Millie too realised that her own work had become a big part of her life, but there had always been something missing. From the day she had met up with Danny again, she had a feeling that she now knew what it was.

It was a happy summer in which they had each given a lot of thought to a shared future. Tentatively exploring the possibility of walking out as a proper courting couple, Millie found it hard to keep her natural exuberance in check. Restrained by the thought of Amy, and knowing instinctively that Danny would be wary of risking another rejection, she vowed to be patient. Things have to be right; they have to be certain; I must wait for Danny to speak.

She didn't have long to wait!

Danny had been so pleased to resume their friendship that he dared not hope for more in case of losing everything again.

As she walked on the shingle towards the gentle shallow waves, the child on her hip the sun warm on her back, she felt a heady freedom from the restraints of work. Millie gazed out across the blue sea at the cliffs in the distance to her left, and to her right The Cobb, where many happy hours of her own childhood had been spent.

Hearing footsteps crunching on the shingle behind her, she glanced over her shoulder and her heart missed a beat. Danny caught up with them. He had watched as she crossed the square and walked down to the beach. Taking his courage in both hands he determinedly followed; the time had come to tell her how he felt.

As she turned to him, he was again aware of her long red gold curls, her pink parted lips. The sound of their happy laughter rang in his ears, as Millie bent low to allow the child's toes to touch the gentle waves.

Millie straightened up as he came to a halt. This was the first time he had taken a half day in a long while. His heart was pounding, as was Millie's. Danny was determined that after all the soul searching, all the 'should he, shouldn't he' this opportunity was not going to be messed up by his awkwardness.

"Millie I 'ope you don't mind. I saw you leave the shop and I 'ave an afternoon off. I'd like to spend it with you an' Amy if that's all right."

"Oh yes Danny, we 'ave too; got some time off I mean. I've bin working evenings when she's asleep. She moved up the beach a little way saying, "I'll 'ave to put 'er down again, she's getting so 'eavy," and placed Amy on the pebbles where she was happy to sit on the uneven beach and play.

They spent another happy hour chatting, remembering their childhood, and the games of tag and kiss chase, and when Amy fell asleep with Millie's shawl tucked under her head, Millie watched as Danny skimmed pebbles across the waves. She was loath to move, but remembering her promise to her Ma, said,

"We were going over to see me Ma; I'd like you to walk with us; if you want to that is."

"I would, an' long as I'm walking with you, why don't I take a turn carrying 'er? That's if she'll come to me."

"Oh Amy won't mind, she always wakes 'appy, an' I could do with a rest, if you're sure." Picking up the child they walked along in companionable silence, it seemed so right. Millie couldn't believe she had been afraid to approach him earlier in the year.

The conversation continued sporadically, but as they walked there was a further rekindling of the old enjoyment of each other's company, helped along by Amy's happy chuckles as she was passed from one to the other. When they approached the door of Millie's old home, Danny took his leave, saying how much he had enjoyed their walk, which was echoed by Millie.

Fanny opened the door and seeing Danny striding off called, "Nice to see you again Danny."

"Aye an' you too," he called back as he waved goodbye.

Millie's face was wreathed in smiles; it didn't take much working out, to know which way the wind was blowing! Fanny put her own interpretation on Millie's flushed face.

Welcoming them inside, Fanny refrained with difficulty from asking any questions; although once she almost forgot herself, and was silenced by a look from Jack. They had always harboured hopes of the two of them eventually getting together, but knew that it would be all too easy to upset the delicate balance of things.

Later as Fanny accompanied them back across the shingle, she looked at Millie's faint smile, noted her silence, and left her to her dreams.

They reached Town Square where Millie voicing her thanks, took the now wriggling child, and waving their goodbyes, continued to walk and daydream. They had seemed like a real family; Danny had been so good with Amy. Fanny walked back just as deeply in thought; that was the trouble with Millie, it was all or nothing.

Danny, walking back to the forge, quietly weaving his own dreams, was suddenly hit like a bolt from the blue with the fact that he had to clear up the Emily business. He decided to call on Millie at the shop to arrange another meeting. The long week passed. He knew if he was to stand a chance of being forgiven for the Emily thing, he had to tell Millie the whole story.

Now it was even harder to muster courage for another meeting. The real possibility of them walking out together, and the fear of Millie's reaction to his confession, could stop it all before it even started. In the blacksmiths jargon he had to 'strike while the iron's hot.' He would set up a meeting with her. He couldn't just drop it into conversation when they were out walking.

He washed his face and hands in the trough, wiped them on a neckerchief, and screwing up all his courage threw off his leather apron. Calling that he wouldn't be long, he walked out of the smithy, and purposefully crossed the street. Reaching the dress shop, he pushed open the door.

Miss Sybil looked up from the hat pins that she was sorting into sizes, and walked the length of the counter, to where he was standing just inside the door.

"I believe it's Danny isn't it? Well it's a while since we saw you." She waited for him to make known his reason for calling, although she knew perfectly well why he was there. Disapprovingly, Miss Sybil still thought there was a possibility that he was the young man responsible for Millie's fall from grace.

"Yes m'am, I'm Danny, I need to talk to Millie an' I wondered if you would allow me to talk to her here, in private, when it's convenient for you that is."

Danny made a big effort to be extra polite. Miss Sybil watched his demeanour with interest, and made a decision of her own giving Danny the benefit of the doubt, and not at this point involving Miss Mabel.

"If it is important Danny, then I am sure we can accommodate you, shall I call Millie now?" This was easier than Danny had expected, but he quickly said,

"Oh no, if it's all the same to you I'll call again, say - two days from now, just after mid- day; an' could you tell Millie it's nothing to worry about?"

"Very well, said Miss Sybil, I'll do that for you, providing Millie agrees." With profuse thanks Danny left the shop, hoping against hope that he was doing the right thing, or at least doing it in the right way.

He pondered on Millie and her child. All his original feelings of hurt and sadness had died, leaving him with a deep longing to slip his arms around her and offer his love and protection...

Miss Sybil was as good as her word, and the day that Danny was due to call again she had arranged a meeting with their accountant, in order that they should have privacy.

Since she had mentioned Danny's impending visit and although his reassuring words had been relayed to her, Millie had begun to worry. She turned it this way and that, her imagination working overtime.

Just what was so important that Danny needed to talk in private? She had been so happy with her dreams of them becoming a family, and had hoped he felt the same. Was Danny having second thoughts about Amy, being another man's child an' all? What else could it be?

She had thought long and hard and still been unable to understand why he needed privacy to talk with her. And why come here, ask her employers? By the time Millie took charge of the shop, she had worked herself up into quite a state.

The sisters would be gone from noon until the hour of one o' clock, giving Danny ample time to talk to her in the break he took at mid day.

They set off on time and within a few minuets the shop bell rang.

Danny, Millie's heart pounded. It was a false alarm. She measured off two yards of blue half-inch satin ribbon, and pleasantly inquired if blue thread were needed. Placing the purchase in a small roll of thin paper, she reckoned up the price, and the transaction completed wished her customer a good day.

A moment or two later the bell rang again, the door was pushed open, and there was Danny standing in the doorway. He quickly stepped inside, closing the door behind him to stop the bell jangling. Millie slowly came around the counter, hands clutching at the folds of her dress.

"Hello Danny, just turn the key in the lock, it's me lunch break now." Even to her, her smile seemed artificial.

"I 'ope it didn't make it difficult for you Millie, me coming 'ere; but there's something I 'ave to tell you an' I didn't want us to be out anywhere, in case"....

422

He stood looking at her. He looked uncomfortable inside the domain of 'ladies haberdashery,' if indeed that was the cause of his expression. Millie glanced down at Amy in her small makeshift cot behind the counter. She was quiet and sleepy. Millie waited a moment and then as was her want, a tide of words burst from her.

"If you've changed your mind about us; if you can't forgive me Danny, if you don't want Amy..." she paused and glanced down at the child. "Don't ask me to part with 'er Danny, she's me flesh an' blood, an' 'er father's nothing to me. I can't go on seeing you if you don't want Amy." She stopped for breath. The outburst had taken the wind out of Danny's sails; he wasn't sure now how to start his own confession.

"No no, it's nothing like that Millie; I 'ave to tell you something about *me* before we go any further. When you met *him*, we, that is your Ma an' Pa an' me, were forced to look on. We knew you were going to get 'urt... Then when Jack came to me an' told me... well, it was a shock. You went away an' 'ad the babby an' then when you came back 'ome, well I was pretty cut up like, an' things got out of 'and.

Me an' Emily - well we sort of got a bit close, an' she thought that we would... get married, an' I couldn't, 'cause I knew that it was *you* I loved Millie. I 'ad to get away from the inn and that's why I got the job with the blacksmith. An' I *can* love Amy, I do, she's part of you Millie, of course I love 'er... who could 'elp it? Well I've said it all now. I really love you both; an' that's why I 'ad to talk to you, an' get it all off me chest like".

It was Danny's turn to stop for breath. Millie had been staring transfixed at *his* outburst. Suddenly she sat down on Miss Sybil's stool, and putting her hands up to cover her face, sat very still for a moment. *Danny loves me...but Danny and Emily, they...*

She thought of one statement and then the other, all the other words were blotted out. Danny *loves* me, but Danny and Emily, together? The silence was strangling both of them.

Danny hardly dared to speak, but after a few moments he quietly said, "Millie?" in an enquiring tone and tentatively laid his hand on her shoulder. Millie's hands came down, uncovering her face, and she took in a deep breath. She must decide *now*, which was the most important piece of information that he had given her.

When her head cleared, there was no doubt about it in her mind He loved her, he loved *them*. She had been given a second chance, and so should Danny. It could be a fresh start for both of them.

The fact that Emily was her friend could hurt deeply - if she thought about it, so Millie simply decided not to think about it, not now or ever. Her hand reached up to cover his, still resting on her shoulder.

"Danny the only thing that matters to me is that we don't go losing each other again." Danny reached down and drew Millie close to him.

"There's not a moment I don't think of you," he pulled her closer, murmuring little endearments against her hair, cemented by baby kisses along her forehead. It seemed that he had wanted this for as long as he could remember; the warm enveloping feeling, of holding Millie in his arms. He stepped back, "Forgive me Millie I shouldn't 'ave, not 'ere; but I want us to be wed." She smiled and drew Danny into an embrace of her own, murmuring quietly, "Yes oh yes, I want that too, more than anything an' I'm so sorry I 'urt you." Sinking her cheek against his chest her sigh told him all that he needed to know.

Miss Mabel stepped from the doorway of the accountant's office where they had finished their business earlier than expected. Miss Sybil again called her thanks as she joined her sister outside. What they saw next was an extremely happy young man leaving their premises, pausing only to wave exuberantly at their shop window, before running across the street, neatly missing a farmer's horse and wagon, and a peddler. Turning to raise his hand in apology to the startled pair, he disappeared into the yard of the smithy. The sisters looked at each other both with the same thought, *are we going to lose Millie again?*

Greeted by smiles and a flurry of words, Millie told them the good news.

"An' don't you go worrying cause if we're wed, an' we will be, I want to go on working for you. Danny's got rooms so we won't be needing the attic, though I'll miss it I will, except that I'll still 'ave to take Amy up there in the day, away from the dressmaking room for a while yet. But I 'aven't even told me Ma or anything. We're going over to see 'er on Sunday."

She stopped for breath. Miss Mabel, wreathed in smiles looked across at Miss Sybil.

"Didn't' I say there's never a dull moment with Millie around?" and to Millie, "everything will fall into place my dear, the whole business will work out very well, I'm sure of it."

On the next Sunday well before noon, Millie and Danny with Amy set out to walk to the harbour cottage as arranged. A different kind of butterfly danced in Millie's tummy. This was a warm anticipation of imparting good news, and confirmation of something that you know others will be overjoyed to hear. They took it in turns carrying Amy and making plans.

When Fanny opened the door she hardly dare believe her eyes. Hope and relief welled up inside her as she called to Jack.

Danny was looking down at the rosy cheeks of the sleeping child in Millie's arms, his own arm protectively around her shoulders. Millie's smile was contented as she met her Ma's eye, and murmured, "Here we are Ma, the three of us from now on." Danny looked proudly at Fanny, and his smile, told her all she needed to know.

CHAPTER THIRTY ONE

"Come in, come in." Fanny ushered the group inside, delighted to welcome them. After all her daughter had been through in the last two years, she was still smiling, and if she wasn't much mistaken the grin Danny exhibited meant they had finally come together.

She looked again at Millie's excited, smiling face, and fleetingly hoped that her natural exuberance wasn't running away with her yet again. But no, Danny was a steady solid sort, and Fanny knew instinctively that at last things were going to turn out the way everyone had hoped; even if Millie had been the last to realise it.

Hearing voices, Jack, home again, hurried through from the kitchen, a welcoming smile on his face.

"Now," said Fanny, "is anyone going to tell me what's going on?"

"We're getting wed," announced Millie, Danny nodded in agreement.

"Well I'll be damned," exclaimed Jack. He strode across and shook Danny firmly by the hand. "That's the best news we've 'ad in a long time, 'cept for babby's safe arrival." The cottage was buzzing. Jamie came charging downstairs, his gammy leg now almost good as new.

"Getting wed, when?" He voiced what was on Fanny's lips.

"As soon as we can," Danny asserted, "we don't want nothing much, just a simple ceremony.

I was going to ask you proper like Jack, only Millie burst out with it as usual, can't keep nothing to herself this one." He squeezed her arm affectionately. Jack winked at Fanny, they laughed together, but Fanny couldn't help remembering how Millie had certainly kept a secret to herself in the past.

Stepping quickly to Danny's side she patted him lightly on the cheek, "I'm glad that I am, glad," and slipping her arm around Millie and her still sleeping granddaughter, guiding them to the old armchair.

"No-one I'd rather give 'er to," laughed Jack, "this, calls for a tipple. What do you say Fanny?" Jack turned to grin as he took a jar of cider from the dresser cupboard.

"Aye," Fanny replied, "an' I got something special for Millie an' me, an all." She followed Jack to the dresser; "couldn't 'ave 'oped for better news," she muttered, as the parsnip wine was retrieved from the back of the same cupboard. "I got volunteered to pick up the left over's from farmer Cole's crop; 'e knows I don't waste nothing, I 'ad as many as I could manage in return for a bottle of the finished wine."

Fanny poured two glasses of the rich golden wine, and passed one to Millie, lifting her own on high. Jack, Jamie and Danny raised their tankards too, as Jack firmly stated, "I always knew they'd finish up together."

"I 'ave to say it looked unlikely at times," Fanny murmured. Millie changed the subject.

"Where's Lazurus? I must tell 'im too,"

"He takes a walk this time o' day, but 'e should be back 'afore you go. Well when *are* you getting wed then?"

"We've not 'ad time to work anything out yet. Millie pulled a face; maybe Ely could do it, same as he

428

christened Amy like." Fanny wasn't too sure, hoping there would be plenty of time to think it through.

Lazurus returned, and was quickly told the exciting news and a tankard of cider thrust into his hand. After drinking the happy couple's health all over again, the conversation continued.

"There's going to be a lot to do maid, 'ow soon do you want this wedding?" Fanny looked at her daughter's happy face. Millie sipped her wine, her cheeks now matching Amy's rosy glow.

"Well I don't want it too quick, 'cause I like thinking about it, an' planning. Aye an' I like the thought of telling the blacksmith an' his missus too. Then there's Miss Sybil and Miss Mabel to tell; do you think they'll come to me wedding?"

Danny answered her quickly, "They'll come, they wouldn't miss it. First we'll get you an' Amy over to meet me boss and Dora, proper like." Jack nodded.

"Old Walter's a good sort, bit sparse on words, til you get to know 'im; but Dora, why she can talk the 'ind leg off a donkey!" Danny agreed, and seemed pleased that Jack already knew and approved of his gaffer and missus, as did Fanny, nodding her agreement.

"They're good to me. They already know I bin sweet on Millie for a long time." He grinned; his own excitement as infectious as Millie's, "Dora can't wait for me to bring 'em over to see babby at close quarters. Right motherly she is. I've known pair of 'em since I was knee 'igh to a grass'opper!"

They chatted idly for some time, Jack being particularly interested in the way Danny had changed course and adapted to the smithy's trade. He would never be out of work as long as there were horses and farm implements around. He could rest assured that Danny was well able to take care of them both. At last Fanny could stop worrying.

Jamie's antics, after his second pint of cider had them all laughing. And Lazurus, after adding his good wishes to the proceedings, and enjoying his cider with the rest of them, was now fast asleep in the corner. Jack put the stopper back in the jar. Millie was all too aware of her sleeping child, and so declined a second glass of her Ma's parsnip wine, much as she loved the sweet warm taste.

At last it was time to exchange goodbyes and retrace their steps. Danny's mind was working overtime as they walked back. Walter and Dora could be told the news as soon as he got in. Danny was in no doubt how pleased they would be.

All that remained was for them to discuss where the new family would live. Danny knew that Millie as his wife, and Amy would be made welcome in his rented rooms. He already knew by Dora's remarks that having a child wouldn't go against them.

Later in conversation with the blacksmith, he was assured just how pleased his employer was with him, when just before they finished work, Walter tossed him two small silver coins.

"Here lad, let's see just how skilled you are now. Smelt 'em down an' make yer young lady a ring; like I did for my Dora many years ago. Make a good job of it. That's yer wedding present, from us." Danny had caught the coins deftly and stared down at them in his hand. He looked at the burly smith and was overcome by the sentimental kind heart that was behind the gruff exterior.

"I will that, aye I will, an' thanks."

"No thanks needed lad, just make a good job of it."

When Danny finished work the next day, he waited until he saw the 'closed' sign in the door of the dress, shop and walked across to fetch Millie.

Amy had been fed, and was in her usual contented frame of mind. Millie, although slightly nervous, was ready to meet the blacksmith and his wife. Holding hands they walked across the street and down the alley to the side door. Danny stepped inside, turning to the door on his right he knocked and gently pushed his head around, calling at the same time, "anyone there?"

With one hand Millie clasped Danny's, and with her other arm held tightly on to Amy who was struggling to be set down. After a moment an answering voice called back, "come in, come in we're all chained down," followed by a loud chuckle.

On entering the homely room, Millie's eyes rested first on the dumpy little woman, and then quickly on the blacksmith himself. She had only ever seen them in passing, and separately. When she looked on them at close quarters she was amazed at the difference in their height.

The burly blacksmith was head and shoulders taller than his dumpy little wife. They looked a most unlikely pair, and yet in those first moments Millie could almost feel the warmth and closeness emanating from them. She quickly passed Amy to Danny and stepped forward to shake first Dora's hand, then the large sinewy hand of the smith. Dora was the first to speak.

"Danny's told us that you wish to be wed, and that you'd like to make your'ome 'ere with him. Well my dear there's nothing we'd like better, you will be most welcome." Millie smiled and gulped a "thank you." Walter added his agreement, and that was that. That was all there was to it. She was going to be a part of this happy family; she needn't have worried at all.

Dora was talking rapidly, partly to herself and partly to anyone else who was listening. She held out her arms for Amy, and Danny passed her over.

She chucked and cooed over the child, who immediately grinned back and made a quick grab at Dora's cap which was already sitting precariously on her wispy grey hair. Rocking her quite vigorously, which raised delighted gurgles; she raised her eyes to Millie saying, "I'd love to 'elp with the babby; anything I can do, you only 'ave to ask."

Millie and Dora took to each other immediately and Walter was pleased for everyone. Dora could hardly wait to install them and have an infant to fuss over, but she managed to rein in her excitement, when it was pointed out that first they had to find someone to wed them. She tut- tut-ed, and muttered again against the 'wrong thinking' among certain people who called themselves God fearing folk!

"But take 'er on Danny; show 'er where she'll be!" Millie was shown Danny's rooms and her imagination leapt ahead. She could see immediately how to make the two rooms more comfortable.

With Dora's assurance that the scullery was at her disposal, she looked forward to the day when they would start their new life as a real family, and with a certain satisfaction Dora thought again of how it would be a good move all round.

Danny managed the situation on one side of the street, and Millie on the other. Miss Sybil and Miss Mabel were delighted at the turn of events. This young girl had managed to turn their ordered lives upside down, and in the nicest possible way, had given them a new outlook on life, drawing then into her warm circle.

The only thing that had troubled them was the fact that Millie's status as unwed mother had been well and truly brought home to her at the time of Amy's christening. But she seemed confident that Ely Hembrow would tell them the best way to manage the situation, regarding the nuptials.

Millie, with her Ma, sought out Ely to talk the matter over. Although he would be pleased to marry them, he felt that a wedding in the woods would be stretching things just a little bit too far. After some deliberation he offered to act as 'go between,' and make enquiries of the minister of the small Baptist Chapel on Coombe Street, a friend and colleague of many years standing.

Millie took the news back to Danny and they awaited a reply.

Another week passed; by which time Millie was convinced that no one would be found who would wed them 'legal like' as she put it. Fanny felt for her, remembering how difficult it had proved for Jack and herself. They had wed the old way. But surely times had changed? At last there was some positive news The Baptist minister, a compassionate man, agreed to talk with the young couple at his home, and make a decision at his discretion.

A meeting was arranged, and the day arrived. They walked to Coombe Street in near silence. Approaching the front door of The Manse, Danny squeezed Millie's hand before lifting the heavy iron knocker. They waited in silence until the door was opened by a young maid in sombre dress.

"Please wait in the hall," she whispered, and held the door for them to enter. Moving away, she tapped on the door to her right. There was a long pause in which Millie noticed the stained glass windows above, and to the side, of the front door, giving the hall a yellowish, dimly lit appearance. After a moment they were ushered into the room, there to come face to face with an elderly, kindly man, small framed and with a shock of white hair. He stood to greet them with outstretched hand.

"Come in, Danny and Millie, I believe. The reverend Hembrow has spoken of you to me. After a brief conversation, he requested that they kneel together, while he prayed for guidance. They hardly dared hope, inwardly making all sorts of promises of the 'if only' variety. After an agonizing wait he rose from his knees and turned to them in silence, bidding them rise too. They held their breath, and then quietly the reverend spoke.

"I have known of you both for many years, but sadly not as one of my flock. Although attendance at Sunday school, and Millie's attendance at the Sunday morning service at Saint Michael's, is in your favour... well until that is, her - um... " He cleared his throat and continued, "I can see that you truly want to enter into the state of holy wedlock, I am sure, for all the right reasons. But I am unable to perform the ceremony myself, because of the teachings of my faith.

Of course the most common way of entering into the married state, is for you to declare yourselves 'man and wife' before two witnesses," he paused again, and seeing Millie's tears threatening, continued quickly, "However, I see no reason why Ely, himself a man of the cloth for many years," again he cleared his throat, "shouldn't carry out a short ceremony for you. After prayer, and talking to you both, I shall allow this to be carried out in my chapel. Forgiveness is everything." he murmured the last phrase half to himself.

Silence filled the small room, Danny and Millie digesting the news. They had been certain that he was going to turn them down completely, but instead he was allowing a ceremony to take place in his Chapel, turning a blind eye to the service that Ely would conduct.

They were overwhelmed with relief, and quietly thanked the reverend as he gently placed his hands on their bowed heads, and bid them 'go in peace.' After the pair had left, the minister again contemplated his actions.

Surely it was better to forgive a young girl's error of judgement, in the face of their desire to be joined as man and wife. The choice was stark, no one else would marry them, not the vicar of St Michaels certainly, and not the congregational Minister. The alternative was to live together as such anyway, as did all the other young couples of their class. Very few actually made it to the alter in Church.

It was more than they had dared hope for, and later, relating the happenings to all concerned, and agreed that the minister had done all in his power to help them. He was as Ely said, a compassionate man. Millie vowed there and then never to let anyone down, and was to remember many times in the future the trust that he had placed in them.

The arrangements set Miss Sybil and Miss Mabel's mind at rest. Millie would be wed, in their eyes the only union they could condone. Everyone was happy, though in truth Jack would have entrusted his girl to Danny with or without the ceremony. There were few of their standing that made much of it, trust Millie to be different! The marriage act was for folks with wealth to safeguard, but the likes of them had little to worry about, *half of nothing was still nothing, whichever way you turned it.*

Christmas approached, and there was another important date to celebrate. Amelia reached the first milestone of her young life. Her first birthday was celebrated in style; and then two weeks later the Christmas jollifications took place. The whole family and Danny too, could spend a memorable day together. This time last year Jack was on the high seas, and Millie was at Clifftops, forcing them all to spend Christmas apart. The small cottage echoed to the sound of Jamie's tin whistle and Lazarus's reed pipe. It wasn't until almost midnight that the house became still and quiet.

The rest of the household had retired to bed and Amy was sleeping soundly in her cot, settled in her grandparent's room, an arrangement that had helped Millie out many times. Sitting together huddled close to the dying embers of the fire; Danny stared into the face of his young wife to be. She was eighteen, with the responsibility of a child and steady work. To Danny, she still looked as fresh faced and innocent as she was in the earlier years, when his awakening feelings for her first stirred.

He leaned towards her his hand behind her neck; his fingers loosely entwined in her hair, and gently drew her to him.

"I love you Millie, never forget that. I love how you feel warm when I hold you close, I love how you raise your face to be kissed; I love the softness of your lips. We will be happy for ever, I know it." He stared deep into her beautiful blue green eyes before he kissed her; gently at first, then with more urgency. Something stirred in Millie and she found the answering passion that she had secretly feared would be missing. The more Danny kissed her the more she wanted to be kissed. They were young, in love, with their whole lives in front of them; there would be many more celebrations in the future, and doubtless some heartache too, but they would face it together. It was going to be a wonderful New Year ahead of them.

Millie's choice of a summer wedding set Fanny in an industrious mood; planning with her, all sorts of items for her bottom drawer. Towels and tea cloths to be hemmed, bed linen to be acquired and crockery and kitchen pans to be purchased from the market stalls. The lead up to the wedding was thoroughly enjoyed, even if it did leave the men folk baffled by all the fuss.

The months wore on until the summer was suddenly on them, and with it the wedding day grew closer. With Amy safely tucked up in bed at her grandmothers, Millie sometimes wandered the lanes above the town during the long summer evenings, collecting petals from the dog roses that lined the hedgerows. These were to be dried and scattered on her wedding day.

The vision of herself with Danny beside her, took on an ethereal quality, although once during these quiet times she came too with a start, as the face in her daydreams gently turned into the face of another.

The only thing that marred her plans was that Amy couldn't be there. It was one thing standing in the chapel with Danny, but to bring her illegitimate child with her, would be pushing the boundaries a little too far. This sadly included only allowing immediate family to stand with her, whilst Ely performed the simple ceremony that was to unite them. There would be just her and Danny, her Ma and Pa and Jamie. Talking with Ely, they realised just what a big concession the minister had made.

Millie and the sisters put their heads together regarding the dress that she would wear for her big day. It was with some fast thinking that Millie had convinced them, and her Ma too, that the cream silk dress would make her feel uncomfortable, that she wanted something less grand, something to fit in with her family and surroundings.

She knew just how much she would miss Emily. The more she thought about it the more she could see the whole matter from Emily's point of view. That was the trouble, Millie could always see everyone's side of the argument, but goodness knows she had needed people to see hers. It had landed her in so many dilemmas. They had all been at fault, but hadn't she herself been the start of it all?

Mentioning it, Danny showed his total reluctance to meet up again with Emily, but true friendship is a funny thing; no matter what happens, time eventually heals, and Millie wanted Emily to meet and get to know Amy. They still had so much to share. Was it asking too much? Maybe now wasn't the right time, but maybe sometime in the future...

But first things first, Millie had to make her choice of which dress she would wear. No more precious money was to be spent on material, so the best of her three dresses was to be refurbished. She chose the plain grey. The dark grey with the green trimmings had been worn to see her blood father. Millie deemed this unsuitable on her wedding day, for Jack's sake. The dusky pink was now worn almost threadbare, and was far too tight. It had to be the plain silver grey. The material was good, and she set to work to renew and replace edgings and buttons.

Lilac taffeta scraps had been gleaned from the off cuts of a grand gown, which had been created that summer, matching ribbon happily given by her employers.

When Millie stood back to inspect the finished dress, she was really pleased with the result. There was enough lilac material leftover to make a large bow for her hair, which she would pile up high on her head, and fix somehow at the back.

Millie's wedding day dawned and she awoke to bright sunshine. Washing and dressing quickly, she hurried down to the kitchen Miss Mabel was brewing tea, and Miss Sybil surprised and delighted Millie, by sitting her down and serving her with a lightly boiled egg and a thin slice of buttered bread.

"We think it fitting on your wedding day, for us to wait on you," said Miss Mabel as she poured the tea and continued. "We appreciate all you have done for us, and know that when we lose you to Danny, you will still only be across the street. But it's right and proper that your first allegiance must be to your husband and family. Never the less we hope you will still find time for this pair of old maids, outside of working hours."

Miss Mabel came to a halt as tears threatened to overtake her, and Miss Sybil finished off by raising her cup of tea and drinking a toast to the young family's future. Millie spluttered into her cup, quite moved by the unexpected outpouring of emotion. She reached for their hands.

"Not too much will change, I've grown to love having you both in my life and couldn't step into the future without you being a part of it." There was a gentle silence in the warm kitchen as they finished their breakfast and Millie, aware of time, stood up saying, In the kitchen "I must collect all I need now, an' get over to me Ma's. I'll leave you to make your way over to Coombe Street just before ten o' clock. Then you can see me an' Danny, before we go into the Chapel and again, when we come out wed!"

She left the house and quickly walked to her old home where her family would be waiting. Her mind was full of the enormity of the changes that would surely take place, even though she had reassured the sisters otherwise.

Arriving at the cottage, dress over her arm, she pushed the door open, encountering Jamie sitting by the window.

"You're early; Ma said you would be, she's getting Amy up. Are you nervous sis? Danny should be, I feel sorry for 'im, does 'e know 'ow bossy you are?" Jamie grinned as Millie answered lightly, "Good job I am, it's kept you from trouble more than once. Look what 'appened when I wasn't around! An' aren't you supposed to be getting ready for me wedding?"

She swished past him and called up the stairs, "I'm coming up Ma." Fanny appeared at the top of the stairs.

"No need, I'm just bringing Amy down. Lazurus is going to look after 'er while we're gone, then we're coming back 'ere anyway. 'Ave you looked in the kitchen yet?"

Millie stepped away, as her Ma reached the bottom stair and Jamie pushed his way up.

"No not yet, why?" She moved into the kitchen, taking a delighted Amy who was straining from Fanny's arms to reach her.

"Hello my pretty maid, how are you this morning then, did you miss your mama?" She nuzzled Amy's soft skin and set her down on sturdy legs, supporting her by holding both her hands and 'walking' her to the kitchen.

Fanny stepped to the table in front of them and whipped off the covering cloth, watching Millie's face as she did so. Millie drew in a deep breath as she saw the spread laid out before her.

"Oh Ma, me wedding breakfast, oh it's wonderful, you done everything proper for me, oh Ma, thank you."

"It's looking quite a respectable feast," said Fanny proudly. "We all chipped in, an' one or two of me friends brought round some savouries for you, an' all." Well come on now we best be getting ready. Leave your dress for a minute an' I'll 'elp you with your 'air. It'll 'ave to be brushed out special."

"Oh I wanted to put it up, and pin this bow at the back." Millie produced the lilac bow.

"You can still wear your bow, but your hair should be brushed out long till after you're wed, then you can start wearing it up - that's the usual thing for a *married* lady!"

Fanny sat Millie in the chair by the window, and proceeded to brush her long shiny curls. It seemed only yesterday that the excited young girl, with all her dreams and aspirations, was telling of her longing to leave the harbour work and steer herself in an entirely new direction. Look at her now- she's done everything she'd set out to do. Aye an' some things she never dreamed of too!

Fanny was brought back to the present by a crawling Amy tugging at the hem of her skirt, and Millie saying, "That's all right now Ma, you'll brush it away, just fasten me bow for me." Fanny did as she was bid and stood back to admire her handiwork.

"You'll do," she said with a wide smile. "Step into your frock and you're ready." Millie duly stepped into her dress so as not to disturb her hair. Gently she pulled it up over her shoulders and buttoned the bodice, and both of them proudly admired the finished result.

"Now then, Jack will be back in a minute or so, he's walked down to the Cobb to clear 'is 'ead, 'e can't believe you're flying the nest for good. Now I'll just take off me apron and I'm ready too.

"You look real nice Ma. It's a shame Amy can't be there." Millie picked her up and cuddled her.

"It wouldn't be proper and Lazurus will mind her well enough, it won't be that long."

Jack came through the cottage door.

"My stars, what a little beauty you turned out to be, nearly as good as yer Ma," his eyes twinkled. He gathered Millie into his arms; "can't believe we're losing you, but sharing's the better word. It does me heart good to know it'll be Danny taking care of you. Now maid, do you think I've scrubbed up good enough?"

"Oh Pa, you an' Ma look real nice, oh an' look at Jamie." Jamie reached the bottom of the stairs and struck a pose to illustrate his sister's remark.

"It's only for you sis, only for you." He grinned as he added, "this u'll be sold on at market stall again the morrow." Laughing together they watched Lazurus's face as he followed Jamie downstairs.

"Well I'll be darned; looks like you're off to London Palace." His humour hid his disappointment at not going with them. But the rules had been bent far enough already and someone had to look after Amy, and besides his old legs wouldn't carry him that far. He contented himself with the knowledge that there would be a rare old shindig when they all got back.

"Off you go then, I'm all set 'ere and I promise we won't eat all the food while you're gone"... He chucked again as he practically pushed them all out of the front door, "go on then," he patted Millie's back, "you can't be late for your wedding." Picking up Amy with some difficulty, he waved the happy group off.

Reaching Coombe Street, with her nerves almost getting the better of her, Millie's heart leapt at the familiar figure of Danny at the Chapel door. She scuttled into a handy doorway as Jack hurried ahead, and reaching him steered him into the dark interior of the Chapel.

"We 'ave to wait inside until she comes lad, stay in the front pew, an' I'll go an' walk 'er in when t'others is settled. An' don't let on if you saw 'er just now, 'tis bad luck!"

Ely came towards them and shook Danny by the hand, motioning him towards the front pew. Danny inclined his head, feeling slightly nervous, and felt in his pocket for the small silver ring.

"Aye Jack you go an' fetch 'er in an' I'll tell Danny 'ere what he as to do." Ely stretched his hand out to Jack, "no need to worry about your girl, she's a fine maid; young Danny an' 'er are well suited." He sent Jack out to await his daughter at the gate, and Fanny with Jamie, walked past him to take their places inside. Millie took her Pa's arm and he squeezed it warmly.

"Look back there," he whispered. Millie glanced over her shoulder to see Miss Sybil and Miss Mabel just beyond the gate, straining to see her. As she caught their eye, their delicate little finger waves conveyed how proud they were of 'their' Millie. Jack patted her hand

and with a last peck on the cheek, led his daughter, *his* daughter into the chapel.

As they drew abreast of Danny he stepped into the aisle beside Millie, and together, with hands clasped they at last stood before the old minister, to be declared man and wife.

Outside Miss Sybil and Miss Mabel, and now the blacksmith and his wife, waited with the dried rose petals, ready to set them on their way to their new life.

Moments later the happy couple left the chapel, their faces wreathed in smiles. Looking into each other's eyes, they knew that the feelings they had for each other would help them weather whatever else life could throw at them. Millie was radiant. Pink and white rose petals fluttered in the warm summer air.

THE END

In the impoverished fishing, community of 18th century Lyme Regis, young Millie seeks to better herself. Turning away from harbour work, she is overjoyed to secure a position as seamstress, and milliner, drawing on her natural flair and skills. The influence of her benefactors, bring her closer to a world she is drawn to, and her secret, brief but naive liaison with the squires charming son Gerard, has far reaching consequences.

Millie's Lyme is a dramatic family saga, encompassing intrigue, seduction and wrongful imprisonment, set against a smuggling background. Will help from an unexpected quarter rekindle hidden feelings? Through a fast moving series of events, the tale unravels in the small community on the Dorset coast, in the second half of the eighteenth century.

Lightning Source UK Ltd.
Milton Keynes UK
UKOW04f1053070115

244093UK00001B/1/P